GIRA SOLÉ

Renovate My Heart

Content Warning: This book is intended for mature audiences and contains explicit language, explicit sexual situations, violence, mental illness, and references to miscarriage. Discretion is advised.

First edition

ISBN: 978-1-7366121-1-8

Advisor: Charisse C. Marcato

This book was professionally typeset on Reedsy.
Find out more at reedsy.com

For M & C
You can read this when you're 30!
Maybe.
I'll think about it.
But, probably not.

For CRE
You are and will always be my Finn

Foreword

Authors Note

Content Warning:

This book contains explicit language, explicit sexual situations, violence, mental illness, and references to miscarriage.

Gira Solé

Acknowledgement

There are so many people I would like to thank. If I wrote them all down, it would fill another hundred pages, and it would make the book a little too long. And still, there are some people I would especially like to thank because, without their support, I couldn't have done this.

Kathryn Di'Orio, Shushma Fraizer, & Jennifer Warowitz.

Thank you for your love, support, and being the best cheerleaders anyone could ask for during this process. I really couldn't have done any of this without you.

For more information on Labyrinths:

World Wide Labyrinth Locator: https://labyrinthlocator.com

For the Labyrinth information referenced in this work:

Church of the Redeemer

108 S 20th Ave, Longport, NJ 08403

-Gira Solé

Spotify/Apple Music Playlist

1. *I Will Remember You*. Sara McLachlan
2. *Cranes in the Sky*. Solange
3. *IDK You Yet*. Alexander 23
4. *Good Enough*. Sarah McLachlan
5. *Million Reasons*. Lady Gaga
6. *Save Me.* Aimee Mann
7. *Blackbird.* The Beatles
8. *Wise Up.* Aimee Man
9. *I Don't Wanna Fight.* Tina Turner
10. *The Sex is Good.* Saving Abel
11. *So Unsexy*. Alanis Morrissette
12. *When We Dance*. Sting
13. *Fear*. Sarah McLachlan
14. *Fumbling Towards Ecstasy.* Sarah McLachlan
15. *Love.* John Lennon
16. *Strong Enough.* Sheryl Crow
17. *Take Me To Church.* Hozier
18. *Halo.* Beyoncé
19. *Delicate.* Taylor Swift.
20. *Bad Day.* Fuel
21. *The Reason.* Hoobastank

1

22. ***I'd Die Without You.*** P.M. Dawn
23. ***Ain't No Sunshine.*** Bill Withers
24. ***Never Break.*** John Legend
25. ***Surrender.*** Natalie Taylor
26. ***Thousand Years.*** Christina Perri
27. ***Say You Won't Let Go.*** James Arthur
28. ***Perfect.*** Ed Sheeran

PROLOGUE

I t seemed dark in the room. Even with the sun shining outside. The curtains were drawn, and the window faced a pathway between the two wings of the hospital. It was quiet except for the beeping from the machines keeping Lottie Howard alive. Lottie would take a gasping breath with every swoosh of the device, then return to normal breathing. Kara sat at the bedside, watching her mother die. She'd been there for the last two days since the doctor told her, Lottie refused treatment. Comfort Care was the best they could do for her. They would make sure she left the world feeling no pain.

Kara had been watching the numbers on the machine decline steadily during the two days she'd been there. Every ninety minutes or so, the nurses would come in, check the machines then leave. Every four hours, the nurses would come in and inject the I.V. in Lottie's left arm with morphine, then go out again. A tv hung on the wall in the room, but Kara didn't turn it on. She wasn't much of a tv person anyway. The only thing on tv during the day were talk shows, and Kara hated those. Kara simply sat by her mother's bedside, working on her computer, waiting for it to all be over.

While Kara was in the middle of sending an email, Lottie finally took her last breath. The machine beeped once, then turned into a long continuous beep, as her mother's heart finally stopped. Kara rolled the table she'd been using as a makeshift desk to the side and looked at the woman who used to be her mother. Lottie had changed so much from the towering stern mother of Kara's youth to a shell of her former self lying in the hospital bed.

"Goodbye, Mom, I love you," Kara whispered to her mother. She left the room and went to the nurse's station to let them know, her mother had finally passed away.

Kara sat next to her mother's bed as the doctor came to officially call the time of death. She watched him as he examined Lottie and wrote notes in the chart. Kara had to admit, the doctors at South Jersey University Hospital were much better than the other quacks her mother had been going to for years. Kara had spent months trying to convince her mother to come here and be seen instead of going where she usually went. It wasn't until she was forced to go to the emergency room, Lottie finally agreed. But of course, by then, it was too late. After being in the hospital for a week, doctors determined there was nothing they could do. Lottie had waited too long for them to treat her. Everything they suggested, she refused. Their hands were tied.

The doctor came over to the side of the bed and faced Kara.

"I'm sorry, Kara." Dr. Mitchell whispered. "My condolences to you and your family during this difficult time," he said gently. "Take as much time as you need, and when you're ready, we will have your mother taken to the morgue." He patted Kara on the shoulder gently and looked at her with sincerity.

Kara nodded, "Thank you, Dr. Mitchell. I appreciate everything you did for my mom." Dr. Mitchell nodded and walked out of the room.

When Kara was alone with her mother, she finally allowed her eyes to fill with tears. Kara let them fall down her cheeks onto her blouse. Even though Kara knew it was coming, she still couldn't believe her mother was gone. It was just so unnecessary. She took a deep breath. There was no point in sitting here feeling sorry for herself, she thought to herself. She looked over at the table she was using as her makeshift desk to find her cell phone.

When she had to leave the room earlier for the nurses and the doctor to come in, she left it on the table. She got out of the chair, walked over to get her cell phone, picked it up, and called her brother. It was just after ten in the morning in New Jersey. Her brother was in New Orleans, so it was only after nine there. It went right to voice mail.

"Hey, it's me. Mom passed away this morning. Call me back. Bye." Kara tapped the button to end the call, sighed, and shook her head.

She scrolled through the contacts on her phone, letting everyone know Lottie passed away. She started to feel like her calls were scripted. Everyone she talked to got the same speech.

"Yes. This Morning. A little before eight. No, she wasn't in any pain. Thank you. I appreciate it. I know. Of course, I will. I'll let you know as soon as arrangements are made. Thank you again."

Forty-five minutes later, and her brother still hadn't called her back. Although she wasn't surprised, she was annoyed. She'd been waiting for him to call her back. Kara looked at the time on her phone. It was time to go home. Kara started to gather her things and the things she brought to the hospital for her mother. There wasn't a lot, but it was enough she would have to make two trips. She took her stuff out to her car first. Putting everything in the front seat. She was shutting the door when she felt her phone vibrate. She tapped the screen.

"Hello." She placed the phone between her ear and shoulder to use the key fob to lock the door.

"Hi, Mom." Matt's voice was groggy with sleep.

"Hi, Honey." Kara leaned against the car and held the phone against her ear. "Are you Ok?" she asked gently.

"I'm ok. Are you ok?"

"Yeah," Kara said. Honestly, she was exhausted and wasn't sure how she would do all of the million things she needed to do, but it would only worry him.

"I'm ok. I promise." she lied.

"Ok. Then I'll call you later. I'll fly out for the funeral, but then I have to come right back. I'll get a couple of days off from school, but I have midterms next week, so I'll have some things to shift around."

"I know, honey, don't worry. I'll tell you as soon as the arrangements are made. Ok?"

"Ok. I'll call you later. I have to get ready for class."

"Ok, Darling. I love you."

"I love you too," Matt said before Kara tapped end to hang up the call.

Kara walked back into the hospital towards her mother's room. She looked at people as she passed them. It felt surreal. Some people were happily carrying balloons for a new baby, some people had flowers for loved ones. She wanted to go up to all of them and scream, "I just lost my mother. How can you be so happy?" but she just thought it to herself. She gave the nurses a weak smile as she walked by them into her mother's room.

The bed was empty. While Kara had been outside, her mother had been moved. Looking down at the empty bed, Kara felt the loss a little more. She touched the pillow where Lottie's head had lain. Closed her eyes and took a deep breath. Then she collected the last of her mother's belongings and, without turning back, left the room.

Kara got into her car, and before turning on the ignition, she looked out over the parking lot. She was tired, stiff, hungry, and needed a nap. Cars passed by on the street in front of her, life was moving on. Kara started the car to drive home. Today, silence was her companion. She usually would listen to the radio or plug in her phone and play one of her many playlists.

Silence sat with her as she drove through town. Silence followed her when she got out of her car after parking in her driveway. Silence was with her when she walked into the house. Silence stood by her as she forced herself to eat a bowl of cereal while standing at the kitchen counter. It wasn't until Kara was sitting in the bathtub, scalding hot water falling on her, did silence leave while she sobbed.

Finn Wilson had a problem.

He was sitting on the pristine couch in the living room of the house he "shared" with his girlfriend Shelly, scrolling through the internet on his old laptop. He was supposed to be looking at engagement rings for Shelly. Because it's what she wanted for her birthday in three weeks. Instead, he was looking through Yahoo, reading articles about nothing. He'd been doing the same thing for hours. Actually, he'd been doing it for months. Every time he went to look for engagement rings, he would spend hours scrolling through the internet looking at everything other than rings.

Finn and Shelly had been together for almost six years. They met when she came into the bar where he worked part-time "Neighbors." She was there with some of her girlfriends for a Bridal Shower Bar Hop. Shelly had come up to the bar to order a drink and spent the whole time talking to Finn. When the bridal party was ready to go to the next bar, Shelly gave Finn her number and told him he was taking her out the next night. Shelly got what she wanted. She always did. Finn took her out the next night, and when she said they were dating, they were dating. When Shelly said she wanted Finn to move into her house, Finn broke the lease for his apartment and moved in with her.

Finn always did what Shelly wanted. Most of the time, it really didn't faze him. Finn didn't care if they went where Shelly wanted to go for dinner or if he had to wear the shirt she wanted him to wear. He'd learned very early on to pick and choose his battles carefully. If it would lead to a fight, it was easier for him to let it go.

Since Shelly's thirtieth birthday, she'd been dropping big hints. She wanted to get married. She wanted to start a family. It was time for Finn to "pop the question" and "put a ring on it." All of her friends were married and pregnant, and she and Finn didn't even have a dog. Finn wanted a dog, for the record, but Shelly was too controlled, and her house was too immaculate for a dog. A dog wouldn't fit in the orderly way Shelly liked everything to be. Finn understood the dog, but not the ring. He'd seen it coming, though. Not only was Shelly dropping hints, but her friends and her family were too.

"When are you two going to tie the knot?"

"Why haven't you two made it official yet?"

"When are you two going to finally settle down and get married?"

Shelly's mother was the worst. "I want grandchildren, and you know Shelly, pretty soon, you'll be too old to have kids. The clock is ticking. Tick

Tock, Tick Tock." She'd say in her nasal whine.

With the bridal shower invites turning into weddings and baby shower invites. Finn saw all of the hints. They used to laugh it off. They would tell everyone it would happen eventually. There was no rush. But once Shelly turned thirty, "eventually" turned into "hurry up."

The worst was at Shelly's friend Tracy's Halloween party. Shelly had wanted to force him to wear a couple's costume, which he thought was ridiculous. It started a fight. He didn't wear it, and Shelly was pissed. When they got to the party, Shelly took off for the kitchen and started bitching at her friends as soon as they walked in. Finn walked around and said hello to the few people he knew at the party and eventually made his way to the backyard to talk to Tracy's husband. He wasn't a bad guy, just a little boring.

Finn was standing in front of the fire pit, talking to Tracy's husband. Finn would occasionally look up for Shelly, hoping the brain waves he was sending her would reach her and she would get the hint, he wanted to go home. Tracy's husband was talking about yard work. The food, which was catered supposedly, had no flavor. Finn wasn't a big foodie, but fuck, the food was horrible. The beer he'd been nursing since he got there tasted like piss. He worked all day and then to have to come home and fight about wearing something stupid. His patience for all of it was almost gone.

Finn was nodding along to the hum of the conversation around him, not really interested in autumn lawn care when Tracy corned him.

"You know Fin," looking at him like he was dying to hear what she had to say. "Fall is really a great time of year. The holidays are coming. Friends and family and get-togethers. It's a really great time to get engaged, don't you think?" Finn looked at her like she was an idiot. He smiled to be polite, then walked away.

He had to deal with it again at Thanksgiving. They spent it with Shelly's family. While they were all in the living room watching the football game, Shelly's sister, who was sitting across the room from him, yelled during a commercial. "So Finn, when are you going to finally make an honest woman out of my little sister?" Everyone laughed and thought it was so funny.

Finn didn't.

They spent Christmas with his family. It wasn't any better. His family did the same thing, just not as obnoxiously. New Year's Eve came, they went to a friend's party, and it happened there too. All the same questions, "When are you two going to get married?" It was all anyone asked them anymore.

Finn sighed and put his laptop on the couch next to him. From New Year's Day until Valentine's Day, Shelly dropped hints about "popping the question" and "surprise engagements." Finn did buy her a diamond. It was just in the form of a tennis bracelet, not the ring she wanted. She was disappointed and to prove it, she didn't wear the bracelet. It was still in the jewelry box it came in, sitting on top of her dresser. That was three weeks ago. It was almost spring, and in three weeks, Shelly would be expecting a ring. Finn sighed, picked up his laptop, took a deep breath, and typed engagement rings in the search bar.

CHAPTER 1

Anthony Howard sat at his mother's kitchen table surrounded by papers. He hated having to do paperwork. It's why he always had his mother do everything for him. Now she was gone. "Carolina should be doing this shit," he thought to himself. At fifty-one years old, Anthony had spent most of his life having women do things for him.

He was tall, with smooth brown skin. Large brown eyes, short curly black hair with just a few gray hints make him look distinguished. He had a nice body because he took care of himself. He exercised every day and stayed away from sugar. He was handsome, and he knew it. He used it to his advantage.

He picked up one of the papers with one hand and tried to find another form with his other hand. He couldn't figure any of this shit out.

"Carolina," he called out in frustration. "What do I have to do again?" Anthony put down both of the papers and scattered the rest of the documents on the table until they were all over. He saw one of the highlighted pages and picked it up. It looked like it was written in another language.

"What the fuck does this mean?" He mumbled to himself and put the paper down. "Carolina," he yelled again.

He ran his hands through his curly hair, making sure as he did, it was still in place. He couldn't wait for all of this shit to be done with so he could go home and see his barber. He needed to get his hair cut.

Kara walked into the kitchen and stopped. Her brother had made a mess out of all the paperwork she needed him to sign. She walked over to the kitchen table and stood in front of him.

"Stop calling me Carolina," she said, sighing. "And what are you doing? All you had to do was sign where the sticky tabs say sign here."

"I call you Carolina because that's your name unless you want me to call you bitch. Like all these other hoes," he said curtly. "And I don't see no fucking sticky tabs."

Kara sighed and pointed to the post-it arrows labeled "Sign Here" at the bottom of one of the pages. Anthony didn't say anything. He picked up the paper, read it, then placed it back on the table to sign it. Kara just shook her head. Her brother had been there for their mother's funeral, and she couldn't wait for him to leave. They had never had one of those "close" sibling relationships.

He was five years older than her and was a "Momma's boy." Growing up, he, with his mother's blessing, went out of his way to make Kara miserable. Kara was a "Daddy's girl," and when she lost her father eight years ago, she'd lost the one person in her family who loved her. It's not that her mother and her brother didn't love her. It's just they didn't know how to show it in any way that wasn't toxic.

Anthony moved more papers around, and Kara pointed to the next arrow. Shaking her head slightly every time she had to point out where they were. Dealing with her brother was like dealing with a child. There was no point in arguing with him because he simply didn't understand.

"Make sure you put today's date next to your signature?" she reminded him.

"What's today?"

"March thirteenth."

"Why do I have to sign all of this shit?" Anthony whined.

"Because we have to file the claims for mom's insurance policies." Kara sighed. "Did you think about what we should do with the house?" she asked slowly.

"I told you we're keeping it."

"Why? Are you going to live here and take care of it?"

"No, but where are you going to go?"

Kara almost told him where he could go but stopped herself just in time, thinking better of it. "I can live somewhere else. If we don't sell the house, then all the money we get from the insurance policies would have to go to paying off the house. We could probably get more money if we sold it."

"I don't care. I'm not selling."

"I can move to a smaller place. This house is too big and needs too much work for me to take care of by myself."

"What about Matt? Where is he supposed to go?"

"What do you mean, where is he supposed to go? He's going to college in California. He's got a job lined up for the summer. He's not coming home. He's practically a grown man. And when he does come home, I'm sure between his father and me, we can find a place for him to stay."

"What job is he going to do?"

"He's going to work for a company called Anogami."

"What the fuck kind of company is that?"

Kara shook her head. "It's a gaming company in L.A." Kara didn't go into further detail. It was always "less is more" when it came to her mother and her brother. The more they knew, the more they would try to manipulate her. "Not that it matters. He still has two years left before he graduates. So he's not coming home anytime soon."

"Yeah, well, I don't care. I'm not selling the house. You're just going to have to suck it up. I'm through with it." Anthony said, waving his hand, dismissing her. He picked up more papers that needed signing and shuffled them. Kara held her temper by counting to ten in her head. Only her mother and her brother could make her lose her temper. They knew how to push her buttons. Now their mother was gone, Kara wasn't going to fall into the same trap with her brother for the rest of her life. She took a deep breath and walked over to the counter to pour herself another cup of coffee. They had to go to the lawyer's office today to settle her mother's will and finish all the estate stuff. Then her brother would be gone. She just had to get through the rest of the day.

"Annntthhoonnyyeee" came a shrill, high-pitched wail from down the hallway.

"What?" Anthony yelled back.

"Can you bring me my edge gel? I left it in the bedroom."

"I'm busy. Get it your damn self."

"Anthony. Pllleeeaaassseee."

"What the fuck do I look like?" Anthony got up from the table, knocking papers onto the floor and causing the chair to fall back against the wall. "I'm fucking tryin' to handle my business, and you fucking asking me to get some fucking edge gel."

"Annnnttthhhooonnneee"

"Wait a fucking minute. I'm coming." He walked out of the kitchen, mumbling to himself. "This bitch, what the fuck?" Anthony stormed down the hallway.

Kara closed her eyes and shook her head. Diedre, Anthony's latest fling, had come with him for their mother's funeral. For the last four days they had been in the house, they had done nothing but argue and yell at each other. "DeeDee," as she liked to be called, was petite, curvy, with long box braids that went past her ass. She was a beautiful girl in her early twenties. Which meant Anthony was probably old enough to be her father.

DeeDee looked like she just walked in from the club. She wore a cutout dress barely covering her. Her makeup was impeccable, and when she walked up the driveway to the house, she tossed her hair with her hands. Her nails were long and had jewels on them. When she walked into the house with Anthony, she took one look at Kara, her head moving up and down, and said, "Oooh, you bouchée" in a thick southern drawl. Kara had to close her eyes and pinch the bridge of her nose under her glasses to stop herself from throwing both of them out of the house.

From the time they had been in the house, it was "Bitch this." and "Boo that." "Fuck this." and "Shit that." There was also a lot of "Oker." and "Periodt." Kara couldn't get through a complete conversation with DeeDee without having to close her eyes and pinch the bridge of her nose. Anthony and DeeDee were nothing but drama. Everything turned into a fight, and within five minutes would be all over each other. Kara couldn't wait until they left so she could have peace in the house again.

Kara could hear them screaming at each other in the bathroom. She felt the tension creeping up her spine and settle in the sweet spot right between her shoulder blades. Her head was beginning to pound so hard she could hear it in her ears. She took a deep breath, trying to slow her breathing and calm herself. "Just get through today," she whispered to herself.

Kara and Anthony had always been polar opposites. Their mother had always enabled it to the point where Kara could barely stand to be in the same room with Anthony for longer than an hour. Anthony had always been their mother's favorite. Lottie Howard only wanted one child, and with Anthony, she had everything she could ever hope for. When Kara came unexpectedly, Lottie was not happy and let Kara know it every chance she got. It was Kara's father who loved her. Kara was his little girl. Her father would be the one to step in when her mother and her brother got too bad. Kara felt the pain her father's death caused all over again. She missed him every day.

Thankfully, Anthony and DeeDee were leaving soon, and Kara would once again have a quiet, drama-free house. Although as pleasant as the thought of it was, it also sent a shiver down her tense spine. She would be alone. Really alone for the first time in decades. The shudder shocked her. It's not like she hadn't been on her own before. She had been on her own for years, but Matt had been there. She hadn't been really alone since right after college.

When Matt graduated high school, she planned on living alone. Then Lottie got sick, so Kara had to move back into the house to help take care of her. Anthony wasn't about to do it. Kara wanted to hire a home health aide, but Lottie refused. Lottie didn't want a stranger in her house. Kara didn't have a choice.

Lottie's health problems started with dizzy spells, which led to falls. Kara had to drag her mother to the doctor to find out, it was the beginning of a heart condition. From there, it was a toxic mix of different medications that led to kidney failure. Four unnecessary procedures later, Lottie had water retention so severe it caused her kidneys to fail. Lottie had to use a wheelchair. Because she didn't move around, she got bedsores, which led to sepsis and her mother's eventual death.

Throughout all of it, Kara pleaded with her mother to get second opinions. Go to different doctors. To question why she needed the same procedure multiple times. All of Kara's pleas fell on deaf ears. Kara even begged Anthony to step in and get their mother to see another doctor. Anthony ignored her too. Kara eventually just accepted they both weren't going to listen to her and gave up. She'd been fighting the same battle with them her whole life. They weren't going to change now. And she didn't even have her father there to help her.

Kara sighed and straightened her glasses. She took a deep breath. She needed to focus on getting through today. She would have plenty of time to think through all the anger, exasperation, disappointment, and sadness after Anthony and DeeDee left the house and she was alone. For right now, she had to get ready to meet the lawyer with Anthony and DeeDee. They had to get the estate settled, and then she would be able to move on with her life. Or at least, that was the plan. Kara took a sip of her coffee and set the cup down in the sink.

Kara stood in the driveway and waived as she watched Anthony and DeeDee drive away. She was happy they were finally gone. She couldn't help but smile. The past twenty-four hours, she'd literally counted down to this moment. She didn't want to have to speak to her brother for a long, long time after this. She already knew she wouldn't ever see DeeDee again. She sent up a small prayer of thanks for that.

Kara walked back into the house and closed the door behind her. She leaned back against the door and looked around. Kara always seemed to be tied to this house. Her parents moved here when she and Anthony were younger. She grew up in the house. She slept in the same room she grew up in. She went to college, moved out, got a job, got married, and then moved back when she got divorced. Back into the same room. She had redecorated it when she came back the first time. She brought new furniture and updated the room as much as she could. She still had to deal with her mother. But at least her father had helped her.

When she moved out again, she left everything behind so her parents would have at least one grown-up guest room. When her mother got sick, she moved back into her old bedroom. If that wasn't bad enough. Now she was stuck with the house for the rest of her life.

Lottie Howard made changes to her will not long after Kara moved back home to take care of her. Forty-two percent of the house went to Anthony. Forty percent of the house went to Kara. Eighteen percent went to Matt as her only grandchild. Anthony would have a controlling interest in the house, and should he have children, they would inherit his interest in the house.

If Anthony passed away before Kara and left no children, then his remaining interest in the house would go to her. Of course, Anthony had to say something about that,

"Don't worry about babies, Kara, it ain't ever going to happen, you know what I'm saying. You know I got the old, snip, snip." Using his hand to make the scissors gesture. Kara just shook her head.

Lottie added the part about the potential for Anthony to have kids a year ago. Apparently not realizing he had gotten a vasectomy. Matt and DeeDee laughed at Anthony's joke. Kara just looked at the lawyer, embarrassed. Matt had already flown back to California. He came home for the funeral and flew out the next day because of midterms. The lawyer had him on the conference call for the will reading. If Kara and Anthony passed away before Matt, he would then inherit the house. Lottie also set aside ten thousand dollars for Matt. He would receive it once he graduated from college.

Because Lottie had given Anthony controlling interest in the house, if Kara wanted to sell the house, she would have to get Anthony to agree. Or she would have to buy both him and Matt out, then try to sell the house. Kara sat in the lawyer's office, seething in rage as she listened to the will being read.

After it was done and they waited for the papers to sign, Kara excused herself to go to the bathroom. She went to an empty stall and cried angry tears. Kara felt like she had been screwed. She wasn't surprised, just once again disappointed by her mother. She wondered briefly if the disappointment would ever go away.

Lottie Howard favored her son Anthony over her daughter since Kara was born. Kara had lived with it her whole life. She had always been treated as if she was less than when it came to Anthony. Kara would have to ask Anthony's permission to sell the house if she wanted to move on with her life, and to make matters worse, she would also need her son's consent. After all the papers were signed and arrangements were made for Matt to sign and return the forms to the lawyers Anthony, DeeDee, and Kara came back to the house.

Kara only saw two options she could take in order to get through this. She would have to either convince Anthony and Matt selling the house would be in their best interest as well as her own. Kara knew she could persuade Matt because he was in California. He didn't really care because he was young. The other option she had was to say, "Fuck it." and just walk away and let Anthony deal with the house on his own. She knew option two wouldn't work. Somehow, Anthony would force her to take care of the house because he would manipulate Matt. Matt would then ask Kara for help, and she would be forced to take care of the house anyway.

She really wanted to do option two, but she knew she couldn't do that to Matt. Anthony would hound Matt until Kara did what he wanted. Matt is still her child. Although he was about six inches taller than her. She'd always made sure to keep him away from the craziness of her mother and her brother. She knew she still would. Kara would have to swallow her pride and do what would be the best thing for Matt.

Kara walked around the house, looking at everything. She started cleaning up. She went to the kitchen and cleaned up from breakfast. Then she went to the master bedroom to remove all the traces of Anthony and DeeDee. Anthony decided to stay there instead of in Matt's old room because it had a queen-size bed. Matts room only had a full-size bed from when he was younger. She started to strip the bed so she could wash everything. She looked around the room, thinking about everything that happened over the past week.

From the funeral to this morning, Kara felt like she had been living in a lousy movie. She picked up the bedding from the floor where she had thrown it to put it in the hamper. She went to the linen closet to get fresh sheets and grabbed the bottle of fabric refresher she kept in there. She walked back over to the bed and started spraying the mattress.

Kara had spent the majority of her life trying to get away from this house and her family. Especially since her father had passed away. She felt like an invisible cuff chained to her ankle, kept her tied to the house. She may be able to keep her distance from Anthony, but she would still have to take care of the house.

As Kara cleaned the house, she wondered how she would manage the house by herself. It wasn't really about money. Her mother's insurance policy would cover the mortgage. She would have to pay the taxes and insurance, and that wasn't a big deal. There were the utilities, but it wasn't as much since she was by herself. Really, she not only had a full-time job, but she also worked part-time at a grocery store. She made more than enough to afford the house financially. Since she had moved back home two years ago, she had actually saved a lot of money.

Kara was more worried about the maintenance of the place. The house was old and needed a lot of work. Her parents had renovated the house when she moved in during her divorce, and then they only renovated the bathrooms and the deck. That was sixteen years ago. Since then, they hadn't so much as painted. The roof would eventually need to be replaced, and she should probably get new windows. Kara went into the bathroom to clean up there and looked around as she started wiping everything down. The bathroom was small, even though it had a double vanity.

She looked around and noticed the mold appearing on the ceiling above the standing shower. "Really?" she thought to herself. Shaking her head, she picked up the used towels and threw them into the bedroom. She would put them in the hamper when she was done.

There was another problem Kara would have to deal with when it came to maintaining the house. Her mother had been a hoarder. There was shit everywhere. Not just the regular pockets of clutter every home has. There were piles of stuff. Lottie did not like to throw things away. Lottie still kept all of Kara's father's things in the closet, and he died years ago. Lottie kept everything.

It didn't matter if it was broken, didn't work, or old. It either went into the attic or the garage, but it never went in the trash. Kara would have to go through every room and get rid of all the hidden crap her parents had accumulated over the years.

After Kara finished cleaning the bathroom, she walked back into the bedroom, picked up the dirty towels off the floor, and put them in the hamper. She pulled the hamper out of the bedroom and down the hallway to start the laundry. That's another thing she would have to update. The washer and dryer were downstairs in the family room/basement, and they were old. She would have to get new ones, and it would be easier if there were a washer and dryer upstairs.

She carried the hamper down the steps when the idea struck her. Why didn't she just renovate the house the way she wanted to. If she were stuck living here, shouldn't she at least make it something she wanted to live in? She could update the house. Then if she still didn't' want to live there, at least she may be able to rent it out or finally convince Anthony and Matt to sell it.

As Kara finished cleaning the house, she made a mental checklist of everything she would want to replace and what needed to be replaced. If she planned it out just right, renovating may actually work in her favor. The house would be comfortable for her, and she would remove all the past remnants she needed to move on from.

She did need to consider the matter of cost. There was some money left over from paying off the house. She could tap into it if she needed to. It wasn't much, but it was something. She also had money in savings. The expenses of the house had been covered by her mother's retirement and social security deposits. Kara didn't really have a lot of expenses, so she was able to save a lot. She also had some money saved in different retirement accounts. Although she didn't want to have to tap into her retirement if she didn't need to. She knew it would actually pay off if she did eventually sell the house. She could also apply for a home equity loan if she needed to.

She had options.

Kara followed the home inspector around the house as he went through each room and looked at everything. She asked for a thorough inspection because she wanted to see exactly what she would be working with. She wanted to know what needed to be fixed, replaced and remodeled. The inspector walked around and took a lot of notes. Every now and then, he would ask a question, and then he would move on to the next thing.

Kara asked people at work who she knew had just bought a house about finding an honest home inspector. She knew of horror stories from people who worked with some bad ones. She heard the stories about home inspectors undervaluing Black-owned houses, and she didn't want to get screwed.

When she called to schedule the appointment for this guy, she asked a lot of questions and asked to see a copy of some of his previous reports. All of which, he did without hesitation. From some of the other horror stories she'd heard, she was afraid of paying five hundred dollars for a report that would have bogus repairs that needed to be done and serious repairs that were glossed over. Since it was a pre-renovation inspection, she had requested he be as detailed as possible with everything.

When the inspection was done, Kara sat with the inspector to review his notes.

"You'll have to re-wire the house. The electrical circuit breaker will need to be replaced. The furnace is still in good shape, but it would be in your best interest to replace the air conditioning unit. Maybe not this summer coming up, but before next summer. If you want to remodel the bathrooms, you will need to replace the pipes. If you plan on gutting the house all at once, you could fix a lot of it at one time. If you're going to do it in smaller pieces, then it will take a little longer, but depending on who you hire to do the work, it may not be as bad." The inspector got up, and Kara walked him to the door.

"The good news is you do have some options. You may be able to do a lot of things on your own, which could save you some money in the long run. Keep in mind, renovating is costly, so finding someone who will give you quality work is going to be the most cost-effective thing you could do." Kara shook the inspector's hand.

"I'll send you my final report when it's ready, which should be in about two business days." Kara thanked the inspector and watched as he walked down the driveway.

In the end, the inspection estimated it would cost anywhere from fifty – seventy-five thousand dollars to renovate the whole house, inside and out. It was also dependent upon having all the work done by a contractor. If she did some of the work herself and shopped around for materials, she could save a lot of money. She also wasn't planning on renovating the outside just yet. Although the siding and the windows did need to be replaced, she still had a year or two before it was an absolute necessity.

Based on the inspection, Kara would be able to complete the majority of the renovation and not have to get a loan to do it. She may need to tap into her retirement, but she would be broke if she did it all on her own. It was better to be broke and not have to get a loan than have to pay for the loan for the next twenty years. Being broke was the more preferable option.

Kara started looking for contractors. She called around and got some estimates. From the ones she talked to, they were way too expensive. She would have to take out a loan to afford them. She complained to her best friend, Charlie, about it, and Charlie made a brilliant suggestion.

"Why don't you place an ad on South Jersey Marketplace? You can find pretty much anything there."

Kara at first dismissed it. She tried calling more contractors, and after several failed attempts at finding a contractor, Kara placed the ad.

Wanted: A Handyman who can help renovate a dated split-level house. You would be the contractor responsible for getting the permits needed from the county and making sure inspections took place. You would help me renovate the whole house one room at a time. Additional workers will be brought in for specialty work and as needed. The total project will take several weeks to months, depending on how much we can get done on weekends.

Experience in electrical, plumbing, drywall, and flooring a huge plus.

Must have experience in construction and demolition.

A background check and drug test will be completed.

Serious replies will only be considered. Please contact me at 856-555-1234.

Kara took a deep breath and hit submit. Sending up a silent prayer, the universe would send her someone who would be able to actually help her.

CHAPTER 2

Finn watched in horror as Shelly sat on the couch with her head in her hands, sobbing. He wasn't sure if he should try to comfort her. Should he say something, or should he just let her get it all out? He'd been watching this nightmare for the past hour. An hour. Part of him wanted to say fuck it and just turn on the tv. There had been moments during the past hour where she had stopped and looked at the jewelry box in her lap. It would bring fresh tears, and then the sobbing would start all over again.

At the beginning of this shit show, he had, in fact, tried to comfort her. He sat down next to her on the love seat and wanted to take her in his arms. She'd flung his arm off of her and told him to leave her the fuck alone. So he went and sat back down on the couch. He did as she asked him to. He left her alone.

After a little while, he tried another approach. He went and brought her the box of tissues from the bathroom. Then he went and got her a bottle of water from the kitchen. With all the crying, she had to be dehydrated. He thought to himself as he set the bottle of water down on the coffee table in front of her. He wasn't trying to be a dick, but fuck. She had been crying for an hour. A muffled "thanks" came from her before there was another sob.

He sat down on the accent chair next to her and tried once again to talk to her.

"Shelly, you've been crying for an hour," he said gently. "Are you going to tell me what's wrong?"

No response.

"Shelly, talk to me, please?" A muffled sob and a hiccup.

"Shell, Please. Tell me what's wrong?"

Silence.

Finn sat back in the chair, sighed, and ran his hands through his hair. This was getting old. Shelly did this every single fucking time. It didn't make him mad anymore. It didn't make him feel bad anymore. It was just making him tired. This was the reason they rarely fought. Finn would do something that Shelly either didn't like or was disappointed about. Shelly would cry, cry, and cry some more. He would beg her to talk to him. She would cry some more. He would eventually admit to being an asshole. She would stop crying and then proceed to tell him all the ways he was an asshole. He would agree with her and spend the rest of the night feeling like shit.

This was turning out to be the same thing. A train wreck, on top of a plane crash, with a caravan of dumpsters overflowing with trash, all on fire. Shelly leaned over and took a tissue from the box, and blew her nose. She was sniffling softly. Finn looked at her, expecting her to finally say something, but she didn't. She started crying again.

Finn leaned his head back against the chair and stared at the ceiling. This was the reason why most of the time, Finn just did what Shelly wanted. He hated this. Whenever he disagreed with her or didn't do what she wanted, she cried and kept crying until he took the blame. Most of the things she wanted, he didn't care enough about, to fight with her. It wasn't worth the aggravation. This time, he was just over all of this. Tonight it was actually his fault, but he didn't feel like he was being an asshole. He just didn't do what she wanted.

He did try, though. He really did. He looked online. He went to the jewelry store. He talked to the salesgirl. He'd walked in, intending to buy Shelly the engagement ring she wanted. He looked at the rings in the display case, and he just couldn't do it. When the salesgirl came over to him, he asked to see diamond earrings.

Shelly was crying because instead of the diamond ring in the platinum setting and the surprise proposal she wanted, she got diamond earrings in a platinum setting. There was also no proposal. When she opened the box, her face fell in front of him. It went from hopeful excitement to bitter disappointment. Then there was crying.

Lots and lots of crying.

Finn thought about taking out his phone and playing a solitaire game or start scrolling through social media. He knew if he did, Shelly would just say he was a bigger unfeeling asshole. He wasn't. He just didn't feel like sitting here watching Shelly cry anymore. It's been over an hour, for fucks sake.

The sniffling abated, and Shelly reached for another tissue. Her shoulders were slumped, and she shuddered slightly from her weak hiccups. Finn looked over at her expectantly. Hoping this would be the end of this because if it were going to go on for much longer, he was going to go to bed. He still had to work in the morning. Shelly shifted on the love seat and put the jewelry box on the coffee table in front of her. She looked up at Finn. Her eyes and nose were red and puffy from crying. Finn sat forward and folded his hands in his lap, waiting.

"I don't understand," she said quietly.

"You don't understand. What exactly?" Finn said hesitantly.

Shelly sighed. "I don't understand why you bought me earrings instead of what I really wanted?"

Warning bells were going off in Finn's head.

"DANGER, DANGER. TREAD CAREFULLY. THIN ICE AHEAD."

"What do you mean, Shelly? What did you really want?" As soon as he said it, Finn knew this wasn't going to end well. He knew exactly what she wanted. He just didn't know how to say "I couldn't do it" without sounding like an asshole. It really didn't matter at this point. Anything he said was going to hurt her feelings. Shelly straightened on the loveseat and stared at him. He wondered if it was too late to go seek shelter. Shelly was about to lose her shit, and it was going to hit the fan.

"What did I want?" her eyes widening. "What the fuck do you think I wanted?"

Here we go, thought Finn. Shelly stood up, a small pile of tissues landed on the hardwood floor. "Really, Finn, are you really going to do this right now. On my fucking birthday?"

Finn sighed, sat back in the chair, and leaned his head on his hand. All of a sudden, he was exhausted. He was tired of this. And it seemed to happen a lot more often lately. The bullshit. The expectations. He was tired of pretending this is what he wanted. Finn couldn't remember a time when he wanted any of this. It all seemed to happen, and he'd just gone along with it because that's what Shelly wanted.

Finn had been so lost in his own thoughts he didn't hear what Shelly was saying until she screamed, "Are you going to fucking answer me?"

"What?"

"You're not even fucking listening to me."

"What the fuck do you want from me, Shelly?" Finn had lost his patience.

"What do I want from you?" Shelly screamed. She was standing in front of him. Hands on her hips. Rage radiating off of her. Finn sighed and took a deep breath.

"Yes. What do you want from me?" he said.

"I want to get married, Finn." Shelly waved her hand in front of her. "I want to have kids. I don't want to waste my fucking time sitting here waiting for you to man the fuck up."

Finn lost it. "Man the fuck up? For fucks sake, Shelly. Maybe I don't want to get married and have kids. Did you ever fucking think of that?" Finn stood up and ran his hands through his hair. "It's always about you and what you fucking want. Maybe I don't want the same things you want."

The color drained from Shelly's face. Finn rarely fought back during an argument. Although he had been doing it more often lately. When Shelly paled, it was always the part in the argument Finn would lower his head, agree he was wrong, and Shelly would get her way. Finn just couldn't do it this time.

"What are you saying?" Shelly's voice was quivering.

"I'm saying, I don't want to get married because your friends are getting married. And I sure as shit don't want to have kids and bring them into this shit show because your friends have kids."

"Do you expect me to sit around and wait for you to get ready? Is that what you're saying?"

"I'm saying." Finn took a deep breath. "I don't want to plan my life around what your friends are doing or what they think we should be doing."

Shelly narrowed her eyes at him, "Is this because of money? Are you intimidated because I make more money than you do?"

"Fuck Shelly, are you serious?" Finn yelled. "I don't give a fuck if you make a hundred times more than I do."

"Well, I don't know. What is it?" Shelly said, shrugging her shoulders.

"I just fucking told you what it is. I don't want to get married because all of your friends tell you we should, and you fucking ask me if it's about money."

"If you don't want to get married and have kids, then what the fuck are we doing here?"

Shelly's questions hung in the air between them. Finn thought the same thing. He looked at her and shook his head. "I don't know." Finn walked out of the living room and out the front door, slamming it behind him.

Randy hit Finn's foot. "Dude, wake up." Finn heard him but rolled over. Randy hit his foot again. "Dude, come on. Wake up." Finn opened his eyes and looked at his best friend.

"What?" he muttered.

"Morning Sleeping Beauty." Randy smirked at Finn. "Time to rise and shine."

"Alright." Finn sat up slowly and immediately regretted it. "Fuck. What happened?" His voice was sounded like sandpaper. His whole body hurt. And the room was way too bright.

"What time is it?"

"Easy there, tiger, one question at a time. First, what happened." Randy smirked. Amusement was written all over his face. "You came into the bar late last night and proceeded to drink and bitch about Shelly until you got so shitfaced, I had to bring you here."

Finn groaned. He remembered going to Neighbors, he remembered being pissed at Shelly, but he didn't remember drinking that much.

"It's also 11:30," Randy continued, "I also called your boss last night and told them you wouldn't be making it into work today. You can thank me for that later."

Finn sat up on the couch and put his head in his hands. He rarely drank. Since he was a bartender, he witnessed how people were when they had too much to drink, and he liked to be in control.

"Did anything else happen?" Finn asked.

"You made an ass out of yourself."

"What did I do?"

"Nothing crazy, don't worry." Randy laughed. "Just a lot of fuck this, fuck her and her friends."

Finn sighed. "Is that all?"

Randy laughed, "Of course not."

Finn looked up at Randy. He was bracing himself for the worst of it. "What?"

"You went up to almost every girl in the bar last night and asked them to marry you because it would piss off Shelly." Randy laughed.

"Nuh, huh?"

"Oh, yes, my friend. You only stopped because one of the last girls you asked said she was already married, and her husband was behind you."

"Fuck!"

"Calm down." Randy laughed. "It was Lynn. And Nick was behind you, but he knew you were wasted. He helped me get you into my car."

Finn put his head in his hands and slowly shook his head in disbelief.

"I do want to congratulate you on your engagement, though." Randy was enjoying this.

Finn looked up at Randy. "What?"

"Well, you did get a yes from one girl last night. It was after Lynn said no, but before Nick and I could get you out of there, so you may have a lot of explaining to do."

Finn sighed and took a deep breath. "FFUUUCCKKK!"

"So, you want to tell me what all of it was about?"

Finn shook his head. "Shelly didn't like her birthday present."

"What did you get her?"

"Two carat Diamond Earrings."

Randy looked at Finn, expecting him to say more. "And?" he asked.

"And…it wasn't what she wanted."

"What did she want?"

"An engagement ring."

"Oh."

"Yeah."

"Fuck."

"Yeah."

"What are you going to do?"

"I don't know." Finn sat back on the couch. Covering his eyes with his hands. "I don't know what happened. I looked online. I went to the store. I looked at the rings in the display cases, and when the salesgirl came over to me, I asked for earrings."

"Fuck."

"I know."

"You're going to have to figure something out."

"Thanks," Finn said wryly, looking up at Randy.

"Bro, I'm not trying to be a dick, but it has been like six years."

"I know."

"If you're not feeling it, I get it, but you can't leave her hanging."

"I know. I know. I'm not trying to leave her hanging. I just don't want to get married because all of her friends said we should."

"I get it. But you also don't want to get married if you're not feeling it. Marriage is hard, but you don't want to do it, then have kids. Divorce with kids is a lot harder."

Randy knew from experience. Finn had been there when Randy got married. Finn had been there when both of Randy's boys were born. Finn was also there when Randy's ex-wife decided she had enough of Randy's shit and didn't want to be married anymore, and they got divorced. Randy spent months miserable.

Randy sighed, "You know I got you, though," reaching his fist out for a fist bump.

Finn nodded his head. "Thanks," returning Randy's fist bump.

"No Worries. You should probably call Shelly and your brother while you're up, though."

"Why?"

"Because both of them have been blowing up your phone, and when your phone died, they started blowing up my phone."

Finn groaned, "Really?"

"Yup." Randy sighed. "There's coffee in the kitchen, and I think there's something edible in the fridge. Help yourself to whatever you can find. I gotta go. I have to go to the bank and then to the bar for a delivery."

Finn nodded and looked up at Randy. "Thanks."

Randy waved Finn's thanks away and turned towards the door. "Later."

Finn stood up, and nausea and pain went through his body. The room began to spin as his stomach lurched. "Maybe I should try again in a little while," he mumbled to himself as he sat back down. He lay down on the couch, closed his eyes, and passed back out.

"In one point two miles, stay in the right lane to merge onto Route One Thirty South towards Camden." Finns GPS said in a calming voice. Finn was already in the right lane. He looked at the highway signs to make sure he was going in the right direction. He wasn't sure what he was doing. He was in his truck, driving to a stranger's house for a job he didn't really need. The only thing he knew after the past couple of days, he needed to find something else to do.

He needed to get his shit together, and to do that, he needed to keep himself busy. It's how he cleared his mind. He made himself so busy he didn't have time to think, and somehow it helped him sort out the mess in his head, so he could think clearly. And, he had a lot to think about. After he woke up the second time from Randy's, he called his brother, then he called

Shelly. Neither conversation went well. His brother was pissed because Shelly blew up his phone. Shelly was pissed he walked out and hadn't come home.

At least his brother Mike wasn't so pissed at him, he wouldn't be forgiven. Finn could make it up to him with some beer. Shelly was another story, though. When he finally went home, Shelly wanted to fight, but she didn't. Which was a bonus because Finn was not in the mood to fight. He was still hungover, dehydrated, he needed a shower, and he had to work. Fighting with Shelly was not on his list of things needing immediate attention.

None of this explained why Finn was currently on his way to pick up another job. He already worked full-time as a maintenance supervisor for Tenby School District. He also worked two days a week at Neighbors for Randy. He didn't really need this job. He didn't need the money. He only found out about it because while working at Neighbors, one of the regulars told him about the South Jersey Marketplace's ad. Finn briefly read the ad, and at first, he didn't think much about it. But as the night wore on, the ad circled around his mind. He kept trying to push it away. It kept coming back. He went home and slept on it. It was the first thing he thought about when he woke up.

Sunday was usually the day he and Shelly would spend together doing all the things she wanted to do, but things were still tense between them. When he got up, Shelly was gone. She left a note saying she was going to the spa with her friends and would be back in time for dinner. Finn decided to call the number on the ad. What difference would it make if he just talked to the woman, right?

Finn called and talked to the woman. Her name was Kara, and the first thing Finn thought was he liked the sound of her voice. It was gentle, a little musky, and he could hear the warmth in it. He asked her about the ad, and she wondered if he had time to meet with her today. He did. He asked for the address, and they agreed to meet that afternoon. It hadn't been a long drive for him, only twenty minutes or so.

It wasn't far from the school, Neighbors, or from Shelly's. Not that any of it mattered. He was just going to have a conversation with the woman. He told himself he didn't have to accept the job or agree to anything.

Finn pulled up in front of the blue split-level house. The house was in a planned development, which was popular in the late seventy's early eighties. All the houses were pretty much the same except where the garage was placed. The home was well maintained, but Finn could see where it needed some work. There was a black SUV in the driveway and a path that led to the front of the house. There were two planters on either side of the front door, filled with small topiary bushes. As Finn walked up the driveway, he wondered why he felt so nervous. He got to the door and took a moment to slow his breathing. He took a deep breath and pressed the doorbell.

"Just a minute." Finn heard a muffled voice say. He shifted his weight as he waited for the door to open. He heard sounds running towards the door. The door opened, and when Finn looked up, his breath caught in his throat.

"Fuck, She's beautiful." The warning voice in Finn's head screamed. Sirens immediately going off in his head. She was tall, maybe five foot seven. Long black hair framed her heart-shaped face and fell loosely on her shoulders. Soft brown skin. Her dark brown eyes, outlined behind tortoiseshell glasses, were sparkling.

"Hi, can I help you?" She smiled at him, exposing perfect white teeth in a delicate full mouth. "Fuck Me." Finn thought to himself before actually speaking. His voice sounding rougher than he intended.

"Hi, I'm Finn. I called earlier about the ad." Finn was about to extend his hand and thought better of it and awkwardly put his hands in his pockets.

Kara's smile widened. "Hi, I'm Kara McNulty." She extended her hand, and Finn clumsily took his hand out of his pocket to shake her hand.

It was a mistake. Her hand felt unnaturally soft. It was small and warm in his rough hand. At the touch of her skin against his, Finn felt desire travel from his hand straight to his dick.

"It's nice to meet you," he said faintly, realizing a little late, he was still shaking her hand. "Let go of her hand, shithead," he yelled at himself. Finn let go of Kara's hand and felt the warmth of her touch leave his body. He felt colder.

"It's nice to meet you too. Come in." Kara said, ushering Finn into the

32

house. She stepped aside to let him in.

Finn looked around when he stepped into the house. He was in the living room, with stairs that led up to the kitchen and another stairway that led down to what he assumed was the lower level. The layout was a typical split-level floor plan. The living room had a modest dated couch and love seat. A glass coffee table was in the center, with matching end tables and lamps. There was a fireplace with a mantle with pictures and candles on it. A small tv was in the corner on a tv stand, on the other side of the bay window. Between the door and the window was a small table with a bowl for keys and a purse on top of it.

Kara shut the door behind him and walked up the stairs signaling for Finn to follow her. Finn watched her walk up the stairs. Kara had a medium build. She was wearing a blue top and jeans that enhanced her full ass, hips, and thick thighs. Finn almost tripped up the stairs because his eyes were glued to her. When he got to the top of the stairs, he folded his hands in front of him to hide the erection bulging in his jeans. Finn had not expected this. He was unprepared.

"Would you like something to drink?" Kara asked as she ushered him to sit at the kitchen table. "I've got coffee, tea, soda, or bottled water," she said, standing next to the fridge.

"Bottled water would be great." Finn said. His voice sounded weird to him. He coughed to clear his throat.

"Sure thing." Kara opened the fridge and grabbed two bottles of water, closing the door with her hip. Finn watched her as she walked over to the table and sat in the chair opposite of him. She handed him the bottle of water.

"Thank you," he said softly.

"You're welcome," she said as she pulled her chair closer to the table.

Finn opened his water and took a long drink. Closing his eyes, hoping the water would wash away her captured image branded on his brain. She had high cheekbones, and her smile was slowly causing him heart palpitations. "Don't look at her mouth," he thought to himself when he opened his eyes. "Concentrate on the center of her forehead. That's safe." Kara's hair was falling into her eyes, and he had to force his hands in between his legs to stop them from reaching out and gently brushing the hair away. "This was a bad idea," his mind screamed. Kara took a drink of her water and set the bottle down on the table.

"Well. I guess we should get started." She picked a copy of the official appraisal and handed it to him. "It's the appraisal, just to give you some context." Finn took the report from her and flipped through it. "I should probably start at the beginning, too," Kara said, watching him. Finn shifted slightly in his seat, feeling her eyes on him.

Finn listened as Kara explained why she was renovating the house. She told him how she had taken care of her mother, who recently passed away.

"I'm sorry," Finn whispered.

Kara smiled at him. "Thank you."

Finn looked down and tried to focus on the appraisal, trying not to react to her smile. Kara continued telling him about why she was renovating and what she hoped to accomplish. Finn tried to focus on what she was saying, but the way her voice filled his head, he knew it was futile. He would look up to show her he was pretending to pay attention and briefly study her face. "Were those freckles across her nose and under her eyes" Of course they were because it just made her seem even more beautiful. "Fuck, Finn, pay attention." He told himself. When Kara mentioned her son, he looked up and interrupted her,

"You have a son? How old are you?" he asked in disbelief. Kara laughed, and the sound pierced his heart and made him want to do whatever he needed to do to make her laugh again.

"Yes. My son's name is Matt. He's twenty years old. He'll be twenty-one soon. He goes to college at USC for video game design. And I'm forty-six years old."

"Really?"

"Yes, how old did you think I was?"

"I thought you had to be the same age as I am. Thirty-nine," he said.

The smile Kara gave him almost made him fall out of his chair. It spread across her face and made her eyes sparkle. He wanted to put his hand over his heart to make sure it was still beating because he wasn't sure it was.

"Well, now I have to hire you." she chuckled. "You just became one of my favorite people."

Finn smiled. "Well, I was trying to."

"You succeeded," Kara said kindly. "Well, now we have to be best friends."

"Best friends do help each other renovate houses."

"And move couches." They said simultaneously. Each of them laughing, their eyes met for a brief moment.

"Well," Kara said, delicately breaking their gaze. "I'm afraid it's not going to pay much. It's only one or two days a week. Mainly on Saturdays during the day because I work Saturday nights. I also work on Wednesday nights as well, apart from my full-time job."

"What do you do?" he asked.

"I work as an employee relations analyst in H.R. for a small printing company in Riverside."

"Oh, and where do you work part-time?"

"At the grocery store. It's only about twelve to sixteen hours a week, depending on what's going on. I've been working there on and off since I was in college. When I moved back home to take care of my mom, I started again as a distraction." she said.

Finn nodded his head, "I understand. I work part-time at Neighbors for my buddy Randy." Finn handed Kara back the appraisal he barely paid attention to.

Kara smiled. "I like working a lot. I can't sit still, and it helps." Taking the appraisal back and setting it down on the table. "Even though we're best friends," she said teasingly, "I still need to do a background check and drug test. I can't be too careful about who is coming into my home."

"Of course."

Kara looked at him, and Finn met her eye. "You should probably research me as well," she said softly.

Finn raised his eyebrow, "But you're my best friend." He smiled. "Of course, I trust you completely." Kara rewarded him with her smile, and he knew his heart stopped again. Then she laughed. Her laugh was rich, and the melody of it sent shivers down his spine.

"I know," she started, "But as your best friend who works in HR, you still want to make sure. It could take several months to finish this project. Because we are working on it part-time, it's a lot to have to commit to if you can't count on your best friend."

Finn studied her. There was something that snuck into her eyes. It was a hint of sadness, and it made his heart ache.

"You can count on me. I'll be there," he whispered. "Where the fuck did that come from?" he said to himself. "What the fuck is happening here?" his mind screamed. Kara nodded.

After exchanging their information, Kara put all the papers into a neat pile on the table.

"I still have some other contractors to speak to about the ad, but I'll call you within a couple of days to let you know, either way."

"I understand," Finn said quietly. He stood up from the table and pulled his phone out of his pocket to check the time. He'd been there almost an hour. Kara stood up as well, and Finn followed her out of the kitchen, downstairs to the front door.

"It was really nice to meet you," Kara said. She smiled warmly as she extended her hand for Finn.

"It was nice to meet you too," Finn said, shaking her hand. He liked how her hand felt in his. He didn't want to let it go. He had to scream at himself again to let her hand go. Finn stepped out of the house and walked down the path to his truck. He looked back and saw Kara as she stood in her front door. As he pulled away from the curb, he saw her go back into the house.

He wasn't sure what just happened. Thoughts swirling in his head like a tornado. Whatever happened, he would have to get his shit together if he would be working for her. He'd never reacted to someone the way he'd responded to Kara. From the moment he saw her when he shook her hand and the way she smiled at him. It wasn't just something about her. It was her. She made his body react in ways he wasn't sure he could keep under control. It scared him. A lot.

CHAPTER 3

Kara knew as soon as she opened the door and saw Finn, she would hire him. She knew he would be the one to help her renovate the house. When she shook his hand, she also understood just how much of a mistake it would be. When she thought about it after he left, she made a mental list of all the mistakes she'd be making.

Mistake number one was the minute he shook her hand, and it sent chills down her spine. It would be a terrible mistake to hire him. Mistake number two was when she felt his eyes on her as she walked him upstairs. It would be a huge mistake to hire him. Mistake number three was when he met her eyes while they were talking, and her heart felt like it would explode in her chest. She realized just how big of a mistake it would be to hire him.

She called in some favors to get the background check and drug test processed. She had to pay for it, but she got the results back within a day. Both came back squeaky clean. She wasn't surprised by it. She was actually kind of disappointed. If something came back, she would have an excuse to call him and tell him he couldn't work with her. The fact she felt that way scared her even more.

After Finn, she met with three other contractors, hoping one of them would get him off her mind. Of course, it didn't work. None of them even came close to Finn. They all had similar work experience. They were all qualified. But in the end, Finn was all she could think about.

She counted all the reasons why she shouldn't hire him. First, he was too good-looking. It shouldn't be a problem but considering Kara hadn't felt an attraction to anyone in what felt like forever, it was a big problem. How was she going to renovate her house if he were there? What if, when it was hot, he took his shirt off? Kara's breath caught at the thought of Finn without a shirt. His broad shoulders.

When he came to meet her, he was wearing a long-sleeved t-shirt and jeans. The t-shirt was loose, but you could tell he had a muscular build under it. He was taller than her, about six foot two or so. She had to look up at him, and when she did, he looked strong. He looked safe.

This led to the second reason she shouldn't hire him. Finn had long blond hair that had been pulled back when they met. It looked to be shoulder-length. He had deep blue eyes. Kara realized she could very easily drown in them, and honestly, she didn't know how to swim. His golden-brown beard framed his kind mouth. When he smiled at her, she felt it everywhere. She had to keep looking away when they talked because between his eyes and his mouth, Kara couldn't concentrate. That would be a problem.

The third reason was his hands. He had excellent hands. They were big and looked strong. She noticed that they didn't look cracked or feel calloused for a man who worked with his hands. They didn't feel rough against her skin. She didn't see a wedding band. Which means he probably took care of himself for a girlfriend. Again, this shouldn't be a problem, but Kara didn't want to spend any time thinking about someone else's boyfriend. This was one of the reasons she shouldn't hire him, which bothered Kara the most.

The thought he may have a girlfriend made her a little sad and a little jealous. She shouldn't feel one way or another about her "contractor" having a girlfriend. The whole reason he would be there would be to help her renovate her house.

The fourth and final reason she shouldn't hire him was she enjoyed talking to him. Sitting in the kitchen with him felt right. They spent an hour talking about the house and what she wanted to do with the renovation. She was comfortable around him, and Kara wasn't comfortable around anyone.

By nature, she was an introvert. It usually took a while before she became comfortable with someone. It didn't happen with Finn. She was relaxed with him when he walked in. The only reason she had been anxious was because he was so hot. It completely threw her. When she met with the other contractors, it lasted less than twenty minutes with each of them. She tried to get them to engage in conversation or at least be somewhat interested in what she wanted to do, but none of them seemed interested in anything other than what the appraisal said and how much she was going to pay them.

Despite the fact she had stupid reasons for not hiring him, Kara still hesitated before calling Finn and asking him to start on Saturday. She typed up the contract and made sure to put everything in writing. She didn't get the feeling he would screw her or anything. She felt like she would be able to trust him. Kara hadn't been able to trust someone in a really long time. Kara's phone rang, and she knew by the ringtone who it was.

"Hello, Darling," she said as she answered. It was Charlie. Kara's best and longest friend. They have been best friends since they were nine when Charlie's family moved across the street. Although Charlie's parents moved decades ago, Charlie and Kara's friendship remained. They went through everything together. They were closer than sisters because the universe chose them to be. They also looked alike, although Charlie was four inches shorter than Kara.

"My Kara senses were tingling. What are you doing?" Charlie said sarcastically.

"Wow. You have Kara senses?"

"Of course I do. I've known you for most of your life."

"Although that's true, I didn't know you developed a six sense when it came to me."

"Well, I have one, and it's tingling. Which means you are about to get into trouble."

"You know, I can't even lie. I am having a problem."

"What's the problem?"

Kara told Charlie all about Finn. Then she told Charlie all the reasons why she shouldn't hire him.

"So wait a minute. I'm confused. You find the perfect contractor who will help you renovate the house, but you don't want to hire him because you're attracted to him?"

"In a nutshell, Yes."

"I don't see a problem."

"He's White. And I don't think that would be a good idea."

"What does that have anything to do with this. Kara, you were married to an Irish White guy. You spend every Sunday eating dinner with his White family. Why all of a sudden, after years of saying you don't care, you are against it? Or.." Charlie said sarcastically, "Are you just afraid of this particular White man?"

"What's that supposed to mean?"

"Exactly what you think it means. That you are afraid of this man for whatever reason, and you are trying to find reasons not to hire him?"

"I'm not afraid of him," Kara whispered. She knew she was lying.

"Yes, you are. He disrupts your normal boring life." Charlie said, laughing.

"I don't have a boring life."

"Oh my God, Kara. You are the epitome of boring. It's one of the many things I love about you, but you aren't a risk-taker. You are very cautious, logical, and overthink everything." Charlie said. "You weren't expecting this guy. He's hot, passed a drug test and background check, and he happens to be White. You've been hiding in at your parent's house for the last two and a half years. And when you finally decide to come out of hiding, the first thing you run into is this guy. What's his name again?"

"Griffin Wilson is his full name, but he goes by Finn."

"Finn. The name sounds like a Disney Prince."

"You're crazy, and I have to go," Kara said, laughing. "I'll call you later." She pressed end on her phone.

Kara didn't want to actually have to talk to Finn. She remembered how he sounded when he first called and thought it might not be a good idea. She liked the sound of his voice too much. She sent him a text instead.

Kara: Hey, it's Kara. Would you be willing to start this Saturday? If you can't, it's no big deal. I know it's short notice.

Finn: Sure. I can be there Saturday. What time?

Kara: Is 9:30 ok? Saturday is the only day I get to "sleep" in.

Finn: lol, I get it. 9:30 it is.

Kara: Great, see you then.

Finn: Ok, see you then.

Kara set her phone down and sighed. "I'm an asshole," she said to herself. She took a deep breath and tried to think about the situation logically. First, there was no way someone like Finn would be interested in her. Number one: he was younger than her. She found out from the background check his birthday was five days before hers. If that wasn't scary enough, he was also almost seven years younger than her.

She was too old for him. "Ok, maybe not really old" she thought to herself, but old enough to know better, how about that. Someone like Finn would want a younger woman who would be able to give him kids. Someone, he would be able to grow with.

Number two: Kara was not thin. She wasn't big either. She was of average build. But she did have thick thighs, and her hips were wide. They had been since she was pregnant. And she had a FUPA. Kara knew there was a whole body positivity thing happening in the world, and although it had started to rub off on her, she wasn't fully there yet. Kara knew she was a beautiful woman. It had just been a really long time since someone else made her feel that way. She hadn't been on a date in years, and the last guy she did date made her feel like shit. He'd always saying hurtful things to her. It rocked her confidence.

Number three: this is going to be a professional relationship. Finn probably has a girlfriend. She's probably hot too and perfect, and all the things Kara wasn't. Not that any of it mattered, she realized because she was going to be Finn's boss. That was a line she would not be crossing.

And lastly, Number four: Kara needed to renovate the house. She needed to focus on moving on with her life. Charlie had been right about a lot of what she said. Kara had been hiding away for the last two and a half years taking care of her mother. Honestly, she'd been hiding for a lot longer than that. Since her previous boyfriend, Kara, hadn't so much as tried to date again. All the things she was feeling were just her projecting her loneliness.

The truth was Finn scared Kara. She hadn't been expecting him, and it had thrown her off. She just needed to accept this so she could get past it and move on.

Saturday morning Kara woke up at 4:30 in the morning. She lay in bed for an hour, trying to fall back asleep, but she couldn't. She finally decided to get out of bed and make some coffee. She walked out of the bedroom to the kitchen and turned on the coffee maker. It was set to start brewing at eight, but she manually turned it on. She knew she woke up because she was nervous about Finn starting today.

The original plan was to start at the top of the house and go room by room until everything was done. She changed her mind at the last minute and decided to clean out the garage today, so they would have the workspace needed to tackle everything else.

It was also kind of a trial to see if they would be able to work together. Kara was still working on getting her feelings on a more professional level. It's not that she had feelings for Finn. It was more that she could see herself having them. For her, it was all about the old saying, "An ounce of prevention is worth a pound of the cure." She made a cup of coffee and sat at the kitchen table to drink it.

Everything was so quiet. Kara looked outside over the backyard. Everything was still outside since the world was asleep. She wished she could quiet her mind. Thoughts of Finn had been haunting her all week. She took sips of her coffee and tried to focus on the plan for the day. She could do this.

Finn rang the doorbell at 9:25am. Kara checked her hair in the mirror. Then sighed and shook her head. "You're an asshole," she muttered to herself. She hurried down the hallway to open the door. When she opened the door, she was a little breathless. Finn was smiling at her.

"Hey," she said, smiling at him.

"Good Morning," he said as she ushered him in.

"How are you today?" she asked, closing the door behind him.

"I'm good. How are you?" Finn was looking at her intently, and it was a little unnerving. She smiled at him and shook her head slightly.

"Oh, you know, I feel like I have a million things to do and no time to do them." She ushered him to sit in the living room. Finn sat down on the love seat, and she walked around the coffee table and sat down.

"Do you want something to drink, coffee or something?"

"No." Finn shook his head. "I'm good." Finn sat back on the love seat. Kara felt so awkward.

"So, the plan for today is to clean out the garage and make some space for us to be able to work comfortably." Kara couldn't seem to meet his eyes. She was looking down a lot. And she felt like she was mumbling.

"That works for me," Finn said. He shifted in his seat, and Kara looked at him and met his gaze. "God, his eyes are so blue," she thought to herself.

"It's a good idea to set aside some space," Finn coughed to clear his throat. "It will also help to move things around when you're ready to start on the other rooms."

Kara smiled at him. "That's what I was thinking," she sighed. "Besides, my parents were hoarders, and they have stuff everywhere. We're going to be spending a lot of time just clearing stuff out."

"Should we get started?"

"I guess now is as good a time as any." Kara stood up and led Finn downstairs through the lower level towards the garage door.

They spent most of the morning taking everything out of the garage and putting it in piles. Kara forgot her father used to have a lot of tools, and most of them were buried behind boxes of things her parents didn't want to throw away. Boxes of old magazines and old books, none of them remarkable. Finn found a box of her father's old records. Most of the stuff in the garage was broken.

When it was time to break for lunch, Kara called and ordered a pizza. They took the trash out to the curb while they waited for it to be delivered. When the pizza came, they went into the house and washed up. Kara was sitting at the kitchen table waiting when Finn came out of the bathroom.

Strands of his silken blonde hair slipped out from his hair tie. Kara wanted to reach out and push the stray hair out of his eyes. She wondered if he noticed her hand shaking as she handed him a plate for the pizza.

During lunch, they made small talk. They talked about some of the records and books they found. How much junk was in the garage, and if any of the tools could be salvaged. Most of her father's tools were rusted, but they could still be used with a little work. After lunch, they finished cleaning out the garage. Some of the things could be donated, but most of it went out to the curb. They made space for all the lawn equipment her father owned when he could still mow the lawn. For the last couple of years, Kara paid a lawn service to come and take care of the yard and the flower beds.

When they finished, enough space was cleared to park the SUV in the garage if Kara wanted to. Kara tried to make a mental checklist for all the things they would need for the renovation. They talked about what small things she should need to have ready for when they started the following week. They were done by four that afternoon. Kara was exhausted. Since she hadn't slept well, she needed a nap and a long hot shower before she went to work.

She looked over at Finn as he carried the last of the trash out to the curb. They worked well together. Kara was surprised at how quickly they got into a flow. It still amazed her how comfortable she was with him. They had been able to talk effortlessly about things. And, the silences which fell between them weren't the awkward kind she had with other people.

She went into the house to give Finn the contract. When she handed it to him, she told him to look it over before signing it. He took it, signed it, and gave it back to her. When she questioned him about at least reading it or taking it to a lawyer, he looked at her with his penetrating blue eyes and smiled, "I trust you." Kara wanted to tell him, no, don't trust her. Not because of the contract. It was reasonably drawn up and benefited both of them. But, because she wasn't sure she was going to be able to keep it professional.

She smiled as she paid him for the day through the app on her phone before he left. She watched him get in his truck and pull away from the house. As she closed the garage, she tried not to think about how empty it seemed without him there. She shook her head slowly, then went back upstairs and took a long hot shower. Trying really hard not to think about how he kept looking at her and how much she liked it.

CHAPTER 4

Finn met Shelly when she came into Neighbors with her girlfriends for a bachelorette party. They were doing a Bachelorette Bar Parade. Going from bar to bar, drinking and buying the bride-to-be shots.

Shelly had come up to the bar to order a drink, started flirting with Finn, and spent the rest of the time her friends were at the bar, talking to him. Finn thought Shelly was hot. He hadn't met anyone like her before. When the girls left, Shelly told Finn he was taking her out the next night, and he did. That was almost six years ago.

Finn had never had a problem getting hard for Shelly. She was practically perfect. She was petite at five foot five. From her regular workouts, her body was slim and toned. Big full breasts, a tiny waist, and a round ass. Long light brown hair framed her round face with light brown eyes. She had a full soft pout from lip fillers, by her own admission. Shelly was smart, ambitious, and assertive. She always got what she wanted. Finn liked those things about her.

Shelly was now sitting on Finn's lap, kissing him and rocking her hips against his crotch, and Finn's dick was not having it.

"Fuucckkkkk," Finn thought to himself.

Since her birthday, things had been strained with Shelly. They've had fights in the past, but never for this long. Their relationship had changed, at least for him anyway. He knew she felt it too. Now Shelly was trying her best to bridge the distance. They used to have sex at least twice a week. Since her birthday, they'd had sex three times. Although that wasn't bad, it still averaged at least once a week. Something had changed. Finn kept trying, but he just couldn't seem to get his head or his dick into it. Finn knew the problem wasn't their relationship changed. The problem was their relationship had gotten worse since Finn met Kara.

At the thought of Kara, Finn's dick woke up. "Damn it," he thought to himself. He silently called his dick a traitor. He tried to think of anything else to help him. Models – nothing. Girls in bikinis – nothing. One of his favorite actresses who never failed to make him hard – slight movement . It was a little better, but it wasn't enough to get his dick to fully cooperate.

His mind wandered, trying to grasp at anything to help him respond. Kara flashed in his mind. She was smilin g and laughing . Her plum p full lips, dark red from the lipstick she wore, curved, showing her white teeth. He wondered if her lips were as soft as they looked. What she tasted like. If her skin was as silky as it looked. Finn's dick came to full attention. Shelly moaned.

"Fuck me," Finn screamed to himself inwardly. He was so screwed. He tried to push the thoughts of Kara away. It's not like he hadn't fantasized before. Of course, he had. He's human. Thinking about Kara wasn't good for him. It was like trying to stay away from sugar, only to have someone hand you a box of fresh-baked donuts. Kara's soft brown skin. Her dark brown eyes. "Fuck Finn. Focus," his mind screamed. But it didn't stop thinking about Kara. He remembered how soft Kara's skin was. He had accidentally brushed against her while cleaning out the garage, and Finn felt the curve of her hip as he walked by her. His hand burned at the memory of how she felt.

Shelly got off of Finn's lap, and took his hand to lead him to the bedroom. His dick was so hard it was almost painful to walk. "What the fuck am I doing?" he thought to himself. He was following his girlfriend of nearly six years to the bedroom they shared, so they could make love. He told himself. He was trying to stop the anxiety from creeping up his spine. He was going through the motions or at least trying to, but he could see it all slipping.

Shelly was standing by the bed, getting undressed. Finn stood in the doorway, watching her. Shelly's beautiful, she's sexy, and he shouldn't have a problem fucking her. He told himself. His dick disagreed and started to soften.

"Aren't you going to get undressed and come to bed?" Shelly said as she climbed into bed. Finn nodded. She had interrupted his reverie.

"Uh yeah," he said as he turned out the lights. He walked over to his side of the bed and got undressed. As he climbed in, Shelly slid into his arms and kissed him. Thoughts of Kara flooded Finn's mind. Instead of trying to stop them, he let them drown him.

Finn rang the doorbell and waited for Kara to answer. It was the second Saturday he was working with her, and they were going to start with the attic. He was holding his toolbox with one hand and kept shifting it between both hands. Kara answered the door, smiling at him.

"Hey," she said breathlessly. "You're right on time." She stepped back to let Finn into the house.

"Hi," Finn said as he stepped through the doorway. Kara closed the door behind him.

"Do you want some coffee or anything?"

"No. I'm good. I brought a bottle of water," he said, tapping his toolbox.

"Ok then," she said as she started up the stairs. Finn followed her, trying not to stare at the fullness of her ass. Finn had been telling himself he needed to stop thinking about Kara. He'd been doing a pretty good job, but now she was in front of him, he was slipping again.

"There's a lot of stuff in the attic that hasn't seen the light of day for years." Kara continued, causing Finn to snap back to attention. "My parents used to put anything up there they didn't want, but as they got older, they stuck stuff in the garage. I haven't been up there in years, so I have no idea what condition it's in other than what the inspection says. I know we're going to have to replace the insulation and probably the floors." Kara stopped in the middle of the hallway and looked up at the drawstring. She tried to jump up to pull it down, and Finn couldn't help but smile at her.

"Would you like some help?" he chuckled.

"Yes, please. Would you mind? I'm not tall enough."

Fin walked over to her. Smiling. "Fuck, she's adorable." He thought himself as he pulled the drawstring, lowering the ladder to the attic.

"Thank you," Kara whispered.

"No problem."

Finn stepped aside and watched as Kara climbed the stairs ahead of him. Kara was wearing jeans, seeming to hug her curves and made her ass look amazing. Finn closed his eyes as his dick started to get hard. "Stop it." He told himself. He waited until she got to the top, then he started climbing the stairs.

When he got to the top, he looked around. The attic was small with low ceilings. If he stood at full height, his head would bump the raisers. He had to slouch a bit. Kara turned around as he walked in and started laughing. The rich sound of her laughter filling the room. Finn smiled at her. He loved the sound of her laugh.

"I'm sorry," she said, smirking at him with a wry smile. "I forgot how tall you are and how low the ceilings were. There's a chair in the corner over there if you want to sit down instead of hunching over."

"Thanks," Finn said as he walked past her over to the chair and sat down. He could smell her perfume when he walked by. What was it? He thought to himself. It was floral and musky at the same time. He liked it.

The attic was filled with boxes and various pieces of furniture. There was a standing oval mirror and different odds and ends throughout the room. The beams were exposed in the walls, and some of the insulation was missing. The floor had spots where it was dry-rotted, so you had to be careful where you stepped.

"We had a bat problem last year," Kara said as she walked toward him. "Of course, I was completely freaked out. We called someone who got rid of them, and they were able to fix the hole the bats got in from, but you can see where the damage was done."

Finn looked around and saw where the hole was fixed in the roof. "Where should we start?" he asked.

"I thought we should clear everything out of here. Then we'll know what we're dealing with."

"Sounds good."

They started moving the boxes towards the hatch opening so it would be easier to take them downstairs. Clusters of things were sporadically throughout the room. Once one of the clusters were by the hatch, Finn would climb down a few steps, and Kara would hand him boxes to take down.

"Where do you want me to put them?" He called up to her.

"Put them in the living room for now. Then I can look through them and either put them in the trash or re-box them to bring up later."

Finn stacked boxes in front of the fireplace. Careful not to block the tv and still leave room for Kara to sit on the couch. After clearing out most of the clusters, there were still two hefty boxes Kara couldn't move. Finn climbed back into the attic and walked over to where Kara was sitting next to the boxes.

"These are too heavy for me," she said as she started to open one of the boxes. "I thought it would be easier to see what was in them before trying to move them."

"I can carry them down for you," he said as he knelt down beside her. Kara looked at him, smiling. "I'm stronger than I look," he said, smiling back at her. She wiped her brow to move the hair out of her eyes. She was wearing it in a ponytail, and strands came loose and fell, framing her face.

"I have no doubt about your strength," she said sarcastically, trying not to laugh. "I didn't think you were a delicate flower." The smile she was trying to hide, escaping. Finn laughed. Kara opened the box, and it was filled with old encyclopedias.

"Wow," she said, holding up one of the books. "I remember these. No wonder these boxes were so heavy."

"I haven't seen encyclopedia's in years."

"I know. No one has them anymore now that everything is on the internet."

"My parents had a set too. I think they are still in my father's office," he said.

50

Kara looked through the book. "Well, it was printed in 1982. None of this stuff is true anymore." She put the book back into the box. "Are you sure you're not too delicate to handle the boxes?"

Finn smiled at her, "I promise. I can handle anything you need me to." Kara looked at him, and he met her gaze.

"I'm sure you can," she whispered. Finn felt it pierce right through him. He thought he heard something in her voice, and he had to stop himself from leaning forward and kissing her.

Kara got up and brushed off the dust from sitting on the floor. Finn picked up the box. It was heavy but not too heavy. He carried it to the hatch and set it down so he could climb down some stairs. He picked it back up and brought it to the living room. Kara waited upstairs while he came back to get the second box. Kara climbed down the stairs and walked to the living room. Finn set the last box down. He turned around when he felt her looking at him.

"I think it's time for some lunch," she said, her eyes looking over all of the boxes. They were neatly piled up. The furniture and odd pieces in the attic, Finn put down in the lower level. "What time is it?"

Finn pulled his phone out of his back pocket to check the time. "It's 12:30." He noticed he had six texts from Shelly. He had been so busy, he hadn't even felt his phone vibrate.

"Are you hungry?" Kara asked him.

Finn put his phone back in his back pocket. "I could eat."

"Are sandwiches ok?"

Finn nodded. "I like sandwiches."

Kara smiled at him. "Good. I'll go clean up a bit, and I'll meet you in the kitchen in five. And we'll make some lunch."

"Ok." Finn watched as Kara walked down the hallway towards the bedroom.

He fired off responses to Shelly's texts. She knew he was working, but he didn't say where. Only he was going to pick up some extra hours. When he started working with Kara, he told himself he would use the money to save up for the engagement ring Shelly wanted. The extra money would help.

He wasn't sure why he didn't just tell her the truth at the time. He was going to tell Shelly he was remodeling a house. But, as he told her about working more, she didn't seem to care, so he just stopped talking and instead asked her about her day.

He climbed the stairs and went down the hallway to the bathroom. He needed to wash his hands and clean off some of the grime. He rolled his sleeves up and washed his face. He dried off using the paper towels that were in the bathroom. When he came out of the bathroom, he felt a little more human. Kara was already in the kitchen when he got there. She was looking in the fridge and didn't realize he was there until she closed the door.

"Can I do something to help?" he asked lightly.

Kara held some of the things in her hands. She straightened up and smiled at him.

"Sure," Then she looked down and noticed his ink. "I didn't know you had ink." Finn looked down at his arms, turning them to show Kara.

"Yeah, I got most of it a while ago. I haven't gotten anything new in years," He stood next to her at the counter as she put things down. "I should probably have some of it recolored." He noticed she took her hair out of the ponytail and brushed it, so it fell lightly on her shoulders.

"I was always a little too chicken to get a tattoo, even though almost everyone I know has one. But I've been thinking about it a lot in the past couple of weeks."

"Really? What are you going to get?"

"I'm not sure. Probably something small. I'm still not into the whole needle pain thing."

Finn smiled at her, "Yeah, I can't lie. They hurt. But it's not too bad. It only hurts for a little while, then it goes away."

She looked at him skeptically and smiled. "That's what everyone says, but I'm still not sure." Kara organized everything on the counter. She had it set it up like an assembly line. "What kind of sandwich would you like?"

"What have you got?"

Kara picked up a package of lunch meat. "We have turkey, ham, and roast beef." She set it down and gestured towards some cheese. "We also have American and provolone cheese."

"I'll take turkey and provolone, please."

"I've got wheat bread, is that ok?"

"It's fine."

"Mayo or mustard?"

"A little mayo."

"Lettuce and tomato?"

"Sure." Finn laughed. "What do you want me to do?"

"Can you grab some chips?"

"Ok. Where are they?"

Kara turned and pointed to the cabinet across the kitchen. "They're in there. They're in a variety bag." She started making the sandwiches.

Finn walked over to the cabinet and opened it taking out the bag. "What kind of chips would you like?"

"Barbeque"

Finn took out two bags of barbeque chips and put the bag back into the cabinet. "What else?"

"Can you grab some plates? They are in the second cabinet."

Finn looked in the second cabinet and took out two plates, and walked them over to Kara.

"Thank you," she said. She was done making the sandwiches. Finn noticed she cut them in triangles, and it made him smile. Kara handed Finn his sandwich, and they both walked over to the kitchen table.

"I forgot, what did you want to drink?" Kara said as she set her plate down and walked back over to the fridge. Finn sat down and turned around.

"A bottle of water is fine." Kara grabbed two bottles of water and handed one to Finn before sitting down. They ate in silence for a while. Finn didn't realize how hungry he was. He was mid-bite when Kara asked him,

"So Finn, tell me about yourself."

Finn took his bite, hoping it would give him some time to think about her question. When he was done, he wiped his mouth.

"What did you want to know?"

"Not the normal stuff everyone always talks about." She put a chip in her mouth and chewed. "Where did you grow up stuff? We'll save all that for later."

Finn laughed. "Ok. Then what?"

"Tell me something random." She ate another chip. She was thinking about what to ask. "You know what, never mind, let's do something different. I do this at work when I have to teach a training class. I'll ask you a question, and you can either answer or pass. Then you get to ask me a question."

Finn sat back in the chair and put his napkin on his plate. "Ok. Sounds fun."

Kara smiled at him. "It is. And we're going to keep it simple. Nothing too deep or too personal. I think that may be a little much for a Saturday afternoon."

Finn laughed. "Very true."

"Ok," Kara said, putting her bag of chips down on her plate. "We have to play Rock, Paper, Scissors to see who goes first." They both held out their hands.

"Rock, Paper, Scissor, Shoot." They said in unison. Kara had paper, and he had rock.

"Paper covers rock," Kara said triumphantly as she covered his hand with hers. Their eyes met, and Kara gently pulled her hand away. Finn felt the loss of her warmth.

"You win," Finn whispered. "Ask away."

Kara folded her hands in front of her on the table.

"When you were seven years old, what did you want to be when you grew up?"

Finn thought a moment. "A Transformer."

"A Transformer? Really?"

"Yes. I wanted to be an Autobot and protect the earth with Optimus Prime."

"That's funny. OK, your turn."

"What was your favorite tv show as a kid?"

"That's a good one. I'm going to go with Family Ties."

"Really?"

"Oh My God, yes." Kara laughed. "I loved Alex P Keaton. I was so in love with him. He was the first 'Hot nerd.'"

"Hot nerd? What's a hot nerd?"

"Yes. It was an eighties thing. All the tv shows had a nerdy kid who would become hot. Alex was the first one. And not for nothing, the feathered hair, the sweater vest, and tie." Kara waived herself with her hand. "It's still hot."

"I'll have to keep that in mind." Finn laughed. "Your turn."

"What is your favorite Christmas Movie?"

"Die Hard."

Kara burst out laughing. Finn loved when she laughed like that. "You're one of those."

"One of what?"

"Die Hard is not a Christmas movie," she laughed again. "It's a movie about what happened during an office Christmas party."

"That's what makes it a Christmas movie. It's also a love story. It's a romantic Christmas comedy." Finn was trying not to smile. Kara's eyes were sparkling as she laughed.

"Wait, what?"

"It's a love story. A hard-working detective breaks into a hostage situation to save his wife and win her back before she divorces him."

Kara took a sip of her water. "That is such a dude thing to say."

"No, it's not," he said, feigning disbelief. "You just don't get true romance."

Kara laughed even harder. Finn soaked it all in. Her laugh, the way her mouth curved into a smile. The expression on her face.

"I didn't realize Die Hard was a Christmas Rom-Com. I've been mistakenly thinking Pride and Prejudice was true romance."

"See, that's the problem. Pride and Prejudice is nowhere near as romantic as Die Hard. No buildings blow up, and I'm pretty sure no one walks on broken glass."

"That's true. There's no mention of buildings blowing up or anyone walking on broken glass. I've been so blind. I'm going to have to rethink my definition of romance and watch Die Hard again. Seriously, I've wasted the last thirty years."

"See, I've just changed your life."

"You really have. I will forever be in your debt." Kara smiled at him. Finn felt like his heart was going to stop. He could hear the warning bells going off in his head and wondered if they were loud enough for Kara to hear them. Kara looked past him at the clock on the microwave behind him.

"It's almost two o'clock," she said as she stood up from the table. "We should probably finish up in the attic."

Finn got up and picked up his plate. Kara waved her hand at him. "Don't worry about it. I'll clean it up later."

"Are you sure?"

"Yeah," she said, smiling at him.

Finn set the plate back down on the table and finished the last of his water. He followed Kara back down the hallway and watched as she climbed the ladder to go upstairs. Before he went up the ladder, he took a deep breath. His heart was still beating too fast.

An hour later, they finished measuring the attic to replace the floors. They measured the room for the amount of insulation needed and how much drywall to cover the walls. As they were going back downstairs, Kara looked around at the floor.

"I'm surprised the weight of all that stuff didn't fall through the ceiling with half the floor dry rotted." She stepped on the ladder to climb down.

Finn followed her. "It wasn't that bad. It was just old." When he got to the bottom, he slid up the ladder, so it folded up to close the attic door.

"I guess so. I'll call and place the order for all the stuff we need. I'll get the insulation and drywall first."

"Sounds good." Finn put his hands in his pockets. Kara was walking down the steps looking at all the stuff now piled in the living room. "Do you need some help with all of this?" Finn pointed to the boxes.

Kara shook her head, "No, I should be able to manage." She took out her phone. "I'll Venmo you the money for today. I better do it now before I get distracted and forget."

"It's not a big deal."

"Yes, it is. It's important," she looked at him earnestly. Well, if it's important to her, then it's important to me. Finn thought to himself.

"Thank you," he whispered. Kara nodded. Finn turned and started walking towards the door. He felt his phone vibrate from the notification Kara paid him. He hesitated a moment at the door, not really wanting to leave but not having a reason to stay.

"I'll see you next week then," he said as he put his hand on the door handle to open the door.

"Ok. I'll see you Saturday." Kara walked up behind him as he walked out of the door. The sun was still shining. It was an early spring day. He turned to look at her as he was leaving.

"Bye," he whispered.

"Bye," Kara said as she closed the door behind him.

He walked toward his truck, forcing himself not to turn around.

CHAPTER 5

Kara took a sip from the glass of wine she was holding. She was sitting in the living room, feeling the boxes close in on her. The living room looked like a bomb went off in it. Boxes and trash were everywhere. Pile of clothes on the love seat. Knick-knacks lay all over the coffee table. She still had enough room for her to sit on the couch, and she could even walk from the couch to the stairs. But, it was limited.

She'd been feeling overwhelmed for the last couple of days. She'd gone through most of the boxes and so far had found a lot of old clothes. What she found, she didn't see anything she wanted to keep. Some of them could be donated, but most of them needed to be tossed. She also found a lot of small knick-knacks her mother used to have all over the house. They weren't really worth anything, but she wasn't sure what to do with them. She thought about a yard sale, but she didn't have the patience for that.

She took another sip of wine. She held the glass in both hands, looking at the few boxes remaining. She still had the encyclopedia's and two boxes on top of that. She should have asked someone to come and help, but she didn't want to bother anyone. Charlie would come, but she already had her hands full. Matt was in California, so he couldn't help. There was her brother, but he was in Louisiana, and even if he were here, he wouldn't be any use anyway.

Kara realized she knew a lot of people but didn't really have a lot of friends.

Well, of course, she didn't, she thought to herself. She'd spent the last two years caring for her mother. Before that, she spent all of her time taking care of Matt. She could call Chris, he would come and help, but she didn't want to bother him. He and Teresa had a toddler at home. Teresa would jump at the chance to come and help, just to get out of the house. But they would have to drive almost an hour to get here. It wouldn't be worth it.

She thought about Finn. She could call him and ask him for help. It is one of the things they talked about when she hired him. No, she shook her head. She needed to keep her distance from him. He was spending way too much time in her thoughts as it was. Besides, he was supposed to be helping her renovate the house, not help her get her shit together.

"Why not?" she thought to herself. Because you have to keep this strictly professional. And how pathetic do you have to be to call your contractor to come over and help you sort through your shit? Well, technically, it wasn't her shit. It was her parents. That wasn't the point. The point was she couldn't call her contractor to come and help her clean up her living room. Even if she could. It isn't what she hired him for. "No. You hired him because he was hot, and he said you looked younger than you are," she said to herself.

Kara paused. Two things were bothering her. One. She was having an argument with herself in her head, and she was losing. Two. She couldn't deny Finn was hot. Especially when she saw his ink. And not for nothing, but when did forearms become so sexy to her?

The first thing she was used to. People talk to themselves all the time. She could also admit she lost arguments with herself all the time. The second thing was what she was anxious about. Kara hadn't been attracted to anyone in years. Not since she'd been taking care of her mother. She hadn't had any time. Then she started working part-time, and even though she met some men, she kind of talked to. None of them held her interest.

Finn was different, though. He made her laugh. And on Saturday, when they were eating lunch, she hadn't had that much fun in a really long time. She still wouldn't bother him, though. Kara sighed and put down her glass of wine. She picked up one of the knick-knacks and started wrapping it in a newspaper. She was going to repack them and then make a decision about what to do with them later. Kara's phone rang, and she picked it up.

"Hey Charlie."

"Hey."

"What's going on?"

"I'm calling to remind you about Mia's dance recital Thursday night." Charlie chirped.

"I didn't forget. I took the night off."

"Good. Afterward, we're going to dinner."

"Ok," Kara said flatly.

"What's wrong with you?" Charlie asked.

"Nothing, why?"

"You sound blah."

"I'm just a little overwhelmed."

"Why?"

"Finn and I cleaned out the attic and brought the boxes down. Well, I'm going through them, and there's a lot of stuff. I've gone through a lot of the boxes, but there are still some left, and I just feel like I'm surrounded by boxes." Kara sighed and leaned back on the couch.

"Why don't you just call the hot contractor?"

"Finn?" Kara laughed. "And I don't think I referred to him as hot."

"Oh, yes, you did."

"Well, he is. And that's not the point. I can't ask him to come and help me get all this shit together."

"How do you know? You could ask him for help. I mean, you're going to pay him, aren't you?"

"Of course," Kara said indignantly.

"Well then," Charlie said. "Unless you're still hung up on how hot he is?" she laughed.

"I'm not. And not that it matters, I'm older than he is, and I'm pretty sure he has a girlfriend."

"God, Kara, it's only a little older. It's not like your fifty years older than him or anything. Calm down."

"I feel like I'm ninety, does that count?"

"No, it doesn't."

"I'll think about it." It was as much as Kara was willing to agree to.

"Good. Anyway, I've got to go. I have to do a million things to get Mia ready for her recital."

"Ok, I'll see you Thursday." Kara hit the end button. She needed to do something else. The thought of everything around her was a little too much for her to deal with. She got up and turned on the tv.

Kara was sitting at her desk, finishing up for the day. She wasn't really looking forward to going home and dealing with all the stuff in her living room. She was typing up an email when her phone rang. She didn't recognize the ringtone, so she answered.

"Hello."

"Hi Kara, it's Finn."

Kara stopped typing the email. "Hey, how are you?" She was afraid he was going to cancel for Saturday.

"I'm ok. Are you busy?"

"No, I'm finishing up an email then heading home to the disaster that is my living room."

"Would you like some help?" he asked softly.

Kara hesitated. How did he know she needed help? She did need help but. Should she?

"Hello, Kara, are you there?" Finn asked.

"I'm here," she said.

"Oh, I'm outside my office, so I thought I lost you."

"No, you didn't lose me." Kara sighed. Why did everything they said to each other seem so much more than it was supposed to be? "I would actually love some help, but I don't want you to go out of your way."

"It's not out of my way."

"Are you sure?" she asked, then hesitated. "Wait, why did you call me? Did you need something?"

Finn laughed. "I actually called because I left my toolbox in the living room, and I didn't realize it until I needed one of my tools."

"Well, then it works out. I wouldn't have been able to find it anyway. There's stuff all over the place."

"I'll stop by after work. I should be leaving here in about twenty minutes."

"Ok, I'll see you then."

"Bye."

"Bye." Kara hit the end button and smiled.

Thirty minutes later, Kara pulled into her driveway and saw Finn was waiting in his truck for her. She smiled when she saw him. He got out of the car and walked up the driveway towards her.

"Hi," she said as she grabbed her stuff out of the car. "Thanks for coming over to help."

"No problem. I wasn't really doing anything anyway." Finn said. Kara felt him staring at her. They walked up the path, and Kara opened the door to the house. As Finn walked in, he closed the door behind him. He looked around and whistled.

Kara nodded. "I know. I didn't realize just how much stuff there was until I started opening boxes. I got a little overwhelmed by it all."

"I can see why. Did you get one of those dumpster bags we talked about on Saturday?"

Kara shook her head. "Not yet. I was waiting until I went to pick up all the other the stuff I ordered."

"Well, I'll help you put them in trash bags, and we can go from there."

"That would be great. I'll run and get changed, and then we can get started," she said quietly.

Finn looked her up and down, and Kara could swear she felt his eyes travel her body before he met her gaze again. She was wearing a dress and heels like she usually did for work. She distractedly tugged at her dress.

"Ok. I'll wait here," he whispered.

Kara nodded and turned to go up the stairs to get changed. She came back five minutes later dressed in jeans and a t-shirt. She had taken off her heels and put on some flip-flops. She stopped by the kitchen to grab the box of trash bags. Finn was sitting on the couch when she went down the stairs, looking at the knick-knacks littering the coffee table.

"I grabbed the trash bags on the way down," she said, a little breathless from running around.

Finn stood up and took the box of bags from her. "What's going first?"

Finn held the bag open as Kara filled it with the things she knew were going to be trashed. Most of them were old clothes with holes in them or were so worn it would be pointless to try to salvage them. When the bags were full, Finn would put them by the door, so they could put them out on the curb.

They worked seamlessly. Clearing off the love seat and emptying more boxes. Things going to be donated were put in a separate bag in front of the fireplace. While Finn was going through one of the boxes, he looked over at Kara.

"Does the fireplace still work?" He picked up the box he was going through and put it on the couch. It had more knick-knacks in it.

"The Inspector said it did, but it would need a lot of work. It hasn't been used in probably ten years. I know for sure at least eight years since my dad died."

"Are you going to fix it?"

"I was thinking about it. The Inspector thought it would be better if I converted it to gas. But I haven't decided yet. I like the idea of fireplaces, but I'm not sure if I would really use it."

"Why not?" Finn brought over another bag to hold for Kara. She found another box full of her brother's old clothes. She would donate them.

"I don't know," she said. "Don't you think they're a little cheesy?"

"You could use it in the winter. When it's freezing in January and February. And so what if they're cheesy. There's nothing wrong with cheesy." Finn was standing in front of her holding open the bag. Kara smiled at him as she started to fill the bag.

"Maybe. I'll have to think about it."

All the clothes were in bags, and the ones being donated were put downstairs to go into the garage. The living room didn't seem to be as overwhelming as it was before. Finn sat on the couch, and Kara sat on the love seat as they repacked the knick-knacks and keepsakes her mother had collected over the years. When they finished with the box, Finn carried it upstairs and put it in the spare bedroom to be taken up to the attic when they were done renovating it.

They talked about their day while they worked. Finn told her about working at the high school and the stupid things the students did. Kara told Finn about working in employee relations and all the silly stuff employees did.

Finn's phone rang while he was taping up one of the boxes. When he answered it, Kara motioned she was going upstairs to get something to drink. She wanted to give him some privacy to take the call. She walked up the stairs to the kitchen and looked at the clock on the microwave. Finn had been there for almost two hours. She shook her head slightly, not really believing the time, and got two wine glasses from the cabinet. She got the open bottle of cabernet out of the fridge. She poured both glasses and took a sip out of hers.

She turned and leaned against the counter. She could see Finn standing in front of the window whispering on the phone, so his back was to her. She looked at his blonde hair in the man bun at the nape of his neck. It was slowly unraveling against the collar of his navy blue work shirt. The blue made his eyes look even bluer if that was possible, she thought to herself. She noticed how broad his shoulders looked in the shirt. It fit him just right, even though it seemed a little tight at his shoulders. Her eyes traveled down his back to his ass. His ass looked perfect in his jeans.

"Stop it." She told herself. Seriously, she needed to get it together. She took a gulp of wine and then picked up the bottle to refill her glass. Finn finished on the phone. He put it in his back pocket and walked upstairs to the kitchen. Kara could see the annoyance on his face. His eyes were darker, and Kara thought it was sexy as hell. She almost choked on the wine she was swallowing. When Finn walked into the kitchen, she handed him the glass of wine she poured for him. He took it and drank half of it in one gulp.

"I have beer too if you would prefer that?" she said. She was reading how expressive his face was.

"A beer would be great," he said.

Kara turned and opened the fridge and took out one of the beers she bought when her brother was there. Kara wasn't really a beer drinker, but Anthony was. Anthony complained there wasn't any beer in the house, so to keep the peace, Kara bought some. Finn took the bottle and used the bottle opener on his keys to open it. Then he took a long drink of his beer. Kara watched him closely.

"Is everything ok?" she asked quietly. She didn't want to pry, but she could tell something was bothering him.

Finn set his beer on the counter. "Yeah, it's fine."

"Are you sure?"

Finn looked at Kara directly in the eye. The look was so intense, Kara felt it all the way to her toes. Finn looked away and picked up his beer.

"Yes, I'm sure."

Kara took a sip of wine and looked at the clock. It was seven. "Are you hungry? I could order a pizza."

Finn nodded. "I could eat."

Kara smiled. She put down her wine glass and took her phone out of her back pocket.

"Do you have a preference for toppings?" Finn shook his head. "Ok. Large plain it is." She placed the order through an app on her phone. When she was done, she put her phone back in her back pocket. Finn followed Kara back downstairs to the living room. They finished packing up the keepsakes in silence. Once the boxes were packed, Finn would put them in the spare room.

When the pizza came, Kara answered the door. With the pizza in her hands, she closed the door and looked over at Finn. He still looked annoyed but not as much. Finn looked up at her, and she lowered the pizza box.

"Hungry?" Finn nodded and stood up from the couch. "Go and get washed up, and I'll meet you in the kitchen so we can eat," she said gently.

Kara walked upstairs towards the kitchen, and Finn followed her up but went to the bathroom in the hallway. Kara set the pizza down on the kitchen table, went over to the sink, and washed her hands. She got down two plates from the cabinet and grabbed some paper towels. She sat down at the table to wait for Finn.

When he walked into the kitchen, he looked a little better. "I'm sorry. I feel like I brought down the mood."

Kara waved her hand, dismissing him. "It's fine. Do you want to talk about it now?"

Finn looked down and shook his head. Kara nodded at him and smiled.

"Good. I shall then dazzle you with my brilliance." Finn looked up at her. Kara picked up a slice of pizza, put it on a plate, and handed it to him.

"I shall regale you with tales from my youth. Full of embarrassment, which will distract you and entertain you." Finn smiled as he bit into the pizza.

"The first tale begins when I was seven. I actually believed my dolls were alive, just like people. My brother was mean and tied one of my doll's hair into knots all over her head. So I had the brilliant idea to cut my doll's hair because I thought it would grow back. When it didn't, I went to my dad and told him the doll was sick and needed to go to the hospital."

Finn chuckled. Kara continued, "So you can imagine my surprise when Toy Story came out, and I took Matt to see it. I stood up in the theater screaming, 'I knew it' when the toys came to life. Matt looked at me like I was crazy." Finn laughed.

"I should have sued Disney for stealing an idea I didn't know I had." Kara took a bite of her pizza. When she was done chewing, she wiped her mouth on a napkin. "When I was ten," She continued to tell Finn about all the stupid things she did when she was a kid. She told him about the time she thought she could be a professional wrestler and broke her bed frame. She told him about when she was sixteen, got drunk for the first time, and threw up all over the bathroom. She told him how Charlie had cleaned it up before her parents came home.

She told him about the time she was eighteen, working her first and only waitress job, and how she dropped a birthday cake on the birthday boy and got fired the same day. Then she told him the best story she had. When she was twenty-one in college, and took a trip to New York with her friends.

"I thought I was hot shit, in my mini skirt, and a pigeon pooped on my head. I was absolutely mortified because, of course, the guy I liked was there, and he thought it was hysterical." Finn was laughing so hard she gave him a moment before she continued.

"Thankfully, Charlie was there and came with me. We found a motel room we could rent for a couple of hours. I washed my hair and got changed into an "I Love NY" t-shirt Charlie bought for me. The best part is, I didn't end up with the guy. I realized he was an asshole if he laughed at me. But I still have the t-shirt."

With each story, Finn laughed harder than the last. By the time she was done with her stories, they had finished eating the pizza, forty minutes had passed, and Finn was smiling. He wiped his mouth with a paper towel and put it on his plate. His eyes were sparkling.

"Well, you did it," he said as he pushed his plate forward. "Did what?" Kara asked innocently.

"You successfully regaled me with tales that distracted me."

Kara laughed, "You forgot to add the brilliant part." She pushed her plate forward on the table. "Besides, nothing makes you feel better than hearing about someone else's misery."

"That's true." Finn smiled. Kara met his gaze. He was looking at her so intently. She felt the flitter of her heart. "Seriously, calm down." She told herself. She shifted slightly in her chair.

"Yes, it is." She gave Finn a severe look, "I do have to warn you though," she said in a cautious tone, "If you tell anyone else about what you have heard here tonight, I will find you and torture you until you die."

Finn held up his right hand and put it over his heart. "I promise to take what you told me to the grave."

Kara nodded. "Good, because I would hate to have to kill you."

Finn laughed until he felt his phone vibrate. He pulled his phone out of his back pocket and looked at the screen, the frown returning to his face. He looked up at Kara, "I should probably go. It's already after nine."

Kara looked up at the clock on the microwave. It was 9:17. "I didn't realize it was that late," she whispered.

"Neither did I," Finn said quietly, standing up.

She stood up as Finn picked up his plate to put it in the sink and throw the paper towel away. He walked over to the stairs and waited for Kara to join him. They walked down to the living room. It looked much better since Finn had come and help. Kara didn't understand why she was so hesitant to ask for his help earlier.

Finn walked over to the front door. His toolbox was by the table where Kara left her keys. She followed him to the door and pulled her phone out of her back pocket. She opened the app and paid him.

"Thank you for coming over and helping me with this mess."

Finn got the notification and pulled out his phone to look at it. "Kara, you didn't."

Kara raised her hand to stop him. "Of course I did." Smiling at him. Finn nodded his head. "Thank you." He turned and went to open the door. Kara stepping behind him. "I'll drop off a dumpster bag tomorrow, so we will have it ready for Saturday."

Kara nodded, "Sounds good."

Finn opened the door and stepped out into the chilly spring night. "I'll see you later," he said as he walked down the path towards his truck.

"Bye." Kara said as she closed the door behind him.

Kara leaned back against the door and closed her eyes. Her heart had been pounding from the way Finn had looked at her. It had taken all of her strength not to wrap her arms around him and try to take away whatever was bothering him. She took a deep breath and opened her eyes.

The living room did look much better. She was glad Finn called her earlier. She wondered briefly what had made him so upset earlier and realized it was probably his girlfriend. The thought of Finn with his girlfriend stirred up a knot of jealousy in her stomach.

She had to remind herself, of course, Finn had a girlfriend. And it didn't matter anyway because he was her contractor. She was paying him to help her renovate. Nothing more. It's just business. She started repeating it to herself. Maybe if she told herself enough, whatever feelings he stirred up in her would go away.

She reminded herself, Finn wouldn't be interested in her anyway. She was too old for him. Seven years may not be a lot in the scheme of things, but how much could they really have in common. She was also a curvy woman. She had hips and an ass. She had a belly and thick thighs. Finn's girlfriend was probably perfect. Something she most definitely was not. She was being ridiculous and dramatic. She was just lonely and projecting her feelings onto him.

Kara kept repeating all of these things over and over to herself. Kara sighed and went into the living room to turn out the lights. It had been a long day, and she was tired. She wished there would be a way of just turning off feelings she didn't want. Just like she turned off the lights. The more time she spent with Finn, the more difficult it was to keep things on the professional side. She shook her head, hoping to clear the thoughts swirling around. She walked up the stairs and started to get ready for bed.

CHAPTER 6

Finn had his head in his hands.

He was hoping it would help, but the pounding at his temples suggested otherwise. He was sitting on the couch watching Shelly pace back and forth in front of him, having an epic temper tantrum. Finn sighed. He was mentally, physically, and emotionally exhausted.

In Shelly's defense, she'd been having a bad week. She was busy with a project at work and had been working a lot. Her mother called her, bringing up some past family drama from decades ago. To make matters worse, a woman in her office she didn't like came in the day before with a sparkling shiny diamond ring, bragging about her elaborate proposal. But, the thing that sent her over the edge was, she finally had some time to spend with her boyfriend, and he'd been gone all fucking day.

Finn had been gone all day. It was Saturday. He had spent all day with Kara, helping her paint the attic. He'd come home a little after five, covered in paint. Shelly was mad because it was the fourth Saturday in a row. It had actually been six weeks since Finn started working for Kara. Finn didn't bother correcting her, though. She went off about his already working nights at Neighbors and every weekend. Working all day on Saturdays was too much.

Finn only half paid attention to Shelly's ranting. He was tired, sweaty, and was covered in paint. It was even in his hair. It was Kara's fault paint was in

70

his hair. Kara decided she wanted to make the attic a nicer storage space when she picked up the insulation and drywall. She wanted to add some shelving. Which meant she would have to reinforce the walls after putting in the insulation. The past four Saturdays had been repairing the beams, installing the insulation, hanging the drywall, sanding, and installing new floors. He'd also been stopping over during the week to help.

Today was painting. Kara bought a five-gallon paint and primer in light gray because she said she hated white on the walls. She bought the brushes and tarps, and they started the day getting the attic ready. They taped everything up and put the tarps down. They began painting after lunch and were done relatively soon. While they were in the garage cleaning the brushes, Kara started a paint war by "accidentally" flicking paint on Finn. Finn flicked paint back at Kara. Twenty minutes later, they were both laughing, covered in paint, and Kara was in his arms.

She had run away from him, and he caught her. The problem came when they stopped laughing, and she looked up at him. Her face was covered with flecks of paint, and it was on her glasses. He had one arm around her waist and a paintbrush in the other hand, threatening to splatter her. Kara's hands were on his chest. He had pulled her closer without realizing it. It had taken everything in him not to kiss her.

He spent the ride home trying to calm his dick down. When he came into the house, all he wanted to do was take a long hot shower, eat, and take a nap before he had to go to the bar.

Instead, Shelly had been waiting for him to walk in and exploded. She was mad he was covered in paint. She was angry he was working. She was just mad.

"What the fuck, Finn? Aren't I more important than this job?" Shelly had her hands on her hips. "What about my needs? You've been spending all your time working. Don't you want to spend time with me anymore?"

Finn didn't answer. He was watching her pace back and forth, and all he could think about was taking a shower.

He stood up, "I'm getting in the shower." He walked out of the living room to the bathroom.

"What the fuck, Finn?" Shelly said, following him into the bathroom. "You're just going to walk away when I'm talking to you?"

Finn turned on the shower and started getting undressed. "You're not talking Shelly, you're yelling. And you have been for the last half an hour. I have to get ready for work."

"All you fucking do is work." Shelly was standing in the doorway. Finn stepped into the shower. He wanted to wash the paint out of his hair and get cleaned up. He was tired of sitting there, listening to her. Shelly didn't stop.

"Finn, I'm sick of this shit," she yelled at him over the sound of the shower. He could see her through the shower door. Finn washed off the paint and then rinsed off. It wasn't the shower he wanted but, it would have to do. He turned the water off and opened the shower door.

"So am I," he said as he grabbed a towel off the rack and wrapped it around his waist.

"You're sick of what?" Shelly snarled.

Finn pointed to Shelly and then back to him. "I'm sick of this." He walked past her into the bedroom.

Shelly followed him. "Finn, what are you saying?"

Finn started getting dressed. "I'm saying, I'm sick of this shit, Shell. I'm tired."

"Tired of what? All I'm asking you to do is give up working so much. You should make time for me. If you can't do that, then we're over, Finn."

Finn looked at Shelly. "Ok."

"Ok, what, Finn?"

Finn walked over to the closet and took out his duffel bag. "We're done."

"Wait, what did you say?" Shelly said, her voice shaking.

"We're done. I'm done." Finn went over to the dresser and started taking things out and putting them in the duffel bag. "I can't do this anymore."

"Finn," Shelly's eyes starting filling with tears.

He looked up, "What?"

"Are you serious? You're going to let this job come between us? You're going to throw away our relationship to keep working for no reason."

"I got the job for a reason." He retorted. "I got the job because I was saving the extra money to buy you the engagement ring you wanted."

The color drained from Shelly's face. She hadn't been prepared for Finn's reason. Finn watched her struggle with the information for a moment, then kept packing. When he looked up, she was smiling.

"Finn, you did it for me?" She sounded hopeful.

"I did. But now, I'm done, Shel." Finn picked up his duffle bag and walked past Shelly towards the bathroom. Shelly followed him. Tears were flowing down her cheeks.

"Wait, Finn, I'm sorry." She reached out to grab his arm, and Finn shook her hand off. He was throwing the stuff he needed in the duffle bag. Shelly came into the bathroom and tried to take things out of the bag.

"Finn, please, I'm sorry," she said, pleading with him.

"Stop taking my shit out of the bag. Just fucking stop." Finn yelled at her. Shelly winced and stopped taking things out of the bag. Finn put the stuff she took out, back into the bag.

"Finn," she whispered. "Please, I'm sorry. I didn't know."

Finn zipped his bag and walked past Shelly out of the bathroom towards the living room. Shelly followed him. When Finn picked up his keys from the table, Shelly broke.

"Finn, please. I'm sorry." Her voice cracking. "Don't do this."

Finn didn't turn around or say anything as he walked out of the door, slamming it behind him.

Finn opened the door to Randy's house and shut it gently behind him. He leaned back against the door and took a deep breath. The house was quiet. Randy was at Neighbors when Finn called him from his truck and asked if he could crash at his house for the night. Randy, thankfully just said yes and didn't ask any questions. Finn walked to the spare room and dropped his duffle bag down by the bed. He sat down and covered his face with his hands.

"What the fuck happened today?" he thought to himself. He replayed the day over in his head. He'd gotten up and was at Kara's house by 8:30.

Everything was fine until the moment in the garage. Finn remembered how Kara had felt with his arm around her. He could still feel where her hands were pressed against his chest. Every time she touched him, it was stamped on him. He had wanted to kiss her more than he wanted to breathe during the moment. She was so close. He could have just leaned down, and his mouth would have been on hers. Letting her go had been the most difficult part of his day, that and his erection taking forever to go down.

When he got home, he was already slightly on edge. Shelly having a temper tantrum, just pushed him over. Things hadn't been going well with Shelly since her birthday. He felt like he was walking through a minefield. Shelly's disappointment at not getting a ring had made her angry. It wasn't until today when he told her he was working so much to get her the ring she wanted, she genuinely smiled at him. He hadn't seen her smile like that in months.

Shelly wanted to get engaged so badly it made their relationship worse. It made Finn feel like it didn't matter how he felt about it. She just wanted the ring. Finn didn't have a problem with marriage. He just had a problem with being pushed into it. The truth was he didn't want to marry Shelly and today made that crystal clear.

The last six weeks working with Kara hadn't helped things either. The way he felt when he was around Shelly was nothing like how he felt when he was with Kara. When Finn was with Shelly, he always felt like he was not enough. When Finn was with Kara, although she was technically his boss, she made him feel like being himself was more than enough.

Finn got off the bed. He should probably head to work. He patted his pockets to look for his phone to see what time it was and realized he left it in the truck. He got up and left Randy's, making sure he locked up and got in his truck to check the time. When he picked up his phone, he shook his head.

"What the fuck?" he muttered to himself. He had ten missed calls and thirty texts. Most of the messages were from Shelly. He didn't bother opening them. He just couldn't deal with it right now. The rest were from his family. His brother Mike had texted the group chat, so now everyone knew he had a fight with Shelly, and all of them were responding.

"Fucking hell," he said out loud as he scrolled through the messages. He started typing and hit send.

Finn: Shelly and I had a fight. I love you all, but please stop.

Mike: Shelly's been blowing up my phone. She said you walked out.

Beverly: What did you do? And why did you walk out?

Beverly was Finn's oldest sister. She was two years older than him. Beverly always blamed Finn.

Ellen: Relax, Finn. We were just worried about you.

Ellen was Finn's youngest sister. She was two years younger than him. Ellen always wanted to keep the peace between Finn and Beverly.

Finn: Shelly shouldn't have texted Mike. I told her to knock the shit off. Mike if she texts you again, tell her to stop. Ell, I know you were worried, but I'm fine.

Mom: Everyone, calm down and leave your brother alone. People fight all the time. It's between him and Shelly to sort out. Finn, I love you, and we're here if you need us.

Finn's mother, Dorothy, was the best person he knew.

Finn: Thanks, Mom. I love you, and I'll call you later.

Mike, Beverly, and Ellen all sent sorry texts. Another reason he loved his mother. She could see through the bullshit. Finn loved his family, but it was just too much for him to deal with on top of everything else he had already gone through today. He tossed his phone on the passenger seat and pulled out of Randy's driveway.

Finn walked into Randy's office. Randy was sitting at his desk, entering invoices into the computer. He didn't look up when Finn walked in.

"Hey," Randy said as he picked up one of the invoices.

"Hey," Finn said as he sat down.

"You good?"

"I will be."

Randy nodded and picked up another invoice. He looked it over and put it down as he typed. "What's that mean?"

Finn ran his hand through his hair. "I don't know, man. I'm just tired of it."

Randy nodded again. "I know the feeling." Randy did know the feeling. He'd gone through it. He had been married with two little boys. As the bar got more successful, it had taken a toll on his marriage. His wife filed for divorce when she found out Randy was fooling around with one of the servers.

That was two years ago. The server left shortly after Randy told her he was getting a divorce. By the time Randy realized what he was losing, his ex-wife started dating again. They split the custody of the boys. Randy had recently found out his ex-wife was going to get remarried in six months. Randy hadn't taken it very well.

A light knock on the office door, and Britney came in with a tray carrying a burger with fries and two cokes. Britney set down the burger in front of Finn and then set down the cokes.

"Here you go, Finn." Giving Finn a bright smile. Britney was pretty. Most of the waitresses at Neighbors were pretty.

"Thanks, Brit," Finn said as he reached for some fries.

"No problem," she said as she bounced out of the office.

Finn picked up the burger and started eating. He realized he was starving. He hadn't eaten since he had lunch with Kara.

"Pass the fries," Randy said. Finn turned the plate and pushed it towards Randy so he could reach the fries.

"Thanks for letting me crash," Finn said as he wiped his mouth with a napkin.

"No Worries. I don't have the boys this weekend." Randy took a sip of his coke. "I will have them next week, though, so you have a week to fix things."

"Yeah, about that," Finn leaned back in the chair. "I'm not so sure I want to fix it this time." He took another bite of his burger. "I need some time to think about it," he said after he swallowed.

Randy stopped typing and looked directly at Finn, raising his eyebrow. "Oh, really? It's like that?"

Finn nodded and sighed. "Yeah, it's like that."

Randy reached for more fries. "Ok then," he said as he put fries in his mouth. Finn handed him a napkin.

"Thanks," Randy said as he wiped his hands. "Well, if that's the case, then stay as long as you need to. You know I got you."

"I know, and I appreciate it."

Randy nodded and went back to focusing on his invoices. Finn finished eating the rest of the burger.

Finn woke up Sunday morning stiff and sore. Neighbors had been busy the night before, and he kept getting texts from Shelly threatening to come to the bar. He had to send off a text telling her to stop, leave him alone, and give him time to think. When he got back to Randy's after closing the bar, he plopped onto the bed and passed out still in his clothes. He wanted to go back to sleep. He felt like he could sleep for another ten hours.

He got up and stretched. His back hurt. The bed in Randy's spare room was an old mattress, and Finn felt every lump. He walked out of the bedroom into the kitchen. The clock on the microwave showed it was just before noon. The house was quiet. Finn wasn't sure if Randy was still asleep or even home. Randy's bedroom door was closed. Finn made some coffee and went to the bedroom to grab his stuff to clean up while it brewed.

Finn went into the bathroom, washed his hands, and splashed some water on his face before brushing his teeth. When he rinsed his mouth, he dried it off with the towel on the rack and took a look at himself in the mirror. He looked like he had aged ten years in the past twenty-four hours. He had dark circles under his eyes. He looked as tired as he felt. He folded the towel and put it back on the rod. He needed some coffee.

He walked back into the kitchen. While he was pouring himself a cup, he heard Randy's bedroom door open. Jewell, Randy's on again off again girlfriend, walked out wearing an oversized t-shirt and nothing else. She walked into the kitchen and stood next to him.

"Morning." She grumbled as she opened the cabinet and took out a mug.

"Morning." Finn said as he sipped his coffee. Jewell poured some coffee into the mug.

"Can you pass me the creamer?" she said as she yawned. Finn handed her the creamer.

"Thanks." she mumbled as she poured the creamer into her coffee. She set down the creamer, stirred her coffee, and took a sip.

"Ahh. That's good," she said sleepily. She turned towards Finn, squinting and covering her eyes with her hands because of the sun's brightness in the kitchen.

"What the fuck are you doing here?" she said curiously.

Finn sighed. You gotta love Jewell, he thought to himself as he sipped his coffee.

"Randy's letting me crash here a little while."

"Oooh." Jewel leaned back against the counter. "Did your girl finally get sick of your shit and throw you out on your ass?"

Finn almost spit out his coffee. "No."

"Then why are you here?"

"I just need to straighten some things out. Randy, just let me crash here."

"For how long?"

"I don't know. Not long."

"You should just go back to your girl. You were probably wrong anyway," she said. "Besides, who else would want to put up with your shit," she said as she turned and walked out of the kitchen to Randy's bedroom.

Finn sighed. He forgot Jewell would be there if Randy didn't have the boys. Jewell and Randy had been together for a little over a year. Their relationship was nothing but drama. They would be fine one minute and fighting the next. They would go weeks where everything was good to not talking.

Finn wasn't a fan of Jewell's. She had no filter and would say whatever came into her head. She also liked to create drama. She would start a fight with Randy just to make him miserable. The next minute she acted like nothing happened. If Jewell were there now, there would be no peace and quiet in the house. Randy took Sundays off when football season was over. Since Randy would be home all day, it meant Jewell and Randy would be fighting all day.

Finn couldn't deal with it. Jewell was a little too much for him to take right now. Finn took the last sip of his coffee and put his mug in the sink. He walked toward the bathroom to take a shower. He needed to get out of the house.

CHAPTER 7

Kara was sitting in the weekly staff meeting, only half paying attention. Her boss was going through the weekly staffing PowerPoint, which she created as if he had done the whole thing himself. She was sitting opposite of him, facing the window, watching a squirrel jump from tree to tree. Every now and then, she would nod her head so he would think she was in complete agreement with what he said. Even though everything he said was what she already knew because she wrote it.

Kara was tired today. She spent Sunday trying to prep the master bathroom to be remodeled. She usually tried to rest on Sundays, but Saturday after Finn left, she'd gone down an anxiety-filled rabbit hole. The moment they shared in the garage had unnerved her. Finn looked like he was about to kiss her. If that wasn't a problem enough, she wanted him to. His arm was around her, and her hands on his chest felt like they belonged there.

After he left, she fell into the downward spiral of insecurity. It steered her to the rabbit hole of feeling unwanted, undesired, and unsexy. She'd gone to work trying to get lost in the drama of working in retail, and it hadn't helped at all. When she woke up on Sunday, she needed to do something to help her crawl out of the hole she'd put herself into. Working on the bathroom seemed like the best thing to do to distract her.

She nodded her head again, so her boss would think she was paying attention and continued to tune him out. These meetings were the same every week. She would pull together all the information needed to create the report. She would spend hours working on the PowerPoint and all of the charts. She would send it to her boss, and he would nitpick and criticize it, then send it back to her. She'd make some of the changes. Only the valid ones.

Most of his nit-picking wasn't about her improving, just his wanting to use one word over another or finding ways of clipping her wings. Once the changes were done, she'd send him the report in time for the meeting.

The squirrel was now joined by another one, and together they chased each other around the tree. One of them began to climb while the other stayed on the ground. Kara realized she was so bored, she was creating scenarios in her head for them. The second squirrel lived in a neighboring tree and came to borrow some nuts because she'd just run out. The first squirrel went up to his house to get them. Soon they would go from neighbors to friends to lovers. It was spring, after all. Love was all around.

Kara looked at her boss. He was still on the same slide in the deck. She listened long enough to see where he was in the presentation. She stopped looking at the squirrels. The thought of love was something she couldn't handle thinking about after Saturday. She started thinking about the bathroom. She wasn't sure exactly what she was going to do. She wanted a separate bathtub, big enough for her to take a bath. Something she hadn't done in years. The current bathtub felt too small for her to fully enjoy it. She also wanted more space. The bathroom was cramped, even though it was supposed to be big enough for two.

While thinking about all the possible changes she could make, her phone vibrated. She had placed it on her lap during the meeting. Her boss always got annoyed when people had their phones out in meetings. Her boss wanted everyone to be "present." He had a problem with people keeping their phones on the table because of the temptation to look at them. She looked at her phone and smiled when she saw it was a text from Finn. She really needed to stop, she thought to herself.

The effect Finn had on her was not only distracting, but it was also self-damaging. It brought all of her fears and insecurities to light. Things, she thought to herself, she hadn't had to think about in years. Pandora's box of longing and want also opened, and she had buried it years ago.

After the meeting was over, Kara walked back to her desk, and she read the text from Finn.

Finn: Hey, I'm sorry to bother you at work, but I wondered if you needed any help today. I have some free time.

Kara: I would love some help. I've been working on the master bathroom.

Finn: Ok, cool. I'll be there after work. Probably around five, if that's ok?

Kara: That's perfect. I'll see you then.

Finn: Great. See you then.

Although Kara logically knew better, she inadvertently smiled. Despite rationally knowing better, she couldn't help liking Finn. In the past couple of weeks, they'd worked together, she'd had a lot of fun. They laughed a lot. Talking about different things as they got to know each other. They hadn't gotten too personal, just enough to blur the lines of the boss/employee relationship. They were becoming friends. Kara was trying not to blur the line, but Finn was making it really hard.

Kara and Finn pulled up to the house at the same time. An employee came in five minutes before Kara was supposed to leave to talk about one of the supervisors. Kara tried to rush them out, but it didn't work. She left her office later than she anticipated.

Finn was walking up to her car as she opened the door to get out.

"Sorry, I'm late," she said as she stepped out of the car. "I got cornered by one of the employees just as I was about to leave." She closed the driver's side door with her hip and leaned against the car.

Finn didn't respond to her. He was staring at her. He looked her up and down, and Kara felt his eyes travel down her body. The heat the look generated left her feeling flushed.

"What's wrong?" she said curiously. Finn's eyes seemed darker, and his jaw was slightly clinched.

"Nothing," Finn said. His voice sounded a little hoarse. "I'm just not used to seeing you all dressed up for work."

Kara laughed and turned around to open her back door and get her things. "No, I guess you're not. But, you've seen me dressed for work before."

"You look different."

"Different good or different bad?" She teased.

"You look beautiful." Finn blurted out a hint of pink appearing on his cheeks.

Kara laughed as she opened the door of the back seat to get her things. She hung her purse over her shoulder and picked up her computer bag. She was wearing one of her favorite sundresses with a cardigan. The black dress was more fitted and showed off her curves because of the ruching at the waist. It had a pattern of pale pink and white flowers on it. She also had on her favorite black-heeled sandals, which made her feel taller. Her hair was down in loose curls, and she had on a full face of makeup. She looked this way every day she went to work. But, she usually got home and was changed by the time Finn got there.

"Thank you," she said warmly. "It had been a little while since someone noticed."

"Then the people in your office must work with blinders on." Finn took her computer from her. "How could anyone concentrate when you come to work looking like that every day. It's got to be difficult."

Kara looked directly into Finn's eyes. "What the fuck?" she thought to herself. She could feel herself blush and was thankful her brown skin hid it. She was sure she would be as red as a tomato.

"Thank you," she said, looking at Finn intently. "That's the nicest compliment I've received in a really long time," she said sincerely.

"My pleasure," Finn said as he shut the car door.

Kara turned and walked up the driveway, feeling Finns' eyes as he followed her into the house. She was conscious of the way she had a strut when walking in heels. Which made her even more self-conscience. "You're an asshole." She told herself as she walked in the door.

Kara set her purse down by the table at the door.

"Thank you for carrying that," she said as Finn set down her computer bag on the floor next to the table and closed the door behind him. She looked at Finn, "Just give me a few minutes to get changed, and we can start working on the bathroom." She was backing towards the stairs. "Help yourself to anything in the fridge."

"Ok. Take your time." Finn said amiably.

"I'll be right back," she said as she walked up the stairs and down the hallway to her room. She closed the door behind her and leaned back against it. "What the fuck was that?" she muttered to herself. She took a deep breath and started getting changed. She kicked off her heels as she walked over to her dresser to take her jewelry off. She looked at herself in the mirror. She did look pretty today, she thought to herself. Then she shook her head. "You're an asshole," she whispered to herself, smiling.

Fifteen minutes later, Kara emerged out of her room in an old t-shirt and jeans. Fresh-faced and hair in a ponytail. Finn was sitting at the kitchen table, scrolling through his phone, frowning. Why is he frowning? she thought to herself as she walked over.

"Hey," she said as she pulled out the chair and sat down across from him. "Is everything ok?"

Finn shook his head.

"Are you going to tell me what's bothering you?" She leaned forward on the table and folded her hands in front of her. "Every time you look at your phone, you start frowning."

Finn looked up at her. "Do I really?"

Kara nodded. "Yup," she sighed. "Seriously. For the past couple of weeks, whenever you look at your phone, you frown."

"Seriously?"

"Yes." Kara shifted slightly in her chair. "I haven't said anything because I didn't want to pry. And I also didn't want you to think I was being nosy or anything."

"I wouldn't have thought that."

"Well, that's good to know." Kara smiled. "But really, I think it's time you talk about it. Unless, of course, you're going for that whole brooding, mysterious hot guy cliché thing."

Finn laughed, "I'm not doing that. Is that even a thing?"

"Yes, it's a thing. And it's been played to death. Men who are open, honest, can communicate, and express themselves are the new hot thing."

Finn smiled. "Well, if that's the new hot thing."

Kara laughed. "Come on, Finn. Tell me what's bothering you. Maybe I can help."

Finn sighed, leaned back in the chair, and ran his fingers through his hair. Kara noticed he didn't have his hair pulled back like he usually did. Finn then leaned forward again, looking uncomfortable and agitated. Before he began, he took a deep breath.

"I just broke up with my now ex-girlfriend a couple of days ago."

"Oh. I'm sorry."

Finn sighed. "We were together for almost six years, and I lived with her. So I now have no place to live. I'm staying with a friend of mine, but it's only temporary." He hesitated a moment. "So, to make a long story short, I need to find a place to live. I also need to get my stuff, and my ex is not cooperating." Finn was looking down as he spoke. He folded and unfolded his hands. He looked so uncomfortable. It tugged at Kara's heart. She wanted to make him feel better. She leaned over the table and covered his hands with hers. Finn looked up at her.

"I think you're going to have to tell me the long version of the story, Finn." She gave his hand a gentle squeeze. "Talking about it will help," she smiled gently at him. Finn nodded. He took another deep breath and told Kara the story from the beginning.

Kara listened quietly and only occasionally interrupted to ask questions. She was trying to listen without judgment but was failing. To her, it seemed like Shelly was a spoiled bitch. She didn't understand why anyone would want to treat someone they loved that way. More importantly, she didn't understand why Shelly would treat Finn that way. What the fuck was wrong with people? she thought to herself.

Kara immediately felt terrible. She hadn't been in a relationship in so long. She had no idea how people treated people anymore. She hadn't been in a relationship in over a decade, and it had been years since she'd been on a date. Honestly, what the fuck did she know about anything, she told herself.

Finn finished his story and sighed again. "That's pretty much the long version of the story," he smiled. "Only slightly edited."

Kara briefly wondered what part was edited but didn't want to ask. She leaned back in her chair and folded her hands in her lap.

"You know," she started slowly. "I've been married, and I've been divorced." She paused to take a sip of the bottled water she grabbed while Finn was talking. "Marriage isn't easy even in the best of circumstances. It takes work. If you're not ready or if you have some doubts about it, it just makes it that much harder. Everything just becomes magnified when you get married."

Finn looked at her. They hadn't really talked about anything this personal before. Kara met his gaze, knowing her eyes betrayed her feelings. She continued, trying to keep the pain out of her voice.

"I got married young, and although we waited years before I got pregnant with Matt, there were a lot of things I ignored to keep the peace. After Matt was born, things just got harder. No matter how hard I tried, my marriage still ended."

Kara was fidgeting now. She was peeling the wrapper off her water bottle. "It broke me when my marriage ended. I was broken for a long time. And you know what?"

"What?' Finn whispered.

Kara smiled. "I still believe in love, and I believe in marriage. I don't regret being married. Thankfully, Chris and I have always gotten along. I mean," Kara played with her ponytail. "He was a terrible husband to me, but he is a great father, and he's still one of my best friends. Which people don't understand. But we're family. We always will be. Even though he got remarried and has a baby girl. I'm friends with his wife, and I love his little girl."

"Really?" Finn asked in disbelief.

Kara nodded. "Of course. We're family."

"Was it hard?"

Kara looked out the kitchen window taking a moment to think about it.

She sighed, "Yes. Extremely hard. I swallowed a lot of pride and a lot of blood from biting my tongue. But it was worth it to make sure Matt had two parents who loved him and were willing to set aside their differences for him." She took a deep breath. "It also showed him relationships are work, but they don't have to be toxic. A lot of his friends have parents who are divorced and can't be in the same room together. Matt grew up with his father and me, still friends, still having dinner together and spending holidays together. Matt was happy we weren't like his friend's parents."

Finn looked at Kara and hesitated, then he asked her, "Would you get married again?"

Kara smiled. "I would. I loved being married. The first one didn't work, but I have hope. I mean," Kara shrugged. "I believe in love and all of the happily ever after cliché. Although I'm way too old and should know better, I still do." She shifted in her seat and leaned forward. "Anyway," she said, changing the subject. "What are you going to do now?"

Finn sighed and folded his hands in front of him. "I don't know. I need some time to think about it. First things first, I need to find a place to live."

"You could live here."

Finn looked at Kara, shocked. She even surprised herself by saying it. "What?"

Kara swallowed and said slowly. "Well, you could. This is a four-bedroom house, and I live here by myself. Matt's in California for school and has no plans on coming home for months. I have plenty of room."

"Kara, I appreciate the offer, but I'm not sure."

Kara interrupted him. "Honestly, it's not a big deal. You're here anyway, helping me remodel. Instead of paying you, we'll exchange paying you for a place to stay. You can take your time figuring things out, and in the meantime, we'll keep working on the house."

Finn looked hesitantly at Kara. Kara returned his gaze. "Listen, it benefits both of us. You need a place to stay. And I have room to spare. We'll work on the house, and when you're ready, things will go back to the way they are now."

"Kara, are you really sure about this?"

Kara looked at him. No, she wasn't sure. She frankly wanted to tell him she thought it was unquestionably the worst idea she'd ever had. She wanted to say to him nothing good will come from his living with her. But she also knew it was the right thing to do.

What she actually said was,

"Yes. I'm positive. It will be fine," she smiled at him. "Unless, of course, you're a slob. Then we are totally going to have a huge problem and will probably fight all the time."

Finn laughed. "I'm not an animal. I promise I'm housebroken and everything."

"Good. Then we'll get along famously."

"Ok, then," Finn said. He leaned back in the chair. "I guess we'll be roommates."

Kara's heart skipped a beat. She knew it was the right thing to do, but fuck, she thought to herself. The line she wasn't supposed to cross just got even more blurred.

Kara ordered dinner, and while they ate, they talked about how the arrangement was going to work. After Finn left and Kara was lying in bed, she still couldn't believe Finn would be living there. The more she thought about it, the more she realized, although things would change between them, it didn't mean things were going to change in the wrong way. They would still be working on the house. And roommates didn't necessarily mean anything else was going to happen.

Just because he broke up with his girlfriend didn't mean he was looking for anything else. Not that it mattered, Kara wasn't looking for anything either. She was making this out to be more than what it was. She was projecting, again. She reminded herself, just because someone is nice to you doesn't mean they're flirting with you. Their relationship was simply going from employer/employee to friends who are roommates. Nothing more was going to happen. Everything was going to be okay.

As Kara tried to fall asleep, she made a mental list of all the ground rules she needed to set for herself. She would try to keep her distance from Finn.

She would remember to respect his privacy and give him enough space to think about things. She would try to keep her feelings in check and remember the line she shouldn't cross, although things were changing. If she remembered the rules, she might just get through this.

CHAPTER 8

What the fuck was he doing?

When Kara offered to let Finn stay with her, he wasn't sure it was a good idea. Actually, he thought it was a fucking terrible idea. How was he supposed to take time to clear his head when he would be living with the person who kept invading his thoughts. How was that supposed to help him? It was the last thing he needed. But, here he is.

When she got out of her car dressed in her work clothes and smiled at him, it had knocked the wind out of him. He had actually forgotten how to breathe. He could only stare. He knew she didn't realize just how stunning she is. The way her hair framed her face and fell loosely around her shoulders.

Did she even realize her eyes seemed bigger? Her full red lips curved into a beautiful smile. A war broke out between his head and his dick when he told her she looked beautiful. His head screaming to stop, his dick wanting to go full steam ahead. While he waited for her to get ready, he had a long talk with both of them to get it together.

Then he had gotten a text from Shelly, and it brought him back to the present. He opened up to Kara and told her the edited version of everything. He edited the part she played in the story. How she had started to make him feel when he was around her. How he was beginning to look forward to seeing her. How her laugh was becoming one of his favorite sounds. How he couldn't look her in the eyes because if he did, she would see just how much he wanted her. How he had to keep his hands busy so they wouldn't reach for her.

Yeah, living with her may not be the best thing for him to do.

They hadn't even worked on the bathroom. They ate dinner together and talked about their new living arrangements. Finn would stay in the other spare room. He could move things around to make himself more comfortable, and when they renovated that room, he would move into her old room. Finn would live there instead of Kara paying him, and Finn would cover the additional utility costs. He still wasn't sure if it was a good or a bad idea. He knew things would change. He just wasn't sure how much.

Finn took a personal day, and Randy helped him move out of Shelly's house while she was at work. There wasn't a lot, but he wanted to get in and out of there as quickly as possible. Shelly already owned the house when he moved in with her. The things he possessed from his own apartment, he'd gotten rid of. It had always been Shelly's house. When they were done packing his stuff, Finn looked around and could barely tell he'd lived there for almost four years.

Shelly called him when she got home, and his stuff was gone. He'd left the spare keys for her in an envelope in the mailbox. Finn didn't answer it. He let it go to voice mail. He did send her a text, telling her he needed time to think and he would call her when he was ready to talk. Then he turned his phone off. He knew she would just blow up his phone, and he didn't want to deal with it.

The first couple of days of living with Kara felt awkward. They were overly polite to each other, trying to feel each other out. It was also the most comfortable Finn had ever been. Finn began to notice little things about Kara, how she went out of her way to try to make Finn feel welcome in the house. She'd bought new bedding, cleaned, and made up the spare room. Since they had to share a bathroom while the master bath was being remodeled, she made room for his stuff.

She liked to drink coffee in the morning and tea before she went to bed. She didn't watch tv to actually watch it. She used it more for background noise, and it was always cartoons. She read a lot of books. There were books everywhere. In every room, bookcases were overflowing with books. She also liked to feed people. If she were making something for herself, she would make something for Finn.

When she packed her lunch in the morning, she would pack something for Finn. Then she would set out his coffee cup, so it was ready for him when he woke up. There was actually enough food in the house to feed a family of four, and she barely ate any of it. She barely slept. She would stay up late reading, wake up, get ready, and be on her way to work before Finn got up.

She was so used to taking care of people. It was a part of who she was. She thought about everyone else in everything she did. After living with her for a week, Finn was beginning to get used to the peace of it all. The little things she did for him made him feel cared for.

Kara worked a part-time job at the grocery store two to three days a week. At first, Finn enjoyed being alone. Without worrying about having to do anything. By the second week, Finn wasn't sure what to do with himself. He could work on the bathroom, but he didn't want to do it without Kara. The realization surprised him. As he got used to living with her, being in the house without her felt strange. He didn't want to go to Neighbors. He'd rather do something relaxing. Finn decided to do something he hadn't done in a really long time.

Finn pulled into the empty parking space. He turned off his truck and stepped out, making sure he had his wallet, phone, and keys. He walked into the door of the dinner and scanned the room, looking around. He found them sitting in a booth in the back by the window. When the hostess came over, he pointed to the table, and she nodded. Finn slid into the booth across from his parents sitting side-by-side, scrolling through the quarter-operated jukebox affixed to the table.

Sunset Diner was his parent's favorite diner. They'd been going there since they got married. That was almost forty-five years ago. They didn't bother looking over the menu. His parents ordered the same thing every time they ate there. Finn noticed the pile of quarters in front of his father. His father found the song he was looking for and punched in the number. Within minutes, Jim Croche's melodious voice was playing at the table.

Although Finn's parents were both in their sixties and had been married for well over forty years, they acted like newlyweds. Even now, sitting across from Finn, his parents were holding hands. His mother leaning in towards his father.

"Finn, honey." His mother's tone greeting him. "Inviting us to dinner was such a lovely surprise. How have you been, dear?"

"Hi, Mom. Hi Dad." Finn said as he put his phone and keys on the table. "I've been ok. I had some free time today and thought I'd give you a call."

"Griffin." His father said. His father was the only person who ever called him by his full name. It always made him feel like he was eight years old about to get into trouble.

"So, honey, how are you?"

Finn picked up the menu. He couldn't remember the last time he'd been to Sunset. He hoped the food was still good.

"I'm good, Mom. I just missed you. I thought I'd call and see if you wanted to have dinner with me," he said.

"That's sweet," his mother cooed. "I'm so glad you did."

"So am I." Finn smiled at his mother.

Dorothy Wilson was still a handsome woman. Her hair had more gray in it, but you could see the honey blonde highlights. Her sky blue eyes still sparkled even behind her reading glasses. Growing up, she had been a stay-at-home mom until all of her children were in school. She started out working at the school part-time, helping out teachers. Then went back to school to get her teaching certificate. She taught second grade for over twenty-five years. She didn't retire from teaching until a year ago. She still went to help out as a volunteer teacher aid at the same elementary school.

"How's work going?" his father asked.

"It's going. Busy at the school since we're heading into the final stretch of the year, and then there's Neighbors. I'm also helping a friend of mine renovate her house. So I've been swamped." Finn set the menu down.

Finn's father looked like an older version of Finn. He was tall with dirty blonde hair, faded to gray. His blue eyes, the same shade as Finn's, were behind bifocals but still just as sharp as ever. He still looked as fit and as strong as he did when Finn was a kid. Robert Wilson believed every problem in life could be solved with hard work. Throughout Finn's childhood, his dad worked so his mom could stay at home and take care of them. Whereas Finn's mom went to every game, recital, field trip, and school function, Finn's dad was there on Sundays and holidays.

He still worked part-time at the same school his mother worked at. He was able to stay home and be "retired" for about a week when he had enough. Finn's dad nodded his head in approval. Finn's mother, on the other hand, looked horrified.

"Finn, honey, don't you think your working too hard." She shook her head and tisked. "You need to make sure you get your rest."

"Now, now Dottie," his father patted his mother's hand. "Hard work never hurt anyone. It's good for him."

Finn looked at his mother and smiled at her concern. "Mom, I promise. I have more free time now, and Dad's right. Working is really helping."

"Well, just make sure you aren't overdoing it," his mother said, frowning.

"I promise." Finn knew his mother would worry unless he convinced her he was ok.

He felt ok, even though it seemed like everything was all over the place. He felt better than he had in a long time. Finn had always been closer to his mom. While his father worked, his mother was always there supporting him. She was still there for him. He could depend on her.

The waitress came over and refilled their glasses of water, and took their orders. After the waitress left, Finn's father put another quarter in the jukebox to play another song. Finn's mother looked at him with concern. Finn shifted in his seat under his mother's gaze. From the look on her face, he knew the questions were coming.

"Are you going to tell us what happened with Shelly?" His mother asked delicately.

Finn sighed. Even though he knew it was coming, it didn't make it any easier.

"There's nothing to tell. We're not together anymore," he said quietly.

"We know that, honey. Are you going to tell us why?" she asked gently. "Did something happen?"

Finn leaned back in his seat and sighed. "It wasn't one thing. It was lots of things. In the end, we just wanted different things."

His mother nodded. She seemed to accept it as a reasonable answer. His father was playing songs, seemingly ignoring their conversation. Finn knew otherwise. His father always paid attention, even if he didn't say anything. The waitress brought their salads to the table. Finn's dad punched in another song.

"Ooh, I love this song." His mother smiled and swayed to the music. Finn's father looked at his mom and smiled at her. Finn felt a pang in his chest. He wanted that. He wanted to look at someone the way his father still looked at his mother. Kara's face flashed in his mind. "Not now," he thought to himself. His brain ignoring him reminded him. He looked at Kara like that.

His mother continued to sway to the music as she picked up her knife and fork to cut into the chunky pieces of her salad.

"Maybe you two just need a little time. It would be such a shame to throw all that time together away. Shelly seemed like such a lovely girl."

Finn coughed to hide the laugh that almost escaped him.

"He's not throwing anything away, Dottie." Finn's father said. Causing both him and his mother to look at him. Finn's father folded his hands in front of him on the table.

"If you can imagine living your life without her, then she wasn't the one." Finn's father said solemnly. "You'll know it when the thought of being without her is like trying to breathe underwater. You simply can't do it on your own."

Finn's father looked at his mother. Finn saw something he'd never noticed before. The look was full of utter adoration, worship, and reverence. Finn knew his parents loved each other, but today was the first time he'd ever noticed how much his father loved his mother. It was heartwarming and made him a little envious. His father continued,

"I worked a lot, trying to be a good provider and take care of our family. But every day, I woke up thankful I got another day with your mom." Finn's mother looked up with tears glistening in her eyes, smiling at her husband as he continued.

"And at the end of every night, I went to bed knowing that no matter what happened, as long as she was with me, I had everything I could ever need." Finn's father leaned down and kissed the top of his mother's head. His mother closed her eyes and leaned into her husband.

Finn sat on the couch in the living room with his head leaning on his hand as he stared at nothing. The tv was on, but the sound was turned down. Thoughts swirling around his head like an F5 tornado. The rest of dinner passed with light conversation. His parents talked about working at the school, his siblings, and his niece and nephew. After Finn paid the check, he hugged his mother and gave her a kiss on the cheek. Then he turned towards his father, pulled him into a hug, and whispered, "Thanks, Dad."

As he drove back to Kara's, he wasn't quite prepared to call it home just yet. His father's words lingering in his mind. Flashbacks from his relationship with Shelly assaulted him. When they met. Their first date. The first time they were together. Holidays. Family meetings and gatherings. Almost six years of memories. And in none of them could Finn see himself looking at Shelly the way his father looked at his mother tonight. Even after being married for almost forty-five years. It made Finn feel a little sad.

Finn saw the flash of headlights as Kara pulled into the driveway. He sat up as she walked through the front door. His heartbeat quickened as she smiled at him. The smile was genuine. Filled with a bit of surprise and happiness, he was there. He knew she wasn't used to his being there yet, either.

"Hey," she said as she set down her keys on the table by the door. She shut the door behind her and walked into the living room, sitting on the love seat.

"Hey, how was work?" he asked. He tried to sound as casual as possible even though he could hear his heartbeat pounding in his ears.

Kara leaned her head back, closed her eyes, and sighed. "It was ok. I'm just exhausted."

"Can I get you something?"

Kara lifted her head and smiled at Finn. "Some tea would be great. But I'll get it." Kara started to get up.

Finn stood up abruptly. "I'll get it." He walked around the coffee table towards the stairs. "I need to get up anyway."

Kara looked at him. "Thank you," she said, leaning her head back again and closing her eyes.

Finn walked up the steps into the kitchen. He picked up the teapot and went to the sink to fill it with water. He placed it back onto the stove and turned the stove on. He walked over to the cabinet, got a mug, and set it down. He got the teabag from the container on the counter and put it in the cup.

He leaned against the counter while he waited for the water to boil. He needed to get his heart to slow down. It was beating so hard he thought it would burst through his chest. When Kara walked in the door, Finn had been knocked down by a surge of emotions. It happened so suddenly and completely unexpected. It had pulled him under like a rip current. It had caught him so off guard, he wasn't prepared for it. Mainly because, for the better part of the last hour, he'd been thinking about his relationship with Shelly.

He folded his arms across his chest and shook his head. That wasn't it. The wave of emotion shouldn't have surprised him. He was acting like it never happened before. From the moment he'd met her, he felt it every time he looked at her. His body had the same reaction to Kara it always had. His heart would beat. He would feel the flush of heat speeding through his veins. His hands would ache to touch her, and his dick would get so swollen, it was painful. The problem was, now he saw her every day. It meant that it happened every day.

He reminded himself, Kara was helping him out by letting him stay with her. He was supposed to be sorting his shit out. It was only going to be temporary, that she wasn't his boss. She would still be his boss when things went back to normal. Normal being, finding an apartment and getting his life together. He was just reacting to breaking up with Shelly and having dinner with his parents. His father's words affected him more than he anticipated.

The whistling of the teapot snapped him out of his head. He turned around and shut off the stove.

"How do you take your tea?" he yelled down to Kara as he poured the water into the mug he prepared.

"Three sugars and lemon. The lemon juice is in the fridge, just a little." Kara yelled back.

Finn prepared Kara's tea. Grabbing the lemon-shaped juice from the fridge and squeezing some into the mug.

"Do you want me to bring your tea down to you?" he yelled down.

"No," she said as she walked into the kitchen. "I'm right here."

Finn jumped when he turned around and saw Kara behind him. She laughed, putting her hand gently on his back. "I'm sorry. I didn't mean to startle you."

"It's ok," Finn said as he ran his hands through his hair. Kara moved her hand off his back. Finn knew running his hands through his hair was more a gesture to keep Kara from touching him than it was to get his hair out of his eyes. But as soon as her hand was gone, he missed her touch.

Kara stepped closer to him. "Are you ok?" she asked gently.

Finn looked down at her. He could smell her jasmine perfume. He held his arms at his sides, clenching his fists to stop his hands from reaching out to touch her.

"Uh yeah. I'm fine. I was just," he looked away from her.

Kara looked at him, "Off in never-never land."

"You could say that."

"Do you want to talk about it?" Kara asked sympathetically. Concern filling her eyes.

Finn met her gaze. She looked tired, but her eyes were warm. She was smiling at him. His heart started to beat faster. It would be so easy to put his arms around her, lean down and kiss her. The intensity of the desire was so strong he could feel himself leaning down.

"Finn?" Kara said gently. It snapped him out of it.

Finn shook his head. "I'm ok. I'm just a little tired too." He straightened up. He backed up and walked around her. "I think I am going to head to bed. Good night." He walked out of the kitchen, leaving Kara to stare after him.

Finn lay in bed with one arm behind his head and the other resting on his stomach. He couldn't sleep. His thoughts racing in the same direction. His thoughts were driving full speed ahead straight into a brick wall that was reinforced with steel. His desire to kiss Kara hadn't left him. He felt like he was crushing under the weight of it. His cock was still hard and stiff. He reached down and took his dick in his hand. Rubbing his thumb across the tip. His eyes closed, and Kara's face immediately appeared.

He thought about giving in to the urgent need to kiss her. He wondered if her mouth was as gentle and warm as it looked. He thought about pulling her into his arms. His hands caressing down her body and resting on her hips. He could imagine how her body would feel pressed against his. He wrapped his fingers around his swollen cock and gently stroked up and down. He was stiff and throbbing.

He thought about how her skin would feel so smooth under his lips. How he would breathe in her jasmine scent. How her breasts would feel pressed against his chest. The softness of her belly against him. He gripped his cock tightly as he quickened his pace. His breathing becoming hoarse as he struggled to be quiet. He wondered what sound she would make if he spread her legs and kissed her thighs. He guessed she would taste as sweet as she looked.

He shuddered as he came in his hand. It happened faster than he thought it would. His breath coming out course and rough. Cum flowing onto his stomach, causing him to shudder again. He took a deep breath and whispered, "Fuck," as he sighed. Cuming only made him feel a little better. It didn't stop how badly he wanted Kara. If anything, it made him want her more.

He got up and grabbed the t-shirt he had worn earlier. He cleaned himself off and tossed it in the hamper. He got back in bed and felt sleep finally come. He was thinking about doing laundry as he drifted off to sleep.

Finn pulled up in front of the house and shut off his truck. He was having a bad day. He woke up in the morning, sticky from a wet dream. He hadn't had one since he was fourteen. The longing he felt when he woke up crushing him. He'd dreamed he was making love to Kara. He was inside of her, and it felt right. Kara felt so good. Her skin felt so soft. She tasted so sweet. And... He was hard again. He felt like he was nothing but a constant erection. His cock was always hard.

Because he couldn't go to work with a hardon, he'd gotten in the shower and jerked off again. Which made him late. He got dressed and ran into the kitchen to grab his coffee before he left. He didn't have time for breakfast, so he'd have to grab something on the way.

He turned coffee in one hand, lunch bag in the other, and Kara walked in. He forgot she was going to work late today because she was meeting with a plumber this morning. She was wearing a skirt that hugged her hips and a flowy blouse. She was barefoot, and when Finn looked down, he noticed the ankle bracelet she was wearing. "Fuck," he thought to himself. He was hard again. "Damn it. Since when did he think ankles were sexy," he thought to himself.

"Morning," she smiled at him. He could only manage a quick "morning" and raced past her down the steps and out the door.

He made it to work only a little late, even after stopping to grab breakfast. He didn't really need to rush. He didn't have to clock in or anything. It was just the point. Finn hated to be late. He'd just set his breakfast down on his desk when he got a call about a leak in the boy's locker room. The pipe cracked. Then a toilet backed up in the girl's bathroom on the second floor. And to top it off, someone had spray-painted graffiti in the back of the bleachers in the gym.

Finn was the maintenance supervisor of facilities for Tenby Highschool. He had two guys working with him, and it felt like every problem today

100

needed two people. Four weeks were left in the school year. Kids always seemed to go a little crazy before the end of the year. But fuck, didn't they have anything else to do.

Finn was so lost in thought, he didn't notice the red Lexus sedan pulling up behind him. It wasn't until he got out of the truck he saw it. When the car door opened and Shelly got out of the car, Finn looked up to heaven, "What the Fuck. Do you hate me today or something?" he muttered to himself. He walked to the back of his truck and leaned against it. He crossed his arms and felt anger and frustration in every part of his body. The only bonus was his erection had finally gone down.

Shelly walked up to him and stood in front of him.

"Shelly, What are you doing here?"

CHAPTER 9

K ara pulled into the driveway in a rush. She felt like she'd been rushing all day. She met with the plumber in the morning to install the pipes for the new bathtub she wanted. By the time she got to work, she had meeting after meeting. Work had been stressful. The company she worked for wanted to roll out a whole new employee engagement program. She was the one who had to do most of the work. The worst of it was how much work needed to be done. She was late leaving the office, which made her late getting home. It was almost 5:30. She had to rush in, get changed, and run to her part-time job.

She left her purse in the car and just grabbed her computer bag. Her boss had done something nice today and bought the team lunch, so she left her lunch at work. She walked up the pathway, and as she got to the front door, she thought she heard a woman's voice. It had to be the tv, so she didn't think anything of it.

Kara walked in the front door and saw Finn sitting on the couch. A beautiful, furious woman was standing in front of the love seat yelling at him.

"And who the fuck is this?" she yelled.

Finn looked up to see Kara coming into the house. Kara dropped her computer bag in front of the table by the door. Kara looked between Finn and the woman, and anger flared up her spine. Finn looked miserable. He sat on the couch with his arms crossed in front of him. Kara looked at the woman standing in her living room. The woman had her hands on her hips, her face red with rage. Kara closed the door behind her and took a deep breath. "I don't have time for this shit today," she thought to herself. She took a step into the living room and looked at the woman up and down.

"I am Kara McNulty. The woman who owns the house you are currently yelling in. From your behavior, I have to assume you must be Shelly," Kara's voice had a chill in it. She only reserved it for people she really didn't like. Truthfully, after everything Finn had told her about Shelly and what she just witnessed, Shelly was now one of those people. Shelly looked shocked at the introduction and remained silent as Kara continued.

"Now, that's out of the way. I will explain the rules of my house because apparently, you forgot to bring your manners with you when you came into my home today. In this house, we treat everyone with courtesy and respect. If you can't behave in a dignified manner, then I would suggest you see yourself out of my house and don't come back until you can." Kara took a deep breath. She hadn't raised her voice, but from the look on Shelly's face, she had gotten her point across.

"Now, if you'll excuse me," Kara said icily. Kara walked up the stairs and down the hall to her room, seething in rage. "What a bitch," she muttered to herself as she shut her bedroom door behind her. "Who the fuck did she think she was talking to? This is my fucking house." She walked over to her closet to kick her shoes off as she unzipped her skirt. She was late, very annoyed, and wanted to go back into the living room and punch that little rat-faced bitch in the face.

"I'll fucking cut you bitch from navel to nose, and I dare Finn to stop me." She stepped out of her skirt and took off her blouse. She stood in her underwear, ready to go back out to the living room and fight that skinny bitch. She took a deep breath, walked over to where she kept her uniform for work, and started getting dressed.

She stopped ranting as she put her shirt and jeans on. She took deep breaths, trying to calm down. She sat on the edge of the bed to put on her socks and sneakers. "She's such a bitch. How could Finn have been with her for almost six years? No wonder he didn't want to marry her. She's fucking awful." She leaned over and put on her socks, then her shoes. She stood up after her socks and shoes were on and walked over to her dresser.

Her name tag and a belt were on top. Since she worked on the house, she lost some weight, and her jeans were too big. She put her name tag on and put the belt on. She checked the time on her alarm clock. She would have enough time to shove something down her throat and run out of the door, or she'd be late. As she was about to walk out the door, she said a little prayer Shelly would be gone when she went back into the living room. She was just about to open the door when she heard a light knock.

"Kara, it's Finn. Can I come in?"

Kara sighed and opened the door. She wanted to scream at him, but when she saw the look in his blue eyes, her anger faded away.

"Kara, I'm sorry," he said faintly. His eyes pleading with her. "Shelly followed me home. I didn't know she was there until I got out of the truck. And since I didn't want her yelling in front of the neighbors, I brought her into the house. I didn't."

Kara put up her hand to stop him. "You don't have to apologize for her bad behavior. It's not your fault she's a," Kara hesitated. She was trying to think of the right word to describe Shelly. Bitch, heathen, heifer, asshole, there were so many words she could choose from to fill in the blank.

"A bitch," Finn said, smiling.

"I was looking for something a little more expressive but, I guess that will do since I can't think of something polite to say."

Finn laughed. "There's no polite way of describing Shelly. She's a bitch, and I told her she needed to leave."

Kara leaned against the door. "So I guess you don't need any more time to think about it?" She met Finn's gaze and realized she was holding her breath, waiting for Finn to answer.

Finn shook his head, "No. I don't think there's anything more to think about."

Kara released her breath slowly, trying to make it seem like she was breathing normally. Her heart leaping in her chest. "Thank God." Her heart shouted. Her mind was screaming, "Keep cool." Kara hesitated a moment before looking up at Finn.

"Are you ok?"

Finn nodded. "I'm good. Even though today was a horrible day. I'm still glad that's over. I feel like a huge weight has been lifted from me."

Kara smiled at Finn. He did look happy. A sparkle returned to his eyes. It hadn't been there when Shelly was in the room. She was glad it was back.

"I'm glad," she said, smiling at him. They stood there for a moment. Looking into each other's eyes. Kara felt her knees begin to weaken. "If he keeps looking at me like that, I'll never get out of here," she thought to herself. She felt warmth flush her body. Finn broke the gaze by looking away.

"Well," he said hesitantly. "I know you have to go, but I wanted to say I'm sorry about Shelly and to thank you."

"For what?" Kara asked.

"For everything," Finn said. He looked at Kara and then turned and walked down the hallway. Kara shook her head and smiled. She watched him walk away and couldn't help admiring the way his ass looked in his jeans. "Kara, you don't have time for this," she said to herself as she ran into the bathroom to check her makeup and brush her teeth quickly before she had to go. She was late.

Kara and Finn spent the weekend re-tiling the master bathroom. Over the past couple of weeks, they had demolished, cleared away, and had a crew come in to extend the bathroom into the adjoining room. Thankfully, the adjacent room was the office no one used. It was the smallest bedroom, and Kara had the crew cut into the closet to give her the extra square footage she needed for the bigger bathtub she wanted.

Kara and Finn had to clear everything out of the room just in case. The room could still be used as a small office. But Kara liked the idea of making it a large storage area and converting it to an upstairs laundry room.

Kara felt something shift between her and Finn since Shelly's visit the other day. They had become more relaxed with each other. Laughing more often. Talking more about themselves. Actually, it was Finn asking Kara more about herself. He seemed interested in learning more about her. Kara tried not to overthink it. She kept telling herself it was only conversation. She was the master at deflecting. But Finn wasn't having it. He seemed to see through it and ask just the right questions to get her to open up. It was surprising and a little unnerving.

They fell into a routine on the weekends. They took breaks for lunch and then again to rest before both of them left to go to work Saturday night. Since Finn had moved in, they had spent Sundays sleeping late and going back to work later in the day. They would break again for lunch and keep working until it was time for dinner.

They were temporarily sharing a bathroom. During the week, it wasn't a big deal. Kara was up and gone before Finn got up. But on weekends, things got complicated. Kara caught Finn going from the bathroom to the bedroom wearing nothing but a towel. His hair was wet and hanging over his shoulders. His skin still damp from the shower. He had another towel he was drying his face with, so he didn't notice her standing in the hallway. She was on her way to get something from her room. When she saw him, she stopped frozen. Her brain turned to slush. She moved her mouth, but the sound got caught in her throat. She absently wiped her mouth because it felt like she was drooling.

His chest had the faintest blonde hair going down to his stomach. It was like the yellow brick road. Leading the way to where the wizard would give Dorothy and her friends what they desired. Kara's eyes followed it, wondering if she were to follow it would it lead her to what she desired.

The heat she felt between her legs told her it would. Finn walked into his bedroom and shut the door behind him. Kara closed her eyes, keeping the image of him imprinted into her brain. She took a deep breath and walked back into the kitchen. She completely forgot what she needed from the bedroom. She was also afraid if she went down there, she wouldn't be able to stop herself from opening Finn's door and taking the yellow brick road. She told herself she would have to find the Wizard of Oz and stream it.

She reminded herself, all the reasons she shouldn't have feelings for Finn.

She reminded herself of all the reasons Finn wouldn't be interested in her. She reminded herself of lines that shouldn't be crossed. She also waited until she was alone Saturday night while Finn was at work at Neighbors to use her vibrator, hoping it would help. It didn't. It made it worse.

She laughed at herself as she laid in bed. Why did she think it would help her get Finn out of her head? All it did was make her want him more. She was in heat. She had to do it again the night before when he went to work at Neighbors because after retiling the bathroom, it had gotten hot, and he used his shirt to wipe the sweat off his face, and Kara sucked in her breath. Heat flooded her body. It had taken all of her willpower not to walk behind him and press against his back, using her hands to feel her way down the yellow brick road.

Today they both could sleep in. Kara tossed and turned in her sleep. She kept having fitful dreams, and Finn kept appearing in them. She woke up feeling like her body was on fire. She was sweating and panting. Her ovaries ached so badly, she wasn't sure she was going to be able to get out of bed. She got up before Finn and took a quick shower. Much colder than she usually took. The shower only helped a little. Sunday was just as warm as Saturday, so Kara put on multiple layering tank tops.

She was already working in the bathroom when Finn joined her. The conversation was slow at first. Kara was distracted, and Finn seemed more tired than usual. She wondered if he started seeing someone since the Shelly thing was finally done. Jealously almost overwhelmed her. "What the fuck?" she thought to herself. She needed to get her feelings under control.

The problem was she didn't really know what her feelings were. Kara hadn't been interested in anyone for so long. She only knew how to be alone. Another thing was no matter how she felt, if it weren't reciprocated, she would once again make a fool of herself. At this point, wasn't it better to be by yourself than risk getting hurt again? Kara's heart had been broken on more than one occasion. She wasn't sure she would survive another heartbreak.

They took a break for lunch. As they made lunch together, Finn was trying to draw Kara out of her head. It wasn't working. Being around him was distracting her. Finn could cook and was pretty good at it. Kara was amazed at how well he knew his way around the kitchen. They even worked well in the kitchen together. Both of them able to do what the other one needed. Kara sighed. "Was there anything he couldn't do?" she thought to herself.

After lunch, they went back to working in the bathroom. The tile work was done, and they had to add the grout. They finished later in the afternoon. Hot, tired, and sweaty. Kara got up and stretched.

"I'm going to get cleaned up. I feel sticky and gross," she said.

Finn nodded and smiled at her. Kara walked out of the bathroom and right into the one they shared. She turned the shower on, waiting for the water to get so hot it was scalding. She stepped into the shower and let the water cascade down her body. She shaved and exfoliated to scrub away the dirt and grime. Hoping it would wash away the blech she felt. She emerged from the shower with her skin glowing and feeling a little bit better.

She put on her bathrobe and picked up her dirty clothes. She walked out of the bathroom to go into her room to get ready. She dropped something and bent down to pick it up, and Finn caught her as her robe opened, exposing her thigh. She saw him staring, and when she looked up to meet his gaze, he looked away.

Kara rushed into her room, not sure if she was embarrassed or hurt. She put the clothes in the hamper and sat down on her bed. Did he turn away because he was disgusted? Her thighs had stretch marks and cellulite. "See, this is why she didn't bother trying to date," she thought to herself as she started moisturizing. She wasn't ready for all the insecurities and the constant questioning herself. If she didn't open herself up, then she wouldn't have to think about all the ways she felt she wasn't enough for someone else.

She thought about Shelly. She was the complete opposite of Shelly. She was taller and weighed a lot more. Shelly was tiny, probably a size four, maybe if she was bloated. Kara was a size twelve. Shelly was young and still had perfect breasts not plagued by age and gravity. She didn't have a belly full of stretch marks or a FUPA from being pregnant and having your body never fully recovering.

Kara looked in the mirror. Shelly didn't have freckles across her nose or skin full of age spots. Although Kara looked younger than her age, she felt older than she was. She shook her head. She knew she shouldn't compare herself to someone else, but it's what happens when you thought about opening yourself up. You not only had to allow the good to come in, but you also had to keep in mind all the negative thoughts and insecurities would follow right along with everything else.

Kara sighed heavily as she put on a simple sundress. She remembered the last time she opened up to someone after she got divorced. She'd gotten the remaining pieces of her heart broken. Since she had to take care of Matt, she'd decided being on her own was better. She'd also been younger then. It wasn't as if she didn't get hit on. She did. She just wasn't interested.

Then her father died, then she had to take care of her mom. Now her mom was gone, and Matt was away at school. This was supposed to be her time to focus on herself and start living. None of these thoughts were helping her feel any better about Finn. Kara closed her eyes and took a deep breath. She had to get over whatever feelings she felt for Finn.

"Do you have any plans today?" Kara asked Finn. He was standing in front of the coffee machine, pouring some coffee. It was Memorial Day, and both of them were home. It was a beautiful day outside. Sunny and warm. Kara didn't want to spend the day working on the house. She needed a break. She had been feeling overwhelmed lately and needed to relax.

She was sitting at the table, looking out the window over the backyard. Pretending not to stare at Finn. He wore a t-shirt and shorts. His hair was down, falling on his shoulders like a golden halo. Kara had never been into the whole long hair thing. She'd always liked clean-cut nerdy types. Finn was the furthest thing from what she thought her "type" was.

Kara had been trying to keep her distance since he'd seen her coming out of the shower the week before. It wasn't working as well as she would like. Finn wasn't making it any easier, either. The worst part was he didn't even realize it. The more she tried to pull away from him, the more he sought to draw her out. She had to look away from him because all she wanted to do was walk up behind him, wrap her arms around his waist, and press herself against him.

Finn turned around and leaned against the counter. He took a sip of his coffee and shook his head. "No. Why?" His voice was still husky from sleep.

"Well, I've been invited to a barbeque. I have no choice but to go because I've been stalling and making excuses for the last couple of weeks, and if I don't go today, I'm going to be in trouble." She smiled. "I think you should go with me because I shouldn't have to suffer by myself."

Finn laughed at her. "So you want me to go and suffer with you?"

"Of course. I hate to suffer alone. Besides, Matt would normally go with me, but he's three thousand miles away. And...you're here and will make for a very nice replacement."

"Nice. I'm the fallback, guy?" Finn said, chuckling.

"You're not a fallback guy."

"Second choice guy, then?"

"You weren't the second choice."

"Oooh, so I was the third," Finn laughed, his blue eyes sparkling.

Kara laughed. "Stop it. You know you were my first choice." As soon as she said the words, she flushed. Why did he have the ability to make her say things she didn't want to say.

Finn smiled at her. "So, where is the barbeque?"

CHAPTER 10

Kara was standing on the deck talking to her ex-husband, Chris's wife, Teresa. Kara was holding Katie, their one-year-old daughter. Katie was cooing and gabbing away to Kara. Teresa was smiling as Kara talked to Katie like she completely understood what Katie was saying. Chris walked over and put his arm around his wife's shoulders.

"Kara, stop trying to steal my daughter. She's all mine," he said as he leaned over and kissed Katie on the head.

"I don't have to steal her. It's not my fault she likes me more than you." Kara said dryly. She smiled. "Honestly, can you blame her? I'm amazing."

Chris laughed. "You are. But seriously, you're already the favorite in this family. And now you're trying to take my daughter, and my wife is letting you."

"Again," Kara mock rolled her eyes at Chris. "You're jealous. Because honestly, Teresa loves me more than you too, and you're mad."

Teresa nodded. "She's right." Taking a sip from her Diet Coke. "You're fourth in line, after Matt."

Chris shook his head. "I'm ok with fourth. It's better than tenth." He took a sip of the beer he was holding. As Kara and Teresa laughed.

Chris was tall. Six foot three with broad shoulders. He'd played basketball in high school and college. He still looked as lean as he did then, even though he was forty-eight. He still looked young, with only a few gray hairs in his jet-black hair, making his green eyes stand out. Even though whenever Kara looked at him, she could only see her son Matt who looked like Chris 2.0, except Matt's eyes were brown and his skin a warm olive.

Despite Chris and Kara's divorce, they were still close. They spent every holiday together. Even after Matt went to college, Kara was still expected to come every Sunday for family dinner. Kara had avoided it the last couple of weeks because Finn moved in, and she hadn't wanted to leave. Chris finally had enough when it came to Memorial Day. He told Kara if she didn't come today, he would tell his mom on her. Chris's mother, Marion McNulty, was the stern matriarch of the McNulty family. Kara loved Marion as much as her own mother. Kara would never do anything to disappoint Marion. Kara knew better.

Chris took another sip of his beer and nodded towards Finn. Finn stood by the grill talking to Chris's brother Pete and his father, Dave.

"So…. Who's the dude?" Chris asked.

Kara rolled her eyes for real this time. "I told you. He's a friend of mine. He's helping me renovate the house."

Chris looked at her. "So you're saying your just 'friends.'" Using his hands for air quotes. "But he's staying with you?"

"He needed a place to stay, and I have plenty of room. I brought him today because he didn't have any plans and you," Kara said, pointing at Chris. "Threatened to tell on me if I didn't come today."

"Chris," Teresa said, looking at her husband. "Did you really?" She shook her head.

"Your damn right I did. She's been blowing us off for weeks. And I would do it again," he said, then sipped his beer.

"You act like you're her father," Teresa said.

"I am nothing like her father. Her father was mean. He didn't like anyone talking to his princess. And he was scary."

Kara laughed. "My father was not mean, and he definitely wasn't scary. And you're one to talk. Look at how you are with Katie. You're just as protective of her."

"Katie is never getting married and will stay my princess forever," Chris said, looking stoically at Katie.

Kara and Teresa laughed harder. Katie wanting to add her opinion in the conversation, started clapping her hands and laughing too.

"What's happening over here?" Chris's younger sister Lori walked over and rested her arm on Chris's shoulder. It looked weird because Chris was a good six inches taller than Lori.

"You guys are having way too much fun over here. Don't make me have to separate you," Lori used her most stern teacher's voice.

"Your brother is just being his usual overprotective self, again," Teresa said.

"Big shock there," Lori said wryly. "Over who this time?" Walking around, Chris to stand in front of Kara to play with Katie.

"Kara," Teresa said, laughing.

"Oh. Is it because her new boyfriend is hot?" Lori said without sarcasm.

"He's not hot," Chris said at the same time as Kara said,

"He's not my boyfriend."

Teresa looked at Lori and said, "Yes."

Lori laughed as she took Katie from Kara. "Come here, pumpkin. Give your favorite Aunt a hug." Katie went to Lori, and Lori showered her with kisses until Katie giggled.

"Seriously, Kara, he's hot. If I wasn't married already." Lori said.

"He's not my boyfriend. He's just a friend who is helping me remodel the house."

"And living with her," Chris said.

"Temporarily," Kara said. "Until he finds another place."

"Is he looking?" Christ asked doubtfully.

"Ooh, he's looking all right," Lori said. "But only at Kara."

"Lori," Kara said, shocked.

"Seriously, Kara. The way he looks at you, you expect me to believe you're just friends?" Lori said skeptically.

"We are," Kara said. "He's my handyman," she thought to herself. "Wait. How is he looking at me?"

"Like he's in the desert, and you're the oasis," Lori said. Katie squirmed in her arms. "Oops. It smells like someone just went potty. Come on, pumpkin, let's get you cleaned up."

Teresa stepped forward to take Katie from Lori, and Lori swatted her away. "I can do it, relax," she said as she walked away with Katie cooing.

"She's crazy," Kara said, shaking her head as Lori walked away.

"She's right," Teresa said, finishing the last of her Diet Coke. "I'm going to get a burger from your dad. I'm starving." She leaned over and gave Chris a kiss on his cheek.

"Do you guys want anything?"

"No," Chris said.

"No, I'm good," Kara said.

"Ok," Teresa said as she walked towards Dave, who was still at the grill talking to Pete and Finn. Kara and Chris watched her as she walked away.

"They're right, Kara," Chris said, turning to look at Kara. Kara turned and looked up at Chris.

"About what?"

"About the way he looks at you."

"No, he doesn't. No one looks at me like that."

"Yes, he does. You don't pay attention to it. You never have."

"What are you talking about?"

"Kara, you've always been oblivious to how beautiful you are. You have the entire time I've known you." Chris smiled at her. "Your head is always running in so many different directions. You've never noticed or paid attention to how people look at you. Or anything else for that matter."

Kara thought about what Chris said and started frowning. Chris laughed at her and shook his head.

"See, even now. Your mind is spinning so fast, trying to find all the reasons why all of us are wrong about something that's so obvious to everyone else but you."

"Because you're wrong. Seriously, Finn isn't interested in me as anything other than a friend."

"Kara, he's not looking at you like a friend. I have lots of friends who are women, and I've never looked at any of them the way he looks at you. You always think it's something other than what it is." Chris drained the last of his beer. "Anyway, all I'm saying is, Finn likes you. I just want to make sure this guy is ok."

Kara nodded her head. "I promise he is. Besides, you know I wouldn't."

Chris interrupted her, "I know. I know. You wouldn't do anything if you weren't sure. Still, you're family and Matt would kill me if I let anything happen to you." Chris laughed. "If you think I'm overprotective, Matt is crazy protective of you. He's a total momma's boy."

"He is not," Kara laughed.

"See, you just proved my point. You're totally oblivious to how much people are attached to you. And you're one of the smartest people I know."

"Shut up," Kara said, laughing. She looked over to see Finn walking towards them, chatting with Teresa.

"Hey," Finn said, standing next to Kara.

"Hey," Chris and Kara said.

"Did my father finally release you?" Chris said.

Finn laughed. "I told him I'm a maintenance supervisor for Tenby High school and also did renovations, and we talked shop."

"Yeah, he used to work construction. Now he goes around to everyone's house and fixes everything." Chris laughed. "You have now become my father's favorite person." He turned towards Teresa. "Come on, I'm starving. And you should probably see if Lori is alright."

Teresa took the hint, "Yeah, she's been gone an awfully long time." Kara frowned as she watched them walk away.

"Are you ok?" Finn asked, looking at Kara.

"Yeah, I'm ok. I think I'm just hungry." Kara said. She realized she hadn't eaten anything since breakfast.

"Well, let's get something to eat."

Kara nodded as they walked over to the picnic table set up. Joining everyone already surrounding the table.

As they were driving home, Kara's mind traveled a million miles away. She barely heard it when Finn said,

"Thanks for inviting me today. I had a really good time."

Kara turned to look over at him and quickly went back to focusing on the road.

"It was no big deal. Chris's family is my family, and they also happen to be good people."

"I can't believe you're still so close, even though you divorced and Chris remarried."

"I know. I get that a lot. But they're still my family because of Matt. And Chris and I got divorced almost fifteen years ago. It was extremely important to me Matt grow up with both parents able to put aside our differences and focus on what was really important," she sighed. "Once we did, everyone else just kind of went along with it. That and Marion loved me, and she wasn't going to let me go. Matt is the first grandchild. She wasn't about to lose any time with him because of me and Chris."

"Marion is a tough lady," Finn laughed. "She cornered me before I went out and talked to Dave. She grilled me for over an half-hour. Then she nodded at me and left. I was actually nervous."

Kara laughed. "That's Marion. She's a momma bear. Always has been. When Chris and I got together, Marion was brutal. Chris is the oldest. Not only was I not Catholic, but I was also a Black Baptist." Kara shook her head at the memory. "I thought she was going to explode when I refused to convert to Catholicism."

Finn laughed out loud. "That's the first thing she asked me."

Kara laughed and shook her head. "Marion's faith is essential to her. Chris and I almost didn't get married because of it. Dave stepped in and defended us. Dave never says anything, especially against Marion. No one does. But because Dave said something, Marion stopped." Kara sighed. She remembered all of the fights she and Chris had before getting married.

"What happened when you broke up?" Finn asked quietly.

"Believe it or not, that's when Marion stepped in. She told everyone I was family, and it didn't matter if we were married or not. She wasn't going to be separated from her grandchild. Dave agreed." Kara took a deep breath. "Honestly, by that point, I didn't have the energy to fight both of them.

Besides, they were much more supportive than my own family. Even my dad was brutal when it was over."

"You don't really talk about your family, except maybe Matt."

"Neither do you." Kara laughed

"Fair point," Finn said. "Ok, what do you want to know?'

"I don't know. Tell me everything. Your parents, do you have siblings? Where did you grow up?"

"That's a lot," Finn laughed.

"Well, then you better get started because we're almost home."

"Ok," Finn said. "My parents are Robert and Dorothy Wilson. Married for forty-five years. Together for forty-seven years. My dad is retired. He used to be a salesman, but he worked three jobs when I was younger. My mom is a retired second-grade teacher. She used to be a stay-at-home mom when we were younger, then went back to work. I have an older sister Beverly, and a younger sister Ellen and my younger brother Mike. All of us are two years apart."

"Four Kids, two years apart? God bless your mother."

"Yeah. We were a handful. We are all still close. Both of my sisters still live within blocks of my parents. Ellen lives with her boyfriend. Beverly is married and has two kids."

"What about your brother?"

"Mike lives about thirty minutes north of my parents. On the other side of Princeton."

"Is he married?" Kara asked.

"God no, he's a man whore." Finn laughed and smiled when he heard Kara laugh. "I'm not slut-shaming him. He really is a man whore, and he knows it."

"So is my brother Anthony. I get it," Kara said. Kara pulled into the driveway. They got out of the car and walked up the driveway towards the house. Kara didn't want the conversation to end. When they got into the house, Kara turned on the living room lights and sat down on the couch. Finn sat down next to her, and she turned towards him.

"So where did you grow up?" she asked him.

"Lakehurst, it's almost an hour away," Finn said. "My parents still live in the same house I grew up in."

"Really?"

"Yes. It's in Ocean County. We all grew up, went to college, and then went our separate ways. Still close enough to go visit, though."

"Didn't you go to Ocean County Community College?"

"Yup. I was going to transfer when I graduated, but I needed money, so I got a construction job. During the winter, I started working at Neighbors and became friends with Randy."

"Neighbors, is where you met Shelly, right?" Kara hated even saying the woman's name made the bile rise to her throat.

Finn nodded and shifted his position on the couch, so he was facing her. "Yeah."

Kara noticed he didn't say anything else about Shelly. She was happy about it. If she never had to hear Shelly's name again, it would be too soon.

"How did you end up working at Tenby?"

"Randy told me about the Job. He knew the superintendent of the school district. Randy pulled some strings to get me the job." Finn looked at Kara. "Can I ask you a question?"

"Sure, ask away."

"How did you meet Chris?"

Kara smiled. "I was going to Stockton and got an internship working at the same casino as Chris. Hospitality wasn't my major, but a part of the internship did cover HR. Chris was a dealer at the time, and we met in the employee cafeteria. We were reading the same book at the time, so Chris sat down at my table, and we started talking."

"You both worked at casinos?"

"Yes. I hated working in a casino. So as soon as I could, I got another job. Chris stayed for a while. Even after we got divorced. When things in AC got bad, Chris got another job as a store manager. He's still doing it. He met Teresa there a couple of years ago."

"Isn't it weird?"

"Chris and Teresa?" Kara asked. Finn nodded. "It was at first. But Teresa's great. And she loves Matt as much as I do. I also love Katie as much as she does. We didn't try to compete with each other. Which helped." Kara said carefully. "She also didn't do some of the bullshit some of Chris's other girlfriends did. She loves Chris, and when he told her I was family, she accepted it. We went to lunch to get to know each other and laid everything out on the table. We talked about any doubts either of us had, and by the time we paid the check, we were the best of friends and have been ever since."

"It's amazing you were able to do that. Not many people would go out of their way to make friends with their ex's new girlfriend. When Randy got divorced, he and his ex-wife could barely be in the same room without fighting. Even when it was for their boys."

"That's exactly what I wanted to avoid for Matt."

Finn looked over and smiled. Kara met his eyes and felt her heart flutter. Everything Chris and Lori told her earlier playing in her mind. She shook her head to clear away the thoughts. Finn looked over at the clock on the cable box. He stood up and stretched. Kara got a glimpse of his stomach and felt heat spread through her body.

"It's getting late," Finn said after he was done stretching. Kara couldn't seem to stop staring at his body. Finn yawned. "I should get some sleep." Kara looked up at him and nodded.

"Yeah, I should go to bed too. But I think I'm going to make some tea first, though."

"Good night," Finn said as he walked out of the living room up the stairs.

"Good night," Kara said. She turned out the light and walked upstairs to make some tea.

CHAPTER 11

Finn's phone vibrating on the nightstand woke him up. He reached over to pick it up. Fourteen new messages.

Mom: Happy Birthday, Finn. I love you.

Dad: Happy Birthday, Griffin. Love you.

Mike, Beverly, and Ellen: Happy Birthday! The Big 40!

Randy: Happy Birthday, Bro.

The rest were from his crew and other friends from both jobs. He texted 'thank you" back to everyone. He debated staying in bed, but he might as well start the day since he was up. Finn got up, put on a t-shirt and shorts, and walked out of the bedroom to the kitchen.

When he walked into the kitchen, there were Happy Birthday balloons tied all over the kitchen. In front of the coffee machine was a brand new travel coffee mug. There was another wrapped present and a card.

Finn smiled and shook his head. "Kara," he thought to himself. He opened the card and couldn't stop himself from smiling as he read it. She did all this and also promised him dinner later. He set the card down and opened the gift. His heart caught in his chest. Inside were four bracelets made to symbolize the elements. Earth, Air, Fire, and Water. They were small, polished beads tied together with leather. He leaned back against the counter and stared at the box.

On one of their many Lowes trips, Finn noticed the associate who was helping them wearing them. They had gone in to order the bathtub Kara wanted along with new fixtures. The guy who had them on was probably in his fifties or so. Finn had asked about them when he thought Kara wasn't around. The guy told him his wife bought them for him because they were cool. The bracelets apparently had some meaning, but he couldn't remember what it was. His wife had gotten them for him so long ago.

Finn wasn't really a jewelry guy. He owned a watch, but he really didn't wear it unless it was a special occasion. He had other pieces of jewelry, but most of them were gifts he didn't wear. Another reason was jewelry would just get in the way of construction and working at the school. But something about the bracelets appealed to him.

"Did she have to be so fucking perfect all the time?" he whispered to himself. Since Memorial Day, Finn had been crushing on Kara hard. Everything she did was sexy.

Angry Kara was sexy.

Happy Kara was sexy. One of his favorites.

Work Kara was sexy. Day job or part-time didn't matter.

Home Kara was sexy. Another favorite.

Quiet Kara was sexy.

Laughing, Kara was really sexy. His absolute favorite and never failed to make him hard as a rock. Since he always tried to make her laugh, it meant he walked around with a constant erection because her laughter was his favorite sound.

For the last two weeks, Finn had been trying to control his feelings for her. But she was making it so fucking complicated. It was little things she did. She would look at him and smile, and he would stop breathing. She had a habit of playing with her hair without realizing she was doing it. Finn wanted to tangle his fingers in her hair and lean her back and kiss her breathless.

He'd even caught her coming out of the shower, and her bathrobe exposed part of her thigh. Finn had to force himself to stay where he was. Everything in him wanted to rip her bathrobe off and fuck her in the hallway.

"How did she even know?" he thought to himself. Of course, she would know. Of course, she would find them and get them for him. Finn took the bracelets out of the box and put them on his left arm. There was a card inside the box explaining what each one represented. They matched the ink he had on the inside of his forearm. Blue, green, white, red, and silver. He looked at his ink and thought it was about time to get them recolored. Most were almost eight years old. Some of them were older and starting to fade. He took his phone out of his pocket. He had one new message.

Kara: Happy Birthday! I hope you enjoy your morning and are relaxing. Thanks for waiting around for the plumber. I appreciate it.

Finn: Thank you. And thank you for everything. The mug, the balloons, the card. And especially the bracelets. BTW, how did you know?

Kara: Because. I'm amazing!

Finn: Yes, you really are amazing.

He set the phone down on the counter and made himself coffee in his new mug. Kara made fun of his old one. It was battered and peeling. Of course, she got him a replacement of the same cup. "God, she really is fantastic." he thought to himself as he took a sip of coffee. Forty was turning out to be a great birthday.

Finn did have a great day. Actually, it had been a damn good day. One of the best birthdays he had in a long time. The plumber came early to install the pipes for the upstairs laundry room Kara wanted. Everything had gone smoothly. Kara called the same plumber who had worked on the master bathroom, and Finn liked the guy. He did good work and didn't try to price gouge.

Finn and Kara had finished the master bathroom and were almost done with the master bedroom. They were working on the shelving in the walk-in closet. They also ripped up the floors in the smallest room, so Kara could convert it to an upstairs laundry room. Kara was waiting for shelving and cabinets to be delivered. Then they would finish both the walk-in closet and the new laundry room.

When the plumber left, Finn cleaned up his room and did some of his own laundry. When he went downstairs, some of Kara's clothes were folded on top of the dryer. While waiting for the washer to finish, he took Kara's clothes and put them on her bed. Her bedroom smelled like her. Finn breathed it in. He was losing it. This woman was making him ache in a way he'd never had before.

By the time Kara came home, Finn was showered and ready. He sat on the couch in the living room when she came in. "She looks fabulous as usual," he thought to himself. She was smiling and had a sparkle in her eye, Finn hoped was for him. He walked over to her and took the grocery bags filling her arms. They walked up to the kitchen to put everything away. She'd bought steaks, lobster tails, potatoes, and stuff to make a salad. There was a bottle of champagne and a small cake.

They put everything away, and Finn leaned against the counter. He couldn't believe how she was going all out for him.

"Kara," he said docilely. She turned and looked at him. Her eyes were literally sparkling. She seemed so happy. "Fuck, she's beautiful," he thought to himself. He was about to say something but forgot what. It didn't matter because she stopped him.

"I know what you're about to say, and I'm going to stop you before you do."

Finn looked at her, smirking, "Oh, really? And what is that?" Even he didn't know what he was going to say.

"You're wondering if all of this is too much." She was leaning against the counter with her arms folded across her chest. Her eyes took on a mischievous look. "And I personally don't think so. I think it is just enough for a fortieth birthday. So..since I've decided it's not too much, that's what we're going to go with." She stood in front of him and put her hands on her hips.

"And to make another thing perfectly clear, we are not going to work on the house today. We are going to relax and celebrate your birthday. Because it will make me happy."

Finn laughed. "Fuck, now she's reading my mind," he thought. "Ok. I was going to say that," he admitted. He would have admitted to anything she wanted him to if it made her happy.

"I know," Kara laughed. "You've got that look on your face that says, 'it's too much, and you didn't have to do this'" Kara used her fingers for air quotes.

Finn could only smile at her. She was right. He shook his head. "Ok. You win."

"Good." Kara looked at the clock. "We have some time before we have to start dinner. I have an idea."

Kara's idea before dinner was to play Monopoly. Finn hadn't played Monopoly in forever. Finn liked how Kara made everything so easy. He didn't have to pretend to be having a good time because he was having a good time. He could just be himself, and it was enough. They played until it was time to start dinner, then they both washed their hands and started cooking.

On nights they didn't have to work, they made dinner together. Finn liked cooking with Kara. It was Kara's favorite thing to do, and she was a good cook. They talked as they chopped and would make the other taste something. Tonight, Kara put on some music, and they sang and danced in the kitchen. At one point, Finn took her hand and twirled her, catching her in his arms. If it weren't for the timer going off for the steaks, Finn would have kissed her. He was a moment away from letting them burn.

They ate dinner in the dining room using the good plates. Because Kara said, they should. They ate, talked, laughed, and Finn loved every minute of it. Finn sat across from Kara and just looked at her. She was smiling and looked serene. It made her happy to do all of this for him. Finn thought his heart was going to burst. Kara's happiness made him happy.

They finished eating, and Finn was sitting back in his chair. Dinner was delicious. He was full, happy, and couldn't remember the last time he'd been so relaxed. "Yes, you do. You feel the same thing any time you spend with Kara," he thought to himself. He couldn't even argue with himself because it was true. They cleared the plates from the table and decided to clean up the kitchen. The music went back on as they cleaned up. Finn didn't twirl Kara this time. He didn't think he could keep his hands to himself if he did.

After cleaning up, Finn decided he wanted to sit and watch tv. They went downstairs and turned on the tv. Finn wasn't really paying attention to what they were watching. He didn't really care. He needed some time to come down from the Kara high he was on. She'd made his birthday perfect. And she'd done it without even trying. Finn realized he couldn't come down even if he wanted to. Honestly, he didn't want to. He was falling in love with Kara.

"Fuck. What?" His brain screamed. His heart started beating faster, ecstatic his brain ultimately understood. He got up to go to the bathroom. Just because he didn't think he could sit next to her and not fall at her feet. He wanted to grovel in front of her and declare his love for her. In the bathroom, he splashed some water on his face.

He was in love with Kara.

It felt so natural. Of course, he was in love with her. Hadn't he been trying to talk himself out of it for weeks? No, it had been longer than that. He'd been in love with her the moment he saw her. When he shook her hand and felt it throughout his body. Every time she smiled. Every time she laughed. He even loved how she was quiet in the morning before she had coffee and fully woke up.

Finn washed his hands and went back to the living room. While he was gone, Kara got the cake, a candle and filled two glasses with champagne. He went downstairs and sat next to her on the couch. She lit the candle and started singing.

"Happy fortieth birthday to you, Happy fortieth birthday to you, Happy fortieth birthday dear Finn, Happy fortieth birthday you. Make a wish."

Finn closed his eyes. He could only think of one thing he wanted more than anything else. He made his wish and blew out the candle. Kara handed him a fork. They ate the cake straight from the container and drank the champagne.

As they went to bed, Kara hugged Finn tightly and whispered,

"Happy Birthday Finn. I hope your wish comes true." Finn held her longer than he should have, and she pulled back. He could have sworn she heard his body screaming in protest.

Finn drifted off to sleep, thinking about his wish. He smiled because he knew what he wanted was sleeping in the room next to his.

Finn woke up the morning after his birthday happy. He was forty years old. Although he wasn't where he'd thought he be, he was pretty satisfied with where he was. The fact his life had changed so much in less than six months stunned him. Six months ago, he was living with Shelly and struggling under the burden of marrying her. Now, he was living with Kara, feeling weightless. He was in love. It was so unexpected. He thought he loved Shelly, and a part of him did, but it was nothing like what he felt for Kara.

Finn thought about what his father said to him when he took his parents to dinner. He knew he could live without Shelly. He wasn't so sure when it came to Kara. The thought made him happy and scared at the same time. He was glad he felt something like what his father did but were his feelings for Kara so strong already? When did that happen? What was he going to do about it?

As Finn went about his day, Kara filling his thought, he knew he had to do something. Finn knew Kara's birthday was coming up. Marion had told him Memorial Day and reminded him every Sunday since then. After meeting Finn and deciding she like him, Marion had let him and Kara know they were expected to be at family dinner on Sundays in no uncertain terms. Marion was not someone you wanted to disappoint.

Finn also knew Kara didn't celebrate her birthday. He'd overheard a conversation Kara had with her best friend, Charlie. He'd been in the living room watching tv while she was on the phone in the kitchen. From what he heard, Kara said she liked to celebrate everyone else's birthday, but not her own. Finn wondered why and was quickly rewarded when she told Charlie, her birthday was always a major disappointment.

Finn wanted to change that. Kara had made his birthday one of the best he'd ever had. He wanted to celebrate her. Knowing her had changed his life. He knew exactly what he needed to do. He would need some help. He called Randy.

"Hey," Randy said when he answered the phone.

"Hey. I need a favor. Actually, I need a couple of favors."

"That escalated quickly," Randy laughed. "It went from one to a couple real quick."

Finn laughed. "I know, but it's important."

"Ok, what do you need?"

Finn told Randy what he was hoping to do. He wanted to do something for Kara, expressing how he felt about her. He also wanted to let her know just how amazing she was. If she hated her birthday in the past, he wanted to change that. She really was the best person he knew. He didn't want to do something stupid to ruin it. He needed to keep it simple and genuine.

"I got you, bro," Randy said.

"Thanks, man, I appreciate it."

"No problem. I'll call you back."

Finn hit end on his phone. When he got back to his desk, he turned on his computer. While he responded to emails, he took out his notepad and started making a list of all the things he needed. If he was going to pull this off, he didn't want to forget any details.

Randy called him back within thirty minutes.

"Hey," Finn said when he answered.

"Hey, you're all set."

"Thanks, man. Last favor, can I borrow your car?"

"My car?" Randy asked.

"Yeah, I can't do this with my truck."

"Wow, You're really trying to impress your girl, aren't you?"

"Something like that."

Randy laughed. "Yeah, pick it up when you want."

"Cool, I'll see you Thursday."

Finn hit end. He had work to do.

CHAPTER 12

Finn lay in bed Wednesday night, too excited to sleep. He was anxious, nervous, and hopeful. He felt like it was the night before a big test, and he wasn't sure if he would pass or fail. He knew he prepared, and it was the best he could do. He'd done things for girlfriends in the past, but Kara wasn't his girlfriend. He just wanted her to be. He wanted her to be more than that, actually.

He turned over in bed and tried to quiet his mind. He needed to relax and get some sleep. Everything would be ok. Everything will work out. Everything would go according to plan. He repeated it over and over again like a mantra. After what seemed like an eternity, Finn fell asleep.

Finn sat at his desk in the morning, picking up his phone and checking it every five minutes. He texted Kara when he woke up to say Happy Birthday, and she texted back thank you. He hadn't heard anything else since. Even when he'd gotten the delivery notification. He shifted in his seat, bouncing his leg up and down. He got up, walked over to the window, looked outside, and walked back to his desk. He thought he heard his phone vibrate. It didn't.

He looked at the clock on the wall and got disgusted because he didn't think it was moving. It was. Just not as quickly as he wanted it to. The two guys who were a part of his crew were completing many of the end of the school year maintenance tasks. Tonight was the high school graduation ceremony, so things had to be done to get ready for it. Usually, Finn would have to be there for the ceremony just in case anything happened. Sean, who had been with Finn the longest, offered to cover for him so Finn could have the night off.

Finn paced in his office. He needed to burn off the extra energy he had. He sat back down in his desk chair, staring at his computer screen. He should be focusing on catching up on emails and filing incident reports instead of acting like a teenager. He was forty years old, for fucks sake. He opened up his email and was starting to read the newest one when his phone finally vibrated.

Kara: I love them. Thank you so much. They're lovely. And I would love to go to dinner. What time?

Finn pumped his fist into the air and whispered, "Yes!" He leaned back in his chair and let out the breath he'd been holding all morning.

Finn: I'll pick you up about 6:30

Kara: Ok, but won't you be home anyway?

Finn: No. I have to help with the graduation ceremony tonight, so I'll pick you up.

It wasn't technically a lie. It just wasn't the whole truth.

Kara: Ok. Where are we going?

Finn: It's a surprise.

Kara: Lol. Ok. What should I wear?

Finn: Something nice.

Kara: Lol. You're being cryptic, but Ok.

The rest of Finn's day seemed to drag on at an annoyingly slow pace. When he was at last done, he rushed out of the building like he was being chased. He still had things to do. First, he stopped by the store to pick up Kara's gift. Glad he'd paid extra to have it professionally wrapped. He would have made a mess of it. He went to the dry cleaners and picked up the suit he'd dropped off the day before. By the time he got to Randy's, he had just enough time to get ready.

Finn pulled up to the house at 6:25. He put the car into park and turned off the engine. His palms felt clammy from gripping the steering wheel. He closed his eyes and took a deep breath, exhaling slowly to calm his nerves. He got out and walked up the driveway to the front door. Then he pressed the doorbell.

Kara answered the door, and Finn stopped breathing. His heart was pounding so fast in his chest, he thought it would break free from his body. He sucked in a breath, and his brain screamed at him to remember to breathe. His eyes feasted on the sight of her.

Kara looked stunning. She wore a long-sleeved navy blue lace dress. It was off-shoulder, exposing her neck and collarbone. It was fitted at the waist and flowed at her hips. It fell about an inch above her knees and showcased her legs. It was flowy yet accentuated her body, giving her the perfect hourglass figure. She had on matching heels with crystal accents at the toe.

Her hair framed her beautiful face and fell prettily onto her shoulders. She was wearing a blue crystal necklace matching her dress. Her skin looked like it was shimmering. It made her look like she was literally glowing.

"Hey," Kara said affectionately.

Finn forgot how to speak. He was afraid if he opened his mouth, nothing but gibberish would come out. All he could do was stare. His eyes drinking her all in. Kara's full mouth was slightly parted into a small smile.

"Finn?" she said and tilted her head to meet his gaze. Thankfully, it triggered the part of his brain that actually formed words reminding him to speak.

"You are the most beautiful woman I have ever seen."

Kara's mouth widened into a big smile. "Well, that's the nicest way I've ever had anyone say hello to me before."

"It's the only way someone should say hello to you."

Kara smiled. "You know, you don't look bad yourself."

Now Finn smiled. He'd chosen his charcoal suit with a matching gray shirt and tie.

"Thank you." Finn extended his arm out to Kara, "Ready?"

She nodded as she stepped forward to close the door behind her. She locked the door and put her keys in a small blue purse matching her shoes. She turned and took his arm, and Finn led her down the driveway to Randy's silver BMW parked on the street.

As they walked, Finn was glad Kara took his arm. If she hadn't, he might float away. He felt like he was walking on air. When they got to the car, Finn opened the door for her. She smiled at Finn as she got into the car. Finn caught a flash of her creamy brown calf as she sat before he closed the door.

They drove in silence. The radio playing one of Randy's preset jazz stations, Finn hadn't bothered to change. He tried to concentrate on driving while simultaneously trying not to glance down at Kara's legs. He noticed how she occasionally glanced over at him as she looked out the window. Finn could feel the blood flowing through his veins as his thoughts raced. "When did she get the ability to cause him to act like a complete idiot?" he thought to himself. Then he realized she'd always had it.

Kara reached over and gently placed a hand on his forearm, and everything came to an abrupt halt. His mind calmed. He looked down at her hand and over at her.

"Are you ok?" she asked gently. "You seem like you're a million miles away."

Finn took a deep breath before he spoke. He wasn't sure going with his first thought of "You look so fucking amazing that you've completely shut down the parts of my brain that I need to function as a rational human being" was the best way to go. It probably wasn't the wisest thing to say, even if it was the truth. He decided to simplify it.

"Yeah, I guess I'm just a little anxious."

Kara laughed, and his heart beat faster. "If he didn't get his heart under control, he would ruin tonight by having a heart attack and going to the emergency room," he thought to himself.

"Why would you be anxious? It's just us, only a little better dressed than normal," she said gently.

Finn glanced at her quickly before turning back to the road. "God, did this woman not know how she affected him?" he thought to himself. Didn't she realize that simply being with her was turning him into mush? No, of course, she didn't. How could she be one of the smartest women he knew and be so clueless.

Finn smirked, "It is just us," as he pulled into the parking lot of the restaurant.

Bernard's On The Water was a seafood restaurant offering a piano player and a dance floor. One of the favors Finn asked Randy was to get him a reservation for tonight. Randy knew the owner because, honestly, Randy knew everyone. Finn knew he was going to owe Randy big for this.

Finn parked in one of the few empty spots. As he shut off the car, Kara went to open the door, and Finn shot her a look. She smiled at him and leaned back in the seat. He got out of the car and walked around to open the door for her. She laughed and looked up at him with her sparkling dark brown eyes as she took his hand.

The planets didn't align.

The earth didn't move and shake the ground.

Fireworks didn't magically light up the sky, and lightning didn't flash through the night.

It was quiet. Like the sound when you turn on the light, and it chases all the darkness away in a room.

The sound a butterfly makes when it flaps its wings and lands on a flower.

Finn was drowning, deeply in love with Kara.

When he'd realized it after his birthday, he didn't know how much. Now he knew, he was more entrenched than he could have ever imagined. Loving Kara made him feel calm and brought a sense of peace like all was right in the universe. He felt like he was exactly where he was supposed to be and with the person he was always meant to find.

Finn kept Kara's hand in his as he gently closed the car door behind her and pressed the key fob to lock the car. He led her into the restaurant, gently intertwining his fingers with hers. Her hand was soft and warm. At her touch, Finn felt all the nervous energy he had disappear.

He opened the restaurant door and unwillingly let go of her hand as he led her inside ahead of him. He followed her over to the maître d.

"Hi, I have a reservation at seven o'clock. Wilson party of two."

"Of course, follow me, please." The maître d said. He was an older man, tall with black hair graying at the temples. He wore a high-quality, tailored suit. Finn wondered if he was the owner.

The maître d ushered them through the crowded restaurant to a table by a big bay window, facing the water. Melodic piano music played in the background. The table was close to the dance floor, but far enough away it wouldn't be too loud to talk. The restaurant had dimmed lighting, and each table had candles floating in bowls of flowers in the center.

The maître d pulled out Kara's chair for her to sit down and handed her a menu. Finn sat down across from her and picked up the menu in front of him.

"Can I start you off with something from our wine collection?" The maître d said as he poured water from a small pitcher on the table into their glasses.

"Can we have a bottle of Lancaster Estate Cabernet, please," Finn said.

"Excellent choice. I'll have your waiter bring it over right away."

"Thank you," Finn said as the maître d walked away.

Finn looked over at Kara from above his menu. She was suffused in candlelight. He could see the twinkle in her eyes behind her glasses as she looked through the menu. Her beautiful mouth curved in an easy smile. Her head tilted slightly, causing her hair to fall into her eyes. If he had ever tried to imagine what the woman he would fall so helplessly in love with would look like, it wouldn't have come close to the perfection Kara was right now. He couldn't help but smile to himself.

Kara looked up at him and met his gaze. "What?" she asked serenely.

"Nothing," he said, shaking his head slightly. Finn realized he was staring at her.

He opened his menu and was surprised to find he wasn't hungry. He should be starving. He hadn't eaten anything since lunch, and that was at noon. "Was it possible to lose your appetite when you were in love?" he thought to himself. He tried to focus on his menu, trying not to be so obvious he couldn't stop staring at Kara. He failed.

"You're looking at me as if you haven't seen me every day for the last eight weeks," she said without looking up from her menu.

Finn smiled sheepishly, "I'm sorry. You're right. I should stop, but," he hesitated.

"But what?" Kara looked up at him meeting his gaze.

Finn looked down for a moment and sighed. For a moment, when Finn lifted his head to meet her gaze, he was afraid to speak.

"But, I can't seem to help it. My eyes are naturally drawn to the most beautiful woman in the room, and she just happens to be sitting across from me."

"You're smooth," Kara said, smiling. "Are you flirting with me on purpose?"

"Yes. Is it working?"

"Maybe," Kara said as she lifted her menu, trying to hide her smile.

The waiter came over, poured their wine, and set it in the silver bucket by the table. The waiter told them the specials and, after taking their order, took the menus and left to place their order. Finn leaned forward and folded his hands in front of him on the table.

"So," he said, watching Kara. "How's your birthday been so far?"

Kara took a sip of her wine and set the glass gently on the table. "Well, so far, it's been the best birthday I've had in a really long time."

"Really? Why?"

"Well," she hesitated. "I don't actually celebrate my birthday anymore. I stopped after a particularly awful one. Since then, people have tried, but I always seem to be alone at the end of the evening, crying." She paused to take another drink of her wine.

"But today has been very different. I received the loveliest bouquet of all of my favorite flowers. My friends from work took me out to lunch today. Which was nice. Charlie took me to get my nails done this afternoon, which was a nice surprise. I got to talk to Matt today, and that always makes me happy. I also heard from Chris and the rest of the McNulty clan, and that was good." She took another sip of her wine and set her glass down gently again. She leaned forward slightly and smiled at him.

"And the best part is earlier today, I received an invitation to dinner. It was out of nowhere and completely unexpected. Then as if out of a movie, the most handsome man I've ever seen, wearing a suit and tie, rings my doorbell and whisks me away. Now, I'm sitting in an excellent romantic restaurant with the person whose company I happen to enjoy immensely. And he is looking at me like I've never been looked at before."

"How is he looking at you?" Finn whispered. His voice was a little hoarse.

Kara hesitated. She looked at her wine glass and slowly traced the opening with her finger. After a moment, she looked up at Finn. The look was intense, and Finn felt it surge through his body.

"As if I were the reason God created woman. Like I was the answer to every question he'd ever had, wrapped in the prettiest package he's ever seen. And he's not sure if he deserves it or not."

Finn didn't respond at first, letting her words sink in. "Maybe he's not sure," Finn whispered.

"But why not? Why would he think he didn't deserve it?"

Finn leaned back in his chair.

"Maybe because it makes him realize he's not good enough, smart enough, or worthy enough. Maybe because he doesn't understand how something so amazing could be for him."

"But isn't that the point?"

"The point of what?"

"Everything. The people who feel the most undeserving are actually the ones who need it the most." Kara sighed. "Because they will do everything they can to keep it."

Finn didn't know how to respond. Kara was looking at him so intensely he wasn't sure if he was still breathing. How did she do that? How does she say exactly what he was feeling and make it sound like it's the most natural thing in the world? Like they were talking about the weather. Not if he was worthy enough for her. Because he still wasn't sure if he was.

The waiter brought the first course over and set it down in front of them. They ate in silence. Each of them lost in their own thoughts. As the waiter brought over the other courses, they still hadn't continued speaking. Soothing music floated through the air. Finn turned and looked around the restaurant. Couples were dancing slowly around the dance floor. Light was cascading through the windows from the setting sun. Shadows were dancing across the table from candlelight.

Finn wiped his mouth on his napkin and set it down by his plate. He stood up, and Kara's eyes followed him. He walked over to her and reached out his hand.

"Will you dance with me?"

Kara nodded, taking the napkin from her lap and placing it on the table. She took his hand and allowed him to lead her to the dance floor. Finn swung her around, and she stepped into his arms. Finn held her hand in his as he placed his other hand on the small of her back. Swaying her to the music. Kara leaned her head on his shoulder. Her hand resting lightly on his back.

Finn held her close to him and wondered if she could feel his heart beating. He was distracted by her jasmine perfume. The way she felt in his arms and how her body seemed to melt against his. "Was it possible to get drunk off a woman? Because if it was, then he was smashed," he thought to himself. Kara leaned back and looked up at him. Finn meeting her eyes, bent down, and kissed her.

Finn felt time stop. Everything fell away. The softness of her lips. The warmth of her mouth. How sweet she tasted. Finn's hand moved up her back, and he tangled his fingers in her hair. Gently guiding her so he could deepen the kiss. He felt her body press closer to his. Kara gently bit his bottom lip, and Finn felt his knees weaken and his dick get harder.

Kara broke the kiss and gently pulled away. Finn wanted to pull her back into his arms. But as the room came back into focus, he realized the music stopped, and people were surrounding them. "Fuucckk," His brain and his dick said simultaneously. Comprehending they were in public and ripping off Kara's clothes and making love to her on the dance floor would probably land them in jail.

Kara brought him back by gently placing her hand in his, and he led her back to the table. He pulled out the chair for her to sit down. Then sat down across from her. Within minutes the waiter brought their entrees. Finn watched Kara cut her chicken and took a small bite. Her face serene as she closed her eyes and savored the taste. Finn stared at her, wondering if he should knock everything off the table and make love to her or if he was just jealous of the fork.

"Aren't you going to eat?" Kara asked as she cut another piece of her chicken.

"Uh-huh." Was all he was able to mutter. He shook his head, hoping to clear it so he would regain the ability to speak. Finn picked up his knife and fork and began to cut into his tenderloin. They ate in silence. Both of them savoring dinner. The food was exquisite. Finn would have to thank Randy for the reservation. As he was finishing his tenderloin, he was mid-bite when Kara smiled at him.

"You know, I have a theory about dancing," she said matter of factly.

Finn wiped his mouth. "Really? What's that?"

"You need to be really careful about who you dance with?"

"Why's that?"

"Because you fall in love when you dance with someone."

Finn put his knife and fork down in front of him and looked at Kara. "So," he said hesitantly. "If I ask you to dance with me again, will you say yes?"

"Yes," Kara whispered.

Finn took a sip of his wine. His mouth had gone dry. Then he wiped his mouth on his napkin. He stood up and walked over to Kara. He held out his hand,

"Will you dance with me?"

Kara took his hand, and as he was about to lead her to the dance floor, the waiter came and asked if they were finished and would like everything wrapped. Finn barely heard him but nodded.

All Finn wanted to do was feel Kara in his arms. He wanted to feel her body pressed against his and breathe in her scent. As he held her in his arms, he kissed the top of her head. He didn't think he would be able to kiss her again and stop himself from fucking her on the dance floor.

When the song was over, Finn led Kara back to the table. The remains of their dinner were neatly placed in white boxes in front of their seats. Finn pulled out Kara's chair for her, and as he sat down, the waiter came to the table.

"Would you like something from our dessert menu or coffee, perhaps?"

"Can I please have two coffees and the special order brought over, please?" Finn said. Kara looked at Finn with a raised eyebrow. Finn just smiled at her. The waiter nodded and went back to the kitchen.

The waiter returned a few minutes later with two coffees and a slice of Tiramisu with a single candle already lit. The waiter set down the tiramisu in front of Kara and gave each of them a coffee.

"Thank you," Finn said to the waiter as he left the table. Kara's smile lit up her face.

"Happy Birthday Kara. Make a wish." Finn whispered.

Kara closed her eyes and blew out the candle. She took the candle out of the cake, set it on the side, and picked up her fork. Finn got the same pleasure watching her take her first bite of tiramisu as he did while she ate her chicken. Her eyes closed, and Finn was frozen, watching her savor her first bite. He could watch the way her beautiful mouth moved forever and never get enough.

Kara opened her eyes, and Finn could see the happiness radiating around her. "This is it. I want to be the person who makes Kara look like this every day," he thought to himself. He wanted to be the one who made her happy. As happy as she made him.

They finished their coffee, and Kara finished her tiramisu. She offered some to Finn, but he shook his head, only wanting to watch her enjoy it. He motioned to the waiter to bring the check. Kara excused herself to the lady's room while Finn paid the bill. He left a huge tip and slid a fifty to the maître d. as he stood at the entrance waiting for Kara, carrying the bag with the leftovers.

Finn took Kara's hand when she stood by him and led her out of the restaurant to Randy's car. When they got to the car, he leaned over to open the car door. Kara stepped in between Finn and the door and kissed Finn.

The kiss took Finn by surprise. He wrapped his arm around her and leaned her back against the car, trying not to drop the bag in his hand. He pressed his body against hers and ravaged her mouth. Desire filled his veins like he had been given a drug. His dick was stiff and throbbing. Kara's hands were behind his neck. She nipped his bottom lip, and he couldn't hold the moan escaping his lips.

"This woman is killing me," he thought to himself. He pressed his erection against her, and when he heard her gentle moan, Finn stepped back from her.

"We should go now," he said, his voice rough. Kara smiled at him, and Finn returned her smile. He opened the car door, and Kara got in. He closed it and opened the back door to place the bag on the back seat shutting the door a little too forcefully. As he walked around to the driver's side to get in, Finn smiled to himself. He'd almost lifted her up and fucked her on Randy's car.

CHAPTER 13

Finn held Kara's hand in his as they drove home listening to the radio. When they stopped at a red light, he brought her hand to his lips. He kissed the inside of her wrist, inhaling her scent and letting it fill his lungs. Finn felt euphoria coursing through his veins. Their date so far was incredible. He hoped Kara felt the same way. He would glance over at her occasionally just to see if she was still smiling. With less traffic, the drive home was faster, and Finn was soon pulling up to the front of the house.

Finn turned off the car and looked over at Kara.

"Wait one minute," he said. He got out of the car and opened the trunk to take his duffle bag out. He closed the trunk, got the bag out of the backseat, and walked over to Kara's side to open the door for her. They walked up the driveway, and Kara opened the door. Finn followed her in. He closed the door behind him and turned to Kara. She stood in the living room, turning on the lights.

"Wait here. I'll be right back," he said. Kara sat down on the couch, and Finn ran up the stairs. He put the bag from dinner in the fridge and ran to his room. He placed his duffle bag on his bed and took out Kara's gift bag. Then ran back out of the room to the living room. Finn stopped at the top of the stairs, taking a deep breath before he walked down. As he walked down the stairs, he walked with the gift bag behind his back, hiding it from

Kara. He walked into the living room and stood before Kara.

"Ok, Close your eyes," he whispered lightly.

Kara leaned back on the couch and closed her eyes. Finn put the gift bag on the coffee table and sat down next to her.

"Ok. You can open your eyes now," he whispered.

"Finn," Kara whispered. "You didn't."

Finn put his finger to her mouth to silence her. Then he turned her face to look at him.

"Yes, I did. Open it."

Kara carefully opened the gift bag and gently slid the box out to open it. She pulled out the styrofoam packaging and placed the box on the table. When she opened it, her eyes grew wide, and a smile lit up her face. Kara carefully removed the Faberge egg globe, decorated with blue and green gems. A gold latch attached to the front opened the trinket box.

"Finn," Kara whispered breathlessly.

"It's a music box too. Turn it over." Finn said quietly.

Kara carefully turned it over and turned the key. The melody was a familiar song, pleasant and soothing.

"Do you like it?" Finn whispered, searching Kara's face as she held the globe. Kara took a deep breath and sniffled. Tears glistening in her eyes.

"It's the most beautiful birthday gift I've ever received ," she said, barely above a whisper.

Finn wanted to jump up and whoop but didn't. When he saw it, he'd known it would be perfect. He remembered Kara telling him she wanted to travel the world. She didn't get the chance to. She had somehow ended up stuck in New Jersey. It was something she'd never meant to do.

"I wanted to give you the world," Finn whispered to her. Kara turned and looked at Finn, searching his eyes. She had tears in her eyes, but they were happy tears, he thought. But she looked sad.

"Kara, are you ok?" he said, reaching for her hand.

She nodded her head. Finn reached up and gently wiped away a tear from her eyes, caressing her cheek. She held up her hand, signaling she needed a minute. She took a deep breath and gently put the globe on the table. When she turned and looked at Finn, tears were still in her eyes, and Finn gently wiped them away. Kara took his hand, reached for the other one, and held them in her lap. She took another long deep breath before looking up and meeting his eye.

"I stopped celebrating my birthday a little over ten years ago. The truth is I've always had bad birthdays. Ever since I can remember. I either wouldn't get what I wanted, or people would bail at the last minute. Something would happen, and I would always end up crying by myself at the end of the night." She hesitated for a brief moment, sniffling to stop the tears.

"It wasn't until I stopped celebrating them that they even became tolerable." She paused to take another deep breath. "To me, it was just another day. But people would make all of these grandiose promises. I knew if I ignored them, then it would be ok because I wouldn't be disappointed when it all fell apart, and it always did." She took her hand and caressed his cheek. Gently rubbing her thumb across his cheek.

"You have made today the best birthday I've ever had. If every birthday I ever have for the rest of my life sucks, it won't matter because of how perfect you've made today."

Kara leaned forward and gently brushed her lips against his. It was the softest, lightest kiss.

"Thank you."

Finn did the only thing he could do. He pulled her into his arms and kissed her. Gently and tenderly. He felt the dampness of her cheeks from her tears. He wanted to tell her how he felt about her without having to put it into words. He took her face in his hands, gently kissing her cheeks, eyes, and forehead. Then he retook her mouth, this time hungerly. He kissed his way down her jaw to her neck. His hands caressing her back. Kara moaned quietly, and Finn pulled her into his lap. Kara arched her back as he kissed her collar bone and across her chest.

Finn lifted his head and claimed Kara's mouth again. The more he kissed her, the more he wanted her. He hungered for her, and he didn't think he would ever get enough. "God, she tasted so good," he thought to himself as his hands caressed her body.

Kara's hands cupped his face kissing him just as hungerly. Her hands moved down his neck to his chest. She inched off his jacket and was loosening his tie. Never taking her mouth from his. She undid his shirt buttons, exposing part of his chest, and touched his chest gently. He breathed gently against her lips as his hands glided over her hips.

Finn pulled away from Kara and looked at her. Desire making her dark eyes look glassy. Finn gently slid her off his lap. She looked at him questioningly. Finn stood up, took her hands, and pulled her up off the couch. Without letting her go, he leaned across her and turned out the lights, and led her upstairs. He stopped at his room, but Kara walked past him to her room. He ran into his room, grabbed one more thing out of his bag, and ran after Kara into her room.

Finn didn't go into Kara's room too often. She had a queen-size bed. Her mattress was so tall, she had to use a step stool to get into it. He stood at the door, watching her as she turned around to face him. He was about to turn on the light, but he heard her whisper, "No, don't."

Finn took a moment to let his eyes adjust to the darkness. Kara's room faced the back of the house. The motion lights from the backyard filled the room, so it wasn't too dark. Finn walked slowly over to her. When he reached her, he cupped her face in his hands. He leaned down and kissed her. Kara reached up and pulled Finn's shirt out of his pants to finish unbuttoning it. Then she slid her hands over his shoulders to take his shirt off. It landed on the floor with a noiseless swoosh. Kara's hands caressed Finn's chest. At her touch, Finn shivered, a sigh escaping his lips against her neck. He reached around and slowly unzipped her dress. As it slid down, Kara caught it before it could fall.

"Wait," she whispered. Finn stepped back.

"What's wrong?" His arms falling to his side.

Kara reached out and pulled him to her. "It's not what you think," she looked up at him smiling. She took a deep breath and leaned back against her bed. "It's just," she hesitated, embarrassed.

Finn stepped closer to her and turned her face to his. "What is it?" he whispered.

Kara sighed. She used her free hand to reach up and pinch the bridge of her nose, causing her glasses to shift to her forehead. Finn looked down at her, confused. He took her hand away from her face.

"Kara, tell me?"

Kara took her glasses off and set them down on the nightstand. She lowered her head and shook it slowly.

"It's just, I'm wearing shapewear. It's not the sexiest thing, and it's hard to get off," she said, slightly embarrassed. She sighed again. Finn cupped her face in his hands and forced her to look at him.

"Kara, are you serious right now?" he whispered.

Kara looked away. "I haven't had to think about it for a really long time. I'm not like Shelly."

"What are you talking about?" At the sound of Shelly's name, Finn flinched.

Kara sighed. "Finn, I have a real woman's body. I have a belly and stretch marks and wide hips. I have cellulite. This shapewear is holding everything in. I'm real. But, I'm not perfect, and I don't have a perfect body. I'm fine with it, but," Kara stopped.

Finn wasn't sure if he was angry, sad, or both at the same time. He couldn't believe he was having this conversation. It was making his heart ache. First, did she really think he was a shallow prick? Second, whoever made her believe she wasn't the most beautiful, sexiest woman on the planet needed to be hunted down and beaten. Third, didn't she realize the effect she had on him? Finn shook his head. Seriously, it was just Kara. It wasn't an attempt to seek compliments. She just never saw herself as she really was.

Finn kissed her lightly. "Kara, you really are one of the most frustrating women I have ever met." Kara looked at him.

"What?" she said vaguely.

Finn smiled at her. "You have no idea. You don't see yourself the way I see you. When I look at you, honestly, I see you as the sexiest woman I have ever seen." Finn sighed and shook his head.

"You don't know how long I've wanted you. Or how badly. And not just right now, I want you all the time. Since I met you, I've wanted you. Every day I'm with you, it takes all of my energy not to pull you into my arms and fuck you."

Kara looked at him uncertainly. Finn seeing her hesitation, took her hand and placed it over his cock. At her touch, he immediately regretted his decision. His intention had been for her to feel how hard he was, not to cum in his pants.

"I probably shouldn't have done that?" he whispered hoarsely.

"Why?" she whispered.

Finn laughed. "Because I almost came in my pants, and that would have been really embarrassing."

Kara laughed faintly. Finn leaned down and kissed her tenderly. He moved her hand away from her dress to let it fall on the floor. He pulled her into his arms. Trailing kisses down her neck to the hollow of her throat.

"Fuck Kara," he said against her skin. Her hands were in his hair. A moan escaping her. Finn went to tug at her shapewear, and Kara stopped him.

"Let me," she whispered.

Finn kicked off his shoes and took off his pants as Kara shimmied out of her shapewear. Under it, she was wearing blue lace underwear. Finn wasn't prepared for that. The sight of her took his breath away. He let out a deep breath. Kara stepped onto the step stool and backed onto the bed, moving over to let Finn climb up.

He moved next to her and turned on top of her. He lowered his head and kissed her. Devouring her mouth. He got lost in how her body felt under his, and he didn't want to hold back. Kara wrapped her legs around him, moving her hips to grind against him. He moaned as he kissed her neck and her chest. When he got to her breasts, Kara sat up slightly to unhook her bra, slipped it off, and let it go over the side of the bed. Finn kissed her breasts, taking her erect nipple into his mouth and biting gently. Kara arched her back and moaned. His hands slid down her body. Over her stomach down to her mound. Kara sucked in a sharp breath. Finn gently spread her legs apart, kissing her stomach.

"Kara, your so soft," he said against her hip. He breathed in her scent. She smelled delicious. Like happiness and warmth. He kissed her above her panties and gently pulled them down. Kara lifted her hips so he could take them off. Finn's hands gently touched her legs, kissing her inner thigh, and just as he reached her mound, he gently bit her inner thigh. Kara whimpered as she arched her back. Finn had to grab his swollen cock and squeeze it tightly to stop himself from cumming immediately. He moved up and kissed her, gently stroking her mound with his fingers. Tracing circles over her folds. She groaned against his mouth. He stopped kissing her and looked down at her. Her eyes were slightly open. Her lips parted. Her chest falling and rising with her harried breath.

Finn climbed off Kara and almost laughed out loud when he heard her cry of frustration. He found his pants and removed the box of condoms from his pocket. He climbed back onto the bed and moved next to her. "I just had to grab these." He ripped open the box and took out the package of condoms ripping one off and opening it. He took off his underwear, put the condom on, and climbed back on top of her.

Finn kissed her again. He covered her mound with his hand letting his finger enter her. She was so wet. His thumb gently circling her clit as his finger moved in and out of her. Kara's moans filling his mouth.

"Finn," she whispered breathlessly. "Please,"

"Tell me what you want, Kara," His voice raspy. Not stopping his hand. He leaned down and kissed her. His thumb teasing her clit. Kara arched her back and thrust her hips to match Finn's rhythm. "Kara, you taste so sweet." he whispered against her mouth.

"Finn." Kara panted breathlessly.

"Yes," Finn whispered. Never slowing his pace.

Kara clutched the blankets. "Please, Finn."

Finn stopped, and Kara cried out. He kissed her hungrily. "Sorry, Baby, I can't wait anymore." His voice was hoarse.

Finn gently guided himself into her. Both of them crying out as they joined. He let out his breath, "Kara, I can't move. I'm too close." Kara thrust her hips, and Finn thought his body was going to explode. He squeezed his eye's shut. Kara moaned and moved her hips under him. Finn kissed her and matched her pace. Each thrust into her felt like heaven. "Kara, holy shit," he rasped against her mouth.

"Finn, I'm cumming," she breathed. He felt her shudder beneath him.

Finn lost it and came hard as Kara's climax caused her to tighten around his dick. He kissed her as he came, her nails digging into his back.

Finn went to the bathroom to take care of the condom, and Kara used the other bathroom to clean up. He went into his room and put on a pair of shorts. When he went back to Kara's room, she wore an oversized t-shirt and put her glasses back on. Finn walked up to her and pulled her into his arms. He held her, her head resting on his chest and her arms around his waist. He closed his eyes. He wanted to enjoy how it felt with her in his arms. Everything felt like it happened so fast, even though it had taken forever to get here.

"Do you want a cup of tea?" Finn whispered. Kara nodded against his chest. "Ok, just one more minute, though. I've waited so long for this." Kara leaned back and looked up at him. He smiled at her, then gently kissed her. Finn broke the kiss, then took Kara's hand and led her to the kitchen. He turned on the burner under the teapot and then walked over to the kitchen table. They sat down to wait for the tea to boil. The kitchen was dark except for the light over the stove. Kara always kept it on. Finn reached for her hand, intertwining their fingers. He searched her face, but her eyes were hidden because of the darkness.

"Tonight feels a little surreal," Kara whispered.

"How so?"

"I don't know, it just." She trailed off and used her other hand to run through her hair.

"Just what?" he asked warmly.

"I guess. I can't believe tonight happened."

Finn knew what she meant, but for him, it wasn't surreal. He was glad tonight happened. Now he was wondering why it had taken him so long.

"Kara, I have to tell you the truth," he whispered.

Kara turned her head sharply towards him, "About what?" she said hesitantly, taking her hand away from his.

Finn smiled, "It's not anything bad," watching relief flood her face. "About this." He reached for her hand again.

"I've wanted this for a long time. But, after everything with Shelly, I thought I shouldn't attempt anything with you because, well, actually, I don't know why. I thought of a lot of reasons, but now when I think about them, none of them seem to make sense anymore," he chuckled.

"I thought I should just be on my own for a while. But, I'm an asshole." He shook his head as he gently ran his thumb over her knuckles. "I couldn't stop thinking about you. I tried. I really did. You were all I could think about. I thought I should go out and date. But every woman I saw, I compared them to you. If a woman had pretty eyes, I would immediately think they didn't sparkle like yours. If a woman smiled at me, I would think, yeah, but Kara's smile takes my breath away." Finn felt Kara looking at him. "I don't know what this is, but I'm thrilled it happened, and I'd like it to keep going."

Kara hesitated. Thinking about everything he'd just said. After a few moments, she looked up at him, "Are you sure?" Kara whispered.

"Yes," he answered.

They sat for a moment before the whistle of the teapot broke the silence.

They both stood up, and Kara made her tea while Finn handed her the lemon. When she finished, he put it back in the fridge. She walked carefully out of the kitchen, down the hall to her bedroom. Finn followed her, standing in the doorway. She set the cup on the nightstand and turned to look at him.

"Aren't you coming in?"

Finn smiled. "I wasn't sure if you were comfortable with me being here with you."

Kara turned and looked at the clock. It was just after eleven. She turned and looked at Finn.

"Are you comfortable with staying?"

"Yes. But aren't you sleepy?"

She nodded. "Stay," she whispered gently. "Please,"

Finn stepped into the room and walked over to her. "As long as you want." Kara reached out and hugged him. Wrapping her arms around his waist and holding him tightly. Finn put his arms around her and held her. He sensed something was wrong, but he also knew she was tired, and a lot happened today. He let her go unwillingly as she pulled away and turned down the bed. She stepped on the step stool to climb in. Finn walked around to the other side and got in.

Kara inched closer to him, and he opened his arms for her. She put her head on his chest, and he wrapped his arm around her. He reached for her hand with his free hand and interlaced his fingers with hers. Within minutes Kara's breathing slowed, and soon after, Finn drifted off to sleep. Thinking about how happy he was and how Kara never drank her tea.

CHAPTER 14

Kara woke up with her body intertwined with Finns. The house was still and quiet. She could hear his steady breathing. His arms wrapped around her and her head buried in the crook of his neck. She could feel his heart beating under her hand resting on his chest. She gently untangled herself out of his arms. The clock on the nightstand confirmed how early it was. 5:15. The sun wasn't even up yet. Finn stirred slightly but didn't wake up.

Kara reached over and turned off her alarm clock so it wouldn't wake him up. She eased out of bed. She picked up her glasses and put them on, then she picked up the cold cup of tea from last night. She quietly walked out of the bedroom towards the kitchen. She set the cup down in the sink and then remembered she hadn't programmed the coffee machine last night.

She tried to be as quiet as possible as she made coffee. While she waited for her coffee to brew, she cleaned up the few dishes in the sink. She grabbed a coffee mug from the cabinet and the creamer from the fridge. When the coffee was done, she poured herself a cup, poured creamer in, and put it back in the refrigerator.

She picked up her cup and took her first sip. This is precisely what she needed. She needed the coffee to wake her up. She walked over to the kitchen window looking outside. It was still early and peaceful out. She enjoyed the quiet moment before she would start her day. It was Friday. It should be a pretty easy day.

She didn't see it when it came in. To be fair, she had her eyes closed, savoring her coffee and the silence. Because of its silent stealth-like approach, she didn't hear it. She didn't realize it was there until its coldness sent shivers down her spine. By then, it was too late. It had already roared to life. Washing over her and pulling her under like a twenty-foot wave.

She held her coffee mug in both hands to steady her shaking hands. She felt her chest tighten and her heart pounding in her ears. Her mind racing, thoughts coming at her so quickly she couldn't keep up with them. An ear-splitting scream cut through her swirling thoughts. She felt a little queasy and light-headed.

"WHAT THE FUCK DID YOU DO?"

"YOU SLEPT WITH FINN?"

"YOU RUINED EVERYTHING."

"FUUUCCCKKK."

She set the coffee mug on the counter because it almost slipped from her hands. She leaned against the counter to keep herself from falling. She began to dry heave and had to cover her mouth with her hands. She could feel the bile rising in her throat, and she didn't think she would make it to the bathroom.

"THIS IS WHY YOU'RE ALONE."

"YOU'RE DAMAGED."

"YOU'RE BROKEN."

"HE MIGHT LIKE YOU NOW, BUT JUST WAIT UNTIL HE FINDS OUT WHAT YOU'RE REALLY LIKE."

Kara's mind kept up the steady stream of attack. Tears spilled from her eyes, gliding down her cheeks. She squeezed her eyes shut, trying to stop them. She slid to the floor and leaned against the cabinet door. She brought her knees to her chest. She took a long deep breath. Slowly breathing out. She noiselessly whispered, "Breathe," to herself. Taking a deep breath and then slowly exhaling. She said the words out loud quietly, hoping the calm, soothing words would drown out her mind's screaming.

After what felt like eight lifetimes passing, Kara's breathing returned to normal, and her heart stopped pounding. She opened her eyes, her vision still blurry from tears and from squeezing them shut. When she regained her focus, she stood up slowly. Afraid she would fall over, she gripped the counter to keep herself steady. She looked over at the clock on the microwave. "Fuck," she whispered. Now she was late. She ran down the hallway to the bathroom. She had to get ready for work.

Kara stepped out of the shower and wrapped herself in a towel. She used the spare bathroom because she needed to hurry and thankfully had some of her stuff hidden under the sink she'd left behind when she moved everything to the master bathroom. She crept into her room quietly to grab some clothes to wear and some of the things she needed to get ready.

Finn still peacefully asleep, lying in her bed. She looked over at him, smiling to herself. The sun was slowly starting to fill the room with light. Casting sunlit over Finn's face. He was on his back with an arm above his head. The same arm he used to wrap around her last night. "God, he's beautiful," she thought to herself, feeling her heart flutter. She wanted to crawl back into bed and wrap herself up in his arms. It was safe there. Nothing could hurt her there. "Except your mind," she thought to herself. She shook her head, hoping to clear it.

"Focus," she thought to herself sternly. Since it was Friday, she was allowed to wear jeans. She grabbed a pair of jeans, a blouse from her closet and picked up a pair of sandals. She walked out of the bedroom, put her stuff in the bathroom, and then went back in to get the rest of the things she needed to get ready.

Within ten minutes, Kara was moisturized, dressed with makeup, and hair done. She'd put her hair up in a ponytail. And did her makeup light to save time. She looked in the mirror. She looked like she was somewhat put together. Hopefully, she would be able to fake it for the rest of the day. She left the bathroom and walked into the bedroom for the last time. She glanced around to double-check if she'd left anything. She walked over to the bed, stepped on the step stool, and lightly brushed her lips over Finn's. He stirred slightly. She stepped down and quietly left the room.

She stopped into Finn's room to make sure his alarm was set so he wouldn't oversleep. Then went back down the hallway to grab her stuff before rushing out the door and locking it behind her. It was just after seven when she got into her car. Her whole morning was thrown off. As she pulled out of the driveway, she realized she hadn't packed lunch. She left her coffee on the counter and still had the purse from last night.

"I just have to wing it today," she muttered to herself. If she was going to be late, she might as well be late with coffee and breakfast. She felt her stomach growling. She took a deep breath and shook her head to clear it. She needed to focus on driving.

At 9:15, Kara was in the last stall of the ladies room crying silently. She'd carefully looked in each stall to make sure she was alone. She leaned against the wall, put her head in her hands, and started crying as soundlessly as she could. She was surrounded. Her demons, dancing around her bullying her into submission. Anxiety, Depression, Insecurity, Fear, and Doubt. The gang was all there, chanting as they twirled around, taunting her as if she was a Maypole.

"YOU'RE NOT SKINNY ENOUGH FOR FINN. NO MAN WANTS A FUPA"

"YOU'RE TOO OLD. YOU HAVE SPLOTCHY SKIN AND AGE SPOTS, THOSE AREN'T FRECKLES AND THEY AREN'T CUTE."

"FINN SHOULD BE WITH SOMEONE YOUNGER. HOW COULD HE POSSIBLY WANT TO BE WITH YOU?"

"YOU'RE JUST A REBOUND. AS SOON AS FINN GETS BORED WITH YOU, HE'LL DROP YOU SO FAST YOUR HEAD WILL SPIN."

"HE'LL NEVER LOVE YOU. YOU'RE DIFFICULT. YOU'RE IMPOSSI-BLE TO LOVE."

"HE ONLY WANTED TO GET LAID LAST NIGHT. NO ONE REALLY WANTS YOU."

"YOU DON'T DESERVE TO BE HAPPY. YOU SUCK AT RELATION-SHIPS. YOU ASK FOR TOO MUCH, AND THAT'S WHY EVERYONE LEAVES YOU."

Round and round, they danced. Taunting and singing merrily in their high-pitched shrieking voices. Kara let the tears fall as she leaned against the bathroom stall, covering her mouth. Thankful no one else was in the bathroom.

Kara had struggled with depression and anxiety all of her life. It wasn't until she had Matt and suffered post-partum depression she was fully diagnosed. She spent most of her days lying in bed crying, only getting up to take care of Matt. She also hid almost all of it from Chris. Chris didn't actually find out the truth until years later. After they had been divorced for years, she had casually mentioned it to Teresa. Chris didn't take it well when he found out.

She would fake having everything together. She was good at faking it. And it worked for a while until it didn't anymore. Her job at the time was causing her hair to fall out. Matt was in his terrible twos, and she felt guilty, leaving him to go to work. Chris was ignoring her and acting like she didn't matter. She spiraled down the warm whirlpool, hoping she would drown and everything would be over.

At the worst of it, she tried different kinds of therapy. She tried various combinations of pills. Most of them causing either horrible side effects or made her feel like a zombie. Behavior therapy seemed to have the best results for her. She was high functioning. She'd been so used to hiding it and coping, no one ever noticed.

Since she'd been in therapy, it had started getting better. Panic attacks and episodes were few and far between. With her mother's failing health and eventual death, dealing with Anthony, and trying to renovate the house, this year had been stressful. Work was becoming demanding. Add to that her complicated feelings for Finn, Kara had pushed herself beyond her breaking point.

And now she'd slept with him. Making it even more complicated. This is why she didn't date. This is why she didn't open up. She was safer, being hidden away. If she kept to herself, her demons couldn't attack her. If she didn't allow herself to feel so much. If she hadn't allowed Finn to get to her, she would have been fine. She should have just avoided it. Being alone was comfortable. Being alone was safe.

Finn scared her. With Finn, she was in unknown territory. He wasn't like anyone else. He'd made her feel things she'd never felt before. Look at last night. It was the first time in decades, she'd had a good birthday. It wasn't good. It was perfect. No wonder he scared the shit out of her. Fear was causing her to spiral.

"YOU'RE GOING TO DIE ALONE."

"NO ONE REALLY LOVES YOU. THEY JUST PRETEND TO."

"YOU'LL NEVER BE ENOUGH. FOR ANYONE"

Kara slid down the bathroom wall and huddled into the corner. Slowly rocking herself, waiting for the attack to be over.

"You did what?" Charlie squealed. The look of sheer excitement and happiness made her face light up. Kara took a sip of her sweet tea and sighed as she set it back down on the table.

"I slept with Finn last night," Kara repeated quietly. After everything she had to deal with earlier, she wasn't sure how she felt about it. She was exhausted from all the battles she'd fought this morning.

"Oh my God, Kara! Finally." Charlie exclaimed. She sounded triumphant.

"What's that supposed to mean?" Kara snipped.

"It means," Charlie exaggerated. "That you're finally starting to put yourself out there, instead of hiding. No more living like a hermit." Charlie took a sip of her diet coke. They were having a belated birthday lunch at one of Kara's favorite places Olga's Diner, near Kara's office. Even though Kara saw her the day before, Charlie insisted on having lunch today. Kara was glad because she needed Charlie to help ground her.

"Yeah, well, I'm paying for it this morning," Kara said inaudibly. Charlie knew all about Kara's struggles with depression and anxiety. Charlie had been there for Kara, through the worst of it. The best part was Charlie didn't judge Kara or tell her to "just suck it up" like so many other people did. Charlie understood, which not many could.

"Tell me everything," Charlie said. Concern and worry clouding her face. Kara sighed and told Charlie everything. About the date, dancing with Finn, the globe music box he bought her, their making love, and both of the panic attacks she'd had this morning. When she was done, Charlie reached across and placed her hand on top of Kara's.

"You know, none of that is true, right?" Charlie whispered. Kara looked at her. Tears filling her eyes, and she nodded her head. "Then what's really the problem?" Charlie asked.

"The problem is, even if all the fear and anxieties aren't real, there are still a million reasons why Finn and I shouldn't be a thing."

"No, there aren't. You're just doing what you always do."

"What do I always do?"

"You hide, Kara. You run away. You've convinced yourself you don't deserve to be happy. You're looking for reasons to say no, instead of seeing all the possibilities if you were to say yes." Charlie took another sip of her diet coke, and when Kara didn't say anything, she continued.

"Finn scares the hell out of you. But Kara," she said, gently putting her glass down on the table. "Love is scary. You have to open yourself up and be vulnerable. And every time you've done that, it's blown up in your face. I know it seems easier to just avoid it. I get it."

"No, you don't." Kara sighed. "You're happily married to a man who worships the ground you walk on."

"That doesn't mean I haven't had my heartbroken, and you know it," Charlie said quietly. "Kara, you can't keep avoiding everything in your life."

"I'm not," Kara said defensively.

"Yes, You are," Charlie said sympathetically. "Kara, you deserve to be loved. You deserve to be valued. You deserve to have someone who wants to take care of you."

The waitress came and brought their orders. A salad for Charlie and a ham and cheese omelet for Kara. Her episode earlier in the morning meant she missed breakfast. They said thank you, and the waitress left the table. Charlie started eating her salad, and Kara looked at her omelet. She should be starving since she hadn't eaten anything since the night before. Her appetite was gone. It left as soon as her demons showed up.

"What if I'm not ready for all of that?" Kara whispered. Looking down at her plate. Knowing she should eat something. She picked up her knife and fork and started cutting her omelet. Charlie looked at her.

"You are ready, not that it matters," she said, pointing her fork at Kara.

"You've waited a long time to start actually living your life for you and not because you have to make everyone else happy."

Kara took a bite of her omelet. Forcing herself to eat. If she took one bite at a time, she might be able to eat enough, so she wouldn't be sick later from not eating. Charlie watched her intently. Kara knew Charlie worried about her. Kara was worried about herself. What the hell was wrong with her. Why was it every time she was on the brink of happiness, she has a panic attack? How was that even possible?

"You know, this probably wouldn't have happened if you weren't already so in love with Finn," Charlie said matter of factly. "And from the sound of it, he's just as in love with you. You can deny it if you want to, but it doesn't change it. It snuck up on you, and you didn't have time to overthink it and analyze it to death."

Kara raised her head up sharply and stared at Charlie. "In love with Finn? What the hell?" she thought to herself. Charlie was smirking at her. Sometimes, Kara thought to herself, and not the first time, she really can't stand her.

"Don't look at me like that. It's not my fault. I had nothing to do with this. You did this all on your own. Don't be mad at me because I'm right,"

"I can't stand you," Kara whispered as tears filled her eyes.

Charlie laughed. "I love you too. Now eat." Pointing to Kara's omelet.

Kara nodded and ate more of her omelet as Charlie told her everything happening with her.

When they finished lunch, and Kara was about to get into her car and go back to her office, Charlie gave Kara a big hug. "Remember, you deserve the love Finn so freely wants to give you. It's ok to be scared, but Kara, don't run away. Don't push him away. You deserve this, more than anyone."

Kara hugged her tighter. "I love you."

"I love you too," Charlie said.

157

Kara went back to her office, her day not getting any easier. Meetings, emails, and people coming to her desk to talk to her. She was exhausted from this morning, and although she felt better after lunch with Charlie, it wasn't enough. Her boss was continually calling her over to his office to ask her about her progress on the project. An employee came to her desk to ask about a transfer. Kara put on her "everything is fine, nothing to see here" mask and tried to keep going.

By the end of the day, cracks were beginning to show in her mask. At least two of the emails she sent were on the snarky side. She snapped at her boss after he called her into his office for the third time within five minutes. When four o'clock came, she ran to the door. To make it worse, she still had to work her other job tonight. She wasn't sure she was going to be able to make it.

CHAPTER 15

Kara pulled into her driveway, turned the car off, and sighed. Today had lasted ten years, and it still wasn't over. She still had to get changed, eat something, and go to work. Even though she only had to work a few hours, it still felt like she was being asked to crawl through the desert. Her brain was fried, and a migraine was lingering at the base of her neck.

She got out of the car and walked up the pathway to the house. Before she could get to the door, Finn opened it. He took one look at her and took the computer bag from her hand as she walked in. He set it down by the table and closed the door behind her.

They'd been texting each other throughout the day. Although he knew she had a rough day, it wasn't until she walked in that he could see how rough. Kara had never been good at hiding her feelings once she took off the mask. Her face always showed precisely what she was feeling. Finn turned Kara around gently by the shoulders to face him. He pulled her into his arms and held her. He didn't say anything. He just held her tightly against him.

When she tried to pull away, he held her tighter. He didn't let her go until he began to feel the tension release from her body. Eventually, her body relaxed against his, and her breathing began to slow. She took a deep breath, filling her lungs with his scent. Finn smelled good. He smelled of soap, and his cologne smelled like the air after a fresh rain.

"Are you ok?" Finn whispered. Not letting her out of his embrace. Kara shook her head against his chest. She definitely wasn't ok.

"What can I do to help?" he asked.

No one other than Charlie had ever asked Kara that question. Kara felt tears form in her eyes again. She'd been periodically crying all day. Seriously, how did she have tears left? Kara shrugged.

"Kara," Finn whispered. "Talk to me. Tell me what you need." He held her tighter. "Don't shut me out."

Kara flinched, Charlie's words coming back to her. She sighed. She might as well get it over with. If her fears were correct, the minute he found out, he would leave. If Charlie was right, and he was in love with her, then.... She wasn't sure what would happen. She'd never talked seriously about her anxiety and depression with anyone other than Charlie and her therapist.

Kara tilted her head back to look at him. His blue eyes filled with concern. She stepped out of his arms and took a deep breath.

"I suffer from high functioning depression and anxiety. And today, I had a panic attack that caused an episode." She paused to take another deep breath. The only way she was going to get through this conversation was to keep her breathing under control.

"Most of the time, I'm ok. But sometimes, something will trigger it, and it will cause me to spiral. Today I just happened to spiral a little farther down than I have in a while, so it's taking me a little longer to climb out of it."

Kara stopped, letting what she said sink in. When she started talking, she looked up at Finn, and now she was looking down at her shoes. She was never this honest about her depression. She wasn't ashamed of it. It was a part of who she was. She just never had to talk about it.

She couldn't talk about it with her family because they simply didn't understand. So she never brought it up. Even though she was close to Chris's family, she often withheld the hard parts. When she did talk about it, it was always after the fact. Charlie knew the most and still didn't know all of it. The only person she was one hundred percent honest with was her therapist.

Kara continued. "I do see a therapist. I don't take medication, though.

When I did, I either had terrible side effects like night terrors, or I felt like a zombie." Kara sighed and started wringing her hands. Finn reached down and took her hands in his. At his touch, Kara calmed. She took a deep breath. Slowly exhaling. Finn let go of her hand and lifted her chin to look at him. His thumb gently wiping away a tear she didn't realize had fallen.

"Kara, you are the strongest woman I've ever met," he whispered. "You've had to be strong for so long that your acting like having anxiety and depression is a weakness, and it's not."

He pulled her into his arms and held her tightly to him. She began sobbing noiselessly. Shuddering against him.

He caressed her back, whispering "Shhhh." and "It's ok. I'm here," soothingly. Over and over until she stopped crying, and her shuddering stopped.

Kara leaned back to look up at Finn and saw the concern in his eye.

"Thank you," she said faintly.

"For what?" he whispered.

"For being there for me."

Finn looked at her. "Always." He leaned down and kissed her. Tenderly and gently. His hands reaching up to cup her face. The kiss sent shivers down her spine, filling her with warmth. A moan escaping her lips. Finn's hands moved down her body, pulling her closer to him.

"Work," Kara whispered. Pulling away from him. "I have to get ready for work," she looked at her watch. If she hurried, she could get changed and try to find something to shove down her throat and still get to work on time.

Finn nodded and let her go reluctantly. She could feel his eyes on her as she walked up the stairs to her room to get ready. She was surprised when she walked into her room, and her bed was made. When she left this morning, he was still asleep. The clothes all over the place from last night, neatly put away. Her dress hanging in her closet. Kara smiled to herself.

As she got changed, she thought about what she'd told Finn. She hadn't opened up to anyone in years. He'd told her she was strong. Kara knew she was strong. She just didn't want to be anymore. She wanted to be allowed to be vulnerable and still feel safe. She'd been strong for so long. She wasn't used to not being strong.

Finn actually made her feel safe in a way she'd never felt before. She tried thinking about when the last time she actually felt safe with someone. She couldn't think of one. She'd always kept some part of herself hidden. She always held some part of her back. She never felt safe enough to simply be herself, including the broken pieces. Kara leaned over to put her sneakers on. She went into the bathroom and touched up her makeup, and brushed her ponytail.

She still tried to find a time when she last felt utterly safe. Not on edge, worried about something, or anxious about something else. When she wasn't depressed. Safe enough, she didn't think about what she looked like to someone else. Safe enough, she didn't have to pretend. She didn't feel like she should be doing something else. The kind of safe where she could be herself, and it was enough.

Kara left the bathroom and walked into the kitchen. Finn waited for her and handed her a plate with a sandwich, chips, and a water bottle.

"Finn, you didn't have to," she said, smiling at him.

He interrupted her. "Stop saying that," he smiled at her. "I know I don't have to. I want to. I like doing things for you." He raised a hand and gently caressed her cheek.

"Thank you," she said warmly.

"You're welcome," he said, smiling at her.

Kara took the plate from Finn and sat down at the table. Finn sat down across from her. She took a bite of the sandwich. When she was done chewing, she looked at him.

"And thank you for making my bed and cleaning up. I was running really late today."

"It's no big deal. I got up a little late to," he smiled at her, and she looked down smiling. Finn laughed.

"Are you embarrassed?"

"No," Kara said a little too quickly. "Maybe a little. I don't know. I don't talk about it."

"Talk about what? Sex?"

"Yes, Sex," Kara said shyly.

Finn laughed harder. "Well, you should because it's fun to talk about." He leaned forward and stared into her eyes. "And fun to do."

"I'm not a prude," she cried, laughing. "I happen to like sex very much, actually."

"Oh, really?"

"Yes!" she said, throwing her napkin at him, causing him to laugh more. "I just always feel ridiculous talking about it. I feel like such a faker," she chuckled. "I always think to myself, who says these things, when I hear some of the things people say." As she took another bite of her sandwich.

"Maybe you should start small," Finn said with a mischievous smile. "Then, with a little practice, I think you would be really, really good at it."

Kara laughed. "Maybe." She ate a chip. "So, how was your day?"

"Changing the subject. Nice," Finn laughed. Kara smiled at him as he told her about his day. She liked listening to him talk. His voice was husky and sexy. Kara kept staring at his mouth while he spoke and had to force herself to meet his eye while she finished her sandwich.

When she finished, she wiped her mouth on a napkin. She took a long drink of her water, drinking almost all of it. She got up and picked up her plate to put it in the sink. She had five minutes before she had to leave. Finn got up and walked towards her.

"Are you ready to go?" he asked, standing in front of her.

"Yes, I still have five minutes, though."

"Good." He stepped closer to her. "Then I can kiss you for five minutes."

Kara smiled. "That would be lovely."

Finn pulled her into his arms, leaned down, and kissed her. Kara put her arms around his waist and leaned into him. Allowing herself to melt into him. "His mouth is so soft," she thought to herself. A gentle sigh came from her. Finn kissed her more urgently and pressed her tighter to him. Finn moaned pleasurably as he kissed her jaw and her throat.

"Kara, if we keep this up, I'm going to make you late for work." His hands caressing her back.

"Yeah," she whispered. "We should probably stop." She arched her back as he kissed her neck. He sighed.

"We really should," he whispered. "But, I'm doing it against my will," still kissing her. "Because I don't want to."

Desire flooded Kara. If she didn't step back, she really would be late. "Fuck," she thought to herself. She stepped out of his embrace.

"I have to go," she whispered.

"I know." Finn nodded. She smiled turned to walk down the steps. Grabbing her purse and keys. She looked up at him, smiled, and gave a little wave as she opened the door and stepped out.

For the last two days, Kara had been caught up in a whirling sea of thoughts, all full of Finn. For weeks she'd been telling herself she couldn't, shouldn't, wouldn't, feel anything for him. She had reasons. She had rules. She constantly reminded herself she didn't feel anything for Finn. She did, of course. She knew it when she first met him, and it scared her then. Her feelings were easily controlled at first. She'd only saw him once or twice a week. Once he moved in with her, her feelings were harder to control.

They spent every day together. It wasn't just working on the house. It was all the other things they did that made it hard for her. When they would make dinner together or sit on the couch and watch tv. Even small things like cleaning the house. She and Finn would talk about things, laugh, and joke around. It was fun.

The more she got to know him, the more difficult it became to keep her distance. Kara tried. Relentlessly repeating her rules, over and over to herself. She honestly believed she was projecting her feelings onto him when she thought he looked at her. When they went to Chris's Memorial Day, Lori, Teresa, and Chris had tried to tell her he wanted her. But she couldn't wrap her head around it. She was petrified to believe it was true.

Then he made her birthday perfect. Finn accomplished something many people had promised her and had consistently failed. It had surprised her and scared the shit out of her. It's what still frightened her. Finn was almost too perfect. He made her feel safe and wanted. He made her feel like she was more than she honestly was. He'd told her anxiety and depression weren't a weakness. She knew it wasn't, but hearing it from him, had shaken her.

She'd built up so many walls to protect herself. Finn seemed to be taking a wrecking ball to all of them. She was afraid he would ultimately break her heart. Because that's what always happened. Kara always got her heartbroken. She knew, when Finn broke her heart, she wouldn't recover.

Kara pulled into the driveway and turned off the car. Her body ached from her muscles being clinched all day. Thank you for that, Panic Attack. She was emotionally exhausted from the depression. She was mentally exhausted from the anxiety. She took a deep breath and tried to muster the last of her energy to walk the short distance from the car to the house.

All she wanted to do, was sink into bed, close her eyes, and sleep. Hopefully longer than the four or five hours she usually got. She got out of the car and walked towards the house. She felt like she was ninety. "There are probably ninety-year-olds who feel better than I do," she thought to herself.

The light was on in the living room as she walked up to the door. She opened the door, but Finn wasn't in the living room. "He must have gone to bed," she thought to herself as she set her purse and keys on the table by the door. She walked over to the lamp and turned it off. She sighed as she climbed the stairs to the bedroom. It felt like each of her legs weighed a thousand pounds.

Kara walked down the hallway towards her room and noticed the light was on in the master bathroom. Music was playing quietly as she walked into the bathroom. The speaker she used was on the counter. Tealight candles were lit around the room. Flower petals were placed around the room. The tub was filled with bubbles. The smell of lavender filled the room. It was magical.

Kara felt Finn's presence behind her as she walked into the bathroom. He walked behind her, putting his arms around her.

"I thought you would like a nice hot bath after everything you'd been through today," he whispered in her ear. She leaned back against him.

Allowing him to support her.

"Finn," she whispered breathlessly.

"Umm?" he asked as he turned her around to face him, keeping his arms around her.

She looked up into his eyes, and she saw it. His eyes said it all. "Holy shit, He loves me. Like actually loves me," she thought to herself. Her face must have shown her surprise.

"What is it?" Finn asked gently. "Are you ok?"

Kara nodded. Letting the knowledge sink in. Finn loved her. She almost didn't believe it, but it was hard to miss. She leaned up and kissed him deeply, feeling Finn's arms tightened around her. She stepped out of his embrace and looked into his eyes again. "Nope," she thought to herself, "still there." Finn looked at her with a raised eyebrow,

"What?" he said, smiling. "You're looking at me like you've never seen me before."

Kara shook her head slowly. "No, it's not that," she sighed. "I'm just not used to having someone wanting to take care of me," she said sincerely. Finn smiled at her.

"I kind of like taking care of you." He pulled her into his arms and kissed the top of her head. "Besides, you deserve it after the day you've had." Kara hugged him tighter.

"Come on, get in the tub," he whispered against her head. "I'll make you a cup of tea."

Kara squeezed Finn and nodded. Finn kissed the top of her head and let her go. He walked out of the bathroom on his way to the kitchen. Kara got undressed, folding her clothes, and put them on the counter. She walked to the tub and slowly got in, sinking into the hot lavender water. She stayed in the bath until the tension and soreness from the day left her body. After she had washed, she felt a little more human. As the water cooled down and she thought about getting out of the tub, she heard Finn call her name.

"Kara?"

"Yes?"

Finn stepped into the bathroom. "I made your tea and set it down on your nightstand."

"Thank you, I'm getting out now anyway. The water's getting cold."

Finn laughed, "Do you need anything else?"

"No, I'll be out in a minute," she said as Finn left the bathroom. Kara unplugged the drain and stepped out of the tub. She wrapped herself in one of the big towels Finn left out for her. She felt clean, relaxed, and refreshed. Much better than when she came home. She blew out the candles and set them on the counter, and turned off the speaker. She would deal with the flower petals later.

Finn was waiting in her room when she walked in, wrapped in the towel. Kara walked up to him.

"Thank you," she said quietly.

"You already thanked me."

"No," she said, shaking her head. "I mean, thank you for taking care of me today when I needed it the most," she said earnestly. She wanted to say so much more. She wanted to tell him, he was wonderful, too good to be true, how no one had taken care of her in so long, let alone as well as he did tonight. There were so many more things she wanted to say. But she didn't because merely thinking them was beginning to make her a little sad.

"I wanted to do it. It made me happy." Finn whispered.

Kara stood on her tippy toes and kissed Finn on the cheek. It was a little awkward because she was still trying to hold her towel up. Finn reached his arm out to steady her, and she was pulled into his arms.

"Kara," Finn whispered. His voice was raspy. "You should probably get dressed because I'm not sure I'm going to be able to keep my hands off you." he looked down and kissed her neck. "Wearing just a towel."

Kara smiled. She leaned in and kissed him lightly and stepped out of his arms. "I'll be ready in a minute." Finn grinned and walked out of the room, closing the door noiselessly behind him.

Twenty minutes later, Kara was moisturized, drank some of her tea, and put on an oversized t-shirt. She was ready for bed. She took the pillows off the bed and began to wonder where Finn was. She considered if he went to sleep already. Should she say good night? Was she overthinking it? She laughed to herself because she knew she was.

She walked out of her room towards the kitchen and noticed Finn's door was closed. She knocked gently. Finn answered the door wearing nothing but his boxers. Kara sighed. The light was still on in his room. He smiled when he saw her. "Fuck, he's distracting," Kara thought to herself.

"I came to say goodnight," Kara said. She was staring at his body.

"Good night," Finn whispered.

Kara bit her lip. She suddenly felt embarrassed. "Was that it?" She wanted to scream at him. She didn't know what to do or say. It was ridiculous and complicated at the same time.

"Do you?" She started and stopped. She took a deep breath. She was a grown woman. Why couldn't she just tell him, come to bed with me, damn it?

She started slowly. "Would you stay with me?" she asked uncertainly, not meeting his gaze. She couldn't believe that at forty-seven, she still felt uncomfortable asking for what she wanted.

Finn smiled, "Sure, I'll be right there," he said tenderly.

Kara looked up at him. He was smiling at her, and it eased some of her clumsiness.

"Ok," she whispered. She turned around to go back to her room. She waited at the door as Finn turned out the light and followed her into her room. She was standing by her bed, and Finn walked up and stood in front of her.

"Ready?" he asked quietly. Kara nodded. The room was dark. Usually, Kara kept the tv on and used it as a makeshift night light. Otherwise, her room was sometimes too dark if the motion lights outside weren't on.

"Normally, I sleep with the tv on," she said timidly. Why does everything she do, make her seem like an idiot. Why was she embarrassed about something perfectly normal?

"I usually watch something stupid until I fall asleep," she said.

"Ok," he said, gently reaching for her hand.

Kara let out a deep breath, relief flooding her. Finn accepted it. No further explanation needed. No making fun of her. Just acceptance. She turned on the tv.

Kara stood up on the step stool. Finn let go of her hand and walked around to the other side of the bed. They both climbed into the bed, inching to the center. Finn lay on his back, and Kara snuggled next to him. Lying on her side, resting her head on the pillow next to him. She looked up at him, the light of the tv illuminating him. Finn turned on his side to face her. He was looking at her.

"Are you ok?" he whispered. He reached out and caressed her face gently.

"Yes," she yawned. "Just really sleepy."

"Well, come here," Finn said. He lay on his back and opened his arms for Kara to move into them. With his arms wrapped around her and her head resting on his shoulder. Finn kissed the top of her head.

"Get some sleep," he whispered tenderly.

Kara was asleep within minutes.

CHAPTER 16

Finn was nauseatingly happy.

After his birthday, it was cute. "Great, you're happy."

After Kara's birthday, it was "Ok. I'm glad to see you're happy, but really calm

down."

Now it was getting to the point, he started to make everyone think he should go be happy somewhere else. Kind of happy. He couldn't help it, though. Being with Kara made him happy in a way he'd never been before. It was sickening. It was annoying everyone around him.

Finn wondered if the newness of it all would fade. For some reason, he didn't think it would. The thought was both scary and awesome at the same time. Kara made him feel different, better. She appreciated even the little things he did for her. She'd been on her own for so long. She had been strong for so long. She didn't need him for anything, even to help renovate the house. She could have found someone else. Kara made him feel being himself was not only enough but valued. The things he did for her made her happy. Because she was allowing herself to be vulnerable meant she trusted him. Finn didn't want to screw it up.

Finn and Kara hadn't talked about their relationship since her birthday. Although Finn thought about it a lot. Everything just progressed naturally. He didn't want to rush it, and he didn't want to rush Kara. It was still too new, too fresh, too delicate. If he came on too strong, it would freak her out, and that was the last thing he wanted.

He also didn't want to make the same mistakes he made with Shelly. Although, honestly, Kara and Shelly were nothing alike. The difference between them was incommensurable. When Finn was with Shelly, she determined everything. They never talked about it. Finn did what she wanted because if he didn't, he knew what it would lead to. It was easier to take the path of least resistance. It was the easy way out, he knew, but it kept the peace.

He didn't like the person he was when he was with Shelly. As long as he went along with everything Shelly wanted, it was fine. The minute he disagreed, she would explode. Then he would explode. He would lose his temper and fight back. All the pent-up anger and frustration would come pouring out at him. Shelly would give him a wounded look, and he would immediately feel bad and apologize. He wasn't like that with Kara, and he didn't want to be. He wanted to be a better man for Kara because she deserved better.

Finn was wiping down the bar. He'd just finished stocking the bar for the night. There weren't a lot of people in the bar yet. It was still light outside, and although it was still early, it was already after eight. The early crowd was in the bar. The people who came in before it got too late and the rowdy crowd showed up.

Randy came into the bar, through the kitchen. He sat down in his usual seat at the farthest corner of the bar. Randy had a scowl on his face, and Finn shook his head. Randy had been wearing a grimace on his face a lot lately.

"You ok?" Finn asked as he placed an O'Doul's in front of Randy. Randy owned the bar, but he didn't drink while he was working. Randy picked up the bottle and took a long drink.

"Just because you're so fucking happy all the time doesn't mean everyone else has to be." Randy snapped as he put the bottle back on the coaster Finn set before him.

"Fair enough," Finn said as he leaned against the bar in front of Randy.

He pretended to watch the baseball game on one of the tv's around the bar. Finn knew if he was patient, Randy would talk. Finn didn't have to wait long.

"Fucking Jewell," Randy muttered, taking another drink from his beer.

"Ahhh, Of course, it's Jewell." Finn thought to himself. He crossed his arms in front of him and shook his head slowly.

"What happened now?" Still pretending to look at the game. Finn wasn't really into baseball. He played T-Ball and Little League when he was younger, but once he discovered girls, all sports ceased meaning anything.

"She's pissed because I have to take the boys an extra day next week because Nik has to work another shift." Randy took another sip of his beer. "Not that it matters. Nik said she could use the extra money since they cut her hours. So, of course, I agreed. They're my fucking kids." Randy sighed in frustration. "What the fuck am I supposed to do? Say no, I can't be with my kids because Jewell wouldn't like it."

Finn was looking at Randy shaking his head. "What the fuck?" he thought to himself. Nicole was Randy's ex-wife. Jewell treated Nicole like her arch-nemesis. Nichole worked as a Per-Diem Nurses aid. She worked twelve hours shifts, four days a week, then would be off for three days. Because she was Per-Diem, her hours got cut a lot. She would pick up as many shifts as she could. The arrangement she had with Randy was to take the kids when she worked, so she didn't have to pay for childcare. During the school year, it worked out perfectly. In the summer, it was more of a challenge. When Randy was in his "on-again" relationship with Jewell, she made the situation even more difficult.

Randy began to peel the label off his bottle of beer. The nervous habit when he needed to do something with his hands and couldn't punch something.

"So what did you tell her?" Finn asked.

Randy looked up at him. He looks tired, Finn thought to himself. Randy and Jewell had been on again off again for the last year. They would go anywhere from one day on and one month off to one month on to two days off. They met at the bar, and since they'd gotten together, it was always some new drama. Usually started by Jewell and almost always was about Nicole.

Finn thought the drama was the reason Randy liked Jewell. It was like he was punishing himself for all the ways he'd fucked up with Nicole. Nicole was the polar opposite of Jewell. She was quiet and kind. She used to come into the bar a lot, and Finn liked her. When Nicole had the boys, she didn't work as often because everything revolved around Randy and the boys. Randy didn't appreciate her. One day after finding out Randy had cheated on her again, she woke up and said it was enough and filed for divorce.

"That I had to take the boys," Randy said, bringing Finn back to the moment.

"What did she say?"

"The usual bullshit, man. I don't even know." Randy said. "As soon as she said Nik was getting married and their soon-to-be step-father should do it, I stopped listening." Randy sighed. He drained the last of his beer. Little pieces of paper were littered in front of Randy.

Finn sighed and shook his head. "Aren't you tired of all that?"

"All what?" Randy said, looking up at Finn, confused.

"The drama," Finn said, looking at Randy. "Seriously, it's shouldn't be that hard."

"All relationships are hard, Finn. None of them are perfect."

"They shouldn't be that hard," Finn said, shaking his head slowly. "You shouldn't have to feel like shit because you have to be with your kids."

"Man, what the fuck are you talking about?" Randy said incredulously. "How is this any different than when you were with Shelly? You put up with that shit for years. She wouldn't let you see anybody. Family or friends."

The resentment in Randy's voice hit Finn hard. It wasn't any different. When Finn was with Shelly, she would get mad if Finn did anything other than work without her. He couldn't hang with his friends. She even had a problem with Finn hanging out with his brother. It wasn't like that in the beginning, but it's how it ended up. It was one of the reasons Finn kept working at the bar. Then he could see his friends and his brother without Shelly giving him shit.

"You're right. It isn't any different." Finn said. "Which is why I'm asking, aren't you tired of all that?"

"Man, you acting like you know everything." Randy leaned back from the bar. "You get a new girl, and all of a sudden, you're the relationship expert."

Finn shook his head. "No, I'm not. I'm just saying, being with Kara showed me the difference." Finn couldn't help but smile every time he thought of Kara.

"What's the difference?" Randy muttered defensively.

Finn sighed and looked Randy in the eye. "I was with Shelly for almost six years, and most of the time, it felt like being in prison," he hesitated a moment before he continued. "And now that I'm with Kara, it feels like every day I'm in church."

Randy didn't say anything. He just looked at Finn intently. Finn smiled at Randy and turned around to get a drink for a guy who just came in and sat at the other end of the bar.

Finn didn't get home until after one. The bar picked up after the sun went down. The joys of summer, everyone wants to go out later. Then the rowdy crowd came in, and the bar was packed. Finn didn't get much of a chance to talk to Randy as the night wore on. He'd been too busy trying to keep up with the drinks. It was just as well. Randy would need some time to think. Finn walked into the house and Kara, was fast asleep on the couch. She was curled up under a blanket, with a book next to her. The tv was on, but the sound was low. He decided not to wake her up just yet and take a shower instead. He was sweaty, sticky, and smelled like alcohol. He wanted to wash the night off of him before he went to bed.

Finn quietly walked up the steps and down the hall. He went to his bedroom and got undressed, tossing his clothes in the hamper. Although he now spent every night sleeping with Kara, he still technically had his own room. He didn't want to presume anything. Besides, he liked having his own room. It gave him his own space when he needed it.

Finn left his room and walked into the newly renovated second bathroom. He turned on the shower and waited a few minutes for the water to warm up. Kara had additional spigots installed when she replaced the shower. She wanted to get rid of the tub but changed her mind. You never knew when you would need a smaller bathtub, she'd said at the time.

Finn stepped into the shower and let the hot water cascade down his body. Kara installed a Rain Shower Head, so the water flowed directly upon you. Finn loved it. He let out a sigh as he felt his muscles relaxing. He thought about his conversation with Randy and just how true it really was. Kara was showing him how a relationship could be. It was like being in church, or what he remembered being in a church felt like. Their relationship was peaceful. Neither one of them had to force anything on the other.

Their relationship changed. It changed for the better. They were closer. Not just because it was now physical, they were open and honest with each other. They could be vulnerable and show their faults to each other, and it was accepted. Finn wanted to share things with Kara because he didn't want to share them with anyone else if he were completely honest.

He couldn't do that with Shelly. He would tell her some things but not everything. He found himself withholding more and more as the relationship went on. He couldn't fully be himself. Shelly was hard. And everything with her was hard. She always had to have things her way. Shelly dominated things. She wouldn't give an inch unless it benefited her.

Kara was gentle. She didn't have to push to get her way. She liked to talk about things and compromise. Finn could be himself. He didn't have to pretend to make her happy. Kara felt like shelter after the stormy relationship he had with Shelly. Finn wondered where he would be if he hadn't met Kara. The thought made him shiver, even in the scalding hot shower.

Being with Kara was a totally new experience for Finn. Not just because she was different from almost every woman he knew, but he'd also never been with a Black woman before. It wasn't on purpose. It just hadn't happened. Being with a Black woman was different in little ways. Not bad ways, just slightly different ways. Finn learned something new from Kara every day. Why she had a million lotion bottles. Because she needed to keep her skin hydrated so it wouldn't dry out. She convinced Finn to take better care of his skin. Now he used lotion and sunscreen.

Why she wouldn't take a shower with him. Because she wore a shower cap, and her exact words were, "I wear a shower cap to keep my hair dry because I don't wear it natural. I don't think there's anything sexy about a shower cap." She'd said matter-of-factly. Finn had to ask her what natural meant. She explained about hair texture and styling. She told him about braids, chemicals, weaves, and wigs. She preferred wearing her hair straight. Then she told him all the things she had to do to style her hair straight. Finn suggested they take a bath instead. Kara agreed. Finn decided he loved taking baths. It was better than taking showers anyway.

Kara helped him see things differently. She challenged him to think about something with a fresh perspective. He'd never met anyone who made him do that before. Finn really had become a better man since meeting Kara. He rinsed the rest of the soap off with the handheld shower attachment. He turned the shower off and pulled back the curtain. Kara handed him a towel.

"Thank you," he whispered as he dried his face.

"Why didn't you wake me up when you came home?" she asked, her voice still groggy with sleep.

"I was going to as soon as I was done," he said, wrapping the towel around his waist. Smiling, he walked over to her and put his arms around her. She still felt warm from being under the blanket. She wore one of the many oversized t-shirts she had to wear to bed. Kara wrapped her arms around his waist and gently stroked his back.

"Are you ok?" she whispered into his chest.

"I am now," he said, kissing her on the top of her head.

She leaned back and looked up at him. "Was it a long night?"

"No," Finn said, shaking his head. "It wasn't bad. I just couldn't wait to come home and be with you." He leaned down and kissed her lovingly on the lips. He loved how her mouth felt.

Kara held him tighter, pressing herself against him. Finn felt himself getting hard. Knowing the only thing separating them was a towel. His hands slid down her body, resting on her hips. She stepped out of his embrace, smiling at him.

"Hurry up and come to bed," she said, turning and walking out of the bathroom.

She wouldn't have to ask him twice.

Finn smiled as he hurried to get ready for bed. Walking naked from his room to hers. When he walked in, he was afraid for a second Kara had fallen asleep. He climbed into bed, gently moving next to her, just in case. Kara reached for him in the darkness, pulling him closer to her. She was waiting for him, naked under the blankets. Finn moved effortlessly on top of her and looked down at her as his eye adjusted to the darkness.

He lowered his head and kissed her. His cock pressed against her thigh. She sighed pleasurably against his mouth. Her hands gently caressing his back and gliding up and down his body. Finn loved when she touched him. Finn kissed along her jaw and down her throat. Savoring the taste of her.

He kissed her breasts, taking her hard nipple into his mouth and flicking it with his tongue. He heard Kara sigh as she arched her back. Her hand in his hair. Finn shifted his weight, moving to Kara's side, so he was next to her. She turned to look at him,

"Shhhh," he whispered as he ran his hand down her body. He gently turned her, so her back was against him. He put his arm under her head and wrapped it around her. Using one hand to tease her breast as the other hand gently glided over her mound.

Kara whimpered, pressing against him as he gently parted her folds with his fingers teasing her. Finn kissed the back of her neck and down her shoulder. Kara grinding her hips against him. He bit her shoulder, and Kara cried out.

"Stop it," he whispered huskily into her ear as his finger entered her. She gasped as he slid his finger in and out of her. She lifted her leg over his, spreading her legs as much as his embrace would allow. She was pinned on her side. Finn held her tightly in place as she tried to turn as he used his hands to pleasure her. She was so wet for him. His palm teasing her as his fingers quickened in and out of her.

"Finn," she said breathlessly.

"Ummm?" he said against her shoulder. Rubbing his cock against her. "Damn, her ass." Finn thought to himself.

"Please," Kara whispered helplessly. Lifting her leg higher on top of his.

Finn moved his hand to his cock, guiding it gently into her. Both of them moaning as he entered her.

"You feel so good," he whispered into her ear. She moved her hips with his as he gently thrust in and out of her. His hand rubbing her mound. He kissed her neck as his other hand teased her nipple.

"Finn, don't stop," she whispered as she panted. Finn quickened his thrusts. "I'm," she breathed.

She arched her back against him. Lifting her legs wider for him. He moved his hands, wrapping his arm around her

"Kara, I can't," he whispered in her ear. His voice was coarse against her neck. He gently bit her shoulder. He felt her convulse against him as she came tightening around him, as she cried out in surprise. Finn couldn't hold it and exploded into her. His cock pulsing inside of her. Pressing his lips against her shoulder. Kara leaned her head back, breathing heavily. She lifted her arm around his neck and turned, forcing his mouth onto hers.

Sunday dinner was the McNulty family tradition. Marion McNulty was a firm believer in the family being together on Sundays. None of her children or her husband shared her devotion to Mass. If they weren't going to get together for church, then they should meet for dinner. No one in her family ever argued about dinner. Unless you were dead, in the hospital, or in another state, you were expected to be at dinner, on time, on Sunday.

After meeting Finn on Memorial Day, Marion made it clear, she expected Finn at dinner on Sunday. Finn believing Marion was only being friendly, didn't go. When Marion asked Kara where he was, Kara told her the truth. He's at his brother's house. Marion told Kara to call him.

"I want to talk to him," Marion said.

Kara laughed as she called Finn. When he answered, she told him, "Marion wants to talk to you."

"Why?" Finn asked. He could hear Kara laughing as she handed the phone to Marion.

"Griffin Wilson," Marion said in her firmest mom voice. Using his full name to snap him to attention. "You are expected to be at family dinner on Sundays. Do you understand?"

"Yes, Ma'am," Finn said. He felt like he was seven years old again. And she wasn't even his mother.

"I won't have any more of this foolishness." "No, Ma'am"

"Good. I'll see you next Sunday." Marion's tone softened.

"Yes, Ma'am, I'll be there."

"Goodbye, Finn," she said sweetly, handing the phone back to Kara. Kara laughed when she got back on the phone.

"Are you ok?"

"What the hell was that?" Finn asked, not really sure what happened. With one phone call, he regressed almost thirty-three years.

"That was Marion, putting her foot down."

"Holy shit, she broke out my full name. The only person who ever uses my full name is my father. Even my own mother calls me Finn," he said incredulously. "I was actually scared as hell. I thought I was in big trouble."

Kara's rich laughter filled his ear and made him smile.

"It would be wise to be afraid of Marion. This was tame by comparison. I've seen her when she gets angry, and no one is safe."

"She's only four foot nine. How can she be scarier than men who are three times her size?"

"Just because she's little doesn't mean anything," Kara said. "Marion has mom superpowers. The disappointing tone and the full name are used to ignite fear."

Finn has been to every Sunday dinner ever since.

He took Marion flowers to apologize for missing the previous Sunday. Chris came up to him and shook his hand, whispering,

"Smart man, Mom always forgives everything when you give her flowers." Finn laughed, whispering, "Kara told me." Chris's dad and his brother nodded in agreement. Flowers were the quickest way to forgiveness for Marion. Finn stored the knowledge away for future reference, although he honestly hoped he'd never be on Marion's bad side again.

Finn wasn't exactly sure why he was there at the beginning. It felt awkward to him. But as his relationship progressed with Kara, he thought it was because everyone assumed he was Kara's boyfriend. Teresa, Chris's wife, was the one to explain it to him, although Kara tried.

"For Marion, once she considers you family, you are. It doesn't matter what happens or what changes. When I first came to family dinner and saw Kara, I wasn't sure how I was supposed to feel. I'd only met her once before. But still, I was going to meet my boyfriend's family and his ex-wife is there with their kid. I admit I was freaking out," she said, shame crossing her features.

"Then Marion set me straight, real quick. She told me, 'when it comes to family, there is no pride and no status. Family is not the place for competition. We are all one. We are all there for each other, and just because things changed, your place in the family doesn't.'" Teresa shook her head slowly.

"Marion told me, 'If Kara can welcome Chris's new girlfriend to dinner, in front of her son, especially since it's his fault, they aren't married anymore, then I could be woman enough to let go of my pride and accept in that house only family mattered. If I couldn't, then I needed to leave and not come back.'" There were tears in Teresa's eyes as she finished speaking. She took a deep breath before continuing,

"So I listened to Marion. I let go of my pride and accepted only family mattered. Honestly, it was the best thing I ever did. Because Kara is amazing. I love her. She's one of my closest friends. Sometimes I think Chris was an idiot when he let her go. He knows, though."

After talking to Teresa, Finn didn't question anymore why he was there and just accepted it. Marion saw him as family whether or not anyone thought he was Kara's boyfriend. Then he wondered if Kara was his girlfriend. He wasn't sure how he felt about Kara being his girlfriend. It didn't seem right when she meant so much more to him. He was going to have to think about that later.

The McNulty family was also affectionate. Everyone hugged hello and goodbye. Finn wasn't used to it at first. His own family wasn't affectionate. The only person he'd ever hugged and kissed was his mother. His parents weren't publicly affectionate either. It wasn't until he met his parents for dinner, he'd seen just how much his father loved his mother.

There was a long table set up in the dining room. All ten of them sat together, eating and laughing like it was Thanksgiving every Sunday. Only with a different menu. After they ate, plates were cleared, and dessert was brought out. After dessert, everyone helped clean up. Washing dishes, clearing the table, taking out the trash, and putting away leftovers.

Finn relaxed as he felt his acceptance in the family. He began to look forward to Sunday dinner. That was until Lori cornered him. Lori was identical to her mother. Almost a carbon copy, except Lori, said whatever was on her mind. Because she was the baby of the family, she got away with it. Most of the time. The only person who could keep Lori under control was Marion. Lori was always friendly but reserved. She kept her eye on Finn and how he acted around Kara and the rest of the family. As Lori watched Finn become more comfortable with the family. She had some questions.

CHAPTER 17

O n Sunday, Finn was riding a very lovely Kara, high. He woke up
with Kara in his arms. The previous night they had incredible
sex. He'd slipped out of bed, remembering he was naked because
he'd gone into her room after the shower. He smiled to himself when he
went to the bathroom then slipped into his room to put on some boxers.

The kitchen was in shambles because it was currently being renovated.
Half of it was gutted. There were only two cabinets still hanging. One for
food and the other for dishes. Everything else was being stored temporarily
in the dining room. Finn made coffee, and Kara came in a few minutes
later, wrapping her arms around him to hug him from behind. He closed
his eyes and leaned back against her. When she let him go, Finn felt a pang
of disappointment as he reached up and got a mug to pour her coffee. She
went to the fridge and handed him the creamer.

When he handed her the coffee, he looked at her, his heart beating faster.
She had bed head, her eyes cloudy with sleep, behind her glasses. She wore
a t-shirt and yoga pants. She took the mug, and Finn waited as she took a
sip. Kara's brain was in a fog until she took her first sip of coffee. Then her
brain clicked on, and her world came into focus.

It was the first smile that Finn looked forward to. The smile full of the joy
of coffee and being content. It was one of his favorite smiles. When Kara
smiled like that, it was like a sky full of rainbows after it rained.

Finn slowly drank his own coffee. Keeping his eyes on Kara as the steam from the coffee fogged her glasses. He felt it grow from the pit of his stomach. He wanted her. So badly, his hands started to shake. He set his coffee mug down on the counter and then took her coffee mug from her and set it down next to his.

Kara squealed in protest. Looking up at him with her pouty full lips. He didn't care. He quickly closed the distance between them. He put his hands on her waist and kissed her. Tasting the sweetness of her coffee. He led her to the kitchen table and sat her down on the chair. Pulling her underwear and yoga pants down a little rougher than he meant to.

"Finn," Kara said, surprised.

He kissed her instead of responding. Inching her closer to the edge of the chair. He gently spread her legs. He smiled when he stopped kissing her.

"What are you doing?"

"I'm having breakfast," he said as he got on his knees and leaned in to kiss her folds.

"Oh," Kara sighed. She arched her back. Lifting her legs and placing them on Finn's shoulders as he wrapped his arms around her and buried his face. Gently licking and sucking her. Kara rocked her hips. Finn licked his fingers and entered her. He kissed her inner thigh.

"You taste so good," he whispered huskily. Her thighs tightening around him. He flicked his tongue as he quickened his pace. He had to squeeze his dick over his boxers with his other hand because he was going to come.

He couldn't help it. She tasted so sweet. Kara clenched around his fingers. Her chest heaving up and down as her breathing quickened. She arched her back, moving her hips to match his rhythm. Finn was teasing her, his fingers gliding in and out of her. Licking her up as he did. He knew she was close.

"Kara," he whispered.

"Yes," she said breathlessly

"Are you ready for me to be inside you?"

"Yes," she whimpered. She'd reached her arms above her head, grabbing the back of the chair. Her hips rocking to match his thrusts.

"Are you sure?" he said, stopping.

"Uh-huh," she whined.

Finn studied her face. Her eyes closed. Her head leaning back. He slid her legs off his shoulders and stood up. Kara pulled at his boxers. Freeing his cock and wrapping her hands around him. He pulled her up and sat down on the chair in her place. He gently pulled her forward and slid her down on his cock. Both of them crying out as he entered her. She wrapped his arms around him as she rocked her hips. She kissed him hungrily. She was in control now, and she liked it.

Finn's hands slid under her shirt to touch her breasts. Teasing her nipples as she moved. Finn would have given her anything she asked for right now.

He moaned into her mouth, "Kara. I'm going to come," She leaned back and arched her back, clamping his cock. Finn exploded into her so hard he gritted out her name. Kara shuddering against him. He wrapped his arms around her as she fell against him. He pulled her back and kissed her. He broke the kiss, and he looked her in the eye.

"I love you."

He'd said it without thinking about it. He said it as if it was the most natural thing in the world to tell her. It was when she looked at him and said,

"I love you, too," and kissed him again, he felt the weight of what they just said to each other. She leaned back and looked at him.

"Can I please finish my coffee now?"

Finn heated up her coffee and handed it back to her. He kissed her as he left the kitchen and went to take another shower. He was starving. While he was in the shower, he thought about what to do for breakfast. They didn't have a lot in the house because the kitchen was a disaster. They'd been ordering delivery and heating up leftovers.

He got out of the shower and brushed his teeth. He thought of the perfect place, and while he was getting dressed, he made a phone call. When he came out of his bedroom, he heard Kara in the shower. He went into the kitchen to clean up. He poured himself another cup of coffee and heated it in the microwave. Then he put the dishes in the dishwasher. Cleaned the table and wiped off the chair.

As he was leaning against the counter, drinking his coffee, Kara stepped into the kitchen. He forgot to breathe. She glowed. She wore a white sundress with blue flowers and a light blue cardigan. Her hair falling around her shoulders in silky waves. She was wearing sandals that laced up her legs. She walked up to him, smiling.

"What's wrong?" she asked as she stopped next to him.

Finn shook his head slowly. Setting his coffee mug on the counter.

"You're beautiful," he whispered. He leaned over and kissed her lightly.

"Finn, breakfast!" His mind screamed. "Food," His stomach growled. "We'd better go. If we stay here, I'm taking you right back to bed."

"Where are we going?" Kara asked, smiling.

"You'll see," Finn said as he took her hand. "Let's go."

The day was sunny and warm. They drove in Kara's car holding hands. Finn took Kara to one of her favorite places for brunch. She was thrilled when they entered the parking lot. They got a table next to the window, and Finn couldn't keep his eyes of Kara. Her eyes sparkled. Her smile was turning him into a puddle.

They talked during brunch. About nothing and about everything. They talked about work. They talked about the house. They ate breakfast. Kara had egg's benedict, her favorite. Finn ordered an omelet. Both ordered more coffee. They lingered, neither one quite ready to go.

As they were leaving the restaurant, Kara suggested a walk. Finn drove to Camden Water Front. They walked along the path on the Delaware River. A slight breeze was in the air, but the day was sunny and warm. They stopped at one of the benches, and people watched. Boats and kayakers were on the river. Finn would occasionally look over at Kara and smile, thinking to himself, "She loves me."

They took their time driving to Chris's parent's house for Sunday dinner. Everyone already there. David stood at the grill with Chris and Pete. Marion sat in the kitchen with Teresa and baby Katie. Lori and her husband Sean were sitting on the couch in the living room watching a movie.

They made the rounds, saying hello to everyone. Kara stayed in the kitchen while Finn went to the bathroom. Lori was waiting for him when he came out. She was leaning against the wall, her arms folded, scowling at him.

"I want to talk to you," she hissed at him.

Finn, surprised, pointed to himself. "Me?"

Lori rolled her eyes. "Yes, you."

"What did I do?" he said. What was it about the women in this family? He thought to himself. They were all scary.

"That's exactly why I'm here," she whispered angrily. Pointing her manicured nail at him. "I want to know what your intentions are with Kara?"

Finn looked at her, confused. "What do you mean?"

"Exactly what I said. What are your intentions?" Lori put her hands on her hips.

"I don't," Finn stammered.

Lori held up her hand. "Never mind. Let me get right to the point. Kara walked in here today, and she's fucking glowing." Lori snarled. "She looks absolutely radiant. She hasn't looked like that in a really long time. So I want to know what you," pointing her finger at him. "are going to do to ensure she stays that way."

Finn couldn't help smiling. The thought of being the reason Kara was glowing was making him a little too happy. Lori glowered at him.

"Don't look so smug." She shook her head and took a deep breath. "Look, I've known Kara almost all of my life. She's my big sister. Actually, she's more than that. And if Chris hadn't been such a dick, she would still be my sister legally. Nothing against Teresa. I love her too. To be completely honest, Chris doesn't deserve her either."

Finn saw the memory of what happened flicker in Lori's eyes. It was the second time someone mentioned Chris being an asshole to Kara. Kara and Finn hadn't really talked about why she got divorced. It wasn't that it hadn't come up. It had. Kara was just really good at deflecting. She would say one thing and change the subject. The only thing Finn knew for sure was at the time, Kara was devastated.

Lori continued, "I watched Kara get her heart shattered. And it took a really long time for her to put all of those pieces back together." Lori stopped. Tears were glistening in her eyes. She held up her hand to signal she needed a moment. "And even then, the light inside of her didn't quite shine the same way."

Finn leaned back against the wall and put his hands in his pockets. Lori took a deep breath, trying to force herself not to cry as she continued.

"And after all this time, and everything she's already suffered this year, You show up out of nowhere. The light inside of her is finally starting to shine a little brighter. She's finally starting to come alive again. And I want to know what you're going to do to make sure that light never goes out again." Lori leaned against the wall, her arms still folded in front of her.

"Kara's been through a lot. More than anyone deserves. She's strong and kind and wonderful. She's always been there for me. I love her. and although I can't 'Kill,'" Lori used air quotes around the word Kill. "Don't think for one minute, if you hurt her or break her heart, I won't kill you, regardless of whether or not my mom likes you."

Lori stared at him with sheer determination in her eyes. These McNulty women were tough. Finn had no doubt about Lori's threat. Finn smiled at her, and she rolled her eyes.

"Don't smile at me like that." She glowered at him. "I just want to make sure you're not another asshole, just fucking around with her, and she's so head over heels in love with you, she doesn't see it. I'm not going to let you break her heart."

Finn put his hands up and smiled. "Take it easy," Finn said. "I'm smiling because it amazes me just how much people love Kara. She has that effect on people, and they just love her"

Lori nodded, "Yes, she does. And it's been missing for a really long time. My brother broke her first, then just when she moved on, some other dickhead, broke her heart. I'm not letting it happen again."

Finn reached down and took both of Lori's hands in his. He looked her directly in the eyes.

"Lori, I promise, if it takes all of my life, I won't let anyone or anything," Finn dropped Lori's left hand so he could place his right hand over his heart. "Myself included," He added for emphasis, "dim Kara's light or break her heart." Finn sighed. He ran his hand through his hair, "I've never felt about anyone the way I feel about Kara. I," Finn paused. Lori put her hand up to stop him,

"I know," she said wryly. "It's been all over your face since I've met you." She finally smiled at him. Finn sighed with relief.

"Just to let you know," Lori said. "This is your one and only warning," a scary gleam coming into her eyes. "If you break her heart, I will kill you and hide the body. No one will ever find you."

Before Finn could respond, Sean walked into the hallway.

"Your mom is looking for you." He bent down and kissed Lori on the top of her head. He turned to Finn, "Did my wife just threaten to kill you?" he asked, smiling at Finn.

"Yes," Finn said, nodding his head as Lori said "No," and shook her head.

Sean laughed. Lori looked offended. "I didn't threaten him. I just gave him a very stern warning," she said innocently.

Sean and Finn said simultaneously, "She threatened."

Lori huffed and muttered, "I'm going to see what mom wants," stalking down the hallway towards the kitchen, leaving Finn and Sean laughing as they followed her.

As they were preparing to leave Sunday dinner for the drive home, Kara and Finn made the rounds of saying goodbye to everyone. Lots of hugs were given, and Finn got a kiss on the cheek from Marion. Kara was waiting by the door for him when Lori came up to him and gave him a big hug, whispering in his ear,

"Remember what I said." she smiled at him.

Finn laughed at her, shaking his head. "I will, I promise."

He walked over to Kara, who was watching them with a raised eyebrow. She opened the door, and as they walked out, Finn whispered, "I'll tell you later." As he closed the door behind them.

Finn opened the door for Kara as they got to the car. She got in, and he ran around to the driver's side. He got in, buckled his seat belt, and started the car. Kara let Finn drive on Sundays. He didn't mind, he liked to drive, and it gave her some time to relax and look out the window. Something she liked to do. Finn backed out of the driveway and pulled onto the street.

The McNulty's lived in the woods. The backroads were dark and didn't have many streetlights on them. Patches of open fields mixed in with the woods. You never knew what would jump out onto the street. More than just deer were lying on the side of the road.

Kara turned to Finn and looked at him, smiling, "So, are you going to tell me what happened with Lori?"

"It was nothing. We just had a little talk earlier."

Kara laughed. "She threatened you, didn't she?"

"Yes," Finn laughed. "Although she said it was a 'Stern Warning,' her words not mine."

"Yeah," Kara sighed. "That sounds about right. What did she say?"

"Nothing bad. She told me she would kill me and hide the body so no one would find me." Finn said sarcastically. "But she did mention some other things."

"Like what?"

"Well," Finn said slowly, "That's kind of what I wanted to talk to you about." Finn shifted in the seat to make himself more comfortable, not taking his eyes off the road.

"Ok," Kara said hesitantly. "What did you want to talk about?"

"Lori mentioned how Chris used to be an asshole. She's not the only one, though."

"What do you mean?"

"Teresa said the same thing to me a couple of weeks ago."

"She did?"

"Yes. She told me Chris was the reason your marriage ended, and Lori said the same thing to me today."

"When did Teresa tell you that?"

"I don't remember exactly. I think it was the second time I came to Sunday dinner."

"Really? Why didn't you say anything?" Kara asked.

"I don't know. I guess I didn't want to pry. I figured you would tell me about it when you were ready."

"And talking to Lori today changed that?"

Finn took a moment before answering. Kara's tone changed. It wasn't annoyance. It was something else. It was reluctance. Tinged with a hint of sadness. It reminded Finn of when she'd told him about her depression and anxiety. Like she was unsure about how vulnerable to be because she was afraid of what would happen.

Finn sighed. "I don't want to pry Kara," Finn ran a hand through his hair. Then he turned to look at her quickly before turning back to the road. "I was hoping you trusted me enough to tell me about it anyway."

"What did Lori tell you?"

"She didn't go into detail. She just said you were hurt pretty badly." Finn was starting to get nervous about the way the conversation was going.

"Ok." Kara paused. "What did you want to know?"

"Well, you've only said you and Chris were divorced. But you've never told me why?"

"There's not a lot to tell," Kara said flatly. She turned away to look out the window. Finn could feel her shutting him out.

"Don't do that?" he whispered.

Kara turned to look at him, "Do what?"

Finn met her gaze quickly before turning to look at the road in front of him. There weren't many cars on the road ahead of them, but the road was dark.

"You know what. You dismiss something as if it weren't a big deal and act like you don't care."

Kara didn't say anything. She turned and looked back out the window. Finn reached his hand out to her and took her hand. At his touch, she turned and looked at him.

"Kara, please," he said pleadingly. "Don't shut me out."

Kara sighed, "Fine," she took a deep breath. "What do you want to know?"

CHAPTER 18

Kara didn't want to have this conversation.

What she wanted to say, was "Why do we have to talk about having my heart broken? Again. It happened years ago. Everyone has moved on. We're all good now. Can't we just move on?" she thought to herself. Not because she had anything to hide. But Why? Why did people feel the need to talk about her pain, then make her constantly relive it over and over again?

Finn was driving. He held Kara's hand and tried to look at her and the road at the same time.

"I want to know everything," he whispered. "The whole story."

Kara sighed again. She turned her head, looking out the window. She could have told him she didn't want to talk about it, but that would have been the easy way out. The truth was, she told Finn, just that morning actually, that she loved him. And she'd meant it. Which meant she had to tell him what happened.

Kara thought back to one of the darkest times of her life. She tried to think of ways to downplay it, so it didn't seem as big of a deal as it was. Finn held her hand patiently, waiting for her to begin. She realized her silence was truthfully her stalling. She never talked about herself. She never opened herself up to anyone. She looked over at Finn. He wasn't just anyone. As if on cue, Finn squeezed her hand, even though he didn't take his eyes off the road.

Kara took a deep breath and decided to let her heart choose how much to tell Finn. If the flood gates opened and they drowned, then so be it.

"I told you Chris and I met while working at a Casino. Both of us were really young. And like most twenty year old's, very naïve," she sighed. "We dated for two years before we got married. And there were problems, but I did what most people do. I ignored them. I thought after we get married, it would change. Things became complicated while we planned the wedding. Marion was being difficult about my not being Catholic. David stepped in, and I probably should have said fuck it and walked away. But by that time, the wedding was weeks away. I was in love, and I thought love was going to be enough to save the day."

"Marriage isn't 50/50 all the time. Sometimes it's 80/20 or 70/30. Our marriage was 90/10. All the time. One problem is your not always in love with each other at the same time. Sometimes one of you is in love, and the other is not. After we were married, I wasn't ready to have kids, but I wanted to do other things. I wanted to travel and see the world. I wanted to buy a house and start building our life, and Chris didn't want to do any of that. I thought if I gave him enough time, he would change his mind, so I didn't push."

"When I got pregnant, our relationship changed, as they always do. I already struggled with trying to be the perfect wife, employee, daughter, and everything else, now I would have to add mother to the list. I was overwhelmed, and Chris just wasn't there." Kara hesitated a moment before continuing.

"Chris tried in the beginning. After we brought Matt home, he wanted to help with everything. And for the first two months, neither of us slept much or really did anything other than try to take care of Matt. It wasn't until after I went back to work that our relationship began to break.

"When Matt was just about eight weeks old, I went back to work. The company I was working for at the time closed. So I had to find another job. I didn't want to work in a casino, so I went to work for another company. I was suffering from mom guilt, separation anxiety, and postpartum depression. Chris felt like he was being neglected. The first time, it was with one of the hookers who came into the casino. That was just a blow job."

"Cocktail server number one happened. That was just sex, too, apparently. I knew something was going on, but I just didn't know what. I felt like something changed, and I wasn't sure if I imagined it. Then I noticed the change was actually coming from Chris. He would come home and just shut down. He didn't talk unless it was about Matt. He stopped touching me. He would kiss me goodbye every day, but that was it. I would have to beg him to," Kara stopped. She leaned her head back and sighed. She took a deep breath and continued her voice shaking.

"I would have to beg him to make love to me. It was humiliating because I'd gained weight with Matt, and it didn't come off right away. I had stretch marks, and my boobs sagged, and I already felt like shit, and now I had to beg my husband to fuck me."

Kara felt the tears as they slid down her cheeks. She didn't stop them. Finn let go of her hand and handed her one of the napkins she kept in the dashboard's compartments.

"Thank you," she whispered. She wiped the tears and dabbed her nose. She was being crushed by the weight of feeling unwanted and rejected. "Deep breath," she thought to herself.

"Cocktail server number two only lasted a couple of weeks. Chris sent her dick picks, and she sent him nudes. That was fun when I found out about them. But I didn't find those until he started with the dealer. She was how I found out about all of the others."

"Apparently, she and Chris became close while they were working together. It started out as just friends. They would hang out while on break and sometimes get a drink after work. Then it got physical. After they'd been sleeping together for a while, she gave Chris an ultimatum. When she told Chris she wanted him to leave me, and she would take care of him and Matt, Chris agreed." Kara paused again, letting her words hang in the air.

"Fuck, What a dick," Finn whispered. Kara turned towards him. When he'd given her the napkin, he put both hands on the steering wheel, and now he was gripping it so tightly, his knuckles were white. Kara looked at his face. Finn's jaw was clenched. She could feel how angry he was. She reached over and touched his arm. He turned to face her, and she gave him a small smile.

"Finn," she said his name lightly. He reached over, and she took his hand. "The thing is, at the time, I was really in love with Chris. I knew he was being a dick. I knew something was going on. I just hoped I was wrong. So I ignored the way he treated me and how he lied to me. Because love covers a multitude of sins. And it does." She took a deep breath.

"So I found out about the dealer. Chris actually felt bad and broke it off with her, but things just got worse. I was so hurt I thought he would do whatever it took to save our marriage, and when he didn't, I just got crushed again. We began to fight all the time. We went in circles, trying to save what was so obviously broken. When I found out he was still seeing the dealer, I had enough. So I told him if he wanted her, he should go. And he did. I moved back into my parent's house with Matt, and that's when everything fell apart."

"What do you mean?" Finn asked. "Didn't that happen when you found out he was still cheating on you?"

Kara sighed and shook her head. "Believe it or not, Chris cheating on me and treating me the way he did wasn't the worst of it."

"What could be worse than that?" Finn asked skeptically.

"Not telling my parents why Chris and I were getting divorced is how it got worse." Kara sighed. "My parents acted like it was my fault. They blamed me for driving Chris away because they didn't know what happened. They assumed I was wrong. It was a lot of 'no wonder he left you' and 'why would Chris want you' especially from my mom."

"Are you serious?" Finn whispered, turning to look at Kara. She could feel his eyes on her as she looked down at their intertwined fingers.

"Yup. So, in a matter of months. I lost my marriage, most of my friends, my family abandoned me, and then I got laid off again. Literally, everything fell apart. It was Matt and me in the middle of hell. Thankfully, he was only three and was too young to know what was happening. But I was sinking." She paused.

"No, I didn't sink. I was drowning in depression. The only thing keeping me going was Matt. Honestly, there were so many days I thought about ending it all and if Matt wouldn't be better off with Chris. I didn't do anything, but I thought about it. A lot."

"Then what happened?" Finn asked quietly.

"Then, things started to get better. I met someone else. I thought, now things are going to finally start going right for me."

"And they didn't."

"No. They didn't. They got even worse, if you can believe it. I found another job, although not for as much money. The guy I was seeing was great. Or so I believed. I was finally getting the attention I'd been missing for so long. I lost weight because I stopped eating for months. And he made me feel like I was sexy. But my parents just didn't stop attacking me. And even though I was a grown woman and a mother, my parents were just brutal. Even my dad was awful. Then the guy I was seeing just got so demanding."

"It was chaos. I was trying to deal with Chris, who wasn't helping at all. He was being an asshole at the time. My parents seemed to find some new ways of making me suffer. I went out, they would make snide comments or say I was a bad mother. Then the guy I was seeing started demanding I drop everything for him. I was struggling to pay my own bills because I wasn't making enough. I was afraid my car was going to be repossessed every day. And just when I thought I could finally come up for air, everything dragged me back down. So when the guy gave me an ultimatum, I broke up with him."

"What was it?" Finn whispered.

"He asked for more than I could give at the time. He wanted me to cut off all communication with Chris, even if it meant Matt would suffer. He wanted me to protect him from my parents, who were absolutely rude to him. And he wanted me to commit solely to him and his needs, even asking me to give Chris sole custody of Matt. He said he wanted to marry me and start his own family and didn't want a 'stepson.' He wanted his own children."

Kara stopped. She sat quietly, letting Finn think about everything she just told him. Her heart pounding so loudly she could hear it. Reliving the pain and looking at the scars, although healed but still felt raw. Each wound was tingling even though it all happened years ago.

She continued, "The years after that were pretty much me living scared, alone and keeping my head up just enough above water to keep Matt from seeing just what a mess I was. Even though I was failing in so many ways. I stopped talking to a lot of people and just focused on being on my own."

"Is that why you didn't date much?" Finn asked solemnly.

"Well, yes, that and I was afraid."

"Afraid of what?"

"Everything. I tried going on a couple of dates, and they all just ended up a disaster. I kept getting hurt by stupid little things. I would get my hopes up just to get disappointed. I was afraid to trust people. It just felt like everyone was just trying to hurt me and was against me. So I gave up and decided it was too risky to try."

"So Lori and Teresa were right," Finn whispered. More to himself than to Kara.

"About what?"

"About you going through a lot."

Kara laughed gloomily. "They only know about the part Chris played in all of it. Lori only knows about the other guy because she met him and wondered what happened when I told her we broke up. So I told her an abridged story, but not everything. Chris only knows about my parents because they would attack me in front of him. Only Charlie and my therapist know everything that happened. And even then, I didn't tell them all of it." Kara sighed and took a deep breath. She waited a moment before continuing.

"But, if you take nothing else from all of this, understand after everything that happened, I don't blame Chris. I forgave him because it would have been horrible for Matt, and I didn't want that. Yes, my marriage ended. Yes, it was Chris's fault. Yes, he did mean and terrible things. But I forgave him. I forgave Chris because I loved Matt. And Matt was the only thing that mattered to me. It took me a long time to accept my marriage was over. But I did. The stuff that happened with my parents is what broke me. That's what took a really long time to put those pieces back together."

Kara sighed. "That's the long story, which has been edited for content." She smiled. "Believe it or not, Chris and I do have a happy ending. We are much better as friends than we ever were as husband and wife. We're family. We made peace, and we were able to move past everything and come together for Matt's sake. Chris has come to my rescue more than once since we've been divorced. I can depend on him now, in a way I couldn't when we were married."

"Chris moved on. He married Teresa, who is wonderful, and she loved Matt from the beginning. They have Katie, and I love Katie. With Teresa and Katie's help, Chris is a much better man than the one I married. And we're still family. It wasn't always easy, but after everything we went through, we did it, and that's all that matters."

They were silent for the last few moments of the drive. Both of them lost in their own thoughts.

When they got home, Kara went inside and went into her bedroom. Since being renovated, the master bedroom was one of her favorite rooms. The walls, a grayish-blue, were soothing. She bought new wood furniture, replacing the bed frame, dresser, and vanity. She also created a reading area with an accent chair, a table, and a lamp. She loved that she could sit in her room, read, and look out the window.

She took her sandals off and sat in the accent chair, pulling her legs up under her. She turned her head and looked out the window. The street was quiet, with only the occasional car passing by. She leaned her head back against the chair. Exhausted from talking about what happened with Chris. She had barely scratched the surface with everything she told Finn. There was so much more she didn't say.

She didn't tell him about the loneliness. The fear. The helplessness. The frustration. The times she cried in the shower so Matt wouldn't see her tears. The huge fight she had with her parents causing her to reach her breaking point and move out. How her relationship with her parents never recovered. How it had aged her father when she took Matt away.

Her father changed after that. He began to have panic attacks and would spend days depressed. Sometimes he didn't get out of bed. He would lie in bed and just watch tv. It was the beginning of his downward spiral. When Kara left, she'd bring Matt to see her parents once a week for a half-hour. It was all she could handle. The only time Matt saw them longer was on holidays, and she would need time to recover afterward.

She hadn't told Finn how she avoided her parents, even though she saw her father wither away. She just couldn't fight with them anymore. When she moved out, the attacks never stopped. Kara's relationship with her parents was shattered. So she stayed as far away as possible and remained silent. Kara still carried the guilt of not being there when her father died. She'd asked Matt to call him the day before, but she hadn't wanted to talk to him. He was gone the next day.

She didn't tell Finn about struggling on her own. Constantly afraid for her and for Matt. Even though they lived in a safe place, she was still always scared. Chris did step up when she moved out. Seeing her struggle to keep the lights on caused him to see just how much he caused her to suffer. He went to therapy after that and worked through his own demons.

Kara was so lost in her thoughts, she didn't see Finn watching her from the doorway. She didn't notice him come into the room and quietly walk over to her. He sat down on the floor in front of her and put his head on her lap. It brought her back from the past into the present.

She gently stroked his hair. Feeling the silkiness of his golden locks. She looked down at him. He was looking up at her.

"Why are you hiding?" he whispered. Kara ran her fingers through his hair. Finn closed his eyes.

"I'm not hiding," she murmured.

She liked the way his hair felt under her hand. She liked touching him like this. It was intimate after being starved for intimacy for so many years.

"Yes, you are. You left me and went into your head. I could hear you thinking all the way in the living room." Finn opened his eyes and smiled at her.

Kara smiled back at him. "I'm sorry."

"Don't apologize. I just want you to talk to me. Tell me what you're thinking and what you're feeling."

"It's going to take me a little while to get used to having someone to share my thoughts with." Finn turned and faced her. He got on his knees in front of her and took her hands.

"But Kara, I'm here now. You don't have to keep it all inside anymore."

Kara felt the tears in her eyes. "Finn, I know you're here," she said barely above a whisper. "It's just I'm so used to keeping it all to myself. I've been," Her voice catching in her throat. Tears were starting to fall down her cheeks. She took a deep breath and continued. "I've been on my own for so long. Always being afraid, always being anxious, trying to hide how I really felt so no one would see just how much of a failure I felt I was." Her voice was shaking as she spoke solemnly.

"I know it seems like I'm keeping things from you or hiding, but I'm not." She shook her head. "I haven't had to share myself with anyone. I haven't been able to show someone everything about myself and still feel safe. It's going to take some time for me to get used to it." She sobbed quietly.

She was crying. Tears falling, nose running crying. Finn pulled her off the chair and into his lap, wrapping his arms around her, and cradled her. He gently stroked her back while she sobbed. Kara let all the tears she had out. She had allowed her heart to decide, and the flood gates opened. Tears she hadn't been able to shed before now came with a vengeance. Finn just cradled her in his arms. Slowly rocking back and forth, providing the comfort she desperately craved.

Kara allowed herself to be vulnerable with Finn. He'd broken through many of the walls she built to protect herself. It wasn't just because she loved him. It was more because he loved her. She was willing to receive his love without being afraid she would lose it. She was starting to trust Finn wasn't going to hurt her. Kara hadn't trusted anyone that much ever.

Finn held her until her sobs quieted, and her shuddering stopped. He hadn't spoken at all while he held her. He let her cry. He rocked her and gently stroked her back. When Kara's sniffling was the only thing left, she lifted her head and looked at him. Finn kissed her gently on the temple.

They sat on the floor, Finn cradling her to his chest for what seemed like the longest time. Kara finally slipped off Finn's lap because she thought she was probably going to break him. She stood up and stretched, her body stiff from the way they were sitting. She looked at the clock on the nightstand, and although it was just before ten, it felt much later.

Finn stood next to her and pulled her into his arms. She wrapped her arms around his waist and leaned against his chest. She could feel his heartbeat. She looked up at him.

"What are you thinking about?" she murmured.

"You," he said frankly.

"What about me?"

"Just how amazing you are."

"Really? I would have thought you were thinking how much of a mess I am and how you should run for the hills," she laughed truthfully.

"Nope. Sorry. You can't get rid of me that easily," he said, smiling at her.

"That's good to know."

Finn leaned down and kissed her gently. Kara leaned into his kiss. His mouth soft, warm, and inviting. She liked how he kissed her. As if he savored the taste of her. Finn broke the kiss and stepped out of their embrace. He took her hand, gently turned her around, and started to undress her. Unzipping her sundress and unhooking her strapless bra. Since they had been together, he had become proficient at getting her shapewear off. He placed her clothes on the chair and led her to the bed.

Finn pulled down the blankets, and Kara climbed into bed. He got undressed and slid into bed next to her. He pulled her into his arms, and Kara went willingly. Enjoying the feeling of his naked body against hers. He kissed her gently. His hands gently caressing her. Finn was so tender. Treating her as if she were fragile. He kissed her delicately on her neck, her breasts, and her stomach. He took his time perusing her body.

Lightly following each caress with a kiss. He gently spread her legs, using the faintest touch on her mound. Kara arched her back, her body longing for him. The lightness of his touch sending desire through her.

"Kara," he whispered against her stomach. His hand teasing her.

"Yes," she said breathlessly.

"You belong to me now," he whispered. Kara hearing an edge to his voice. "I'll take care of you. I'll protect you. Because your mine."

Kara didn't know what to say to respond.

"I won't let anyone hurt you," he whispered as he kissed her breasts. His fingers teasing her entrance. Kara moaned. She wanted to scream out, but she had never been overly loud or vocal while having sex. It just wasn't her. Finn's teasing touch and how her body was responding were making her want to change. She moved her hands to caress his back.

"I'm not going anywhere. And where you go, I'll follow you. I'm yours," he whispered against her neck. He moved on top of her. Using his knee to spread her legs wider for him to slip between them. He kissed her as he entered her, muffling Kara's moan.

"Your mine, and I'm yours," he whispered as he kissed her. He possessed her, filling her up. "Say your mine," he said as he thrust inside of her. Kara looked up at him. Her hips moving to match his thrusts.

"Say it," he whispered against her mouth. Looking down at her.

"I'm yours," she whispered. A tear falling from her eye at his intensity.

"And I'm yours. Say it. Tell me I belong to you."

"You belong to me," Kara whispered.

Finn kissed her. Hungerly taking her mouth as his thrusts quickened. He was consuming her. Kara's orgasm was so powerful, she shuddered hard against him. Finn exploded into her as he felt her tighten around him. His mouth on her, suppressing her moans.

Kara fell asleep with Finn's arms wrapped tightly around her. Feeling Finn's possession of her and happy knowing she gave herself willingly.

CHAPTER 19

⚜

Finn scowled as he followed Kara and the Lowes sales associate around. She was trying to find the same cabinets she'd bought weeks ago for the kitchen, and the sales associate was trying to convince her to go with something else. Finn knew the sales associate was really just stalling. From the moment they'd walked over, the guy had looked Kara up and down. Finn decided he would look at something else because he had gotten so annoyed and Kara gave him a look.

Kara had the measurements and knew what she wanted. He'd only come along for the ride. Finn was in a mood. Things had been getting to him lately. He was anxious. He felt like something was wrong somewhere, and it was bothering the shit out of him because he couldn't figure out what it was. He needed to get out of the house.

His mood started with the kitchen. What was supposed to be a simple renovation had turned into a fucking nightmare. Kara didn't want to expand the kitchen. She wanted to update everything and add a kitchen island. Then she would have a breakfast nook built-in. But the carpenters she hired had utterly screwed up.

One of the workmen didn't understand he was supposed to be building a breakfast nook against the wall, somehow knocked down the wall between the kitchen and the dining room. Finn walked into the Lead Carpenter, talking down to Kara and saying her directions weren't clear enough. Finn lunged at the guy, ready to punch him in the face. Both of them screaming at each other and threatening to kick the other's ass. Kara physically stepped in between them, and since she is the epitome of grace, she calmed everyone down.

The wall wasn't a load-bearing wall, which was the good news. But now, there was a gaping hole between the kitchen and the dining room. Kara called the owner the next day to talk about what happened. She told him of the situation and convinced the owner to repair the damage, provide a discount on the work already being done, and complete the custom breakfast nook Kara hired them for. Honestly, the wall being knocked down wasn't the worst thing. It opened up the kitchen and dining area. With the new cabinets, she would add, it would look amazing when it was done.

The appliances were the next thing to set Finn off. Kara decided to convert the electric stove to gas. Which meant gas lines had to be run. Kara called a Master Plumber to run gas lines for the kitchen and fireplace since she wanted to convert it to gas. She also wanted him to install a tankless water heater since she needed to have the water heater replaced. Finn had to work, so Kara stayed home to wait for the Master Plumber.

Finn spent all day at work, growling at people. He texted Kara every thirty minutes. When the Master Plumber was there, Finn texted her every five minutes. When she didn't respond right away, he was practically running to his truck. Thoughts of the house blowing up or on fire filled his head. He was afraid something would happen to her, and he wouldn't be there to protect her.

After terrorizing his crew all day, Finn left work as early as he could. He'd sped home and miraculously didn't get pulled over. He somehow avoided getting a speeding ticket or worse. He pulled up to the house, and it was still intact. Finn wasn't a religious man, but he closed his eyes and actually thanked God. Something, he noticed he'd been doing a lot since meeting Kara.

He got out of the truck and ran into the house. When he opened the door and saw Kara sitting on the couch, he sent another prayer of thanks heavenward. He was so relieved to see her, he fucked her right there. He had to touch her. He had to kiss her. He needed to make sure she was ok. He'd come so hard and so fast, it had made him dizzy.

When Kara asked him about it, he didn't know how to put it into words, so he told her he missed her. Which was true. But it was more than that. It was something he didn't know how to describe. That was over two weeks ago. Since then, Finn had found the words and knew how to describe what he felt. Now, he just didn't want to talk about it.

Finn had been scared. Actually, it was more than scared. He'd been petrified. It had never occurred to him there was even the remotest possibility he could lose Kara. The thought sent chills down his spine. Leaving him cold. Then, it filled him with murderous rage. Because his feelings felt so extreme to him, it confused him. Now he was in a mood.

Finn had never been the possessive, jealous type. He was the lose interest type. If any of his previous girlfriends tried to make him jealous, Finn would lose interest. Even with Shelly, men would practically try to walk away with her, and it wouldn't faze him. He had always believed if a woman wanted to go, good riddance. He wasn't going to stop them.

With Kara, it changed. Finn actually felt very possessive of Kara. It annoyed him when men hit on her in front of him. Like he wasn't even there. He wanted to throat punch them. If that wasn't complicated enough, the thought of living without Kara felt like someone ripped him in half. It made him nauseous, light-headed, and his heart race so much he felt like he had a heart attack. Finn didn't know how to process the magnitude of emotions, just the thought of being without her caused. Finn knew he'd never loved anyone the way he loved Kara. That alone was enough to make him anxious.

Finn was standing next to a countertop display, watching Kara. "She's so beautiful. No wonder everyone is so drawn to her. She's like a beacon. Everyone seeking light simply gravitates to her," he thought to himself. He walked over and stood next to her. The salesman, at least ten years older than Kara, was flirting with her. As usual, Kara was totally oblivious to it. The man practically drooled when he asked if her "husband" would be there for the delivery.

Kara innocently replied, "I'm not married." Completely ignoring the man's hints.

"Really, a woman as pretty as you are, isn't married?" The sales associate said.

Finn almost went feral. With a look the man completely missed, Kara stopped him. Finn stood there seething. "When did he become such a jealous prick?" he thought to himself. Why was he so possessive of her? Because she's yours. His heart screamed. His brain adding, because you're a jerk and didn't realize how much you loved her until you realized you could lose her. Finn sighed because both were right.

Kara paid for the cabinets and countertops she wanted. She smiled and thanked the sales associate for all of his help. She walked over to Finn and looked up at him with her big dark brown eyes.

"Ready?" Giving him a smile that made all the anger and jealousy evaporate.

"Yeah," Finn said, nodding. Finn put his arm around Kara and squeezed her ass as they walked out of the store.

One more thing was bothering Finn. Labor Day. It was two weeks away. Every year, his family had an end-of-summer barbeque on the first Monday of September. It's something his family had done since he was a kid. Labor Day was usually one of the few holidays his father had off from work. For the last five years, Finn had gone with Shelly. The thought of taking Kara was filling him with dread. More dread than when he first went to the McNulty's.

There wasn't anything wrong with his family. His family was great, but he still had alarm bells ringing in his head. The only person from his family Kara had met was his brother Mike. As Finn started going to Sunday dinner, he wasn't hanging out with Mike as often. Sometimes he got together with Mike on Sundays to have lunch before going to dinner with Kara later. Mostly when Kara went to see her best friend, Charlie.

As soon as Mike met Kara, he knew Finn was serious about her. Mike came by the house one Sunday to pick him up for lunch. Kara was going to meet Charlie, and she looked amazing. Finn introduced them, and Mike liked her immediately. As they got into Mike's car to drive to lunch, Mike turned to Finn.

"You know, she's too good for you, right?" he said, starting the car.

"I know," Finn said as he buckled his seat belt.

"If you fuck this up, you're a fucking idiot, and I'd have no problem swooping in there and stealing her from you."

"No, you won't."

"Oh yeah, and why not?"

"Because I'd kill you and tell mom it was suicide."

Mike laughed at him, "Now I know you're serious about her. I used to threaten to steal Shelly all the time, and you didn't flinch."

Finn looked at his brother and smiled.

Mike came over a couple of Saturdays afterward to help out with renovating when he had some free time. Mostly to hang out with Kara, though. Which just proved to Finn how people gravitated to her. Mike followed her around, telling her stories about Finn to make her laugh. On the one hand, Finn loved Mike was getting to know Kara, even if Mike made fun of him.

On the other hand, Finn knew Mike was a man-whore. He wasn't slut-shaming him by any means. He loved his brother. Mike wasn't caught up in labels. If he vibed with someone, that was all that mattered to him. Mike vibed with Kara. They got along so well, they even had their own little jokes. But sometimes Finn would catch Mike looking at Kara a certain way, and Finn would want to punch him in the face.

Finn called his mom to tell her he was bringing someone new to the house on Labor Day. His mother was absolutely fine with it. She was her usual warm, welcoming self. Of course, she wouldn't mind. The more, the merrier. Finn hung up with his mother feeling only slightly better. But, he still couldn't help dreading Labor Day.

Finn pulled into the driveway of the two-story white colonial house. He pulled up behind the other parked cars, turned off the car, and took a deep breath. Next to him, Kara was checking her already flawless appearance in the passenger seat mirror. She looked stunning. She wore a golden yellow sundress with matching sweater. Her hair was down, falling on her shoulders in smooth, loose curls. In her lap lay the bottle of wine she insisted on bringing.

"God, she's beautiful," he thought to himself. She turned to look at him smiling. The anxiety Finn had been feeling momentarily easing.

"Ready?" she asked. She seemed so calm. So at ease. Finn wondered why he didn't feel as calm as she did.

"Yup," he said. Trying to sound more confident than he felt. Finn got out of the car and jogged around to open the door for Kara. He closed the door after she got out and took her hand. He felt better when he touched her. Her warmth spreading through him, easing the knots in the pit of his stomach. She was smiling, and Finn pulled her close and kissed her lightly on the cheek. He could smell her jasmine scent and breathed it in, letting it fill his lungs. Everything about her brought him comfort. She was the calm amid his own mental chaos.

They walked in the house and down the long hallway into the kitchen. Finn's younger sister Ellen was sitting at the table with his eldest sister's nine-year-old daughter. Meg spotted Finn first.

"Uncle Finn," Meg squealed, jumping out of her chair and onto Finn. Finn let go of Kara's hand to catch his niece. Her light brown hair hiding her face as she planted kisses on his face.

"Easy, Princess," he said, laughing as she wiggled in his arms. Ellen got out of her chair and walked over to her brother.

"Hey, Bro. Long time no see." Giving her brother a one-arm side hug. Finn put his niece down and put his arm around his sister, kissing her on the top of her head.

"Hey, Squirt," he said to his sister.

"Don't call me that." Ellen sneered. She turned to Kara and extended her hand to shake Kara's. "My brother is an animal and has no manners," she smiled at Kara. "Hi, I'm Ellen."

Kara took her hand and returned her smile. "Kara."

"It's nice to finally meet you, Kara," Ellen said warmly. "I've heard all about you from Mike because," looking at Finn and pointing at him. "He's being secretive and wants to keep you all to himself."

Kara laughed, and Finn gently shoved his sister's shoulder. "Can you blame me? After she met Mike, he said he would steal her from me. And you would let him."

"No, I don't blame you. Mike's already said she's too good for you." Ellen said, then turning to Kara, "And I would. But, be careful, Mikes a man whore." Ellen lifted her hands. "No judgment, though."

Kara laughed. "I know. I've been told."

Finn looked around. "Where is everyone?" he asked.

"Outside on the deck," Ellen said, pointing outside. "I came in with Meg because she and JJ were fighting." She gestured towards Meg. "JJ is our six-year-old nephew. Jimmy Jr., He likes to fight with his sister," Ellen explained to Kara. "It must be a brother thing," she said and rolled her eyes at Finn.

"Don't listen to her. She's a squirt," Finn said, messing up his sister's hair.

Ellen squealed. "Stop, you're messing up my hair," as she waved Finn's hand away.

Finn laughed, taking Kara's hand in his. "Come on." He led Kara out the back door onto the deck. Everyone was congregating on the deck. Finn's mother noticed them first and patted his father's arm. They walked over to meet Finn and Kara.

"Hey, Mom," Finn said as he gave his mom a hug.

"Griffin," His father said, nodding.

"Mom, Dad, this is Kara McNulty." They both extended their hands to shake Kara's. Exchanging 'Nice to meet you. Please call me Dorothy. I'm Robert.' Kara handed his mom the bottle of wine.

"Oh, you shouldn't have, how sweet," his mother cooed.

Mike was by the grill talking to Ellen's boyfriend, Steve. They both came over to the little group to say hi. Finn glared at Mike as he leaned in and gave Kara a hug and a kiss on the cheek. Mike laughed at Finn as Steve shook hands with Kara. Finn looked around for his older sister. He saw the top of her dirty blond hair on the grass. Finn called out to her,

"Bev?" waving her up.

She turned and waved up at him. She looked down again, and Finn could see the annoyance on her face.

Beverly slowly walked up the stairs from the grass. Her son following her. Beverly walked over and stood in front of Finn and Kara, her son hiding behind her legs.

"Kara, this is my older sister Beverly, and the little guy behind her is JJ," Finn said.

Beverly extended her hand to shake Kara's. "It's nice to meet you." Kara shook her hand and smiled at her. "It's nice to meet you too." She looked down at JJ and smiled at him. "Hi." JJ smiled shyly at Kara and hid his face behind his mother's leg.

Finn looked at Beverly, "Where's Jim?" he asked.

"Oh," Beverly sighed. "He's sitting downstairs on the grass," she said flatly.

Jim, Beverly's husband, climbed up the steps as she said that and came up behind her.

"She's Black." Jim bellowed.

Beverly turned quickly and gave her husband a stern look. "Jim!" she exclaimed.

Jim looked at her, "What? She is," he said obnoxiously.

Beverly closed her eyes and shook her head. Jim leaned towards his wife, looking at Finn.

"Whoa, look, who Finn brought to dinner?" he shouted. Beverly visibly paled.

Jim was swaying behind his wife. Finn could smell the alcohol on him before he got there.

Beverly closed her eyes, "He's had a little too much to drink already," she explained. "And he's barely eaten anything today. You know how it is," she trailed off.

Finn glowered. He looked over at Kara, and he could see the wall going up. Just when he thought he had nothing to be anxious about, Finn forgot about his brother-in-law.

Beverly and Jim were high school sweethearts who got married right after graduation. While their parents insisted Beverly go to college, Jim went to work on the same farm he grew up on. Finn never really liked Jim. Jim had always been obnoxious. Finn didn't understand why his sister married him. Finn tolerated Jim when he had to. Which was only a couple times a year and usually during holidays.

"Look at Finn bringing some color to this party," Jim said. Turning to Kara, "Is your hair real, or is it one of those wigs?"

Kara paled as she winced. Finn stepped in front of Kara, ready to pounce on his brother-in-law. Beverly's face turned tomato red, "Excuse me," as she turned and pushed Jim back down the steps, as he protested,

"I'm just kidding. Can't she take a joke?" Jim reached the railing and leaned over to grab another beer. "It was just a joke, God, don't be so sensitive." Their son JJ ran into the kitchen.

Everyone outside got quiet. Finn's mother went to find JJ. His father went down the steps to Beverly and Jim. Mike and Steve came over to Kara and Finn. Finn turned to Kara and forced her to meet his eyes.

"Are you ok?" he whispered, searching her face. Kara didn't meet his eyes, so he moved until she made eye contact with him.

"Kara, look at me. Jim is an alcoholic," he said, pleading with her. Finn saw the shield go up around her. She took a deep breath and finally answered. "I'm fine," she said quietly. Finn nodded and kissed her on the forehead.

He knew she wasn't, but he didn't want to push her.

He took her hand and led her over to Mike and Steve. He was hoping if Mike started flirting with Kara, her shield would come down again, and she would relax. Finn held her hand firmly in his. When he'd tried to put his arm around her, she flinched. Finn's heart broke a little. The anxiety he was feeling was turning to rage at his brother-in-law.

Ellen came outside and joined them. Finn got Kara a bottle of water, and Mike told Kara stories about all the stupid things Finn would do to him when they were kids. Ellen told Kara about how Finn tortured her when she was younger. Finn's mother brought out trays of fruit, and the five of them ate the fruit. Finn kept taking quick glances at Kara. Her shield was still up, but he could see she was trying. She was eating some of the fruit and holding her bottle of water. Kara would smile while listening to Ellen's stories of Finn's first foray into dating. Mike would add the details Ellen missed. Finn sighed with relief when he saw Kara slowly begin to relax.

Finn noticed Kara barely ate when she put her plate down on the table where they were standing. He stood closer to her and put his arm around her, and she didn't flinch. Meg and JJ were chasing each other around the deck and in and out of the kitchen. Occasionally his mother would look around tell them to be careful. The tension from earlier was beginning to ease.

"What's wrong with what I said?" Jim bellowed from the grass. Everyone got quiet again. Meg and JJ stopped running on the deck and ran into the house, Finn's mother following them. Everyone turned to the grass. Beverly's head was visible, and although you couldn't hear what she was saying. Jim was yelling his responses.

"What, can't she take a joke? Is she too bougie for us?" Jim huffed, "You need to stop acting like you're so good," Jim snarled. "You know you don't like it, either."

Finn felt Kara stiffen next to him. Although she kept the smile on his face, she was so rigid, Finn's heart ached for her.

She turned towards him and whispered, "Where is the ladies' room?"

"I'll show you," Finn said quickly. Hoping if he could get her alone for a couple of minutes, he ease some of the tension radiating from her.

"No, it's ok," she said uneasily. "I can manage." She didn't meet his eyes but gave him a forced smile.

"Ok," Finn said, defeated. "It's just past the kitchen. The second door on the left."

"Ok. I'll be back." She set her water bottle down on the table and walked into the house.

Jim came stomping up the stairs, shouting.

"I'm done. I don't want to hear anymore." He was waving his arms. Beverly and Finn's father behind him. Finn's rage exploded as Jim got closer to him. Finn stepped in front of him.

"What the fuck is wrong with you?" he said through clenched teeth. Finn's hands clenching into fists.

"Me?" shouted Jim. "What the fuck is wrong with you bringing Shaniqua or whatever her name is here?"

Finn didn't realize he'd punched Jim until Steve and Mike pulled him off of Jim. Finn kept lunging at Jim while Steve and Mike struggled to hold him back. Each of them grabbing his arms. Jim was clutching his face. Beverly stood over her husband as Finn's father held Jim back.

Chaos erupted. A chorus of voices shouting at Jim, talking over each other.

Jim shook his head, holding his face. "I'm only saying what all of you are thinking." Raising his voice. "Shelly may have been a snobby bitch, but at least she was White."

Finn shoved his brother away and lunged at Jim again. Steve grabbed Finn by the waist to pull him back. Mike pushing Finn back. Finn's father stepped around Jim and pushed him back towards the stairs. Jim kept yelling,

"Come on, you want a piece of this. I'll kick your ass in front of your black girl." Taunting Finn.

Steve and Mike pulled Finn's back towards the grill. Beverly in front of her husband, crying and pleading with him to stop. Finn's mom was huddled with Meg and JJ by the table, trying to soothe their crying. Ellen, who had been in shock watching everything unfold, turned towards the door with a look of absolute horror. Everyone's eyes followed hers, and everyone became quiet.

Kara stood at the door, quietly with her hands folded in front of her. Finn saw her straining to keep the tears in her eyes from falling. She looked so fragile standing there alone. All the fight left him. The look of hurt on Kara's face broke him. Finn shook off Mike and Steve, and they let go of him. He almost tripped over Ellen as he ran to Kara.

"Mr. & Mrs. Wilson, Thank you for inviting me into your home. I'm afraid I'm simply not feeling well. Please excuse me, but I think I should go home." She looked around at everyone else. "It was nice to meet you."

She didn't look at Finn as he walked over to her. She simply turned and walked through the backdoor to leave the house.

Finn followed her out of the house. She got to the car and waited in front of the passenger door. He walked up behind her. "Kara," he said, panting from running.

She didn't turn around. He put his hands on her shoulders and felt her wince. He turned her around to face him.

"Kara, please. I'm sorry. He's an alcoholic. Please look at me."

Kara looked up at Finn, and he felt the chill down his spine from the coldness in her eyes. She shut him out.

"Kara," he whispered, pleading with her.

"Please unlock the car. I want to go home," she said, barely above a whisper. Finn looked at her imploringly. She turned away from him, and Finn let his arms fall from her shoulders. He unlocked the car, and Kara opened the door and got in, shutting it before he could.

He walked around to the driver's side, got in, started the car, and backed out of the driveway.

CHAPTER 20

Finn drove home, trying to think of anything he could do to get Kara to talk to him. She'd spent the drive looking out of the window. Occasionally wiping a rogue tear from her face. He'd whispered her name and tried to reach for her hand, but she balled herself into the door away from him. He felt so powerless. How could he ever think he could protect her when he couldn't stop her from being hurt by his own family.

Less than five minutes after they left, his family blew up his phone. He reached into his pocket and turned it off. The most important person in the world to him was huddled less than two feet from him, silently crying. He didn't care if he ever talked to his family again after today. He wasn't sure he would ever forgive them.

Finn didn't think Jim would be such an asshole. He knew he was an alcoholic, but he didn't think he was racist. Although, Finn realized it had never come up before. He thought about all of the friends he'd ever had, and though few and far between, he knew Black people but not many. None he would say were friends. Randy was his best friend, but he was Hispanic. Jim never acted that way around Randy, but then Randy owned Neighbors, so of course, Jim was nice to him.

Finn didn't know what to do or think. This was all new to him. He thought about Mike. Yes, Mike was Bi-Sexual, but Mike had never brought a guy home. Now that he thought about it, Finn wasn't even sure his parents knew Mike was Bi-Sexual. As far as he knew, only he and Ellen knew. Mike and Beverly weren't close at all. He wondered if Beverly knew Mike was Bi-Sexual. He didn't think so. Otherwise, would Jim make jokes about that too? Probably.

Finn replayed the afternoon in his head. His parents, Mike and Ellen, all tried to make Kara feel welcome. Beverly tried. Jim was just an asshole. A drunk, racist asshole at that. That's why he'd been so anxious about bringing Kara over. He'd forgotten about Jim.

Jim had always drank, but the past couple of years, the drinking got worse. They all knew it, but somehow, Beverly always made excuses for it. Things happening at the farm. Not making enough money. Family stress. Jim was something they'd all got used to. Even Ellen's boyfriend Steve was used to Jim. Finn took it for granted everyone was used to Jim. Except Kara wouldn't have been used to him.

Finn's hand throbbed as he gripped the steering wheel. He would have to put ice on it when he got home. He glanced over at Kara. What was she thinking? He wondered. She was still huddled against the door. Looking out the window. After everything she'd already gone through, now she had to deal with this. He wanted to force her to talk to him, but he couldn't. He didn't know what to say to her. He felt helpless, and he hated it.

Finn pulled into the driveway, and before he could put the car in park, Kara opened the door and was out of the car. Finn put the car in park and turned it off.

"Kara," He called out to her. Fighting to get his seat belt off, he got out of the car. Kara was waiting at the door. She forgot he had her keys. Finn jogged up the pathway to the door.

Looking at her, his heart broke. Tears were still falling down her cheeks. He reached for her. She turned away from him. Finn winced. The pain of it so deep, he felt it in the pit of his stomach.

"Kara," he whispered. Searching her face to get her to meet his eyes. "Please talk to me."

Kara shook her head. "No." Her voice breaking. "I can't right now," she whispered.

Finn took a step towards her and took her hand. "Please, Kara. I'm sorry. Please. Please talk to me. Please don't shut me out," he pleaded with her. "Please open the door, Finn." She sniffled. "I want to go lie down."

Beaten, Finn said, "Ok," and unlocked the door. Kara ran into the house, up the stairs, and down the hallway. Finn heard the bedroom door slam as he walked into the house. He closed the door behind him. He walked into the living room and dropped onto the couch. He leaned his head back and closed his eyes. He was exhausted, slightly nauseous, and his hand was throbbing. His mind was racing in too many directions for him to focus.

"Kara," he whispered. Jumping up from the couch and running around the coffee table to the stairs. He ran up the stairs and down the hall to the bedroom. He turned the handle. It was locked.

"Kara," with his sore hand, he knocked weakly on the door. "Please let me in."

Silence.

He knocked again. "Kara, please don't shut me out." He leaned his head against the door. He couldn't hear anything on the other side of the door.

Finn turned around and slid down the door to the floor. He lifted his knees to his chest, rested his arms on his legs, and buried his head in his hands. Hopelessness flooded him. Kara was so hurt by what happened today, she shut him out completely. He leaned his head back and banged his head against the door.

"Kara, I love you. Please let me in," he said through the door.

Silence.

Finn sat outside the bedroom door for what seemed like hours. Until his back started to ache. The hallway was dark, the only light coming from the other open doors. He got up slowly, hearing his knees crack. He stretched to try to get some feeling back in his legs. He was tired and hungry. He looked down and saw his hand was starting to bruise. He turned and knocked on the door. "Kara, are you hungry? I'll make you something."

Silence.

"Ok. I'll bring you something." He leaned his head against the door. "I love you." He raised his hand and touched the door. He hesitated a moment, hoping for a response. When none came, he turned and walked down the hallway to the kitchen.

Finn couldn't find a serving tray, so he used a cookie sheet. He made a mental note to buy one. Vowing once Kara talked to him again, he would use it to make her breakfast in bed. Every day for the rest of his life, if he had to. He made soup for both of them, toast for her with a cup of tea, and a sandwich for him. He put her soup, toast, and tea on the cookie sheet and awkwardly carried it to the bedroom. He steadied it against the door as he knocked. "Kara, I brought you something to eat. I'll leave it here for you."

Finn set the cookie sheet on the floor in front of the door. "I love you," he said as he went back to the kitchen to eat and put some ice on his hand.

An hour later, Finn checked to see if Kara at least opened the door to get something to eat. He turned on the hallway light. The cookie sheet was still there, untouched. Finn sighed. His heart ached. He turned off the hallway light and went into his room.

He emptied his pockets onto the dresser and took his phone out of his pocket. His finger hit the touchpad, turning his phone on. His family blew up his phone. There were texts from everyone and even more in the family chat. There were at least fifty texts. Most of them coming from Beverly. He turned his phone off again and plugged it in to charge. He didn't have the energy to talk to them.

He took his clothes off and climbed into the bed he'd never slept in. When Kara renovated the room, she bought a whole new bed. She'd made it up, and when Finn asked her why, she'd said the room should still look nice. He'd smiled at the time, and now it just made him miss her.

He lay in the dark, his body aching for her. He missed the way she felt in his arms. The smell of her perfume. He wanted to hold her. He wanted to take all of her pain away. He closed his eyes, and the image of Kara's tear-streaked face appeared. He opened his eyes and stared at the ceiling, listening to the stillness of the house.

He'd left his door open, hoping he'd hear if Kara came out of the bedroom.

There was nothing but silence, and the silence was deafening. He tried closing his eyes again and eventually fell into a fitful sleep. Tossing and turning all night.

The buzzing of his alarm scared Finn awake. He didn't remember setting it the night before. He looked around the room. The door was closed.

"Kara," he said as he jumped out of bed and looked out the window. Kara's car was gone. "Fuck," he said, dropping back onto the bed.

"What the fuck?" he muttered to himself. "Well, at least she set my alarm," he thought to himself.

He got up and shook his hand, flexing his fingers. His hand was stiff but didn't hurt. His knuckles were a bright red. He left the bedroom and went into the kitchen. His mug was waiting for him. The empty dishes were in the sink, and the cookie sheet was on top of the range. She either ate everything or threw it all away. He thought as he made his coffee. He took it with him as he walked down the hallway to his bedroom. When he walked into his room, he picked up his phone to see if she texted him or even called him. Nothing. Just the texts last night from his family.

He sent her a text to say good morning and to thank her for turning on his alarm. Then he hit send. He added, I love you, Kara. And hit send again. He waited, hoping she would respond as quickly as she usually did, but she left him on read. He sighed.

He was about to put his phone down, then thought better of it. He looked up the florist he used to send Kara flowers for her birthday. He placed an order for immediate delivery. On the card, he wrote Kara, I love you. Please talk to me. He clicked on confirm before he could add anything else.

Finn got the notification when the flowers had been delivered. He picked up his phone every other minute, hoping for something, anything from Kara. He sent her a text, "Hope your day is ok." He was left on read, again. He tried to focus on work to calm his frayed nerves. School started the next day with students on a half-day schedule. He had inspections to do.

The only thing he could think about was Kara. One of his guys Ryan, had to ask him a question three times before Finn even heard what he was being asked. He still hadn't answered his family. He kept looking at his phone, hoping for something from Kara, and with every text he got that wasn't her, he got more annoyed.

He sat in his office, trying to concentrate on work but couldn't. His phone kept vibrating from his family texting him. He read through the texts, most of them pleading with him to answer. He began to feel bad. He was as silent to them as Kara was to him. If he hated the feeling of Kara's silence, he knew his family hated his. He decided to send one text to the family text.

Everyone: I'm sorry I haven't answered. Kara's so hurt, she's not talking to me, and I don't blame her. I can't talk to anyone because I can't handle anything else until I get things straightened out with her. Just give me some time.

He tossed his phone onto his desk and stared out his office window. He knew his family was just as upset as he was about what happened. His sister Beverly had even called him to apologize, but he let it go to voice mail. He was still so angry with Jim that he was afraid that he'd say something extremely hurtful to his sister if he'd answer. He turned and looked at the clock on the wall. Time for another inspection.

When Finn pulled up next to the house after work. Kara wasn't home. She hadn't responded all day. Not a text. Not a call. He sat in his truck for a moment, crushed under the weight of disappointment. He gripped the steering wheel with both hands and leaned his head against his hands. Closing his eyes, he tried to suppress the urge to vomit.

He waited a few moments before he got out of the truck and walked up the path to the house. He walked in and closed the door behind him. He thought he smelled her perfume lingering in the air. He looked around for some sign she'd been home, but everything looked as it did when he'd left that morning.

He leaned back against the door and closed his eyes. He felt like he was suffering for something he didn't do yet was wholly responsible for. The worst of it was just how badly he missed her. The kiss in the morning she gave him when she left for work started his day. The texts from her telling him random things she found funny. Coming home to her. Seeing her. Touching her. He felt like he was locked in a dark room with no light and no hope of escaping. Being without Kara was torture. He didn't know how to handle it. He sighed. He went up the stairs to his room.

He got undressed and put on a pair of shorts and a t-shirt. He needed something to do. If he sat here doing nothing but missing her, he would go insane. He walked out of the bedroom and into the laundry room. He grabbed the cleaning supplies and decided to clean the house. He took his phone out of his pocket and put on a playlist. Some music might help get him out of his head while he cleaned. He went from room to room. Starting in the kitchen, he wiped down the counters. Emptied the dishwasher. Put the few dishes in the sink in the dishwasher. Cleaned off the table. Swept and mopped the floor. If nothing else, he got it cleaned up for the cabinets being installed the next day.

He went into the second bathroom, cleaned and wiped down everything, and put out fresh towels. He dusted the dressers and cleaned the mirrors in the bedrooms. He hesitated outside of Kara's room. When he walked in, he took a deep breath. He closed his eyes, feeling the longing for her sweep over him.

After a few moments, he opened his eyes and started dusting. He changed the sheets and remade the bed. He held onto her pillow a little longer than he should have because it smelled like her. He cleaned the mirror and arranged the things on her vanity. He picked up the globe trinket box he'd given her for her birthday and sighed. He went into the bathroom next. When he was done cleaning the bathroom, he started a load of towels. He walked into the kitchen and looked at the clock. It was almost 8:30. He picked up his phone from where he'd left it by the speaker on the counter. He had new messages, just none from Kara.

By the next morning, Finn was wretched. Kara hadn't come home. He hadn't seen or talked to her since Monday. He texted her and left her messages. None of them were answered. He was tired because he had to be at work at five in the morning since it was the first day of school. Not that it mattered, he hadn't slept well anyway. He thought cleaning the house would tire him out so he could sleep. It did tire him out, but he still couldn't sleep.

He missed her so much, he felt like huge chunks of him were missing. He was trying to function without them, but he couldn't. It frustrated him and made him angry. As he got ready for work, his anger kept growing. He knew Kara was probably at Charlie's last night. He knew she had to come home today because the cabinets and countertops were being installed. He'd sent flowers to the house to be delivered after one. Hoping she would be home by then.

He hated her silence. If she would have yelled, screamed, cursed, or even thrown things at him, he could handle it. But silence, fuck. He didn't know how to fight silence.

Finn made his rounds through the school. He was trying to concentrate on making sure everything was functioning. When he was done his rounds, he would hide in his office until it was time for the next check on the building. He felt the vibration notification of his phone. Mike texted him.

Mike: Have you heard from Kara yet?

Finn: No.

Mike: Shit. Really?

Finn: Yes.

Mike: Are you ok?

Finn: No.

Finn put his phone on his desk and looked out the window of his office. Thoughts of losing Kara pouring into his mind. He leaned back in his chair and rubbed his eyes, hoping the action would force out some of the thoughts. He couldn't think about losing her yet.

Finn managed to get through his day. Fortunately, he got to leave earlier because he came in early. He drove home, and when he pulled up to the house and saw Kara's car, he was filled with relief. He took a deep breath and sent up a thank you to heaven before getting out of the truck.

The relief he felt was quickly being replaced by anxiety. What would happen when he walked into the house? What if she didn't talk to him?

What if she said she didn't want to be with him anymore? Finn tried to push the thoughts away as hard as he could. Nothing mattered as long as she was there. He just needed to see her, then he could worry about everything else as it happened.

He stood at the door, trying to calm his breathing before he went into the house. He reached out his hand and clutched the doorknob. He sent up a prayer to the universe that everything would be ok once he walked into the house. He opened the door and stepped inside the house, shutting the door behind him.

Kara was standing on the other side of the door. Finn's eyes drank in all of her. He wanted to scoop her up in his arms, but he hesitated. He looked into her eyes, and when she met his gaze, everything else faded away. She gave him a small smile.

"I'm sorry, Finn," she said meekly. She was wringing her hands in front of her. She looked so fragile. Finn wanted to fall her feet and beg for her forgiveness.

"I know I punished you because I was hurt," she said quietly. "I know what happened wasn't your fault, but I couldn't help it. I walked outside, and everyone was yelling. You were lunging at Jim, and it scared me. I felt overwhelmed," she hesitated.

"I felt like it was all my fault, and I couldn't handle it. So I shut you out because that's what I always do. And it was the wrong thing to do. I should have at least tried to talk to you about what happened." She took a deep breath and looked up, blinking back tears, then met his eye again.

"If you could please forgive me for pushing you away. I promise to work on not shutting you out when I get mad or upset." She ran her hands through her hair. Tears were trickling down her cheeks. She sighed.

"I love you, Finn. I'm sorry I shut you out. I'll try to be better, I promise," she looked down, sniffling.

Finn walked over to her. Kara looked up at him. He pulled her into his arms and kissed her. He didn't hear anything after she said I love you. Nothing else she said mattered. All Finn could do was savor the feeling of her being in his arms. How it felt to feel her mouth on his and her body pressed against his. He'd missed her so much. He'd been left hollow without her.

Finn sent up a silent thanks to the universe for answering his prayer and promised he would do whatever it took to make it up to Kara.

CHAPTER 21

⟨❦⟩

Kara sat in an empty conference room near her desk. She was holding the bridge of her nose, hoping to keep her head from exploding. Maybe if she squeezed tight enough, her head wouldn't split in two.

"Carolina, are you listening to me?" Anthony yelled into the phone.

"Yes, Anthony," she sighed wearily.

"I want to sell the house. I need the money. Pauline needs to,"

"Who's Pauline again?"

"She's my fucking girlfriend, damn it," he yelled. It was so loud Kara held the phone away from her ear. "She needs an operation and,"

"Let me stop you there," Kara said. "Anthony, you can't just sell the house. I'd have to agree, and then Matt owns eighteen percent of it according to Mom's will."

"It's my fucking house," he bellowed.

"No, Anthony, it's not," she said calmly. "You own forty-two percent of it. I own forty percent, and I'm not selling." She leaned over in the chair, resting her arms on her knees. "You're going to have to figure something else out."

Squeezing the bridge of her nose wasn't working. The only thing it was doing was giving her a headache.

"So what the hell am I supposed to do with forty-two percent of a house," he shouted. "What kind of stupid shit is that?"

"Anthony," Kara said, sighing deeply. "You're a grown fucking man. Get your shit together." She hissed into the phone. "Mom left the house to both of us. If you didn't want it, you should have said something six fucking months ago. I told you to sell the house then, and you said you didn't want to." Kara's voice was getting louder. She tried to control her temper because she was at work, but Anthony pushed her too far.

"Now, because whoever your fucking at the moment gives you a sob story, you're ready to get rid of the house. You always pull the same fucking shit. It's old. It's tired. And mom and dad aren't here to save your sorry fucking ass." Kara's heart was pounding. She took deep breaths, trying to calm herself down. Her mind was racing.

"You know what, fuck it. You want to sell your percentage of the house, fine. I'll buy you out, and then I never. And let me make this perfectly fucking clear, so you don't get it twisted. I never want to talk to you, hear from you, or see you ever fucking again. I'm done with you and your shit. I'll have the lawyer send you the paperwork." She hit end on the phone.

Kara buried her head in her hands. No one ever made her as mad as her family did. Anthony was such a fucking asshole. She was seething.

"I don't have the fucking patience for this shit," she muttered to herself. She took a deep breath, trying to calm herself down. She needed to make phone calls and figure out what the hell she was going to do. She'd spent thousands of dollars renovating the house. How was she going to have the money to buy it?

Kara pulled into the driveway and shut the car off. It had been two days since Anthony called her, and she was still enraged. She grabbed her purse and got out of the car. There was a crispness in the autumn air. Kara shivered after being in the warmth of the car. She looked up at the house as she shut the car door.

Finn convinced her to buy some mums to decorate the house. Purple, yellow, and orange adding some much-needed color to the house. She thought about adding pumpkins and a hay bale to really decorate for fall.

She sighed as she walked up the path into the house. She walked in, closing the door behind her, and looked around. The living room was completely changed. The focal point of the room was the fireplace. She had converted it to gas and altered the mantle. A flat-screen tv hung above it. The wires were hidden cleverly in the wall. Ceiling fans were added, and Kara and Finn installed hardwood floors. She bought a new sectional with an ottoman and a new coffee table and end tables. The walls were a pale yellow to brighten the room.

The only thing she'd kept was the table by the door. She set her keys on the table and set her purse down. She walked into the living room and sat down on the couch. She leaned her head back and closed her eyes. For the last couple of days, her mind had been racing. Thoughts flying in every direction. She'd called the family lawyer who handled her mom's estate and scheduled a meeting with him.

She'd spent months and thousands of dollars renovating the house. Starting from the top and working her way down room by room. Although her plan at the beginning was to renovate to sell the house. Her plans changed along the way. She'd met Finn, and he changed her plans. Finn made the house feel more like home. Their home. That Anthony could once again change her life on a whim made her blood boil.

Kara took a deep breath and tried to calm down. Her thoughts buzzing in her head like angry wasps. She felt like things were spiraling out of control, and she wasn't sure why. The truth is her life always felt out of her control. She always felt like things happened, and she always had to react to them. It was worse before her mother died. She'd taken a bad situation and tried to make something out of it. Her mother left the house to her and Anthony. Knowing fully well, Anthony would go, and Kara would have to take care of everything. She wasn't surprised by the decision. Lottie knew Kara would pay the taxes and maintain the house. Because Kara did everything.

Kara hadn't thought Anthony would try to sell the house after being so against it months ago. That's where she was wrong. She should have known as soon as some chick Anthony was sleeping with told him a sob story, he would change his mind. It had happened too many times before. Today it was Pauline. Six months ago, it was Deedee. It was Niecie a year ago. They were all the same, and all of them had a story.

Kara did talk to Matt, just to ask him what his thoughts were. He didn't care as long as he had a place to come home to. Matt was simple. He also had the luxury of having two separate houses to go to. So if it was this one or his father's, he would always have a place to call home. Kara also knew if she didn't buy Antony out now, he would just pull the same shit again. Except it wouldn't be Pauline, it would be some other faceless woman she would never meet. The woman would need the money, and only Anthony would be able to save her. Because he would always try to save them but couldn't save himself.

Too many people had the ability to alter her life without giving a fuck about her feelings. Kara was going to have to take her power back.

Kara was in the pre-sleep state when she heard Finn come into the house. She didn't open her eyes since she was barely awake. She heard him put his keys on the table and waited as he walked up behind her and bent to kiss her forehead.

"Hey," he whispered as her eyes fluttered open.

"Hey," she said sleepily.

"You ok?" He gently brushed the hair away from her eyes.

"No," she said, shaking her head.

"Do you want to talk about it?"

"Not really."

"Kara," he smiled at her. Gently caressing her face. Kara looked up at him. Sometimes when she looked at him, she still couldn't believe he was there. He hadn't run away.

"What?" she said, smiling up at him. "I'd rather run away and say the hell with everything."

"How about we compromise?"

Kara furrowed her brow. "What does that mean?"

"Get changed. And put on something warm. I'm going to hop in a quick shower, and we'll go."

"Go where?" Kara asked.

Finn bent over and kissed her. "Get changed," smiling as he walked up the stairs.

"Where are we going?" Kara called out after him. Finn just laughed and kept going.

Kara opened one of the two bottles of water Finn grabbed before they left the house. They had been driving for forty-five minutes. When she asked Finn where they were going, he just smiled at her, told her to relax and enjoy the ride. She looked out the window, then looked over at him.

Finn had his blonde hair pulled back with a hair tie. He was wearing a long-sleeve t-shirt and a sweat jacket. The sleeves of both pushed up his forearms.

Kara looked at his profile while he paid attention to the road. "He's so hot." she thought to herself smiling. Finn looked over at her, took her hand, and smiled. Kara liked how he always reached for her. Like he needed to touch her. Finn was affectionate without being clingy. He was attentive to her. He paid attention to her. Finn made her feel loved.

In the short time, she'd known him, Finn had changed her life. Not only had he helped her renovate the house, but he also allowed her to be herself. Something no one else, other than her best friend Charlie, ever had. He had put up with so much because of her. She wondered if she actually deserved him. Finn looked at her, brought her hand to his lips, and placed a gentle kiss on it. "I don't think I do deserve him," she thought to herself, smiling at him.

Kara looked out the window. Thoughts of the house and now worries about Finn invaded her mind. What if she can't buy the house. What would it mean for her and Finn? Could their relationship take another obstacle? Would Finn finally get sick of all of her drama and leave. Was love enough?

Finn pulled up on a side street in front of a church.

"Where are we?" Kara asked.

"Longport," Finn said as he turned off the car.

They got out of the car, and Kara saw the sign in front of the church. The Church of the Redeemer.

"Why are we in Longport, and why are we at a church?" she asked as Finn took her hand in his leading her to a courtyard.

"For this," he said eagerly.

In the courtyard was a labyrinth painted on the concrete. Kara looked at Finn, confused.

"Come here," Finn led Kara to the sign at the beginning of the labyrinth.

"Walk in peace, knowing that God walks with you. And leave in peace knowing that God leaves with you."

Finn took Kara's hands in his and led her to the beginning of the labyrinth.

"Here," he said, gently guiding her in front of him. "Walk in front of me and tell me everything that's bothering you."

"How do you know about this place?" Kara asked, astonished.

"I used to come here a lot in college. Whenever I needed someplace quiet to think, I came here. Walking the labyrinth helps clear my mind."

Kara turned around and stood in front of Finn. She reached behind her and took Finn's hands in hers. She started walking the labyrinth.

"Well," She started slowly. "I'm mad at my brother because once again, his actions are disrupting my life. I'm mad because I've spent thousands of dollars renovating the house, and now he wants to take it away from me. When I wanted him to sell it in the beginning, He refused to do it. Now because he's fucking some chick, I have to drop everything and do what he wants." She paused, taking a deep breath before continuing. Looking down to make sure she was still following the path.

"I know at first I wanted to renovate the house to sell it. But things changed. Now I have to figure out what to do so I don't lose all the money I've invested into it. I'm not sure how I'm going to be able to buy the house from Anthony."

"Why not?" Finn asked.

"Because I pretty much sunk all of my savings into the house, so I wouldn't have to take out a loan. I still have some money, but I'm not sure if it's going to be enough. And if I get a new inspection, the house's estimate will skyrocket because of all the work I've done. I could get screwed."

"Maybe not," Finn said. "All you need is the money to buy Anthony out.

229

You won't have to buy yourself out."

"That's true, I guess. But, if I buy him out, it will wipe out the rest of my savings and part or all of my retirement. I won't have enough money to finish the downstairs. At least not for a little while. And what about the outside. I wanted to replace the windows, and I still need to get a new roof."

Finn interrupted her. "We don't need a new roof right now. And even the windows can wait. The majority of the house is done. And I'm sure we can do something with the downstairs. Maybe not everything you wanted to do, but something. Besides, it's getting colder. We wouldn't be able to do much outside anyway."

Kara noticed Finn said "We" and that led her to another problem.

"If I'm not going to be able to finish renovating the house, then what happens to us?" she asked.

"What do you mean?"

Kara stopped walking and turned to face Finn.

"I mean," she said, looking up at him. "If we're not remodeling the house, which was the point, then what happens to us." Kara ran her hands through her hair. "Or rather, where does our relationship, if that's what it is, go from here?"

Finn smiled at her, "Is this the 'defining our relationship' talk?"

"Well," Kara searched Finn's eyes. "I guess. I don't know. Maybe."

Finn laughed. "I guess?" He shook his head. "Kara, what are your intentions with me?"

Kara punched his arm lightly. "Stop. You know what I mean." She looked down and sighed.

Finn reached for her hands again. "Kara, I love you. And we can be whatever you want us to be. If you want me to be your boyfriend, your husband, your love slave. All of the above," he laughed. "I'll be whatever you want, as long as I get to be with you. I don't care what you call me." Finn looked at her, forcing her to meet his gaze.

"Kara, all I know is I love you." He leaned down and kissed her forehead. "You're mine, and I'm definitely yours," he smiled at her. "You've basically ruined me for anyone else."

"I don't know how," she whispered distractedly. "Wait," she stopped. "Did you say, husband?"

Finn grinned at her, "I was trying to sneak it past you."

"What?" She asked. "Why?"

"Because," he said, looking at her intently. "I wasn't sure it's what you wanted or not."

Kara looked into Finn's eyes. "You'd marry me? Really? After all, I've put you through?"

"Tomorrow," he said quickly, then looked at her questioningly. "What do you mean, 'all that I've put you through?' What have you put me through?"

"Where should I start? I'm a depressed, anxious mess. I'm old. I'm not the healthiest person in the world. I caused you to fight with your family, and last but not least, I don't handle conflict well and have a tendency to shut you out. Not to mention, I'm pretty sure you deserve more than I can give you."

"Are you serious?" Finn shook his head. "I swear, you are so oblivious for someone so smart." Finn pulled her into his arms. "First, just because you have anxiety and depression doesn't make you a mess. It makes you strong because it's something you have to fight every day. I think you're brave," he whispered.

"Second, you're not old. Just because you feel something doesn't make it true. Third. You didn't cause me to fight with my family. My brother-in-law is an alcoholic and an asshole. No one was happy about what happened on Labor Day. But not because of you."

Kara knew Finn was right about his family. The Saturday afterward, Mike came over to the house with flowers for Kara. He apologized and then told her his parents felt so bad about what happened they wanted to make it up to her. Mike told her, regardless of anything else, he would always be there for her. Then Mike gave her a big hug. Which caused Finn to smile and scowl at the same time. Kara laughed at that.

Both of Finn's sisters also called her to apologize. The only one who didn't was Jim. Beverly said he felt terrible, but Kara knew feeling bad about something was utterly different than apologizing and accepting responsibility for your behavior.

Kara looked down, thinking about everything Finn said. He lifted her chin to meet his gaze.

"Kara, I love my family, but if I had to make a choice, I'd choose you."

Kara shook her head. "Don't say that," she said earnestly.

"Why not?"

"Because I would never ask you to choose between your family and me. No one should have to make that decision. Someone did that to me, and it's a horrible thing to do to someone you love."

"Ok. I won't say that. But you don't have to worry because no one is asking me to choose." Finn sighed. "The point is my family isn't an issue between us." Finn held her tighter in his arms. "Kara, I love you. I know it's hard for you to open up when your hurt. It's hard for everyone. And regardless of what you think I deserve, you're exactly what I need," he said assuredly.

"You always have been, from the moment I met you. You took me in when I didn't have a place of my own. You opened your home and your heart to me. I'd marry you tomorrow. Or whenever you tell me. Just tell me when and where I'll be there."

Kara leaned into his arms, taking a deep breath. Finn would marry her. She still wasn't sure she could believe it. Not because of him, but because of her. She had to question people's supposed love for her, so many times she wasn't used to someone's actions actually matching their words. It made her happy. After all, it was Finn and sad because it wasn't until he'd come into her life that she realized how much she'd been lacking.

Kara looked at Finn. "Let's start with boyfriend, and we'll go from there."

Finn leaned down and kissed her. Kara pressed against him and kissed him back. Finn broke the kiss.

"Ok," he whispered. "You can be my girlfriend." He smiled at her. "We'll work up to wife." He kissed her again. So deeply, Kara almost forgot they were standing in the courtyard of a church. She pulled away from him and stepped out of his embrace.

"We're at a church," she laughed. She took his hand and started walking the labyrinth again.

"Is there anything else you wanted to talk about? We talked about the house, and we've talked about us. Is there something else?" Finn asked.

Kara thought about everything going on in her life. Matt was fine. She'd talked to him almost every day. He was happy at school. Charlie was ok. She'd talked to her this morning. Chris and the McNulty's were ok. Teresa texted her, Katie was getting into everything as toddlers do. The only other thing bothering her was work, and Kara wasn't quite ready to deal with that yet.

Kara shook her head. "No. I think that's enough for the moment."

"Good," Finn said. "We've reached the end. Now we can walk back, and I'll lead."

Kara smiled at him as they turned around. Finn standing in front of her, her hands in his. She smiled at the irony of Finn leading her out of the labyrinth. Just like he led her out of her head so many times before.

CHAPTER 22

After leaving the labyrinth, Finn took Kara to Neighbors. They sat at the bar, ate burgers, and talked to Randy. Kara liked Randy. She knew he was a good guy. He told her stories about Finn working in the bar to pay for school. Which always made her laugh. Today he was telling Finn about Meera.

A divorced, single mother born in India but came to the US for school and met her ex-husband. Randy met Meera because she is the boy's Dentist. Nik asked Randy to take the boys to their appointment because she had to work. Randy agreed, and when he met Meera, they hit it off right away. They'd only been seeing each other for about two weeks, but Randy was already hooked.

On their way home, Finn told Kara about Randy's ex-girlfriend Jewell. Kara shook her head as she listened to all the drama Jewell caused. He'd mentioned Jewell before, and Kara was always amazed Randy put up with so much. She was happy Randy was finally moving on.

As they got home and climbed into bed, Kara leaned over and gave Finn a tender kiss on the lips.

"Thank you for taking me to Longport today," she whispered.

"You're welcome," Finn said, smiling at her.

Kara kissed him, enjoying his taste. She climbed on top of him, and Finn held her against him. She kissed down his neck, his chest, sliding down his stomach. Finn moaned, reaching for her, and Kara swatted his hand away, laughing. When Finn slept with her, he always went to bed naked. Kara let her hands gently caress his bare torso. She loved his body. The way he felt. Breathing in his smell. She kissed the head of his cock, and Finn moaned. She gently nudged him to sit up, which he did, as she deeply kissed and licked his length. She wrapped her fingers around him and tenderly took him into her mouth.

Kara sucked slowly, moving her lips up and down, gliding down his length. Finn's breathing becoming hoarse. Kara let her tongue stroke him, wrapping her fingers around him, setting the slightest rhythm. Finn's hips thrusting to match the rhythm. Finn allowing Kara to envelop him in her mouth. Kara relishing the taste of him. The feel of him in her mouth. The way he glided over her tongue.

"Kara, fuck," Finn said in a breathy moan.

Kara took her mouth off of him and looked up at him. Her fingers still moving up and down his cock. Her thumb lightly caressing the head of his cock. Finn grabbed her and pulled her up. She laughed at his eagerness. He kissed her deeply as his hands gripped her waist and positioned him over his cock. She reached and guided him into her. Both of them moaning into each other's mouths.

She leaned back, breaking the kiss. Finn kissing her neck and her chest, and she wrapped her legs around him. Rocking her hips against him. She arched her back, each thrust of their combined movements causing him to go deeper inside of her. "Finn," she cried out breathlessly as she felt her orgasm come. She shuddered as the wave overtook her. Feeling her body clench around him as he pulsed, coming forcibly into her. Grunting her name. She kissed him, both of them breathing heavily into each other's mouth. Holding each other tightly.

Kara could feel Finn's breathless, "I love you" as they were falling asleep. She whispered, "I love you too," as she fell asleep in his arms.

The problem Kara had she hadn't mentioned to Finn while they were at the labyrinth.

Work.

She didn't mention it because she still wasn't sure what to think about it. Kara's boss was misogynistic. If that wasn't bad enough, he was also slightly racist. He would say micro-aggressive things about her in such a way if she called him out on it, he told her, she was too sensitive. Or taking it too personally. Although Kara had gotten used to her boss's behavior, the past couple of weeks had been worse.

The CEO wanted to do an employee engagement project. Kara created three proposals and presented them to the executive team and her boss. During the presentation, her boss repeatedly disregarded what she had to say. Despite that, the CEO was pleased with Kara's idea and put her in charge of the proposal. She later learned, the CEO also talked with her boss and reprimanded his behavior. At first, it actually made her boss change his behavior for a little while, but it soon reverted back. Now it was back with a vengeance.

The EEP (Employee Engagement Program), as it was called, was going fantastically well. Employee morale was up. Productivity increased, and the sales team was achieving their goals. The CEO was thrilled. Everyone was happy except her boss, who was quietly making Kara's life miserable.

Microaggressions were in every comment he made to her. In their one-on-one meetings, he would tell her she wasn't engaged enough during staff meetings. When she spoke up, he would sigh loudly and roll his eyes. He would send her an email, then when she didn't respond fast enough, he said she wasn't following the communications procedure. She wrote the damn procedure. She knew it better than he did. It was becoming too much. But who do you go to when you're the department that people are supposed to go to?

Two weeks after the labyrinth trip, Kara finally broke down and talked to Finn about it. She'd come home after a particularly brutal day. She sat at the kitchen island eating out of a pint of ice cream. She hadn't changed when she got home. She came in, walked to the kitchen, and needed chocolate. Anything to boost the serotonin levels. Thankfully, when she went to work at the store the weekend before, chocolate fudge brownie was on sale. She hid it in the freezer for emergencies. Finn came in from work and walked up the stairs to the kitchen. He walked up to her and leaned in to give her a kiss.

"Hey," he said.

"Hey," she said, eating a spoon full of ice cream.

"You ok?" His hand caressing her lightly on her back.

"No."

"What's wrong?"

"Just work," she said, licking the spoon. "But there's not much I can do about it other than look for another job, and I don't feel like starting over again." Kara got another spoonful of ice cream.

"What happened?" He sat down on the stool next to her. He leaned over and looked at the ice cream container and took the spoon from her. Kara was about to yell at him, but he just took the spoon so he could eat some of her ice cream.

"My boss is an asshole." Kara sighed. "He's sexist, racist, and disrespectful. And the past couple of weeks, it's just gotten worse." She took the spoon back from Finn and scooped out more ice cream.

"Is there anyone you can talk to?" He took the spoon from her to get more ice cream.

"No. You can't really go to HR about HR. Unless I go to the CEO, which will just cause more problems, I'm just going to have to get used to it."

"Kara, why would you want to get used to something like that?"

Kara looked at him. "Finn, I'm a middle-aged Black woman. I'm the only person of color on my team. If I complain, I'm the "Angry Black Woman." If I get annoyed, I'm aggressive. If I ignore it, then I'm cold, distant, and unresponsive. I have no choice," she sighed. "Unless I want to find another job, which I don't," she said, shaking her head. "I have to get used to it. It's not the first time, and it's not going to be the last time. I just have to stay under the radar and do my job because no matter what I do, I'm going to be wrong." Kara sighed. "It is what it is."

"There has to be some way of fixing it?" Finn said. Kara looked at Finn. She saw the concern in his eyes.

"Finn," she said quietly. "I know you like to fix things. That's what you do. If something is broken or damaged or doesn't work," she put her hand on his knee. "Your first instinct is to fix it. But somethings just can't be fixed. You can't fix people."

"I don't care about people. I care about you."

Kara took her hand off of Finn's knee and picked up the spoon. "You can't fix me either."

"Kara," Finn said sharply, causing her to turn to face him. "You don't need to be fixed." He cupped her face in his hands. "You need to be loved. You need to be accepted. And you need to be cared for. All the time, and by me. But you never needed to be fixed." Finn looking into her eyes intently. "I need you to understand that, ok?"

"Ok," Kara whispered.

Finn lowered his hands from her face. "Maybe it's time to think about doing something else. Maybe going into a different field."

Kara shrugged her shoulders. "I don't know," she sighed. "I like my job. I just hate my boss. I don't even know what else I could do."

"If your boss isn't going to support you and is trying to make you miserable, I think you should at least think about looking for another job. You shouldn't stay where you aren't appreciated or valued."

Kara nodded. She knew Finn was right. "I'll think about it. I mean, I've been with the company for over ten years. I have a lot of history there. I have a lot of friends there."

"Yeah, but Kara, you owe it to yourself to be loyal to you, not a company, not history, or the people you work with. Be loyal to yourself first."

Kara sat across from her lawyer and the closing agent in her lawyer's office's conference room. She signed where all the post-it arrows were placed for her to sign. She felt like she was signing her life away. This was her first time buying a house. When she was married to Chris, they'd always rented because they didn't make enough money to buy a house when they started out. Then Matt came along. They needed a bigger place, but renting just seemed more manageable. Especially when you thought about possible repairs.

Anthony and Matt were on the conference call. She hadn't talked to Anthony since he told her he wanted to sell the house. She had her lawyer call him to let him know she was going to buy him out. He'd called her afterward, but Kara let it go to voicemail. After everything he'd put her through while they were growing up and during her life, this was the final straw. Kara was done. She wasn't going to let him disrupt her life anymore. Matt was there merely as someone who would have an interest in the property because Kara kept his name on the deed. Kara made sure the closing took place in between classes for him. He'd been on the call, quietly listening to the explanations from the lawyer and the closing agent. Kara wondered if he paid attention.

Kara signed and dated the last page. She picked up all the papers, tapped them on the table to straighten them, and handed them to the closing agent.

"When will I get the money?" Anthony asked. Kara rolled her eyes and shook her head. That's all that mattered to him.

"Within two business days," the closing agent said. She was a Black woman with silver streaks in her black twists. She was older than Kara and was wearing a stylish, elegant tailored suit. Kara wondered if she was a lawyer too or just worked with them.

"Mom?" Matt said. "Class starts in five minutes. Do I have to do anything else, or can I go?"

Kara looked at her lawyer and the closing agent. Both of them shook their heads no.

"No, honey. You can go. I'll call you later. I love you."

"Ok. I'll talk to you later. Love you too. Bye," Matt said before the low click of his dropping off the line.

"What else do I have to do?" Anthony bellowed. Wherever he was, it was loud. Kara could hear people in the background. It also sounded like someone was watching tv at full volume.

"Anthony," her lawyer said. He was Kara's age, maybe a little older. With light brown hair graying slightly at the temple. He wore glasses and a bow tie with his suit. Although Kara's family had used the firm for years, he was relatively new. New meaning he'd been with the firm for less than twenty-five years.

"You should know, you now have no legal entitlement to the house, and your name will be removed from the title," he said solemnly.

"I know," Anthony said condescendingly.

"Then this completes your involvement with the remaining provisions of your mother's estate. There will be nothing further to be paid out to you. Do you understand?"

Anthony didn't respond right away. Then he asked, "So if Kara sells the house?"

"She would be entitled to all of the proceeds of the sale. You aren't entitled to anything."

Anthony was silent.

"Ok, Kara," the closing agent said. "I just need the down payment, the first mortgage payment, and the costs and fees for the closing." She had reviewed all of the documents to make sure everything was in order. Kara handed the woman the cashier's check, wincing slightly as she handed it over. "There goes my retirement," she thought to herself. It wasn't all of it, but a lot of it. It would take her years to pay it all back. The closing agent took the check and clipped it to the paperwork.

"Anthony, we're done here. You should have the funds wired to your account within two business days. If there's any problem with your bank receiving the funds, just give us a call." The closing agent said.

"Ok, I'm done?" Anthony asked.

"Yes, Anthony. We're done," Kara said. There was a low click as Anthony dropped off the line.

"I'll send all the documents over to the mortgage company, and you should receive your first mortgage statement within the next thirty days. Your first payment to the mortgage company will be due December first. You'll get all of the information when they send you the statement, though." The closing agent said as she stood up from the table.

"Ok. Thank you." Kara said.

"You're welcome. If you have any questions, I'll leave you my business card with your copies of all the documents. Congratulations on the purchase of your home." She placed all the documents in a manila folder. "I'll be right back with copies of your documents." She left the room.

"I'll close out all of the outstanding items with your mother's estate. I'll call you when it's ready." The lawyer said, standing up from the table. Kara stood up too, and he waved his hand, motioning her to sit down. "You're welcome to wait here for your copies. It's going to take a few minutes for her to come back with them. While you're waiting, would you like me to send in some bottled water for you?"

"Yes, please," Kara said. "That would be great."

"No problem. I'll have it brought right into you." He leaned over and extended his hand. Kara shook it.

"Thank you for all your help with this. I appreciate it," she said, letting go of his hand.

"My pleasure," he said, walking towards the door. "I'll be in touch." He stepped out of the conference room, shutting the door noiselessly behind him.

Kara sat back in her chair, looking out the window. Waiting for the bottle of water and her mortgage documents.

Kara walked out into the Autumn sunshine and waited for her glasses to adjust to the sunlight. The best thing about having transitional lenses is she didn't have to carry around separate sunglasses. She crossed the parking lot and found her car. Getting in and sliding her portfolio onto the passenger seat. She turned on the car and took her cell phone out to call Finn while she waited for the car to warm up.

"Hey," she said brightly into the phone when he answered.

"Hey there yourself, beautiful," Finn said cheerily. "How did it go?"

Kara smiled, "Ah. I think it went ok. I was in there for two hours. The Vice President seemed to like me, and then I had to meet with the Sr. Vice President too."

"What's the place like?"

"It's a bigger company. There are over five hundred employees. It's also a call center. They handle calls for help desk requests. Other companies outsource their IT requests to them, and their agents take the calls. There would be a lot of different departments I would have to work with. But, it would be a promotion, more money, and more work. I would also get more PTO time. So there's a lot I will have to consider if I decide to take the offer." Kara ran her hands through her hair. "The people seem nice though, and I would have a team of five working under me."

"Did they tell you how long you would have to wait to hear from them?"

"The Sr. Vice President said I should know within a week because, of course, there are other candidates, the usual spiel."

"I'm sure you got it. How could anyone compete with you?" Finn said.

Kara laughed. "I'm sure the other people are just as qualified."

"But they aren't you. And you would be perfect for it. They are going to be lucky to hire you."

"I hope so. I still can't believe I did it."

"I can, and I'm proud of you. It's about time. You deserve to be appreciated and valued."

"Thank you," Kara said. "Well, it's over, so now I just have to wait."

"We should celebrate. How about we go out for dinner tonight. No matter what happens, we're going to celebrate."

"Celebrate, for what?"

"For the new job. For realizing how wonderful you are and going after what you deserve. And you do deserve it, Kara."

"Thanks, but we don't have to go out," Kara said uncertainly. "Yes, we do. It'll be my treat."

"Well, in that case, I'm in." Kara laughed. "I just bought a house. I won't have any money for the next thirty years. I'll have to eat ramen and hotdogs if I don't get this job."

"Don't worry. I'll make sure you don't have to eat ramen and hot dogs. Although, it's not like you don't eat ramen anyway."

"I know, but before it was by choice, now it's for necessity."

"I'll make sure you can keep eating ramen by choice," Finn said, laughing. "Speaking of ramen. Since you're going to feed me, can we get Chinese food when we go out tonight?"

"Whatever you'd like," he said. "But I have to go. I have to finish up my rounds. I'll call you later, though."

"Ok, I love you, Finn."

"I love you too. Bye."

"Bye." Kara hit the end button and put her phone in the cup holder of the car. She put her seat belt on and pulled out of the parking space to drive home. She had the rest of the day to do whatever she liked.

CHAPTER 23

Finn paced nervously at the entrance of the store. He pulled his phone out of his pocket for what seemed like the hundredth time. No new texts. No missed calls. He put it back in his pocket and ran his hands through his hair. Even though he had it in his typical man bun, it was getting long in the front. "Maybe I should get it cut?" he thought to himself. He rubbed his face. His beard, neatly trimmed, was getting long too. Maybe I should shave? He shook his head before finishing the thought.

"Calm down, she'll be here," he whispered to himself. He glanced around the store. It felt like everyone was staring at him. They weren't. He glanced outside the store window and finally saw who he was waiting for. Finn sighed and sent a thank you to the universe as a wave of relief washed over him.

"Finally," he muttered to himself. Finn opened the door for her as she walked into the store. She rushed in, looking apologetic.

"Sorry. I couldn't get the baby to go down for her nap, and then my mom took forever to get there." Charlie said as Finn leaned down to give her a hug.

"It's ok. I'm just glad you're here," he said reassuringly.

Charlie looked up at him smiling. "I'm glad you called me." She brushed her glossy brown curls from her face. "I'm happy to help you with this. Anything for Kara." Her brown eyes shining with excitement.

Finn smiled at her and ran his hands through his hair again. "I just want to get it right. I know she's not ready just yet. Besides, I want to talk to Matt first," he sighed loudly. "I just want to be ready, and when she's ready, I want to make sure it's the perfect one." He took a deep breath. His heart was pounding. He needed to calm down. His nerves were frazzled.

"Finn," Charlie said. "Don't worry. I promise I will help you find the perfect one for Kara. She'll love it."

Finn nodded. He took another deep breath and put his hands in his jean pockets.

"I know, I know."

They walked to the back of the store, past the long cases of watches, earrings, pendants, and other jewelry types. In the back of the store was a long case. A gentleman wearing a dark custom-tailored fitted suit was standing behind the case smiling at them. Finn noticed his cufflinks. They were gold with a diamond chip in them. Finn assumed he was the owner.

"Giovanni," Charlie said when they approached the counter. Giovanni walked around the counter and came out to give Charlie a slight hug and an air kiss.

"Charlie," Giovanni said. "I'm so glad you called me. I'm always happy to be of service to you."

Giovanni looked at Finn with a slight frown. "You know I wouldn't accept a last-minute appointment from just anyone."

"Giovanni," Charlie purred. "You know I wouldn't call you unless I needed something special." She turned toward Finn. "This gentleman is about to become my family," she looked back at Giovanni. "And you know, I only want the best for my family. How could I let him go to an inferior establishment? That would be leading him astray."

Finn noticed Giovanni straighten up when Charlie said Finn was going to be family. He watched Charlie in awe as she got Giovanni in line. Charlie was small, but she was tough. He knew he'd made the right decision to call her first before trying to do it on his own.

When Finn told Kara he would marry her whenever she said, he wasn't kidding. Although they had only been officially dating for a little over a month, the thought wouldn't leave his mind. He'd been thinking a lot about what he wanted. And what he wanted was to make Kara his. His wife, his future, his forever.

It should have scared Finn. Especially since he had hesitated so long with Shelly. But the thought of marrying Kara didn't scare him. In fact, he'd never felt more sure about anything in his life. Still, he waited for the fear, doubt, and questions to plague him. When after a month, nothing had appeared, he knew his heart was ready.

The only thing that did cause panic was picking the perfect ring. Kara liked simple classic pieces of jewelry. She wasn't flashy or showy. He wanted to get something that would blow her mind and still be something she would want to wear. He knew there was one other person who knew Kara as well as he did. He looked through Kara's phone one day while she was busy doing something else. He wrote down Charlie's number from Kara's contacts. Then he texted Charlie and asked for her help.

Charlie, of course, immediately agreed. She called him back and squealed into the phone, saying yes ten times. Charlie knew the perfect place to go. She just had to call in a favor. She texted Finn the info to meet her here. Now she was schmoozing Giovanni. Charlie turned to Finn as Giovanni went back behind the counter to the back room.

"Do you know what you're looking for?" she asked him. She leaned against the counter and looked at the bands in the case.

"No," Finn said honestly. "I just know I want her to love it."

"Don't worry about that," Charlie said, smiling at him. "She'll love it. I promise. Giovanni is the best jeweler in South Jersey." She looked at the case again and ran her manicured nail along the glass. "You may want to consider getting something that will match a wedding band."

Finn's eyes grew larger. Charlie looked up at him and laughed, brushing the hair from her eyes. "You should see your face," she smirked. "You look like a deer in the headlights. Calm down. You can buy rings that will match a wedding band, so she won't have to take the engagement ring off. It's just a set."

Finn let out a long breath. Charlie shook her head and laughed. "Stop looking so scared. We'll take care of it. Don't worry."

Finn sighed. "I'm just a little nervous because I really want her to be happy with it. I don't want to screw this up." Finn had picked out pieces of jewelry before, but nothing like this. In the past, when he went to a jewelry store, he just got whatever the salesperson said would look nice.

Giovanni came out of the back holding several long trays stacked up. He placed the trays onto the counter and set them down, side by side.

Finn looked at the trays, glancing at the rings to see if any of them caught his eye, and screamed Kara to him. Giovanni lifted the first tray and pointed out different rings, explaining the diamond cut, the carats, and clarity. Charlie looked at the tray and waved her hand. Giovanni nodded, put the tray down, and picked up the next one. Charlie looked at the tray, leaning her head on her hand. She tapped a perfectly manicured nail against the glass.

"Ummm," she said thoughtfully. "Giovanni, I'm thinking we should go more antique." She paused. "Definitely platinum. Maybe an emerald or princess cut," she murmured. "We should also make sure there is a matching wedding band."

Giovanni nodded. "Of course. I have just the thing you are looking for." He put the tray down and picked up the last tray. Finn saw it as soon as Giovanni lifted it up for them to see.

"What about that one?" Finn said, pointing to the ring.

Giovanni nodded his approval. "Excellent choice." He picked up the ring and held it up to the light. It sparkled, colors dancing in the light. It was a two-carat, emerald cut diamond set in a platinum band.

Charlie looked at Finn, smiling and grabbing his arm. "It's perfect." Finn returned her smile. Relief washing over him.

"Finn," Charlie's smile growing wider. "She's going to love it. It's beautiful."

"What about the size?" Finn asked. His brow furrowing.

Out of nowhere, Giovanni pulled out the ring sizer. "It's a six," he said.

"Perfect," Charlie said.

"What about a wedding band?" Finn said. Remembering what Charlie mentioned earlier. "Do you have something that will match the ring?"

Charlie smiled at Finn and placed a hand on his shoulder. "You paid attention."

Finn laughed. "You think I wouldn't." He shook his head slightly. "I told you I want this to be perfect. Kara deserves it."

Charlie looked at Finn, her eyes moistening. "She really does."

Giovanni nodded. "There is a matching band. It can be held for you, for when you're ready. The set includes bands for the bride and the groom."

Finn nodded. "Then that's the one. I'll take the ring and the matching band set."

"Very good," Giovanni said, nodding. "I'll get it ready for you."

Finn gave Charlie a hug when they stopped at her car.

"Thank you for helping me with this," he whispered. "I couldn't have done it without you."

Charlie hugged him back. "I told you anything for Kara," she smiled up at him. "It's a beautiful ring. She's going to love it."

Finn sighed. "I hope so. Now I just have to convince her."

Charlie laughed. "You will. Kara deserves this. She just doesn't know it yet."

"I know. That's what I'm trying to convince her of."

Charlie patted Finn's arm as she opened the car door. "It will take a little time, but don't worry. You will. I have faith." She smiled as she got in the car, and Finn shut the door for her. He waived as she backed out of the parking spot and drove away.

Finn gently held the small bag, smiling to himself, as he walked towards his truck. He had the day off because of the New Jersey Teacher's convention. He had a nice long weekend. He was on his own today, but Kara was taking Friday off. They were taking a weekend trip to Baltimore Inner Harbor.

They were staying at a Bed & Breakfast near the waterfront. Finn's plan for the weekend was to eat seafood, sleep, relax, and make love to Kara over and over again. And not necessarily in that order. He was especially looking forward to relaxing, which is something both of them needed. The past couple of weeks had been a roller coaster. Everything seemed to be happening all at the same time, and it somehow involved both of them.

Since buying the house, Anthony had been trying to reach Kara, and she wasn't having it. She'd been able to get a mortgage based on the appraisal she had done before renovating the house. Since she bought Antony out, she only had to give him his percentage of the house. He apparently thought he should have gotten more. She had to go back to the lawyer and have a letter sent to Anthony explaining the process. She finally had to tell him she was blocking him, and he wasn't her family anymore.

It didn't matter in the long run. Pauline took the majority of the money from Anthony. Not for an operation, she didn't need. She just used him. Now he was sorry about the whole thing, and Kara still wasn't letting him back in. Finn didn't blame her.

His brother Mike met someone. A Hispanic man named Carlos. Mike brought Carlos over to Kara's for lunch. Kara and Carlos got along immediately. It made Finn smile the way Kara and Carlos sat in the breakfast nook while Finn made dinner. Mike stood next to Finn, nervously glancing over at them. Finn liked Carlos and saw Mike really liked him too. Telling the family had been another story. Finn's parents, his sister Ellen and her boyfriend Steve had been fine. Jim acted like such an asshole, Finn's dad finally put his foot down and told Beverly Jim needs to get help or was no longer welcome in their house.

Beverly left the house crying. Apparently, she had told Jim enough was enough, and he needed to get help, or she was leaving him. When Finn called her a couple of days later, she was still trying to decide if she should stay in the house or move back to her parents.

Kara did get the job offer. When she went to turn in her resignation, it got back to the CEO, who called her into his office. When he asked why she was leaving, she told him. Everything. At first, the CEO was upset she hadn't come to him sooner. Then he fired Kara's boss and offered Kara a promotion with increased pay. He not only matched the offer from the other company but sweetened it with a bonus. Kara accepted it. She was happier at work but also busier. Sometimes it would be over an hour before she'd replied to Finn's text.

They both took off from their second jobs to get away for the weekend. Randy had, of course, agreed, but Neighbors had been busier lately. Not only was it football season, but the Eagles were on a winning streak. More people were coming to watch the game at the bar. Randy also was trying to spend more time with his girlfriend, Meera. Things were going really well between them. She came into the bar, and Finn met her. He liked her a lot. She was much better for Randy than Jewell had been.

Finn pulled into an empty parking spot in front of the Cherry Hill Mall entrance. No matter what time of day it was, it was always packed. The mall was decorated for Christmas, even though it was still eight weeks away. He got out of the truck and jogged across the street, trying not to get run over. The mall was full of moms with their kids and teenagers who were enjoying the break from school. Finn dodged people as he walked into the store.

He wanted to buy something nice for Kara since they were going away. He looked around the lingerie selection, hoping to find something she would find comfortable. He'd been doing her laundry for the past couple of weeks to memorize what size she wore. He was looking at a rack of lace nightgowns when he heard his name.

"Oh, My God. Finn, is that you?" A high-pitched squeaky voice called out to him.

Finn turned to see Kaitlyn walking towards him, waving frantically. Finn sighed and forced a smile onto his face. Kaitlyn was one of Shelly's friends. He hadn't seen her in years since she'd gotten married and moved into a bigger house. Shelly had been one of her bridesmaids, and Finn had to go to the wedding. It had been an overly expensive affair. Finn had to rent a tuxedo for the reception. He'd hated every minute of it.

"Kaitlyn," Finn said, startled. She walked up to him with a baby strapped to the front of her. She gave him a side hug and air kiss, trying not to squash the baby's face.

"How are you?" he said.

"Great, as you can see," she laughed, pointing to the baby. "How are you doing? I heard about you and Shelly."

Finn nodded. "Yeah," he said cautiously, "We broke up a little while ago." Finn ran his hands through his hair.

"I guess you've moved on if you're in here shopping," she said, giving him a wry smile.

"Uh yeah," Finn said, shifting his weight. "I am seeing someone else." The conversation was making him uncomfortable. He wasn't a fan of most of Shelly's friends, and Kaitlyn was one of his least favorites. He knew the minute she left, she would be on the phone calling everyone to tell them she ran into him.

"Is it anyone I know?" she asked, looking at Finn.

Finn shook his head. "Probably not." Finn looked around.

A salesgirl came over to them. "Can I help you find anything?"

"Yes, please," Finn said to her. He turned to Kaitlyn. "I have to go. I'm looking for something," he said to Kaitlyn. "It was good to see you." Turning to give her a half hug, being careful to miss the baby. He walked away from her to the salesgirl.

An hour later, Finn was on his way home with a shopping bag full of things for Kara. The salesgirl had saved him from having to keep talking to Kaitlyn, so he bought more than he needed to. She also had some excellent suggestions for things to buy for Kara. He couldn't wait to see Kara in them. Thoughts of Kara filled his head and sent desire right to his dick. It happened every time he thought about her.

He would have to go home and pack everything carefully so she wouldn't see it. He planned on surprising her with them when they were at the B&B. He still had some errands to run. He'd texted Kara to see if she needed him to pick up anything she may need. She texted him back with a list of small things and snacks. He laughed at the snack request.

When he finished with all of his errands, he pulled up to the house and took everything inside. He looked down at the bag with the rings in it. He wanted to give it to her as soon as he got it. He had to talk himself out of going to her office and proposing today. He smiled to himself. He wasn't sure how long he would be able to hold onto it without blurting it out he had it.

He cleaned up and looked in the fridge for something for dinner. Kara worked the night before and brought some stuff home. He decided to have chicken and put it in the refrigerator. He looked around the house. There wasn't much to do since he'd done some stuff before he went to meet Charlie. He went down to the living room and turned on the tv.

Kara coming into the house, woke Finn up. He'd fallen asleep on the couch. He sat up as she walked in the door, stretched, and got up to meet her at the door.

"Hey," he said, smiling at her.

"Hey," she said as she set her stuff down on the table by the door. She looked tired, he thought as he pulled her into his arms.

"Are you ok?" he asked, gently rubbing her back. He kissed her on the side of her head. Breathing in her jasmine scent.

"It was a really long day," she whispered into his chest. "I had a lot to do before taking off tomorrow anyway, and then an employee came in with a problem."

Finn hugged Kara tighter. "It's been a lot for you lately with the promotion and everything else."

"I know, but it will be ok," she said, stepping out of his arms.

She walked away from him, heading upstairs to change. Finn followed her upstairs. When he walked into the bedroom, Kara was sitting on the side of the bed, taking her heels off. She got up and walked over to the closet to put them away. He could hear her getting undressed in the closet, and she walked out wearing only her underwear.

Finn just looked at her. His eyes delighting in every curve. Her full breasts. She looked at him.

"What?" she asked as she reached around to unhook her bra.

"Nothing. I was just admiring you."

Kara huffed, "Really? Because I feel like crap."

Finn walked over to her for two reasons. One, he found it incredibly difficult to have Kara standing in front of him with nothing but underwear on and not touch her. Two, he wanted to hold her, partly because of reason number one and because she looked like she needed a hug.

"Why do you feel like crap?" he asked, wrapping his arms around her.

"It feels like nothing fits right, I'm tired, and I think I'm a little cranky. I probably need some chocolate," she said, leaning against him and letting him hold her. Then she looked up at him. "And if you ask me if I'm about to get my period, I swear to God, I'll punch you."

Finn looked down at her and smiled. "First, I would never say that because I know better. I grew up with sisters, remember?" he laughed. "Second, I think you're the sexiest woman ever. I love your body." He gently glided his hand down her back to her ass. He gave it a squeeze. Kara jumped and squealed, laughing.

"Your body feels like it was made for me. And I love when it's against mine." He nuzzled her neck. Kara leaned back and moaned. "And, if you're tired. We can take a nap. We don't have to do anything this weekend except relax," he whispered against her neck. He kissed her gently.

Kara looked up at him. "A nap would be fantastic."

"Ok, let's take a nap."

Finn let her go, so she could put her t-shirt and yoga pants on. He walked over to the armchair. Kara kept a spare blanket there for when she was reading. Kara climbed on the bed, and Finn climbed on beside her. Pulling the blanket over them. He lay on his back as Kara snuggled up beside him, laying her head on his chest.

"Do you want to watch tv?" Kara asked him, trying to stifle a yawn.

"Will it bother you?"

"No, not at all."

"Ok," he said. Kara lifted her head, and he leaned over to grab the remote. He turned on the tv, making sure the sound was low.

"Finn?"

"Umm?"

Kara was looking up at him. He looked down at her and kissed her forehead. "Thank you for taking care of me," she whispered.

"You're welcome." Finn pulled her against him. She closed her eyes, and within minutes she was fast asleep.

CHAPTER 24

"Hey, Mom," Matt said.

"Hey Babe," Kara said cheerfully. "How are you?"

"I'm good. Guess what?"

"What, Honey?" Kara said. She sat in her office, typing up another email to one of the managers. The third one she'd sent to him.

"I'm coming home for Thanksgiving."

"Oh My God," Kara said, turning her chair around to look out the window. The autumn afternoon was sunny and cold. People were running into the building from the parking lot. Kara could see their breath as they ran.

"Really?"

"Yup," Matt said.

"How, honey. I thought you would have to work."

"I thought so too, but the office is closed on Thursday and Friday. And I can take off on Wednesday. So I can come home."

Kara leaned back in her chair and smiled. "Oh, Matt. I'm so excited. It feels like you haven't been home in so long. I've missed you."

"I've missed you too, even though we talk all the time."

"I know," Kara said, smiling. "But I still miss you. I haven't seen you since your grandmother's funeral."

"I know."

"Besides, the house has changed so much, and it will give you a chance to see everyone."

"Is Finn still there?" Matt said testily.

"Matt." Kara sighed. Shaking her head slightly, even though he couldn't see.

"What?"

"Of course, Finn will be there. We're dating. He's my boyfriend, and he lives there." Kara waited a moment. "I know you're not used to it yet, but I'm really hoping you'll try to get to know him while you're here. It's really important to me."

"I'll try," Matt said unhappily.

"Thank you, Love." Kara ran her hands through her hair. "I think you'll really like Finn once you get to know him."

"Ok," Matt said. "I've got to go. I only had a few minutes to call you and tell you the good news. I'll call you later, Ok?"

"Ok, Honey," Kara said. "I love you."

"I love you, too. Bye, Mom." Matt said as he hung up before Kara could say goodbye. Kara leaned back and swiveled in her chair. She sighed deeply before turning around to finish her email.

Every week on Sunday, Kara would facetime Matt. It gave everyone a chance to talk to him at Sunday dinner. Even though Kara spoke to Matt at least three times a week, she missed him. Matt hadn't been home since his grandmother's funeral at the end of February. He didn't come home over the summer because he was working. Then the semester started in August. Although he had a couple of days, he could have come home, Matt decided to stay with his roommates.

At the beginning of their relationship, Kara didn't tell Matt much about Finn. Not for any other reason than it didn't occur to her to tell her son she was falling in love with her contractor. When Finn moved in, Kara told Matt Finn was saying there in the spare room. Deciding to keep it as simple as possible and not make it a big deal. When they started sleeping together, Kara simply told Matt, Finn was important to her. When she and Finn made their relationship official, Kara told Matt, she and Finn were dating, and it was serious.

On Sundays, when Matt would talk to everyone, he said hi to Finn, and he was always polite. Kara could hear the change in Matt's tone. It was distant. Finn told her he felt Matt didn't like him, and Kara would tell him it didn't matter because she loved him. Matt would come around with time. She attributed it to Matt simply not knowing Finn. And the fact, Matt was a "Momma's boy." Not in the awful, drop everything for your momma type, but the she's my mother, you're not good enough for her pedestal type. Since Matt was in California and not apart of their every day, Matt always seemed like an enigma. It was easy to think of him as a ghost who only appeared on Sundays. Kara and Finn remained in their own little world.

Matt would be coming home for Thanksgiving.

It would be the first Thanksgiving, Kara didn't have her mom or Anthony. Lottie used to do the whole Thanksgiving thing, even though it was just Kara and Anthony. Sometimes Anthony would bring a girlfriend. Lottie would break out all the photo albums and tell Anthony he should settle down and give her grandchildren. Seeming to forget she already had a grandson. The girl would laugh and tell Anthony to put a ring on it. Kara would roll her eyes and spend most of the day in her room reading a book. When Matt did come home, she would ship him off to the McNulty's so he wouldn't have to stay and listen to the nonsense Lottie would say to Anthony. It was bad enough she had to suffer through it. She didn't want Matt to have to listen to all the nonsense and suffer too.

Kara originally planned to stay home and order pizza for Thanksgiving. She thought if it were just going to be her and Finn, they could do without all the drama. Finn usually spent Thanksgiving with his family. When he was with Shelly, Shelly's parents moved to Georgia, and Shelly never wanted to travel there. It didn't matter to Finn where they were, as long as they were together.

Marion shut it down.

Marion decided Kara and Finn would spend Thanksgiving with the McNulty's. Kara tried to protest, but Marion wouldn't hear it. Kara almost volunteered to go to Finn's parent's house to get out of going to the

McNulty's. In the end, she decided against it. Thanksgiving was going to be tense enough. Mike was bringing Carlos to his parent's house, and Jim was still struggling with his new sobriety. Although Beverly and Jim were in marriage counseling, their marriage was strained. Kara didn't want to go and add to the tension.

Kara felt more comfortable around Finn's family since Labor Day. Finn brought Kara back to his parent's house to have dinner. His parents wanted the chance to make amends. Although Kara was apprehensive, the Wilson's welcomed Kara with open arms. The more time Kara spent with them, the more she liked Robert and Dorothy. They already spent a lot of time with Mike and Carlos. The four of them had dinner every other weekend. Sometimes, Mike and Carlos would stop by during the week. Finn and Kara even got together with Ellen and Steve. Although not as often. They met up occasionally to have dinner, or Ellen and Steve would come to the house. Since Labor Day, Beverly tried to make it up to Finn and Kara. Finn kept his distance, though. He was still angry with Jim. Finn did call his sister when he heard about Jim being in recovery, but the reconciliation between them was slow.

When Marion told them to come there for Thanksgiving, Kara squeezed Finn's hand under the table. She wasn't sure if she was ok with it. It's not that Kara didn't want to spend time with the McNulty's. She already spent every Sunday with them. Kara wasn't sure how she was going to feel. Her relationship with her mother and Anthony was strained, to say the least, but they were still her family. Even though, she wasn't speaking to Anthony at the moment. She worried she would get waves of nostalgia from Thanksgiving's in the past. It had been happening since her mother passed. Holidays were already hard without her father. Now she would be without the rest of her family.

Kara was anxious about Matt coming home even though she shouldn't be. So much had changed in less than a year. Not just the house, Kara changed as well. Finn seemed a little uneasy about Matt coming home as well. To Kara, it seemed like one more test in their relationship, which had seen too many difficulties. It didn't help she hadn't been feeling like herself lately.

Kara knew she needed to prepare Matt for Finn and Finn for Matt.

After Finn and Kara came back from their weekend away, they started working on the house's lower level. Since Kara didn't have as much money left for renovations, she wanted to complete as much as she could with what she had left. Kara and Finn started with the walls. They prepped the walls with primer until Kara felt dizzy. The smell of the paint started to make her light-headed, even with the windows and door open. Finn finished with painting while Kara lay down.

When she felt better, she went downstairs, and the room was done. Finn was kneeling in the garage, cleaning the paint off the brushes. The garage door was open to air out the fumes from the turpentine.

"Hey," Kara said as she walked into the Garage.

"Hey," Finn said, looking up at her. "Feel any better?"

"Yeah, I'm just not sure why I got so light-headed," she said absently. She crossed her arms in front of her to brace against the chill in the air.

"I think everything is catching up to you. Between working both jobs, renovating, and everything else, it may be time to take a break."

"We just took a break," she said.

"Only for a couple days. We also walked around Inner Harbor and the Waterfront. So it wasn't as restful as you probably needed."

"Maybe."

"I can see you're already starting to stress about it and think of a million different scenarios," Finn said, standing up. He was covered in paint.

"No, I'm not," she said, smiling at him. "Not a million of them anyway."

"Don't smile at me like that trying to distract me," Finn said, chuckling. "Why don't you call the doctor on Monday? It will save you from having to worry about it."

"Because I have so much to do at work. I don't have time."

"Make time," Finn said sternly. He put his hands on his hips and frowned at her. "Promise me you'll call the doctor on Monday, Kara."

Kara turned to look outside. Although it was chilly, the kids in the neighborhood were riding their bikes past the house.

"Kara," Finn said.

Kara turned to look at him. She could see the concern in his eyes. "Ok. I promise. I'll even text you when I've made the appointment."

"Pinky promise," Finn said, smiling at her. Raising his hand and extending his pinky finger.

Kara laughed, "Pinky promise." Clasping Finn's pinky with hers.

"Good." Finn walked over to her and kissed her on the forehead. "Go upstairs and relax. I'll finish up in here and be up in a minute."

Finn fussed over Kara for the rest of the afternoon. Kara kept telling him she was fine, but he ignored her. He wouldn't let her do anything for the rest of the weekend. The following Monday, Kara did call the doctor, but she couldn't get an appointment until the week after Thanksgiving.

Since Finn wanted Kara to take it easy, Kara called to have someone come to the house to replace the carpets downstairs. Kara and Finn spent their time during the week up to Matt's arrival cleaning the house. The flooring company came on Saturday, and the whole look of the room changed. On Sunday, before dinner, they went to Williamstown Farmers Market. A furniture store Kara wanted to check out was there. She wasn't sure what she wanted to do downstairs. She thought about making it a family room. She wanted to add a bar, a bigger tv and maybe a pool table. She just wanted to do something to make sure Matt would be comfortable when he got there.

On Tuesday night, Kara was exhausted. She came home late from work after an incredibly stressful day. She had so many things going on she wanted to get done as much as she could. She was going to work a half-day on Wednesday so she could pick up Matt from the airport. She wanted to take Friday off, but the CEO wanted something special to show appreciation to the employees, so she had to be there for that.

After dinner, Finn drew her a bath, and she asked him to get in with her. Finn got in, and Kara sat down between his legs.

"Lean forward," Finn said gently.

Kara leaned forward and wrapped her arms around her legs. Finn picked up the shower puff and the bar of natural soap she used. Finn washed her from her neck down.

"Turn around," he whispered.

Kara turned around, and Finn washed the front of her. When he finished, he rinsed her off with warm water from the showerhead attached to the bath.

Kara turned around and leaned back against his chest. Finn massaged her breasts because they were sore. She wondered if she was getting her period soon.

"Is that better?" Finn whispered in her ear.

"Um-hum," she murmured. Kara closed her eyes as she lightly caressed Finn's legs. She could feel him stiffen against her back. Finn kissed her lightly on her temple. Kara sighed contentedly.

"Are you about to fall asleep?" He was rubbing his thumbs over her nipples, teasing them.

"No," she moaned.

She shifted in front of him. She lifted her arm and pulled his head down to kiss her. His hands drifting down her body. He gently spread her legs, rubbing her mound with his fingers. Kara moaned against his mouth. Finn had one hand massaging her breast and the other hand teasing her. Kara arched her back, but he held her in place. Kissing her as she moaned. He teased her entrance. Using his fingers to enter her. Kara gasped.

"Finn," she whispered.

"Shhhh," he said, holding her against him. "Let me." Tightening his hold on her as he moved his hand faster. She leaned her head back and pulled him down to kiss her again. Rocking her hips against his hand. One hand clutching his leg as they gripped her.

Finn kissing her muted her gasping breath and her moans. As she came, he kissed her, grasping her breast with one hand as she shuddered against him. When her breathing slowed, Finn whispered in her ear, "Come on, let's go to bed."

"Ok," Kara said. "The water's getting cold anyway." Finn laughed as she sat up and got out of the tub, putting on her bathrobe. As Finn got out of the tub, Kara let her eyes roam over his body before handing him a towel. She walked over to him and kissed him. Resting her hands on his ass and pressing herself against him. She could feel his erection through the towel.

Her nighttime skincare routine could wait a little while longer, she thought to herself. She tugged at his towel, pulling him into the bedroom.

CHAPTER 25

~ ᥴ᥅ᥲᥴᥲ᥅ᥱ ~

Matt McNulty wasn't much of a drinker.

He never had been. When he was in high school, the guys he hung out with were considered the good kids. They didn't get into trouble. They didn't drink or do drugs. Even though he was in his third year of college and had roommates, they were all gaming guys. It's hard to play video games when you're wasted.

When Matt's eyes fluttered open, and he woke up, he immediately regretted it. He closed his eyes again. Desperately hoping the blinding light and searing pain in his head was a fluke. He thought closing and opening his eyes again would cause a reboot of his brain.

"Ok," he whispered to himself. "Let's try this again."

He opened his eyes and couldn't remember where he was. The room was too bright to be at home. He kept his room cool and dark for his computer system. He looked around the room, waiting for his eyes to adjust to the brightness. He sat up. Searing pain sped through his veins to his head. The pain was competing with his stomach fighting the urge to throw up.

"Uugghhh," he moaned as the searing pain won and nausea stopped.

He lay back down on the bed. He wished the searing pain would lessen enough to reach a bearable level so he could figure out what the hell was going on. His phone rang. He patted himself down, trying to find it in any of his pockets.

"Please stop," he said out loud to the phone. The noise was making the pain worse. He found it under him. He leaned over to pull it out and had to take a few deep breaths because when he moved, everything hurt. By the time he went to answer the call, the person had hung up.

"Fuck," he murmured. He looked at his phone, waiting for his eyes to focus on the screen. He had twelve missed calls and twenty texts.

"What the fuck?" muttering to himself. He scrolled through the texts first. He wasn't in a position to talk to anyone just yet. He read the group text first. The one with his friends Aiden, Jason, and his best friend, Dylan.

Aiden: You good, my man?

Jason: Bro, Call Me.

Dylan: WTF? Why are you being a dick?

All the texts were the same, and all from this morning. He looked at the time at the top of his phone. It was almost one in the afternoon. He shook his head slightly. Too much movement and he would throw up. "It's better to keep still," he thought to himself.

He looked through the missed calls. The last one was from Dylan. He had calls from his mom from last night. His father, last night and this morning, Jason and Aiden.

He called Dylan first.

"What the fuck, Matt? Why were you such a dick last night?" Dylan asked when he answered the call.

"IDK, man. What happened?"

"You were already buzzed before we went to Neighbors. Then you got even more wasted. You picked a fight with the bartender, yelling at him and calling him an asshole. You got us kicked out of the bar. Then when he came outside to make sure you were ok, You threw a punch at him and landed on your ass in the parking lot."

Matt sat up in the bed. He ignored the pain and nausea, causing his head to swim. He closed his eyes, hoping the room would stop spinning.

"I did what?" he asked Dylan slowly. He prayed Dylan was fucking with him.

"You threw a punch at the bartender. The bouncers came and threw you out of the bar. Then you tried to punch them. The bartender came out, asking the guys to take it easy on you. Then you went after the bartender, tried to throw another punch at him. Calling him an asshole and yelling all types of shit about your mom at him." Dylan paused. "You fell on your ass. We were all trying to pick you up and put you in the car. Then you picked up rocks and started throwing them at him. I think you broke one of the windows in the bar."

"FUCK" Matt yelled. "No, No, No, No. Please tell me you're fucking with me? Please," he pleaded.

"Sorry." Dylan laughed. "I think we are permanently banned from Neighbors. But the worst is, you called your mom and started screaming about a fucking loser cheating on her."

"Are you fucking with me right now? You're fucking with me, right?"

"No, man. After you called your mom, you called your dad and started yelling into the phone."

"Fuck my life. I'm so screwed."

"Nah, man, the dude was cool about it. He told us to make sure you get home and in bed to sleep it off."

"Was my mom up when you brought me home?"

"Yup," Dylan said. "She helped us carry you to bed. But bro, you were so drunk. You kept pushing her away when she tried to take your shoes off. We had to hold you down."

"Fuck, Fuck, Fuck." Matt yelled. He made a vow never to drink again.

"Bro, I've never seen you so fucked up."

"I gotta go." Matt hit end on the call and rushed out of the room.

"Mom," Matt yelled, running to the kitchen.

"Mom, where are you?" He ran downstairs to the living room and then downstairs to the lower level.

"Mom," He ran back upstairs and looked out the living room window. Her car was still there, so she had to be in the house. He ran up the stairs and down the hallway to her bedroom.

"Mom," he said as he opened her bedroom door.

Kara was lying in bed. He could hear her shallow breathing and knew something wasn't right. Matt walked over to her lying in bed and pulled the blankets back from her face. She didn't look well. She was pale and would randomly wince from the pain.

"Mom," he yelled, leaning over her.

Kara looked up at him. As she tried to sit up, pain crossed her features, and she let out a cry.

"Mom, what's wrong? Did I do this?" he cried.

Kara winced again as she struggled to get up, and when she couldn't, she lay back down on the bed, breathing heavily.

"Fuck mom, what do I do? Tell me what to do?" he cried. Fear gripping his voice.

Kara shook her head.

Matt did the only thing he could think of. He called his dad.

Matt sat in the waiting area of the emergency room, telling himself repeatedly his mom was going to be ok. He shifted in his seat, trying to stop his leg from bouncing up and down. It was crowded with people, and the tv played a home improvement show too loudly. He sat in the back of the room near the double doors, the nurses wheeled his mother into. He kept looking at the doors, hoping someone would come out and talk to him. Every time a nurse or a doctor came out, he wished it was someone who would tell him what was happening to his mom.

As people walked into the emergency room, he would look up and pray it was his father coming in. The last time he talked to him, his father said he was on the way. That was two hours ago. If someone didn't come out and talk to him soon, or his father didn't show up, he was going to have a nervous breakdown.

"This is all my fault," he muttered to himself. Then he looked around to make sure none of the people sitting near him heard him talking to himself.

The past couple of days played in his thoughts like a bad movie. And he was the villain. From the moment he walked into the door of the house, he'd been a dick. Seeing Finn in the house made him angry, even though he knew Finn would be there. It was like Finn had taken over everything, and his mom had let him. He knew logically it wasn't true. But seeing them together made him think Finn took his mom away from him. So he did what any kid does. He started giving his mom and Finn shit.

He didn't even have a real reason why he was such an asshole. Whenever Finn said anything, Matt would mutter something under his breath. His mom would say something, and he would sigh loudly and roll his eyes. After dinner, he stalked off to his room. His mom came in and attempted to talk to him about it. He was so busy sulking, he blew her off. He'd never acted that way towards his mom before. She gave him a hug and a kiss on the head before telling him good night and left his room. It made him even angrier.

Thursday morning, Finn and his mom made brunch. He didn't bother going. He stayed in his room. He came out while they were getting ready to grab a bag of chips out of the kitchen. Then went right back to his room until it was time to go to dinner. During the drive, he put his headphones in and sulked in the backseat. Silently scowling every time his mom smiled at Finn or when Finn kissed his mother's hand.

When he first walked in, he was ecstatic to see the rest of his family. He almost forgot about Finn. Matt walked around hugging everyone and saying hello. He missed everyone so much. His grandmother held on to him for a long hug. He talked to his grandfather about school and what he did at his job. He hugged his step-mother and got a chance to play with his little sister, Katie. While he was talking to his dad, Matt saw how the rest of his family was so comfortable with Finn. Matt was pissed off even more.

He knew it happened every week anyway, but it was different now he was home. He hadn't been there in person to see it. He kept calling Finn the "handyman" under his breath during dinner, thinking no one could hear him. When he did it in front of his grandmother, she gave him such a look he stayed quiet. He knew better than to cross Marion. Finn had Marion on his side. "Seriously, had Finn taken everything," he thought to himself.

On Friday, his mom and Finn went to work. Matt spent most of the day sitting around the house. He liked how his mother renovated it. It looked great. It just annoyed him Finn was there. When he couldn't sit there anymore, he called Dylan to come and pick him up. They went to Jason's to hang out. The drinking started at Jason's and kept going at Aiden's. The last thing he remembered was going to Neighbors. He didn't remember anything after that.

Matt got up, too anxious to sit still anymore. He walked out the main entrance of the emergency room to get some fresh air. The people in the waiting area were starting to creep him out. He took a deep breath, breathing in the chill in the air. He missed being in New Jersey sometimes. He missed the seasons. He missed seeing the leaves change and the chill in the mornings. He missed the snow and how it got dark by five o'clock. He was an East Coast guy at heart. Living in California had its bonuses, though. Being able to wear shorts all the time was awesome, but it still wasn't like being at home.

Matt rubbed his face with his hands. His face felt rough from not shaving for a couple of days. He ran his hands through his brown curls. His hair had to be all over the place. He needed a shower. "Uugghhh," he said to himself.

He started walking on the sidewalk in front of the entrance. Trying to burn off some of the nervous energy he had. "What the fuck did I do?" he thought to himself. While he sat in the waiting room, he read all of his texts and listened to all the voicemails. He was able to piece some of it together. What Dylan told him was true. He'd done all of it, but he couldn't remember any of it. It was filling in the blanks that was bothering him. Whatever happened, he'd fucked up big time. He wasn't even sure he was going to be able to fix it.

His phone pinged, and he reached in his pocket to see who the text was from.

Aiden: Still at the hospital?

Matt: Yup.

Dylan: Have you heard anything about mom?

Matt: Nope.

Dylan: Ok. Let us know.

Matt: I will.

Matt put his phone back in his pocket. He was happy his friends checked in with him. It made him feel a little less alone. He sat down on one of the benches outside the entrance. He scrolled through his phone, trying to distract himself. It worked because he didn't notice his father until his father sat down next to him.

"Hey," Chris said, giving him a hug and kiss on the head.

"Hey, Dad," Matt turned and leaned into his father's hug awkwardly.

"Have you heard anything yet?"

Matt shook his head. "No, nothing yet."

Chris nodded. "You want to tell me what the hell is going on with you lately?"

Matt didn't answer. He kept scrolling through his phone. He'd heard the disappointed tone in his father's voice. Although it was deserved, it made him feel worse.

"Come on, Matt. What the fuck happened last night?"

Matt leaned back against the bench. He closed his eyes and sighed. He knew no matter what he said, he'd fucked up. His mother was in the hospital, and his father had not only used the "tone" but had cursed as well. He took a deep breath.

"I don't know, Dad." He put his phone in his pocket and rubbed his hand over his face. He felt like shit. He hadn't eaten anything all day except for a bag of chips over an hour ago. He drank a bottle of water then too, but he was still dehydrated. He was tired, hungry, and freaking out about his mom. He knew he fucked up, and explaining it to his dad, just made it seem so much harsher.

"Me and Dylan went to Jason's house and started drinking. Then we went to pick up Aiden, and we drank some more." Matt sighed and shifted in his seat. "I got really drunk. Well, we went to Neighbor's, and I drank even more. I drank more than I should have, and I remember seeing Finn at the bar talking to some woman. Well, she was all over him." Matt sighed and ran his fingers through his curly hair.

"So, from what I found out from Dylan, Jason, and Aiden, I apparently went over to Finn and started a fight with him. The bouncers threw me out, and I tried to fight with them. When Finn came out and tried to talk to me,

I took another swing at him and fell on my ass." Matt paused. Flashes of what happened coming back to him.

"Finn asked the guys to bring me home and make sure I got to bed. Apparently, I picked up some rocks and threw them at him. No one is sure, but I may have broken a window at Neighbors." He leaned forward, resting his elbows on his knees, and put his head in his hands, rubbing his eyes. "Well, when they brought me home, mom was up waiting for them. They all tried to carry me upstairs to bed, but I kept pushing mom away when she tried to take my shoes off. I woke up this morning and didn't remember any of it. And you know everything that happened after that."

Matt felt the tears on the palms of his hands and wiped them away. He felt his father's eyes burning into him.

Chris sighed. "What's your problem with Finn? You didn't act like this when I was dating Teresa. Why are you acting like this now?"

"Like what?" Matt rubbed his eyes and looked over at his dad.

"Like a fucking two-year-old having a temper tantrum." His father said harshly.

Matt looked at his father. He blinked back the tears, ready to fall. "I'm not."

"The fuck you're not." Chris scoffed.

Matt could see the rage in his father's face. He hadn't seen his father this mad since he was ten years old, and he'd scratched his father's new car with his bike.

"What the fuck is wrong with you?" Chris said. Matt knew his father was trying not to scream at him. "You come home after not seeing your mom for almost nine months. She's told you she's seeing Finn. You see him every week on face time at dinner with your grandmother, and you act like you just found out Finn stole your mother from you." Matt flinched.

"Don't look so fucking shocked. Your mother is a grown woman. Who is allowed to have a relationship. She doesn't need your permission to live her life. There is more to your mother than being your mom. Your mother was a grown woman who somehow managed to live twenty-six years before you were born." Chris paused. "Your twenty-one years old, in college, three thousand miles away. Did you think your mother was going to stop living and just wait for you to come home? Was she supposed to just stop being a person?"

Matt shook his head. Chris faced him, forcing Matt to look him in the eyes.

"I don't know, what the fuck you think you saw?" Chris stressed. "But your mom and Finn's relationship is none of your fucking business. It's theirs. Your mother does not need you to go fighting her battles for her. Do you really think your mother would be thrilled you tried to punch Finn? And how fucking happy do you think she was, seeing you so fucking drunk, you needed to be put to bed." Matt felt the intensity of his father's look. He lowered his head, tears filling his eyes.

"I've known your mother for over twenty-five years. I've never seen her as happy as she's been with Finn. I didn't even make your mother as happy as he does. Finn loves your mother." Chris paused. He reached out and took Matt's face in his hand to look him in the eye.

"Matt, Your mom has been on her own for a really long time. She took care of you. Then she had to take care of your grandmother Lottie. And finally, after all that time, there is someone who wants to take care of her. She of all people deserves to be happy."

Chris let go of Matt's face and sat back on the bench. Matt didn't say anything. The weight of how deeply he'd fucked up was hitting him hard. His father was right. He had been the world's biggest dick to his mom and Finn.

"I'm sorry," Matt whispered, choking back a sob.

"I'm not the one you need to apologize to. You have to own up to the mess you made. If your man enough to cause this much shit, you should be man enough to face the consequences for it."

Matt nodded. He was going to have to beg his mother for forgiveness. Then he would have to apologize to Finn and hope Finn would forgive him too.

Chris put his arm around Matt's shoulders to give him a hug. "One more thing." Matt looked at his dad. Chris smiled at him. "Maybe you should think about not drinking for a while. And if you do drink, don't drink so much you act like an asshole and do stupid shit." Chris laughed. "You shouldn't need to have someone else tell you what you did. If you can't handle your alcohol responsibly, you shouldn't drink."

Matt laughed and nodded. "I think I'm done drinking for a while."

"That's my boy," Chris said, ruffling Matt's already unruly hair."Come on. Let's go inside and see if there's any news. Then we can go get you something to eat."

They both stood up from the bench, and Chris pulled Matt into his arms for a hug. Matt shook in his father's arms as he sobbed. Chris didn't say anything. Just held him tightly. The weight of everything finally lifting a little bit. His dad was there. Even though his dad chewed his ass out for what he did, Matt was still happy he was there.

Matt looked like a younger version of his dad, except his hair was curly, and Chris's hair was straight. Matt had olive skin and was also about an inch taller than Chris. Matt had to hunch down a little for his dad to hug him. Not as much as his mom or his grandmother Marion, though.

Matt held onto his dad a little longer. He realized how much he missed his dad. He talked to his mom almost every day, but he only spoke to his dad once a week. Every now and then, he'd talk to him twice a week. He would have to start calling him more often.

"I love you," Chris whispered into Matt's ear and kissed him on the side of the head.

"I love you too, Dad," Matt said.

Matt and Chris were sitting in the waiting area of the emergency room. They'd gone to the cafeteria to get something to eat. Talking about school and how much Matt liked his job. There was still no news about Kara, so they went to the gift shop to look around. They even took a walk outside just to get up and move. There was still no news about Kara. Matt looked at his phone as he received another low battery notification.

He'd been there all day. "If someone doesn't come out here soon," he thought to himself, "I'm gonna start breaking shit."

"Christopher McNulty?" A tall woman with dark brown hair wearing scrubs and a white coat came out of the double doors.

"Yes," Chris said, standing up. The woman walked towards them. Matt stood up just as she walked up.

"Hi," Extending her hand. "I'm Dr. Priya Chopra. I'm the on-call Obstetric ian-Gynecologist here at the hospital." Chris shook her hand.

"I'm your wife's attending physician. Mrs. McNulty is going to be admitted and kept overnight for observation. We were able to stop the bleeding. But, we weren't able to save the fetus. We used medical management, which involves taking medications to help pass the remaining tissue." Dr. Chopra said solemnly.

"Fetus? Do you mean baby?" Matt asked the doctor.

"Yes," she said.

Matt turned to his father. "Did you know mom was pregnant?"

Chris shook his head. "No, but it explains a lot. I wonder if Finn knows," Matt paled. Chris turned to the doctor. "How far along was she?"

"She was still in her first trimester. From what we could tell, she was between eight to ten weeks. She may not have realized she was pregnant. Believing she was going through the beginning of menopause. Although it's prevalent for women Mrs. McNulty's age to miscarry in the first trimester, it doesn't rule out the possibility for a healthy pregnancy should she become pregnant again. Fortunately, she was brought in quickly, and we were able to stop the hemorrhaging and get her stable."

Matt slumped down in his chair, tears filling his eyes. "What the fuck have I done?" he muttered to himself.

"Do you know what caused her to miscarry?" Chris asked. Placing his hand on Matt's shoulder.

"Unfortunately, when it happens in the first trimester, such as this case, it's because the fetus doesn't develop normally. Different factors can cause it, though. Usually, it's not because of something Mrs. McNulty may or may not have done." Dr. Chopra said.

"I understand," Chris said gravely. "Can we see her?"

"She's resting right now. However, she did request not to have visitors.

You can call the main number of the hospital, and they will connect you to the room. Or you can always call and ask for the nurse's station. They will be able to give you an update if Mrs. McNulty doesn't answer." Chris nodded his head.

"She should be able to go home tomorrow morning. She's dehydrated and nauseous from the medications. After she rests tonight, we'll follow up with her in the morning, and she should be discharged."

"Thank you, Doctor."

Dr. Chopra nodded and turned around to walk through the double doors. Chris turned around and sat down next to Matt, wrapping his arms around him. Matt was sobbing. Matt couldn't believe his mom had been pregnant. Matt was ashamed of himself. Thoughts flying at him like daggers.

Not only had he been a dick for the past couple of days. He'd ruined his mom's relationship, and now on top of it, she'd lost the baby.

Chris held him as he cried, giving him a kiss on the head. "Shhhh, Matt, it's ok," he said. Matt shook his head. He didn't believe it would be ok.

"Come on," Chris helped him up. "I'll take you to my house. Let's go home. We'll figure everything out tomorrow."

Matt nodded. He had to lean on his father as they walked out of the emergency room.

CHAPTER 26

Finn sat at the bar, watching the tv but not watching it. The Pre-Game show was on talking about the matchups for the day. The bar had only been open for an hour, and it was already half full. The Eagles weren't playing until four today. By the time it was kick-off, the bar would be so packed you wouldn't be able to walk to the bathroom without bumping into someone.

Finn wasn't really into football. He only watched when he hung out with his brother or went to family dinner. South Jersey was Philadelphia Eagles territory, and they were serious about football. Randy was behind the bar, with the other bartender Michelle, trying to prep for the afternoon and setting up.

"You hungry?" Randy asked Finn as he stocked the station Finn was sitting at.

"Not really," Finn said quietly.

"Have you eaten today?"

Finn drank the last of his coffee and set the cup down. "No."

Randy turned around, "Jenna?" Calling out to the waitress as she walked by. Jenna was pretty with long black hair, big brown eyes, and a cute smile. Jenna was young and bubbly.

Jenna walked over to him. "Yeah?"

"Can you go in the back and tell Joey I need a turkey and cheese club &

fries?"

"Sure," Jenna said cheerily, turning around and walking to the kitchen.

"I said I'm not hungry," Finn said gruffly.

"Who said it's for you?" Randy replied casually as he turned to look at something on tv.

Finn sighed, "Ok." Although he knew the sandwich was for him.

Randy nodded, "I'll get you more coffee." Picking up Finn's empty coffee mug.

Finn nodded as Randy went into the back. Finn didn't have the energy to fight. He hadn't slept in two days. Every time he tried, he couldn't stop his mind from replaying the nightmare of Friday. When he finally managed to actually fall asleep, it wasn't for long. He woke up reaching for Kara, and when he realized she wasn't there, he spent the rest of the night tossing and turning.

Randy came back with a fresh cup of coffee and some creamers. He set them down in front of Finn.

"Still haven't heard from Kara?" he asked gently.

Finn picked up his phone from off the bar and looked."No." He put his phone back down. "I even tried calling Charlie yesterday and today. I left her two messages and nothing from her either." Finn added cream and sugar to his coffee and stirred it.

"Did you go to the house today?"

"No," Finn said and took a sip of his coffee. "I went there yesterday afternoon. Kara's car was there, so I was hoping she was home. But no one was there. I waited there all day until I came here last night, and no one came home."

Jenna came towards them carrying a plate with the sandwich and loaded with fries. She was holding a bottle of ketchup in the other hand.

"Here you go." She set the plate down in front of Finn. "Careful, the plates hot," she said as she walked away.

"Thank you," Randy said as he picked up a fry.

The smell of the fries reminded Finn's stomach he hadn't eaten anything since the day before. He'd gone all day and hadn't eaten. Randy ordered a burger and made him eat it. Finn picked up a fry and ate it. Randy pushed the plate towards Finn. He turned, walked towards the other end of the bar to a woman who came up to order a drink.

Finn picked up a piece of the sandwich and took a bite. He forced the food past the lump lodged in his throat for the last two days. Randy came back and stood next to Finn after he got the woman her drinks. He picked up some fries and ate them.

"You know," Randy said hesitantly. "My boys never had a problem when I started dating. They were perfectly fine with it." He paused to grab some more fries. "I even made sure to talk about it with them. Asked them a million times if they were ok, and every time they were like, 'yeah, Dad, we're fine.'" Randy reached under the bar to get a glass. He filled it with ice and used the soda gun to fill it up with soda. He took a drink and set the glass on the bar.

"But when Nik started dating, it was a whole different story. You would have thought she abandoned them. They started acting out, talking back, getting into trouble at school." Randy sighed and picked up a piece of the sandwich, and took a bite. He chewed thoughtfully, letting his words sink in. When he finished, he went on.

"When Nik and I sat them down to talk about it, they couldn't tell us why they were acting that way. Fortunately, Nik already had us all in family counseling so we could talk about it."

Finn finished chewing and wiped his mouth on a napkin. "So what happened?"

"The boys never had a problem with me dating because they were never worried about me replacing their mom. She was always with them." Randy sighed. "But when Nik started dating, to them, it felt like she was going to replace them. After the divorce, they had all of her attention. When she started dating, they were afraid she was going to be taken away from them, and they rebelled."

Finn took a sip of his coffee, contemplating what Randy just told him. "But Matt is twenty-one years old and in college. He's an adult."

Randy shook his head and looked at Finn. "It doesn't matter how old you are when it comes to your mom, Finn." He picked up his soda and took a sip. "Kara is still his mom. And you're the bad man who is taking her away from him." Randy set the glass down on the bar.

"I'm an asshole," Finn murmured.

Randy nodded at Finn. "You're an asshole. And you shouldn't have asked Kara to choose."

A guy walked over to the bar and motioned at Randy. Randy nodded at him and walked over to him.

Finn watched Randy, feeling the food he'd just forced down try and come back up. He'd lost his appetite. He pushed the plate away from him, wiped his mouth with his napkin, crumpled it up, and set it down by the plate. He leaned back on the stool, reliving the hell his life had become.

Shelly had come into the bar on Friday night with the sole purpose of trying to get to Finn. She came in with her friends, Kaitlyn being one of them. They sat at a table close to the bar. After four rounds of shots, Shelly tried to get behind the bar. When that didn't work, she tried to lure Finn from behind the bar to talk to her.

As soon as he walked over to her, she lunged at him. She was all over him. Hands everywhere, trying to kiss him and grinding on him. Finn got himself untangled. He went over to the table to get her friends to take her home. While they were trying to leave, Shelly was still trying to kiss Finn. She grabbed his crotch at one point, and when he'd smacked her hand away, she'd tried to kiss him again.

Finn didn't even know Matt was in the bar until he walked up and threw a punch at him. Matt was so drunk, he just spun around and wobbled. He'd punched the air. The bouncers came over, and Finn asked them to go easy on Matt while taking care of Shelly. He got Shelly into her friend's car, not before she tried to kiss him again. Then he ran over to where Matt's friends were trying to get him to leave. Finn found out Matt had apparently taken a swing at one of the bouncers.

Finn went over to help get Matt into the car, and Matt took another swing at him. Missed and landed on his ass in the parking lot. Then he started picking up rocks to throw at Finn. He missed, but he did hit someone's car window. Matt's friends finally got him into the car, and Finn watched them drive off. He went back into the bar to find the owner of the car.

He apologized and offered to pay for the damage to the window, and the guy, who was also drunk, started screaming at him and shoving him. Finn almost pushed the guy back, but Randy stepped in, calmed the guy down, and told Finn to wait in his office.

Finn walked into Randy's office and slammed the door. He'd reached his breaking point. First Shelly, then Matt, and finally, the guy's window. It was all too much. He paced in Randy's office so enraged it was boiling over. When Kara called to ask what was going on with Matt, Finn erupted. He didn't even hear anything she'd said. He just went off. Matt was trying to tear them apart. Matt had never liked him. Matt had been an asshole since he'd gotten there. Shelly fucking shows up. Fucking gets drunk. Puts her hands all over him. She grabbed his dick, for fuck sake. He was trying to get rid of her, and Matt fucking walks up and throws a punch at him. Why the fuck was Matt at the bar anyway. Matt gets thrown out of the bar, and when he goes to see if he's alright, Matt is still trying to throw punches at him. What the fuck? And if that wasn't fucking enough, Matt broke some guy's car window, and now Finn had to clean up that mess. If Matt's such a grown fucking man to try to punch Finn, then fuck him. He wasn't going to put up with his shit.

"Finn, please calm down. Let's." Kara said gently. She was trying to use her soothing tone to calm Finn down.

"Fuck this shit, Kara. I don't need it. It's him or me." Finn screamed into the phone.

"Finn, Please. Calm down." Kara pleaded imploringly.

"No, I'm not going to fucking calm down. I'm sick of his shit. Choose Kara."

"Finn, Please. Don't do this." "For Fuck's sake, Kara."

"Matt. I choose Matt. He's my son." Kara said firmly.

Finn stopped breathing. The anger leaving his body. He sank down in one of the chairs in front of Randy's desk. Before his brain could register a response, Kara continued.

"I'll text you and let you know when you can come and pick up your stuff. Goodbye, Finn." She hung up on him. Finn stared at the phone, wondering what the fuck just happened.

Finn was still in the office when Randy walked in, just staring at his phone. When Randy asked him if he was okay, Finn dropped his phone, covered his face with his hands, and screamed, "FUCK."

The rest of the night was foggy. His temper had ripped half of him away, and he couldn't function. He went behind the bar, and as people talked to him, he stared blankly at them. Randy gave him a ride to his place, and Finn spent the night there. When Randy opened the bar on Saturday, Finn got in his truck and drove to Kara's. She wasn't there, and neither was Matt. He went into the house, waiting on the couch, hoping someone would come home. No one did.

He'd come back to the bar last night feeling lost. He called Kara every hour and left messages. He sent her texts, waiting for her to respond, and none came. He hadn't been able to sleep, and the only reason he'd eaten was Randy forced him to. Finn stayed at Randy's again last night. He woke up determined to find Kara and do whatever he had to do, to get her to talk to him.

"No wonder Matt hates me. I'm a fucking dick," he whispered to himself. He ran his hands through his hair. Randy came back over to Finn and picked up his glass of soda for a drink.

"What are you going to do?" he asked before taking a sip.

"Show up at dinner. Crawl on my hands and knees and beg her for forgiveness. And keep doing it until she takes me back." Finn said matter-of-factly.

"Smart man." Randy nodded his approval.

Finn's phone vibrated on the bar. He picked it up so fast, he almost dropped it. It was a text from Charlie.

Charlie: Where are you, right now?

Finn: Have you talked to Kara?

Charlie: Not Yet. Answer me. Where are you right now?

Finn: I'm at Neighbors. Why?

Charlie: Stay there. Don't leave until I talk to you.

Finn: I'm going to find Kara.

Charlie: FINN, STAY THERE. DON'T LEAVE UNTIL I TALK TO YOU.

Finn: Ok. Fine.

Charlie: I'll explain later. I promise.

Finn: Ok.

"Was it Kara?" Randy asked.

"No, it was Charlie. She wants me to wait here."

Randy nodded and went to help someone who came up to the bar for a drink.

Finn jumped every time the door opened and someone came into the bar. The bar was filling up, the Eagles game was about to start. He stared at the door, expecting to see Charlie walk in. He'd pick up his phone and check to see if she sent him any more texts. As the pre-game started, he realized that he would have to leave soon if he wanted to make it to dinner.

Finn didn't expect to see Chris walk into the bar. Fear tore through him. He felt his heart stop. "What's Chris doing here? Did something happen to Kara?" he thought to himself. Randy looked over at Finn and then at Chris as he walked up to the bar. Chris sat down on the stool next to Finn.

"Hey," Chris said to Finn as he sat down. He nodded to Randy and extended his hand. "Chris."

Randy shook Chris's hand. "Randy." Randy looked over at Finn to make sure he was ok. Finn couldn't move. Randy walked to the other end of the bar to help someone.

"Hey," Finn said when he was finally able to speak. "What are you doing here?" Panic creeping into his voice.

Chris looked at Finn and sighed. When Randy looked over, Chris waived and signaled for a beer. Randy nodded. Chris turned to Finn.

"I asked Charlie if she knew where you were, and she told me you were here."

Randy set down a beer in front of Chris. "Thanks," Chris said, reaching for his wallet. Randy shook his head. "It's on him." Gesturing to Finn.

Chris nodded and smiled, turning to Finn. "Thanks."

"Is Kara all right? Where is she?" Finn blurted out. Dread was filling the pit of his stomach. Anxiously he was beginning to grind his teeth.

Chris took a long swig of his beer. He set the glass down on the napkin and turned to face Finn, looking tired. "No, she isn't, but."

"What's wrong? Where is she? What happened?" Finn fired off questions, not giving Chris time to answer them. Chris raised his hand.

"Calm down, Finn. I promise I'll tell you everything, and there's a lot to talk about."

Finn nodded and took a deep breath. He closed his eyes for a moment, trying to stop his heart from trying to break free of his chest. He opened his eyes and looked at Chris.

"First things first." Chris set his glass down after taking another sip of his beer. "The reason why I'm here is that dinner tonight is canceled. I didn't want you to drive all the way to my parent's house, hoping to catch Kara, because no one is home." He picked up his glass, took a sip of beer, and set it back down.

"Second, I want to talk to you about what happened between you and Matt Friday night."

Finn's shoulder's slumped. He really didn't want to relive Friday night. He'd already replayed it enough over and over again in his head to last a lifetime.

"It's not what you think," Chris said, seeing the look on Finn's face. "I'm here to apologize for Matt's behavior and to ask you to forgive him." Finn looked up at Chris, shocked.

"Matt was wrong, and he knows it. He had a temper tantrum about his mom and acted like a spoiled brat. He wanted to apologize to you in person, but he had to fly out today. I dropped him off at Philadelphia International about forty minutes ago. Since he didn't see you and he didn't have any way of calling you because, you know Kara," Chris paused to drink some of his beer.

Finn huffed, knowing what he meant. If Kara didn't want to talk about something, she shut everyone out.

"You know, sometimes she just stops talking, and no one can get through to her. Thankfully, Charlie found me, and I was able to get her to text you for me." Chris paused and rubbed his hand over his face. Finn could see the circles under his eyes. He looked as tired as Finn felt. Chris sighed.

"Anyway, Matt wants to talk to you himself. So I told him I would give you his number and when your ready, you can call and talk to him."

Finn nodded. He shifted nervously in his seat. He hoped this was the end of it, so he could get the hell out of there and drive to the house. If Kara wasn't going to be at dinner, he would possibly find her at home. Chris was looking at him intently, studying him.

"Matt also told me there was a broken window that needs to be paid for. I want to pay for any damage that he caused."

"It was some guy's back car window. I already took care of it." Finn said indifferently.

"Well, at least let me pay you back."

Finn held up his hand to stop Chris. "Don't worry about it. It's not important."

"Ok," Chris said hesitantly. "Well, I also wanted to apologize to you." Finn stopped fidgeting and looked at Chris.

"For what?" he asked.

"Matt acting like an asshole. He acted like that all through Thanksgiving, and I should have dealt with it then, and I didn't." Chris took a deep breath. "I hope you can forgive us both."

Finn looked at Chris and leaned over to give him a side hug, patting him on the back. "Of course," he said.

Chris gave Finn a small smile, then sighed. "Now, the last thing I have to tell you is about Kara."

Finn stiffened. He leaned back on the barstool, feeling his hands clenched into fists. From the look on Chris's face and the tone of his voice, he knew whatever Chris had to tell him wasn't going to be good news.

"Kara's home," Chris said slowly. "Me and Matt picked her up from the hospital this morning."

"Hospital?" Finn whispered. "Why was she in the hospital?" Finn stood up from the stool, and Chris reached his arm out to push Finn back down on the stool. Randy watching from the other side of the bar, came over and stood at the bar next to Finn.

"She started bleeding early Saturday morning. Matt called me, and I told him to call 911 and have an ambulance take her to the hospital. They were able to stop the bleeding, but," Chris stopped. He was looking at Finn, sadness in his eyes. Finn held his breath. The grip of cold fear squeezed his heart as he waited for Chris to continue.

"But what?" Finn said barely above a whisper. Every possible worst-case scenario flew into his mind. He tried to hold on but felt his grasp slipping.

"But," Chris said grimly. "They weren't able to save the baby. I'm sorry, Finn."

The relief that inundated Finn was quickly replaced by shock. The room began to spin and blurred. Chris reached out and grabbed Finn to steady him on the barstool.

"Kara was pregnant? And she lost the baby?" He breathed.

"She was nine or ten weeks. The doctors don't know what caused it. Kara will be ok, though." Chris said hopefully. "That's the important thing."

Finn didn't respond. Images of every time he and Kara had been together flooded his mind. They hadn't thought about the possibility of her getting pregnant. The color drained from Finn's face, and he thought he would throw up. Nausea overcame him. Kara had been pregnant. Explanations shooting daggers at him. She'd been tired all the time. Why she couldn't handle the paint fumes and got dizzy. She'd told him she felt her period coming.

Pregnant. He would have been a father. Kids with Kara didn't seem possible. They hadn't talked about the possibility. He didn't realize he'd even wanted children. Kara's miscarriage forced the hope he denied himself in front of him. Now the hope was gone, and the loss was excruciating.

"Finn?" Chris whispered. Chris's hand was still on Finn's arm. Finn looked down at the hand on his arm, then up to meet Chris's eye.

"I can't tell you how sorry I am, Finn. Teresa is with Kara now. Charlie was on her way over as I was leaving to take Matt to the airport."

Finn stood up from the barstool. He looked around, lost, everything blurry in front of his eyes.

"I've got to go," he said. His mind racing frantically. He had to get to Kara. Nothing else mattered but Kara. Kara was the only thing he could hold onto to save himself from drowning.

Chris grabbed his arm. "Where are you going?"

"Kara. I've got to get to Kara." Finn said. "I'm going home. Kara needs me."

"Ok, Finn, but let me drive you. You shouldn't drive like this." Chris looked over at Randy for help.

"Finn, maybe you should let him drive you," Randy said, looking from Finn to Chris.

Finn looked at Randy and then at Chris. "I don't care how the hell I get there. I'll crawl if I have to, but I'm going to get to her. Kara needs me."

CHAPTER 27

I t was dark.

Kara lifted her head and tried to see, but everywhere she looked was darkness. She huddled on the floor with her knees pressed to her chest. She wrapped her arms around her legs to try to stop some of the shivering. It was cold and damp. Kara shivered again. She felt the cold deep enough to penetrate her bones. It left a block of ice in her soul.

She wasn't sure how long she'd been here. Since Saturday, she guessed. She'd woken up Saturday morning and immediately knew something was wrong. She'd thought it was just her period. But the bleeding didn't stop. Then the cramps came, and she knew. She knew. How could she be so stupid? Why hadn't she paid attention? It was all there, right in front of her. Did she think ignoring it would make it less real?

With the weight of knowledge pulling her down, Kara didn't try to stop it. She submissively let it pull her under and bring her here. She couldn't bear it. Already struggling with the loss of Finn, this loss was just too much.

"How did she not know?" she thought to herself. Because she hadn't been pregnant in over twenty years. How could she be expected to remember something so long ago?

"I thought it was menopause," she cried out into the darkness, choking back sobs. "I didn't think I could anymore." Her eyes filling with tears.

"I'm sorry." She shrieked over and over to nothing. The weight gain, the hormones, the fatigue, they were all the same symptoms of menopause. Her period had been late, but it's been late before. The breast tenderness. All pre-menopause.

She tried to think back to when they had stopped using condoms. It wasn't important, now. The chances of her getting pregnant naturally were slim. She was forty-seven. They hadn't talked about what would happen if. Now the if had happened and was over before she could accept it.

She didn't realize it was a possibility until it wasn't. When it wasn't a possibility, she was fine. You can't miss something you can't have. Then the doctor came in and told her she was pregnant. Hope. Hope for something she'd given up long ago.

She'd wanted more kids, but it didn't happen. She'd accepted it. She'd moved on. She had been on her own, so it didn't matter. She had her son, and it was enough. When times were hard, she had been grateful she only had one child. If there were more, how would she have been able to manage? She told herself she should be glad it hadn't happened, and it wasn't meant to be. She could barely take care of one child. How the hell could she take care of more?

But Hope. Hope is awful.

Why had the doctor given her such a debilitating thing as hope? She would try to save the pregnancy, she said. Bitter tears fell from Kara's eyes. Hope invaded Kara when the doctor said that. She was pregnant. She could have another child. There was a possibility she would make it through this, and the baby would be ok.

Then it wasn't.

The doctor told her they would give her medicine, and it would all be over soon. She'd thrown up afterward.

Now, here she was. In the dark. In the cold. Alone.

She wasn't afraid. She'd been here before. She hadn't been this far down in years, though.

Ironically enough, it was the same last time. It was at the end of her marriage. Before she left, Chris. Her period was late. Really late. Then the cramps came, and she got her period. She hid in the shower and cried for an hour while Matt took a nap. She was grateful, he was too little to pay attention to her puffy red eyes when he woke up and smiled at her. She held him so tightly that day. Grateful for him. He was enough.

Matt pulled her out of here then. She had to come out of the darkness because he needed her. She realized she'd never told him how he had saved her at the time. He forced her to come out of the darkness. He forced her to accept and move on. She'd have to thank him for that one day. He'd been the light that led her out of the darkness when she'd needed it.

This time was different, though. It was more than just the loss of a baby. It included the loss of Finn. Her heart was already broken when she went to the hospital.

Finn.

She felt the sting of pain as the whip lashed her. Each thought of him, another lash of the whip. She put her head on her knee. Her skin tingling from the cuts.

She knew the smell of the blood would draw out her demons. She knew they would come, and they would find her. They'd been right all along. She should've just stayed with them. They were safe. They'd warned her. They'd told her she wasn't enough. They'd told her she wouldn't be able to give him what he needed. They'd told her she was too old. They'd asked her, "What if?" and she'd ignored them.

The impact of the whip hitting her brought her back. She wanted to cry out from the pain of it, but she couldn't make a sound. She tried to scream. She tried to yell.

She'd pleaded with him. Please calm down. We'll work it out. Please stop. Please don't do this. Please don't make me choose. Saying goodbye to Finn, having to say goodbye to a baby she didn't know she had, her voice left her. She heard the crack of the whip before she felt it. She winced. Eventually, she would become numb to it. She just had to wait long enough. She heard the hushed shuffling sound of her demons running towards her.

"Here they come," she said faintly.

She knew she should try to move. She should get up and run. She should try to hide from them. But her limbs were stiff from the cold. She had sat huddled for too long. She wasn't able to move at all. She tried to force her body to follow her brains command.

"Move," she yelled. She couldn't. Kara stopped trying. She didn't have the energy. It was too much. She lay down and waited for them.

She'd fallen asleep. For a few blissful moments, she forgot where she was. She was lying on the hard floor. The stone felt cool under her cheek. She was surrounded by darkness. She didn't know how long she had been there. It didn't matter though, she was safe. She tried to sit up, her body aching. She lay back down. She was so tired. She closed her eyes again. All she wanted to do was sleep. Sleep was good. Sleep was safe. Kara let the silent, cold darkness surround her and lull her to sleep.

Finn walked into the house and looked around. Teresa and Charlie were sitting on the couch in the living room. They were watching tv, and when he came in, they both turned and got off the couch.

"Where is she?" Finn asked.

Charlie got up and walked around the couch to stand in front of him.

"She's in her room, but,"

Finn started towards the stairs, but Charlie reached out to stop him.

"Finn, wait." She pleaded.

Finn turned to look at her with fury in his eyes.

"Finn, Please," Charlie whispered. She held his arm. Charlie looked up at him, tears glistening in her eyes.

"What?" He hissed at her, trying to yank his arm out of her grip.

Charlie took a deep breath. "Finn, she's," she paused, a tear trickling down her cheek. "She's not in a good place," she said uneasily. "She won't come out of it." Charlie looked up and sniffed, trying to stop the tears. "She won't eat or drink anything. She hasn't said anything."

Charlie pulled a tissue out of the pocket of her sweatshirt and dabbed her eyes. "When Matt went in to talk to her, she didn't move. She just cried and stared through him." Charlie blew her nose into the tissue and balled it up in her hand.

"She's just lying there, crying and not making a sound." She sniffed. "I haven't seen her this bad before." Charlie looked up at him. "Finn, I can't reach her. I tried. I begged her to come back, and she just looked through me."

Finn looked down at Charlie and hugged her. Charlie sobbed against his chest.

"Shhhhh," he whispered in her ear. "I'll bring her back," he said soothingly.

Charlie looked up at him. She nodded her head slowly. "I'm scared. She's hurting so much, and we tried, but we couldn't get through to her."

Finn nodded and hugged Charlie again.

Chris came into the house, shutting the door behind him.

"Anything?" he asked Teresa. Teresa shook her head. Chris nodded and walked over to her and hugged her. Chris looked over at Finn. Finn nodded and let Charlie go. He turned, walked up the stairs and down the hallway.

Finn stopped at the door to the bedroom and took a deep breath before opening the door. The curtains were closed, casting the room in darkness. Finn hesitated a few moments to let his eyes adjust. He walked slowly over to the nightstand and turned on the light. He pulled back the blankets, but Kara wasn't in bed. He looked around the room, panic engulfing him, turning in circles, looking for her.

He walked into the bathroom and turned on the light. He found her in the bathroom, lying on the floor.

"Kara," he cried. Relief and sadness flooding him, he dropped to his knees next to her.

Kara was shivering, wearing nothing but a t-shirt and her underwear. He lifted her up into his arms and cradled her. Rocking her gently back and forth. Rubbing his hands over her arms and her back to warm her up.

"Kara, wake up," he whispered. Her skin felt so cold. He wondered how long she'd been lying there. Finn looked around for something to wrap her in. The closest thing he could find was her bathrobe behind the bathroom door. He yanked it down, causing the hook to fall from the door. "I'll fix it later," he thought to himself as he wrapped it around her.

"Kara, I'm here," he whispered. Kissing her on the head. She stirred a little. He rubbed her back and then her arms. Trying to warm her up.

"Kara, please. Wake up," he said in her ear. He thought about lifting her, but he was afraid of hurting her. He could feel the panic rising in him. He felt helpless. He didn't know what to do. She looked so pale and so fragile. He held her to him.

"Kara, please," he pleaded. "I love you, wake up."

Kara felt light. Where was light coming from? she asked herself. There couldn't be light. She closed her eyes tighter. She felt warmth. How is this possible? she thought to herself. When she'd gone to sleep, it was dark and cold. She must be dreaming.

The light didn't go away. She wanted to lift her hand to block it out, but she felt so weak. She could hear someone calling her name. "Was that?" she thought to herself. But it couldn't be. She'd pushed him away. It was over. She'd told him so. He'd made her choose between him and her son. He broke her heart. She was afraid for a moment. Someone was saying her name. But it was so far away.

Kara stirred in Finn's arms. He tried to use his body to warm her up. Even though the house wasn't cold, the floor she had been lying on was cold. "She's lost so much blood," he thought to himself, remembering what Chris had told him. Finn knew he had to warm her up.

"Kara. I'm here," he whispered. He kissed her face. He gave her the gentlest kiss on her lips.

"I love you, Kara. Wake up," he said, his voice breaking. "Please."

Kara's eyes fluttered open. Finn let out a deep breath. "Kara," he whispered. Tears falling from his eyes.

"Finn?" she said weakly. Blinking her eyes so she could focus, her vision blurry.

Finn held her close against his chest. "Yes, baby. I'm here." Her head was against his chest. His heart beating so fast, it thundered in his ears. He pulled her legs up so she was on his lap. He rocked her gently. "I'm here. It's ok." He kissed her head.

Finn looked down when he felt her shuddering against him. Kara was crying.

"Shhhh. I'm here," he said as he cradled her to him.

"I'm here," he whispered over and over. Holding her in his arms as she cried quietly against his chest.

Chris came into the bedroom to check on them and found them in the bathroom. He helped Finn gently pick up Kara and put her into bed. She was so weak from the blood loss and not eating or drinking, she could barely stand. When they got her into bed, Chris went down the hallway and called Charlie and Teresa to make some tea and soup to warm Kara up.

Charlie and Teresa made Kara some soup and some tea and brought it into the bedroom. Finn sat her up and patiently fed her. He was able to get her to eat some of the soup and drink some of the tea. She was still weak, but she didn't look as pale. Charlie took the soup and the tea back to the kitchen. Chris and Teresa stayed a little while longer, then went home. Charlie made something for Finn to eat and left it for him on the nightstand. He thanked her, but he didn't eat it. Charlie didn't argue with him. She put the food away and went back to the bedroom to check on them before going home.

Finn didn't leave Kara's side. He sat in bed with her, holding her in his arms. He said a prayer, sending thanks to the universe Kara was ok. He promised he was never going to let her go again.

Finn sat on the couch, leaned his head back, and closed his eyes. He went into the living room so Kara could rest. He hadn't left her side for the last two days. He held her while she silently sobbed in her sleep. Repeating over and over again, she was safe, and he was there.

He'd ran a bath for her and gently washed her. While she was in the tub, he'd changed the sheets and made the bed. He helped her out of the bath, lotioned, and dressed her.

He sat her in the armchair, wrapping her in the blanket to keep her warm. He then gently brushed the knots out of her hair and put it in a ponytail. After putting her back to bed, he went to the kitchen to make her something to eat. Finn brought her in some soup with crackers and a bottle of water. He had to build her strength back.

Kara was so weak and fragile, she didn't fight him on anything. She simply let him take care of her. He'd called her office and let them know she had been ill and would be out for the week. The CEO sent over a bouquet of flowers from the company. Finn put them on the table in the bedroom, hoping they would help lift her spirits. He called his boss and let him know he would be out for the week taking care of her. He called his crew and told them to call him if there was an emergency. They told him to relax. They would take care of everything.

He cleaned up and done laundry. He ordered groceries online to be delivered to the house. And, when people called, he gave them updates on how she was. Chris, Charlie, Randy, and his whole family called. He told them all the same thing.

"She was getting better. She wasn't as pale. Yes, she was drinking the bone broth and was able to eat some crackers." Then he would remind them it had only been a couple of days. She still needed time.

Kara wasn't ready to talk yet. To him or anyone else for that matter. The loss had shattered her into a million pieces. And even if she could get past all the bullshit between him and Matt, he knew it would take her a long time to get over the miscarriage. Finn made it his mission to put all of those pieces back together. No matter how small.

Finn took a shower and got dressed. He'd left the bedroom with the intention of making himself something to eat. Then he got the notification the groceries were going to be delivered, so he sat in the living room to wait. He wasn't really hungry even though he'd barely eaten, he was simply tired, but he didn't care.

Finn had never been a caregiver before. Even when he was with Shelly. When Shelly was sick with the flu, she'd called her mom. Her mom came over and took care of her. Finn had slept in the spare room while Shelly's mom stayed with her. At the time, Finn accepted the reason Shelly gave him for not wanting to get him sick. But after taking care of Kara for the last two days, he didn't believe it anymore. Shelly hadn't trusted him enough to take care of her, so she called her mom to do it.

He was surprised at feeling hurt by that. Then he quickly pushed the feeling away. What mattered was, he was capable of lovingly taking care of someone. And no one deserved it more than Kara. Between him, Matt, and the loss of her pregnancy, she'd been given more than she could bear. The weight of it all had crushed her.

Finn looked at his phone. It was just after noon. The last message he'd gotten from the grocery delivery driver was to expect him between twelve and one. Finn knew there was one more thing he had to do for Kara. He took a deep breath and swallowed the little bit of pride he had left.

He sent a text. When he got the reply, he face-timed.

"Hi, Finn."

"Hi, Matt."

Epilogue

Six Months Later.

Matt stepped into the hallway and looked at his watch. He slowly shook his head, walked to his mother's room, and knocked lightly on the door.

"Mom, are you ready yet?" he yelled. He wasn't sure she could hear him over the commotion. He heard talking, giggling, and the running of little feet as the door opened.

Charlie's daughter Mia stood looking up at him.

"They're busy taking pictures," she smiled wide, her two front missing teeth on full display. At eight years old, she was the miniature version of her mother. Her light brown hair in ringlets. She wore a flower crown and a pale yellow princess dress. Matt bent down and picked her up, walking into the bedroom.

"Well, they better hurry up, or we're going to be late," he said as she wrapped her little arms around his neck. He looked around the room and didn't see anyone.

"Where are they?" he asked Mia.

"We're in the bathroom," Kara called out. "We're coming out now."

"Hurry up," Matt yelled back.

He twirled Mia around, pretending to dance with her in his arms as he swayed around the bedroom. He was trying not to trip over all the shoes and clothes flung about the floor. He twirled around and stopped. His breath catching in his throat as Kara emerged from the bathroom. He could feel the tears forming in his eyes.

"You look like a princess," Mia exclaimed excitedly as Matt gently set her down.

Kara was wearing an off-the-shoulder, pale yellow lace gown. Her hair fell in elegant curls framing her face. She picked up her dress slightly to walk around the cluttered floor. Charlie came out behind her, gently lifting the back of her dress so it wouldn't get caught on anything. Matt stared at his mother. She was glowing. Kara looked up at him timidly, biting her lower lip.

"How do I look?" she said timidly. "Do I look ok?"

Matt nodded his head. His voice cracked, "You," he coughed into his fist and tried again. "Mom," he said slowly. "I've never seen you look more beautiful than you do right now."

Kara's eyes began to glisten with tears. She smiled, then laughed. Looking up and waving her hand in front of her face.

"Thank God for waterproof mascara," she said. "Otherwise, you'd ruin my makeup, and I think Charlie would kill you."

"I really would," Charlie said jokingly from behind Kara. "Do you know how long it took me to get her makeup just right?"

The clicking of the camera brought Matt back to the present. He looked down at his watch.

"We're going to be late," he smiled at his mother. "Are you ready?"

"Yes," Kara said as Charlie handed her the bouquet of calla lilies, roses, and miniature sunflowers.

Mia ran over to her mother to get her basket. Charlie picked up her bouquet. The photographer walked around them, the shutter of his camera clicking swiftly.

Matt walked over to his mother and looked down at her. He smiled and kissed her lightly on the cheek.

"I love you," he whispered as he offered her his arm.

She looked up at him. "I love you too."

Matt escorted his mother down the hallway, down the stairs to the lower level. The photographer walking in front of them, Charlie and Mia following them. When they reached the patio doors, Charlie moved Mia into position so she would walk outside first. Charlie would follow Mia, and then Matt and his Mom. The photographer walked out the doors and knelt down to take pictures as they walked out.

While he waited for the music to start, Matt looked down at his mother.

"Mom," he whispered so only she would hear him.

"Yes, Honey?" she said, turning to face him.

Matt sighed, trying to quickly get his thoughts in order. He was acutely aware he was running out of time, but he had so many things he wanted to say. Kara looked up at him expectantly, smiling at him. He took a deep breath.

"I never thought anyone could love you as much as I do." He began cautiously. "I didn't think anyone was good enough to deserve you," Matt looked at his mother's face. Her eyes were sparkling. Her smile radiated pure happiness.

"But I was wrong. When Finn called me after Thanksgiving, I thought it was to talk about everything that happened. But he only asked me if he could marry you," Matt sniffed. Feeling the tears wet his cheeks.

"When I tried to tell him I was sorry, he wouldn't listen to me. He told me it didn't matter." Matt whispered, "He only wanted you. He asked me if he could marry you. Then he promised he would love you and do everything he could to make you happy for the rest of his life. I knew then he loved you more than I ever could," he paused.

"Finn's proven he deserves you. and I'm proud to have him as my step-dad."

Matt kissed the tears on his mother's cheek as she looked at him.

"I love you so much," she said, barely above a whisper.

"I love you too."

The music started, and Matt watched Mia walked through the patio door, skipping down the aisle. He heard laughing from the people outside. Charlie sighed and shook her head. She waited a few moments before she walked through the door, following Mia. Matt walked his mother to the door and waited a moment. He looked over at his mother.

"Ready?"

Kara nodded. "I've never been more ready." Smiling at him.

Matt smiled at his mother. He escorted her through the door, following Charlie. Matt walked his mother down the aisle, briefly looking around at the familiar faces standing in the backyard. Then he looked directly at Finn, watching Finn's face.

The expression on his face, full of love and adoration at seeing Kara. Matt looked at Finn and wondered how he could have ever missed, just how in love Finn was with his mother. Finn's eyes alone gave it away. Finn didn't look at anyone else but Kara.

Finn was standing at the altar, in front of the minister, under a trellis of flowers. His best friend Randy was standing next to him. His brother Mike standing next to Randy. Finn was dabbing his face with a handkerchief. Randy kept patting Finn on the back and whispering to him. Finn was wearing a navy blue tuxedo, Kara's favorite color, with a crisp white shirt. His blonde hair was neatly pulled back with a matching blue ribbon. His beard, carefully trimmed.

Matt stopped just before the alter. The minister stepped forward.

"Who here gives this woman away in marriage?" The minister asked.

"I do," Matt said clearly. He guided his mother to where Finn was standing. Finn reached his hand out and pulled Matt into a hug, patting him gently on the back. Matt hugged him tightly and let him go. He placed his mother's hand in Finn's, turned around, and walked over to stand behind Charlie at the side of the altar.

"Dearly Beloved," The minister began, "We are gathered here on this beautiful day to celebrate with and to share in the joy of this moment. The beginning of the sacred journey of Carolina Grace McNulty and Griffin Robert Wilson as Man and Wife in Holy Matrimony."

Matt was standing at the bar, drinking a soda, when his father walked up and put his arm around him. After the ceremony, the caterers changed over the backyard from the wedding to the reception effortlessly. Tables were brought out and covered with linens. A small head table was put before the trellis for the wedding party. After taking a million pictures, everyone was finally able to sit down and eat.

Matt watched Finn twirl his mother around on the small makeshift dance floor. Both of them smiling and laughing at each other. Matt smiled to himself. Their happiness was infectious. Finn and Kara were surrounded on the dance floor. Mike was dancing with his mother, Dorothy. Matt's grandfather was dancing with his grandmother. Randy was dancing with Meera. Everyone was happy.

"She looks beautiful, doesn't she?" Chris said to Matt, watching Kara and Finn.

"Yeah, she does," Matt said, taking a sip of his soda.

"She's barely showing."

Matt smiled at his dad. "I know. I told her to take it easy. I made Finn promise me not to let her overdo it. She needs to be careful."

"She will be. Your mother will do everything the doctor tells her to. Besides, Finn watches over her like a hawk. If she even attempts to do something she's not supposed to, he tells her to stop it." Chris turned to the bartender and asked for a beer. Then he looked over at his son.

"Are you excited about it?" he asked as he took a sip of his beer.

Matt thought a moment before answering. "Yes, but I already have a little sister. This is just a bonus."

"Yes, but she could be having a boy. A little brother would be fun. Imagine all the stuff you could teach him."

Matt laughed, "I don't care if it's a boy or a girl. I just want a healthy baby. And I'm really happy for mom and Finn."

"I'm happy for them too," Chris said, looking over at Kara dancing with Finn. "They deserve this."

Matt nodded. No one deserved a happily ever after more than his mom. After waiting so long, she finally found it with Finn. The man she hired to help her renovate her house had actually done so much more. He brought her back to life.

THE END

About the Author

Gira Solé is a writer, mother of two, hopeless romantic, and constant daydreamer. Currently lives in the South Jersey area. Which is not the same as living in North Jersey. She is an accomplished time traveler. Sometimes in 19th Century England, drinking tea with Jane Austen and the Brontë Sisters. Sometimes roaming the halls at Hogwarts School of Witchcraft and Wizardry.

Lately, she's been following The Witcher, Geralt of Rivera. Because I love him

You can connect with me on:
- https://www.instagram.com/girasoleauthor
- https://www.facebook.com/gira.sole.31924

www.ingramcontent.com/pod-product-compliance
Lightning Source LLC
Chambersburg PA
CBHW061940170626
46813CB00006B/2482